DOUBLE JE[OPARDY]

Mirror Wars Book 1

Alan Bayles

Copyright © 2021 Alan Bayles

All rights reserved

The characters and events portrayed in this book are fictitious. Any similarity to real persons, living or dead, is coincidental and not intended by the author.

No part of this book may be reproduced, or stored in a retrieval system, or transmitted in any form or by any means, electronic, mechanical, photocopying, recording, or otherwise, without express written permission of the publisher.

ISBN: 979-8-50-032925-7

Cover design by: Krisztian Koves

DEDICATION

For my mum and dad, who always encouraged me try my best at whatever I did.

Thank you to my brother, David with his support and encouragement this book would not have been possible. Also special thanks to my wife, Monica, who was the rock that kept me grounded and whose infinite patience and understanding knows no bounds.

This book is dedicated to Karen, Roisin, Alice, Joanne, Linda, Elaine, Brenda, Zoe, Paul, Jeevan, Liz and all the other hard working health care workers during these difficult times.

Thank you Zoe - your nightmares helped inspire me!

In memory of Ruth & Dr P – Gone but not forgotten

ACKNOWLEDGMENTS

Thank you to Claire, whose knowledge and advice was most appreciated.

Special thanks to my editor Kate Chaparro for her assistance in helping to edit this novel.

'To me, writing is fun. It doesn't matter what you're writing, as long as you can tell a story.'
- **Stan Lee**

'Live now; make now always the most precious time. Now will never come again.'

Jean-Luc Picard, 'Star Trek TNG: Inner Light'

PROLOGUE

12 September 1932 – Langley Park, Durham, England

'Brigadier Thornton, I am sorry to disturb you, sir. Just wanted to inform you that we will be shortly arriving at our destination.'

Sitting in the rear passenger seat, Brigadier Albert Thornton peered up from the documents he was reading and squinted at the vehicle's driver. He bobbed his head in gratitude and then gave James a tight smile.

'Thank you, Blake.' he answered gruffly.

Thornton lowered the flashlight he was holding, took in a deep breath and scrubbed his face with his hands. He was now in his late-50s. Years of following a military fitness regime had kept him in good shape physically, but he still found these long journeys tiresome. He adjusted in his seat uncomfortably and blew out his cheeks. Because of the secrecy of their visit, his superiors had asked him to be discreet and wear civilian clothing, rather than his normal military uniform. He had objected initially, but now he was glad he was wearing comfortable clothing.

Double Jeopardy

Yawning, he brushed his hand through his silver hair and looked across to Herbert Samuel. He guessed the home secretary must have been too engrossed in the document he was reading and he hadn't heard James's announcement. He coughed lightly and then reached over to touch Samuel's arm.

'We shouldn't be that much longer, Mr Samuel.' Thornton said, grimacing as he shifted uneasily in his seat, 'It will be good to get out and stretch our legs.'

Herbert Samuel looked up in surprise, nodded and then massaged his temples with his fingers. Thornton was aware that Samuel had been a politician for close to twenty years. Although he had no issue with Samuel himself, it was just that he wasn't entirely comfortable whenever he was around politicians. As a military man he preferred to do things a certain way. But when Prime Minister Ramsay MacDonald, requested that he wanted them both to personally to investigate how the experiment was proceeding and that they were to report directly back to him, he realised he had no choice but to follow orders like the dutiful soldier he was.

As Thornton watched Samuel look down at his documents, he could tell from the wide-eyed look on his face that he could scarcely believing what he was reading. He gave a small grunt and reluctantly conceded that he was having hard time believing it too. He stared up at the car's ceiling and exhaled sadly. He could imagine that there will eventually come a time when they won't need men like him to fight wars – that wars will be fought with huge, automated fighting machines or some other contraption.

'Unbelievable!' Samuel muttered, shaking his head, 'I still cannot comprehend that we are actually doing this. It is like something out of a H G Wells book!'

Thornton huffed in agreement, 'Humph! Which is the reason the PM has ordered us both to investigate this. Apparently, Churchill is on his soapbox again, trying to put pressure on the government into taking action over what is happening in Germany at the present time.'

Samuel snorted back a laugh, 'If Churchill ever read these papers, he would have a heart attack!' he replied, shaking his head, 'When the Secret

Intelligence Service first learned that Germany were looking into developing this technology. What do they call it, matter displacement?' His face darkened as he fixed Thornton with a steady gaze, 'Well, as soon as the SIS learned about it and briefed the PM, it scared them to death: the thought of this technology in the hands of another foreign power. They realised that the British government needed to act.'

Thornton nodded grimly, 'Can you imagine it? Being able to deploy troops anywhere in the world at a moment's notice in a blink of an eye!' He shook his head in disbelief, 'Horrifying to think Germany nearly had that power. It was only by the grace of God that the German scientist, Allen Selyab, is a Jew and was scared at what Herr Hitler would do when he comes to power, and what Germany could do if they got their hands on his research. When we learned he wanted to defect, the first chance they got, we contacted him. We arranged SIS to get him out of Germany by faking his death, making it appear like a motor vehicle accident. Once things died down, they brought him to England. After debriefing him, we set him up here. That was a year ago.'

Samuel stroked his black moustache, nodded silently and then gazed out of the window. Thornton didn't have to be a mind-reader to see Samuel was disturbed by what he had just told him.

'I understand the need for secrecy.' Samuel said unhappily. He frowned and gestured to something outside the vehicle. 'But did we have to set him up this far north? Were we not able to set him up somewhere closer to London?'

Thornton shook his head, 'There are two reasons we chose this location: one being anywhere near London would be too risky. What better way to hide a secret research centre than in an isolation hospital in a mining village.' Holding his torch closer to the paper resting on his knee, he pointed and drew his finger along a line on the map, 'The railway line leading to the mine was perfect for moving the heavy equipment that Doctor Selyab needed. If anybody saw anything suspicious, we would explain it as equipment needed to upgrade the hospital.'

Samuel lifted his chin thoughtfully and turned to the brigadier curiously, 'And what about the hospital staff?'

Thornton gave a wry smile and stared knowingly at Samuel, 'All the hospital staff have signed a non-disclosure agreement and understand the penalty for asking too many questions: and, because the hospital is supposed to be treating people with infectious diseases, civilians aren't allowed to visit their relatives who are being treated.'

Samuel raised an eyebrow and nodded in understanding, 'And the other reason?' he asked.

'There is a natural crystal cavern formation under the village.' Thornton's mouth twitched as he lifted his shoulder in a half shrug, 'I don't understand it myself, but according to Doctor Selyab it is ideal for what he needs to do.'

Samuel frowned and nodded slowly. His face then changed and stared at Thornton with narrow eyes, that held a touch of suspicion. 'I take it you have met Doctor Selyab?' he asked curiously, 'I have read mixed reports about him. What is your opinion?'

Thornton thought for a minute and bobbed his head, 'He is a brilliant man, no doubt about it.' he murmured, 'But he is arrogant and does not suffer fools gladly. There is something about that man that sets my teeth on edge whenever I am around him.'

Before Thornton could say any more, he paused as he noticed that the car was coming to a stop. He leaned forward and could see that they had stopped just in front of a large metal gate. He watched curiously as a plain-clothed man stepped out from a small guard post beside the gate. Samuel opened his mouth to say something, but Thornton raised his hand to silence him as he watched James roll down his car window.

'Can I help you, sir?' The guard asked James brusquely as he shone a light through the car window.

'We have an appointment in the hospital.' James replied, showing his papers.

The sombre faced man shone his light on the documents and nodded slowly, 'They say it is to rain tomorrow?'

'My garden is full of weeds this year, and the rain will help the roses.' James replied.

'It is best to use red roses in a garden.' The guard muttered cryptically, continuing to examine the papers.

'I prefer blue roses, as red ones attract the moles.' James countered.

The guardsman smiled grimly, gave a small nod, and handed the papers back to James. From his position in the rear of the vehicle, Thornton remained silent as he watched another plain clothes man step out from the shadows holding a gun. He could tell he was eyeing the car warily.

'You are cleared to enter.' The guard said grumpily. He then turned and motioned to his watching comrade to open the gate, 'If you follow the road up to the hospital and then take a left turn, it will take you up to the lab's entrance.'

James lifted his hand in acknowledgment, rolled up his window and drove the car forward.

'Gardening?' Samuel raised an eyebrow as he spoke in a hushed tone.

The brigadier smiled back at him knowingly, 'James was given a code phrase. If he gave the wrong answer, they would have shot us all without hesitation.'

Samuel nodded and then gave Thornton a double take. He swallowed and the colour drained from his face, his eyes widening in realisation of what nearly happened.

The car drove forward and followed the road up to the hospital. As the car pulled up to a stop Samuel could see a short blond twenty-something woman, dressed in a white lab coat, was waiting. He searched his memory for the woman's name as he watched her walk over to the car and open his door. *Joanne, something, oh wait that was it – Doctor Joanne Abbott. She's one of the science boffins helping Selyab.* He quickly got out of the car, closely followed by Samuel.

The brigadier bobbed his head in acknowledgement, 'Doctor Joanne Abbott, this is Herbert Samuel, the Home Secretary.'

Joanne moved forward and shook the home secretary's hand, 'Pleasure to meet you sir.' There was a tone of unease in her voice.

Upon noticing Joanne's nervousness, Thornton gave her a reassuring smile and gestured to the building, 'No need to be nervous,

Doctor Abbott. We are only here to see how things are progressing.'

Joanne pursed her lips together, gave a small nod and led them toward a small outhouse beside the hospital. She stopped in front a large wooden door and held up her hand to motion for him to move in closer.

'I am glad you have arrived, sir.' she whispered, dabbing her brow with a handkerchief nervously, 'Doctor Selyab is pushing ahead too fast. We are trying to tell him we need to be careful and need to tread slowly, but I am afraid he is beyond reason. Thank God you are here. He might listen to you.'

Thornton gave Joanne a harsh disbelieving stare, 'That's impossible, Doctor Abbott. I was to understand that we were a year away from a safe test activation.'

Joanne let out a small of snort of frustration, 'Yes, that is correct, sir. By all rights we should not even be this close to a test.' She shook her head and held up her hands in front of her, 'He arrogantly believes it is safe to proceed now. All the studies show if he tries to activate the device we risk a major overload, or worse.'

Joanne then stretched out her hand and opened the door. After letting the two men in she closed the door behind her.

After closing the door securely behind her, Joanne led the two men down a poorly lit metal staircase. As she hurried in front of them, the corners of her mouth curled up in a secretive smile. Thornton and Samuel believed they were coming to investigate an experiment involving matter transference. But little did they suspect it was much more than that and if they ever found the true nature of Selyab's experiment then there was a chance that Thornton would have him arrested and interrogated.

Joanne could not allow that to happen, because if he were to be interrogated then he would destroy everything that she had worked so hard to build. Joanne Abbott wasn't even her true name – in fact she wasn't even English – she was in fact a German spy.

Born in 1906 in Kassel, Northern Germany, Johanna Schöder was the daughter Leisel and Heinrich Schöder. Her father had been a major in the Imperial German Army. Johanna had loved her father and was heartbroken when he died during the Great War. She grew up harbouring a great bitterness and resentment for the people she felt responsible for her father's death, the British and German Empires in particular. As soon as she was old enough, she joined the military, graduating with high honours in all areas of combat.

Upon graduating, she was quickly snapped up by the Abwehr, the German Military Intelligence Service. After undergoing extensive training, including resistance to interrogation and torture, they placed her within an English military research centre.

In April 1931, while working undercover as a research assistant, Johanna's handler contacted her with orders directly from Reinhard Heydrich, the director of the newly formed Sicherheitsdienst. Embarrassed by Doctor Allen Selyab's defection to Britain, they tasked their most proficient spy to locate him and, after learning everything he knew, they ordered that she was to terminate him with extreme prejudice.

After using her contacts within the British government to find him, Johanna placed herself within Doctor Selyab's team. She knew that the ageing scientist was fond of intelligent women, so it wasn't long before he noticed Johanna.

After a rather awkward night of lovemaking, a drunken Doctor Selyab revealed his true intention for his grand experiment to Johanna. He revealed his device was not a matter transporter as everyone thought, but was, in fact, a portal to another world. Despite herself, Johanna became enraptured as she listened to Selyab speak of his plan to open a doorway to a world with a higher level of technology, hoping to acquire advanced technology to enable him to strike back at his enemies.

Having an intense desire to avenge her father's death, Johanna sensed a kindred spirit in the physicist. She knew that this was her chance to avenge her father, so she did not hesitate to inform the elderly scientist of her true identity.

At first the displaced German physician, afraid for his own life, opened his mouth to scream for help, but stopped and listened to the young woman standing in front of him. He quickly saw that she was someone like him, someone seeking to strike back at those who hurt her. Selyab then explained to his young confidante his frustrations about the upcoming government inspection and his fears that they could shut him down. Eager to help, Johanna reassured the frustrated scientist that they could use it to their advantage.

The plan had been simple one. She would distract the government inspection team by casting doubt on Doctor Selyab's credibility. Then, while she was keeping them busy, Doctor Selyab would cause a power surge, making it appear that he had started the experiment too early. With everybody's attention all on the eccentric German, Johanna would discreetly create a pulse so they could establish a connection and open a portal, allowing them both to jump through when the portal opened.

So far everything was going to plan. As she had predicted Thornton and Samuel had bought Johanna's story like the gullible fools they were. Johanna could barely contain her glee as she hurried down the stairs. If everything went the way they had planned, and with luck on their side, they would be through the portal before anybody would have a chance the stop them.

A short time later Johanna was leading the two men down a long dimly lit corridor that appeared to stretch out into the darkness. Samuel tapped lightly on her shoulder and then gestured to ceiling.

'Where are we exactly?' he asked curiously.

Johanna ground her teeth in annoyance. What was it about the English and their incessant need to ask questions! She turned to Samuel, gave him a pretend smile and then waved her hand up at the ceiling. 'At the moment we are walking under the hospital grounds. They built the main lab into a cavern under the village. Doctor Selyab thought the natural crystal formations in the cavern would help amplify the energy needed to create stable matter transmission.' She leaned forward and pretended to whisper in a voice that was heavy with concern, 'Although most of us have a theory that the crystal formations will have the opposite effect and may cause a cascade reaction with the power Doctor Selyab plans to use. We have a theory we may end up opening a dimensional rift or something worse!'

As she made her way down the tunnel, Johanna smiled to herself as she heard a loud rumbling noise coming from all around her. It was closely followed by a significantly large tremor. *Okay, showtime.* Johanna pretended to stumble and placed her hand up against the wall to stop herself from falling. She turned and gave the two men the best horrified look she could manage.

'Oh God! He's done it.' she exclaimed, 'The mad fool has activated it.'

From the shocked expressions on the two men's faces she could see that they were buying her every word. Damn, she was good.

Without saying another word, she raced down the corridor with the two worried looking men following close behind her. A few minutes later she arrived at the end of the passage and barged through the set of double doors that opened out into an enormous cavern. Johanna cast an eye over her shoulder to the two awestruck men behind her. From the stupid expressions that were on their faces she could tell they hadn't been adequately prepared for the scene that lay before them.

Around the cavern, embedded into the cavern's walls, natural crystal formations gave an eerie glow from the artificial electric lights. A hydroelectric generator stood on each side of the cavern's walls. Connected to each generator, two tall circular electric pylons crackled as powerful bursts of energy shot between them. In between the pylons stood an enormous square window shaped device that pulsed with energy.

On the outer edges of the cavern lay various consoles, each with dials and lights that waved or flashed furiously. The cavern shook as streaks of energy flashed out from the pylons and the window device, striking the cavern walls. The crystals pulsated as bursts of energy struck them. It felt like pure chaos as people ran around the cavern, panic and terror etched on their faces, running to each console, double checking the readings.

Johanna frowned as she searched through the pandemonium for Selyab. Where the was he? The plan was that he would greet them as soon as they walked through door. Why could he not stick with the plan? Quietly seething in anger, she pushed past two of her terrified looking colleagues and saw Selyab standing staring thoughtfully up at the portal.

Keeping her irritation in check, Johanna hurried up Selyab and lightly tapped him on the shoulder 'Doctor Selyab! Brigadier Thornton and Mister Samuel are here.'

Doctor Selyab waved his hand dismissively at her, 'Nein, can't you see I am busy here!' he chided. 'You are about to witness my greatest achievement!'

Johanna blinked and took a step back. What was wrong this dummkopf? Could he not remember the plan?

But before she could think of a way to remind him without being too obvious about it, Thornton chose that particular moment to walk up to Selyab and spin him around, 'Doctor Selyab, I demand that you explain yourself sir. I was told that it would be at least a year before you could conduct a safe test. I am ordering you to stop this, now. At once!'

Selyab blinked at him and then shook his head, 'Nein ... nein ... I cannot stop. I am so very close.' He then turned in a circle and waved his hands excitedly over his head. 'We just need a little more time. Then you will see.'

Johanna raised eyebrow as Selyab's eyes locked briefly with hers. She exhaled a small of sigh relief as she realised that he hadn't forgotten after all. The corners of her mouth curled up into a devious smile as she slipped away from the three arguing men. All he had to do was keep the two men distracted long enough for her to do what needed to be done. She took her place in front of the nearest console and gazed slowly around the chamber.

Once she was sure that her colleagues were too busy to notice what she was up to, Johanna carefully slid her hands over the controls and began to alter the power levels of generator. She smiled as she watched her colleagues all stumble back as a large crack of energy erupted from the portal. People around her staggered as the cavern shook. *So far so good. Now to add a little something else just for show.* She twisted one of the dials to as high as it would go. She smiled as she listened to the generators whine in protest and then watched as one of the consoles on the far side of the chamber began to spark and short out.

'We have an overload.' Johanna's voice was thick with pretend fear as she called out to a trio of technicians that were standing around the console on the other side room, 'Stand bac—'

The console exploded with such force it threw the trio against the wall. Johanna held her breath as the unfortunate trio lay unmoving on the floor. She then exhaled in relief as one by one they unsteadily got to their feet and then helped each other out of the cavern.

Eyes widening in shock, Doctor Selyab stared at Thornton and shook his head in disbelief, 'But … but … all the measurements were safely in the green!'

Johanna chuckled to herself. Selyab certainly knew how to lay it on thick. But as she turned her attention back to her console, her blood turned cold as she noticed that one of the power gauges was approaching critical levels. She gasped as a burst of energy shot out from the window device, striking the left pylon in an explosion of light. The people beneath it leapt away as it exploded and collapsed onto the floor below.

Oh my god, we are all in tremendous danger. Panic stricken, Johanna looked at wildly erratically waving gauges, then at the portal, and then turned to Doctor Selyab, 'Doctor Selyab, we are getting feedback on the portal, but it's coming from the other side! Somebody else is trying to establish a connection!'

Selyab collapsed onto the floor, shaking his head, 'Nein … nein … Not possible!'

Johanna shook her head in dismay as she stared at the console and then back up at the portal. Everything had been going so well. She had gone over Selyab's notes herself countless times, so …. She slapped her forehead as it suddenly it hit her. Of course, he hadn't taken in account what would happen if someone were to attempt to lock onto their portal with a one of their one. It would cause a gravitational shear, resulting in feedback like what they were experiencing now. She shook her head and then glowered at Selyab.

'You arrogant bastard.' she spat, 'Your own hubris has killed us all.'

Thornton grabbed Johanna and spun her around, 'Doctor Abbott, I need an answer now. What the hell is going on?'

Trying to compose herself, Johanna blinked and stared back at

Thornton, 'I don't understand it, but somebody else has locked onto the portal and is trying to open it from the other side.' She felt the blood drain from her face as she stared back up at the portal. 'Whatever they are doing is causing a fatal overload. We are minutes away from a catastrophic meltdown.'

Thornton blanched and took a step back, 'Is there anything we can do?'

Not wanting any more innocent deaths on her conscience, Johanna spun round and waved her hand to the two men, 'You and the home secretary need to get out of here as quickly as possible. We must stay and try to contain this.' Her tone held a note of despair as she gestured to the two large flood gates on either side of the chamber, 'Our only chance is to open the doors leading to the river and flood the chamber. Hopefully that might stop the meltdown and cause a small overload. It's risky, but we have no choice.'

Samuel stared at her in open mouthed disbelief, 'But how will you all get out?'

Johanna shook her head in resignation, 'I am afraid that time has passed for us, but not for you. Go ... now!'

Without showing any hesitation, Thornton grabbed Samuel and pushed him through the double doors leading to the corridor they had just come from.

A heavy weight settling on her heart, Johanna let out a breath of sadness and turned to the dozen people who were standing around her and stared into each of their faces. Each person hung their heads in silent understanding and acceptance, each having the look of someone who knew they were all about to die.

'Ladies and gentlemen, it has been an honour to serve with you.' she announced grimly, 'But we still have our duty.' They all nodded and walked over to the remaining consoles still in operation. Doctor Selyab took his place next to her, adjusted his tie, and glasses, and shook her hand.

'Doctor Abbott, it has been an honour to work with you.' His voice had a respectful tone as he spoke, 'On your command, Doctor Abbott, we will activate the floodgates.'

Johanna gave a small nod of gratitude and smiled briefly, giving one last look around the chamber to the men and women who were standing watching her.

'Ladies and gentlemen on my mark … three …. two … on—'

Before she could give the order, the cavern was lit up by a brilliant flash of light, followed by a surge of energy coming from the portal. Johanna squeezed her eyes shut and screamed as a warm pulse of energy encompassed her body.

Breathless and on the verge of collapse from exhaustion, Thornton pulled the home secretary up the stairs.

'Get up, you fool!' he panted, 'We are nearly there. Run damn you. R*un*!'

Not knowing where the strength came from, Thornton wiped the sweat off his brow as he grabbed the exhausted home secretary and carried him on his shoulders the rest of the way up the stairs. But just as he was approaching the top of the stairs he stumbled awkwardly as he felt a large tremor. He then felt a surge of air that was followed suddenly by a pulse of energy that tore up the stairs like the wind from a hurricane. The force of the pulse threw him out of the door, and he crashed hard onto the ground. Stunned, Thornton lifted his head and was relieved to see that Samuel was lying on the ground beside him.

Two days later, after recovering from their ordeal, the home secretary handed his report to the prime minister. An inspection team had tried to get back down into the lab, but found their way blocked by fallen debris.

The prime minister gave the order for the entrance leading to the underground lab to be filled in and all signs of it removed and, in the interests of national security, any record of the experiment classified and expunged from any public record.

1

Location: Reality 001, Earth Prime
Langley Park, Durham, England
Date: 23rd March 1978

Trembling with excitement, eight-year-old Emma Tulley stirred restlessly in her bed. How could she get to sleep when she was this excited? The cause for her excitement – it was because her parents were taking her away to Butlins the following morning. She could barely contain herself. All she could think about was that this time tomorrow night she would going to sleep in a different bed and waking to a different sun rise.

Emma let out a small squeal of delight. She wanted to be awake as early as possible and not miss a precious second of the start of their grand adventure.

'Em, if you don't go to sleep,' she heard Claire grumble angrily from the other side of the bedroom, 'so help me, I will come over there and thump you!'

Emma rolled her eyes as she listened to her twin sister's moaning voice. Fifteen minutes her senior, Claire had taken it upon herself to be the de facto leader of the duo, always telling her younger sibling what to do. Even though both girls were identical twins, they both had completely differing personalities. Emma was more outgoing and considered to be more impulsive than Claire, who was the more level-headed and responsible twin.

'Oh, lighten up, Cee!' Emma hissed, 'Why don't you take that stick out of your bottom and have a bit of fun for once!'

Claire let out an indignant gasp, 'Em! I'm going to tell mam you swore at me, you used the B-word!'

Emma giggled and shook her head, 'Oh stop, bottom isn't a swear word.'

'Tis so!' Claire giggled back in reply.

'Tis not!'

'Cow!' Claire snorted.

'Moo!' Emma giggled, trying to do her best impersonation of the farm animal.

'Flibbertigibbet.' Claire laughed back.

'Hey! No fair, I don't know what that means.' Emma moaned, sticking out her bottom lip, 'You know the rules. Stick to the words we both know.'

'It's what you are, it means chatterbox.' Claire replied haughtily.

'Clever clogs.' Emma snorted back.

'Nincompoop.'

Not able to hide her bemusement, Emma pressed her hands to her mouth and let out a small giggle, 'You said poop.'

'Poop breath!' Claire giggled back.

'Better than having dog breath.'

'Bite me!'

'Ew, cooties!' Emma moaned back in response, screwing her face up in disgust, 'I don't want your germs.'

'Bitch!' Claire snorted back.

'Claire!' Emma gasped, bolting straight up in her bed, and flicking her bedside lamp on. She looked at her older sister through horrified eyes. 'You swore. I'm going to tell mam and dad!'

Emma regretted the words as soon as they were out of her mouth. She knew if their parents found out that they had been swearing then they would both be in trouble. Claire swung her legs over the side of her bed and stared at Emma through tear-filled eyes. She pressed her hands against her chest as she pleaded for her forgiveness.

'Please Em, I am sorry.' Claire whispered, 'I didn't mean it. If you promise me not to say anything, I will do all your chores for the rest of the month, two months even.'

Emma frowned and tapped her lip thoughtfully. That was very tempting. A devious smile danced across her lips as she wondered if she should let her sister sweat a bit. Unfortunately, before she had a chance to decide she was interrupted by a loud woman's voice coming through the wall behind them, from their parent's bedroom.

'Girls, cease that chatter, turn off your light, and go back to sleep.' her mum's voice called, 'We have a long journey tomorrow and need we need to be up sharp. So, lights off, mouths closed, and eyelids shut!'

'Aww, mam.' Claire grumbled. 'Emma started it. She won—'

'I don't care who started it!' mum interjected angrily, 'I'm stopping it, or how would you like to spend two weeks at your nanna's and me and your dad go away by ourselves?'

'Aww, mam that's not fair!' Emma wailed, 'Claire was the who called me a bitch!' She screwed up her face as soon as the words left her mouth and saw the expression of horror that was on her sister's face. Oops! That did it.

Claire stared at Emma, wide-eyed betrayal covering her features. 'Emma, you tattle tale, how could you?' But before Emma had time to take it back. Their bedroom door bust open and a tall, thin, brown-curly-haired woman wearing a pink frilly nightie stormed through the door, her face thunderous. 'Claire! Is that right?' Her mum asked angrily, 'Did you use the B-word on your sister?'

Claire swallowed, hung her head, and whispered meekly, 'Yes.'

With her arms folded across her chest, mum's eyes narrowed as she eyed the sorry-looking Claire, 'Sorry, I didn't hear that. What was that young lady?'

Shooting her strangely silent sibling a look that could kill, Claire rolled her eyes, inhaled a heavy sigh, and nodded slowly, 'Yes mam, I called her the B-word.'

Emma could almost see the disappointment in her mum's eyes as she watched her straighten to full height. 'Apologise to your sister right now, madam.' Mum said harshly, gesturing to Emma.

Claire stared at mum in open-mouth shock. Emma felt her stomach knot as she could almost sense what her sister would be thinking – That it wasn't her fault etc. If backed into a corner, Claire would think she was being picked on and lash out. There was many a time her tongue had gotten her in trouble because she had a habit of opening her mouth without thinking about what she was going to say first. Emma had seen Claire's stubborn streak first hand, so she knew there was more chance of it snowing in the summer than Claire apologising.

'Aww, mam.' Claire wailed, 'That's not fair!'

Mum placed her hands on her hips and shot a withering scowl at Claire. 'Claire Bernadette Tulley!' she hissed angrily, 'You apologise to your sister right now, or there will be hell to pay!'

'No, I won't!' Claire screamed back. As if to emphasise how much she meant it, she petulantly stuck her bottom lip out and folded her arms across her chest.

Before her mum could respond, an angry male voice suddenly piped up from the bedroom next to them. 'Claire, you listen to your mother right now.' Their father shouted in an annoyed sounding voice, 'If I have to come in there, so help me, you'll wish you were never born.'

Emma gulped. That was bad. If there was anything that would change Claire's mind, then it would be the idea of what would happen if their father was forced to intervene. A moment of hope stirred within Emma as she watched Claire turn toward her and open her mouth slightly. Yes, she was going to do it, she was going to apologise. However, she never got a chance to hear what Clare was about to say because it was at that moment her mum chose to shout back at their dad. 'We can have less of that too, Richard.' Mum snapped, 'If I wanted any help from you, I would ask for it.'

Emma inhaled a deep sigh of relief to herself as she heard her father's grumbling reply coming from the other side of the wall. 'Humph, I was just trying to help Barbara. Next time I'll just keep my mouth shut then.'

Barbara pinched the bridge of her nose and sucked in a deep breath. She gave her head a small shake as she stared down at Claire and shot her a cold side-eye that said, *See what you have done now!*

Her cheeks flushed with humiliation, Claire's eyes narrowed as she stared at Emma, who was secretly wishing for the ground to swallow her up. 'Emma, I'm sorry.' she said through gritted teeth, 'I didn't mean to use the B-word on you.'

Not wanting to make things even harder than they were, Emma lowered her eyes and gave her a sister a small smile as she bobbed her head meekly.

'Good girl.' Barbara said, smiling slightly, 'Now switch off your light and go to sleep.' Then just as she leaned into kiss her Claire on the forehead, she frowned as the surly looking Claire turned her head away at the last instant and let out a small grunt.

Her eyes filled with hurt, Barbara's face darkened and pursed her lips as she shot the moody girl a withering look. 'Just for that young lady, you and I are going to have a serious chat first thing in the morning about your attitude. Just because you have apologised to your sister does not mean it is the end of it. It certainly isn't by a long shot.' She then jabbed her finger at Claire. 'If you don't buck up your ideas, madam, I am going to leave you at your nanna's.' She straightened, turned on her heel and started to walk out of their bedroom but stopped in the doorway as she spoke over her shoulder. 'You are old enough now to lean that your actions have consequences, so I want you to seriously consider that while you sleep. Lights off, both of you now!' Her last sentence had a bit of edge to it as she waited for the girls to turn off their bedside lights before slamming their door shut.

As she lay in the darkness, Emma closed her eyes and listened to her sister's heavy breathing coming from her side of the room. Oh, this was not good. She could tell from Claire's loud rapid breathing, that she was deeply upset. She inhaled through her nose and then called out softly to the other side of the room.

'Cee, are you awake?' Emma whispered carefully. She cringed inwardly. Stupid! Of course, she was. When there was no reply, she twisted onto her side and tried again. 'Come on, Cee, I know you are still awake. Talk to me, please.'

'I'm not talking to you.' She heard Claire whisper back.

The corners of Emma's lips twitched in a slight smile, 'If you are not talking to me, then why did you just answer me?'

'I… I…' Claire responded. Emma could almost hear the uncertainty in her sister's voice.

Adamant she was going to get her sister to speak to her, Emma switched her bedside light on and stared hopefully at the small body in the bed opposite her. 'Come on Cee, don't be like that.' She pressed her hands against her chest in a penitence like gesture. 'I'm sorry. You know I didn't mean for you to get wrong off mam.'

Claire spun round, bolted up, and shot Emma a murderous look. 'You still told on me.' she hissed, jabbing her finger at Emma, 'you,' and then into her own chest, 'betrayed me.'

Her sister's words stabbing into her heart, Emma jerked back in shock. Her vision blurred as she struggled to fight back the tears and shook her head as she tried to plead with her. 'Please, Cee, it just slipped out. You are my sister. You know I would never do anything to hurt you.' She gave the angry Claire a thin smile. 'Come on sis, I know you. You know we cannot stay mad at each other for long.' It was true. There was an unspeakable bond between identical siblings that went deep, almost primal in nature, something that was not even shared by their non-identical counterparts. It was a bond that no matter what they did to one another, they would still stand by each other's sides, no matter what. It was this bond Emma was relying on that she prayed would bring her disgruntled sister out of her funk.

Unfortunately, Emma's hopes of reconciliation were dashed as she watched Claire lean forward and give her a contemptuous sneer. 'I hate you.' She hissed, waving her hand across her body in an emphatic gesture, 'I don't want to speak to you ever again.' With that, she lay back down and turned her back on Emma.

Tears of hurt streaming down her cheeks, Emma shot up out of her bed and bounded across to the other side of the room. She sobbed as she knelt beside Claire's bed and reached out to touch her shoulder. 'Please, Cee, I said I'm sorry.' she whimpered, 'I'm your sister. I love you.'

Claire squeezed her eyes shut, grabbed her pillow and threw it into Emma's face. 'Well, I don't love you!' she snarled, 'I hate you. I wish you were dead!'

She may have taken a knife and buried into Emma's heart. Such was the venomous intensity of Claire's angry words. Emma's hand to shot up to her mouth as she staggered back in shock. As she stared down at her red-faced sister, Emma suddenly felt alone. Although deep down, a part of her understood her sister was angry and did not mean the words she had said, they were still just as painful to hear, nonetheless.

Quickly realising that she needed to put some between space between themselves, Emma blew out her cheeks, turned round, walked back over to her bed, and grabbed her pillow. Hoping that Claire would eventually cool down after she had come to her senses, she trudged slowly out of the bedroom door, coming to a stop as she paused in the doorway.

'I'm going downstairs to sleep with Sandy.' She whispered softly over her shoulder, 'That's where I'll be, just in case... you know...'

'You deserve each other.' Claire answered back sourly, 'Maybe we should put you in the pound too.'

Claire's words cut deep into Emma's heart. Emma stiffened and then shuddered slightly as a small whimper escaped from her lips. No, there was turning back now. Her hand trembled as she opened the door and stepped out of the bedroom.

Her stomach churning with a series of mixed emotions, Claire stared forlornly up at the ceiling and let out a small groan of frustration. Oh, why did she have to say that to her? That meant she was going to have to go crawling down to Emma and beg her to come back, otherwise she would be in even more trouble with her parents. She pounded fists on the bed and shook her head adamantly. No! Why should she? If anything, Emma should be the one crawling back to her. She ... she ...

Infuriated, Claire spun round and buried her head into her pillow and let out a muffled scream. Emma was just impossible. She was so ... so ... Emma! Why should she be the one to go crawling down to her, to beg her to come back?

Claire turned on her back and let out a heavy sigh. Because she was the responsible older sister, that's why. She was the one who was supposed to set a good example for Emma. She thumped her hand on the bed as she reluctantly conceded that her sister was right. As much as she wanted to, Claire could not stay mad at Emma. They both loved each other too much to be divided by a petty squabble.

As she lay on the bed, Claire stared across the darkened room to where Emma's bed was and let out a small groan of irritation. Just because Emma was right, that didn't mean she was going to go crawling to her, begging for her forgiveness straight away. No, she was the one who walked out in a huff. Let her be the one to sit and wait.

Turning on her side, the corners of Claire's mouth turned up into a devious grin. No, she was going to let her sister stew in her own thoughts for a few minutes. It was not like she was going to anywhere, was she?

Pillow clenched tight against her chest, Emma fought back the tears as she closed the bedroom door behind her and made her way along the landing. As she came to a stop in front of her parent's bedroom door, she picked up the sound of hushed voices coming from the other side. From the tone of their voices, she could tell her parents were arguing about what they should do with Claire.

Her curiosity getting the better of her, Emma chewed on her bottom lip as she pressed her ear to the door so that she could make out what they were saying. From the tone of her voice, she could tell her mum was still upset by Claire's behaviour, was even blaming herself. Emma so badly wanted to run into the room, give her mother a hug and tell her that her sister did not mean what she had said. To plead with her, to let Claire go with them on holiday.

But as she reached out to knock on their bedroom door, Emma's hand paused as a thought suddenly popped into her head. What if by doing this she makes things worse? Troubled by that idea, she pulled her hand away and took a small step back. She swallowed as she imagined her parent's reaction if she walked into their bedroom. First, she would get wrong for spying on them and second, they would probably shout at her for being out of bed and creeping around like a little spy. She let out a small gasp to herself as she thought they may even punish her by leaving her at home too. No, she could not allow that to happen.

Sucking in a resigned breath, Emma stepped away from her parent's bedroom door. No, as much as she wanted to, she had to leave them alone. She nodded to herself. Once her mother had a good night's sleep, she would see Claire didn't mean what she had said. She would forgive her, and things will go back to normal and then her mum will let Claire go on holiday with them. Yes, she will see she had made a mistake when she wakes up in the morning.

Her brow furrowed in deep concentration, Emma edged attentively along the landing with well-rehearsed practice, avoiding the parts of the floor that creaked. On reaching the top of the staircase, she nimbly lowered herself down onto the top step of the staircase and carefully let the pillow slip out of her hands. As she watched the pillow slide down a couple of stairs, she gently slid her bottom down to the next step, delicately repeating the process as she slowly made her way down, stopping every so often to kick the pillow further ahead of her.

On finally reaching the bottom step, Emma let out a small sigh of relief as she straightened up and rubbed the feeling back into her bottom. She then picked up the pillow off the carpeted hallway floor, turned and crept down the hallway, toward the kitchen. As she gently nudged open the door and stepped into a narrow kitchen, she let out a small gasp as her bare feet touched the cold surface of the chequered linoleum that covered kitchen's floor. Wishing she had worn her slippers, Emma shivered as she walked into the kitchen, but came to a sudden stop as she felt something smooth and wet lick her bare toes.

The corners of Emma's lips curled up into a broad grin as she looked down and saw the brown eyes of a small Jack Russell Terrier staring back up at her.

'Hey Sandy.' She whispered softly to her curious canine companion, 'You don't mind having some company, do you?' She pressed her index finger to her lips as the excitable terrier answered with a small bark, 'Shush! We don't want to wake everyone up, do we?' She patted her leg and motioned for the dog to follow her. 'Come on, go back to your bed.'

Her small tail waggling excitedly, the happy little dog followed Emma over to the kitchen's corner to where a medium-sized wicker dog basket was. Emma gently placed her pillow onto the kitchen floor and gently ease herself down onto it. Sandy gave a small whine of contentment as Emma reached over scratched the back of her ear.

'I don't know what to do, Sandy.' Emma whispered sadly, 'Claire is mad at me, and Mam is mad at Claire. I'm scared if I say anything, then Mam will be mad at me too.' She gave a sad smile as Sandy stared up at her with sad puppy dog eyes. 'I don't suppose you can tell what to do?' She chuckled to herself as the dog cocked her head and let out a small whine. 'You're no help!'

Her hand gently stroking the small dog's head, Emma unhappily leaned back against the wall and stared up at the ceiling. She shook her head to herself as she pictured her sibling lying in her bed, beating herself up at what to do. She knew Claire was just being stubborn, that she did not want to make the first move by crawling and begging for Emma's forgiveness. At the same time, she understood what was going through her elder sister's mind. She just wanted Emma to stew for a bit before she would decide to come downstairs and make up with her.

There was a special bond they shared with one another than ran so deep, they could not stay mad at each other for long. When united, the two Tulley girls were a force to be reckoned with. Nothing could divide them, not even their own parents.

Double Jeopardy

Emma stared up at the ceiling locked in her own thoughts. She yawned and felt her eyes begin to close. But just as she was about to nod off to sleep, she was suddenly alerted by a small growl. Emma opened her eyes and frowned as she realised that Sandy was out of her basket and appeared to be growling at something on the wall. Concerned, she quickly rose to her feet and moved closer to the agitated canine. As she knelt and placed her hand on Sandy's back, Emma's hand froze as she noticed that Sandy was quivering and the hairs on her back were sticking up.

'Hey girl.' Emma asked worriedly, 'What's wrong? What are you growling ab—'

The words died in her throat as it slowly registered with Emma that the dog was growling at the mirror. Her small brow furrowed in confusion as she found eyes being drawn to the strange spectacle on the wall. The mirror's reflective surface appeared to be shimmering like a body of water glittering in the rays of the sun on a brightly lit summer's day.

It's beautiful, Emma thought to herself in wonderment, slowly reaching out her hand to touch the mesmerizing display.

She suddenly jerked her hand back in fright as the fluid-like substance extended and stretched out. Her eyebrows climbed up her forehead in horror as she made out the shape of a strange claw-like hand reaching out through the mercurial-like liquid. It was as if it was trying to climb out and get at her. She let out a small, terrified yelp of surprise as she heard a small pop of air.

Too scared to move, Emma could only watch as a black, scaly skinned monstrosity clambered out of the mirror onto the kitchen floor. The beast was like something out of her nightmares. Roughly the size of a large dog, it had a long black body, covered with shiny, glistening scales, with four legs with what appeared to be three sharp claws on each appendage. As she watched the terrifying beast's gruesome head turning toward her, Emma felt something warm trickle down her legs as its mouth opened, revealing the shark-like teeth contained within.

Then, as if to protect her petrified mistress, Sandy snarled and lunged at the beast. The horrifying monstrosity lashed out and caught the poor animal's body with the back of its claws, sending it flying along the smooth linoleum floor, coming to a stop near the door in a stunned heap.

Scared beyond belief, Emma staggered back and collapsed onto the floor. She tried to scramble away from the hideous thing in front of her but came to a stop as her back struck the hard wooden exterior of the kitchen cupboards.

All alone and frozen in fear, Emma let out a small whimper as she watched the black scaly monster creep toward her. Tears streaming down her cheeks, Emma squeezed her eyes shut as the beast's red narrow eye slits focused on her. Unable to stop herself from defecating, she sobbed as she felt its warm, putrid breath on her face. Her body stiffened, as if waiting for that moment when it would lash out, bringing an end to her brief life.

But that did not happen. As Emma slowly opened her eyes, she frowned and saw that the creature was just standing there, as if it was waiting for something. What was it waiting for? She was at its mercy. Was it going to let her go free? Had it made a mistake was deciding to let her go? Emma let out a small sigh of relief and nodded to herself. Yes, that was it. It had made a mistake. She was not what it wan—

Emma stiffened as she caught sight of something moving behind the creature, near the kitchen's doorway. She tilted her head slightly to get a better view and experienced an enormous surge of exultation on seeing the familiar thin-face, brown-haired head of her sister peering around the door. It was Claire!

Never had she been more overjoyed to see her sister's face. Emma bit into her bottom lip to stop herself from crying out. Yes, it was Claire. She was going to save her! All she had to do was call out and daddy would come and rescue her. Then it will all be over. All she nee—

Emma's brow creased in confusion. Her elder sister had not called out like she had hoped. She appeared to be just standing there. What was she waiting for?

A few moments earlier, Claire let out a disgruntled grunt as she threw back her sheet and bolted up from her bed. Fine! If Emma wanted her to apologise, she would do it, but not before she got some concessions from her sister. Oh yes, her repentance was going to come at a price. Bidding was going to start with that new Barbie Emma had gotten for her Christmas, that she had not been allowed to play with.

Standing next to her bed, Claire frowned at her bare feet and placed her hands on her hips. She looked at her slippers and then back to her feet. No, if she wore her slippers, there was a chance her parents would hear her, and she would be even more doo-doo.

Her mind made up, Claire straightened her back and wrapped a thin black headscarf around her forehead. If she was to remain undetected, then she was going to have to rely on every bit of her childish cunning. She eyed the poster on the wall of the outlandishly dressed Yvonne Craig and her lips curled up in a mischievous grin. She needed to become like Batgirl!

Claire snuck out of her bedroom and along the landing with well-practiced precision. She then climbed onto the top of the banister and slid gently down its smooth vanished surface, coming to a gentle stop as her bottom nudged the square newel post that marked end of the stairway.

Smoothly extricating herself off the banister, Claire nimbly hopped onto the hallway floor. She crouched down and cocked her head to listen for any sounds of movement coming from her parent's bedroom. Energised by the idea that so far, she had gotten away with fooling her folks, she straightened and crept slowly along the short hallway, coming to a stop in front of the kitchen door.

Just as her hand reached up to push the door open, she froze as she heard the small sound of a disturbance coming from the other side of the door. Was that Sandy growling? Surely, she did not think Claire was a burglar coming to rob the house? Her tiny heart hammering in her chest, she gently nudged open the door and poked her head through the small gap.

A small shape shot past her, startling her. Her eyes grew wide as she saw the small furry object strike the kitchen wall and collapse at her feet. Claire stared at the floor in slack-jawed astonishment as she realised the small bundle of fur was Sandy. What had happened to her? Who would dare do such a thing to her loyal companion?

It was then she heard a tear-filled whimper coming from somewhere in the kitchen. Claire frowned to herself. Was that Emma crying? As she peered further through the slightly open door, she felt her blood run cold on seeing the nightmarish like creature standing over her sobbing sister's cowering body.

Not believing what she was seeing, Claire stood frozen to the spot, trembling in fear. She could see the fear in Emma's eyes as they looked toward her, pleading wordlessly for her to do something, anything, so long as it got that thing away from her. But as she opened her mouth to shout for her father, she froze as a thought suddenly popped into her head. No, if she shouted, it would only make the creature even angrier, and it would attack her.

Claire shook her head slightly. No, the best thing she could do was sneak away while the thing's attention was still focused on her sister. Then she could run upstairs and get her father. Yes, that was the best thing to do.

Carefully stepping back into the hallway, Claire turned and crept back toward the staircase. But just as she was about to put her foot on the bottom step, she stopped. She peered over her shoulder and stared thoughtfully at the door. Wait, did she have to save her sister? It was her fault that she was in this mess. She was the one who was responsible for getting Claire into trouble with her parents. Maybe she should let that thing take her and then she might be better off without her. Wouldn't she?

Emma could not believe what had just happened. Claire just stepped back and closed the kitchen door behind her. She'd deserted her. How could she do that? Why didn't she call out for daddy to come and save her?

But before she could make sense of what of what her sister was up to, Emma let out a small sob as the horrifying, black-skinned beast lifted its left claw, as if to strike her. But then something unexpected happened. Instead of striking Emma, the beast held up its left appendage, revealing a strange metallic looking device. Emma gagged as it sprayed something sweet tasting in her face, and she felt her eyelids become heavy as the room spun around her.

Double Jeopardy

As she slowly welcomed the warming embrace of the black void, Emma's last confused thought was why. Why had Claire betrayed her?

Still standing at the bottom staircase, Claire slapped her forehead with the palm of her hand and let out a small groan to herself. What were you doing, you stupid girl! Emma was your sister, and she needed your help.

Full of guilt at the thought of leaving her sister behind, Claire spun sharply round to call out to her, to let her know she was coming to help her. Unfortunately, as she spun round, her arm caught the edge of the hallway table, knocking off the porcelain commemorative plate that had sat on top of it. Claire made a face as she heard the plate shatter on the floor. She gulped and cast her eye at the kitchen door. That must have altered the thing in the kitchen.

Claire stared in dismay at the broken pieces on the floor. Despite her young age, a part of her must have been aware of its dangerous significance because body automatically went into flight or fight mode.

But as she made to race for the staircase, she barely had time to put her foot on the bottom step as she heard a loud crack coming from behind her. She glanced over her shoulder and became frozen in terror as she watched the horrifying dog-like thing burst out of the kitchen.

Trying to get away, Claire let out a hoarse scream of pain as she felt the beast's claws slice through the thin fabric of her pyjama top, raking the flesh in the small of her back. The searing pain catching her by surprise, she lurched forward and struck her head on the hard wooden edge of the staircase's newel post, stunning her into a semi-unconscious state.

A short time later, Claire opened her eyes and blinked. The monster was no longer standing over her. She frowned to herself as she wondered how long she had been lying in the deserted hallway. Dazed, Claire slowly rose to her feet and screwed up her face at the searing pain coming from her back. She gasped as she felt the warm flow of blood running down the back of her legs.

Claire tottered toward the staircase and placed her foot on the bottom step. But that small movement caused the wound on her back to flare, and she inhaled a small intake of air. Ignoring the pulsing pain coming from the small of her back, she painfully crawled back up the flight of stairs, one painful step at a time, until she eventually reached the landing. Desperate to get to the loving embrace of her mother, she dragged herself along the landing by grabbing hold of a handful of carpet a piece at a time.

Exhausted, her pyjamas soaked in sweat, Claire came to a stop in front of her parent's bedroom and pounded her hand weakly on the door.

'Mommy ... daddy ...' she sobbed, her fingernails scratching the surface of the door.

Claire heard urgent panicked voices coming from the other side of the door. After what seemed like an eternity, the door swung open to reveal her mother's frowning face.

'Claire!' Barbara exclaimed in shock. She then collapsed onto her knees and wrapped Claire in her arms. She peered over her shoulder at her husband, who was standing behind her in total shock. 'Richard! Something has happened to our Claire.'

Claire shook her head weakly, tears streaming down her cheeks as she let out a small plaintive whimper. 'Emma.' she pleaded hoarsely. 'You need ... to help ... Emma.'

The adults exchanged startled glances as they heard something unusual in the voice from someone so young – despair. It was enough to break Richard out of his shocked stupor. He wordlessly gestured for Barbara to remain where she was as he charged past her and bolted down the stairs, two at a time.

A few seconds later, Claire squeezed her eyes and buried her head in her mother's arms as she heard her father's grief-filled wails coming from the kitchen.

2

Location: Belmont, Durham, England
Present Day

Detective Inspector Dave Barnes was woken from a restless sleep to the tune of the '*Dance Of The Knights*' coming from his mobile phone. He groaned and opened his eyes and began searching around for his phone. After spotting it on the floor, he realised that he had once again fallen asleep on the couch. He could not remember the last time he had gotten a good night's sleep in his bed.

He picked up his phone and looked to determine what time it was. The display told him it was 11:43pm and that it was Andy Jenkins committing the terrible offence of disturbing him. He took a deep breath and let out a long sigh of resignation; he knew that he had no choice but to answer it.

'Sergeant Jenkins, I hope you realise that you are interrupting my evening of passionate lovemaking with a gorgeous Swedish woman!' he grumbled jokingly.

A half-hearted laugh was heard from the phone's speaker from a male voice that was speaking with a soft Mackem accent, '*Sure Guv and I am going to win the lottery next week! What's wrong, sir, you asleep on the couch again with the dog on your lap?'*

Dave looked down and found two sorrowful eyes looking up at him. He let out a small snort of agreement, Andy had been right, he had fallen asleep again with his dog beside him - a black Cavalier King Charles Spaniel who was also not happy that she had been disturbed from her restful slumber.

'Andy, is there a good reason why you are disturbing me at this time of night, or are you just trying to annoy me?' Dave asked in a rather exasperated voice.

Andy's tone quickly changed, becoming more serious, *'Sorry, Guv, but they need us. There has been a murder in Langley Park, a father and son. From the information they have given me, it doesn't sound good. From what I can gather, it is nasty!'*

Sitting straight up and scrubbing his face with his free hand, Dave tried to make himself more alert and he cast an eye at his wristwatch. He furrowed his brow as he tried work out how far away the crime scene was. 'Okay Andrew, get yourself over there and I'll join you as soon as I can.'

'Right Guv see you soon.' Andy replied, and the call disconnected.

Dave stood up, sniffed himself and gave a bit of a wince at the smell. He walked upstairs to his bedroom and took off his shirt, dashed into the bathroom and started to fill the wash basin. He gazed into the mirror at his own reflection, shook his head sadly and wondered where that eager, youthful young copper had gone.

He was an average man, really; having been tall and handsome in his youth, but as the years and the job took their toll, his face and body began to show the signs of age. He remembered the line from *Raiders Of The Lost Ark* spoken by Harrison Ford *"It's not the years, honey. It's the mileage."* As he stared back at his reflection, he realised that line had never been truer. The years were catching up on him; he was in his mid-50s, his salt and pepper hair thinning on the top, his youthful, slim figure spreading out along the middle. He sighed sadly to himself. Age was a bitch!

Fifteen minutes later he arrived downstairs, clean shaven and properly dressed. Walking over into the kitchen, and after making sure

Jenny had enough dog food and water in her bowls, he put on his glasses, grabbed his car keys and ID. After casting a quick around to ensure he had left nothing behind, he quickly put his jacket on and left the house.

Twenty minutes later a black Audi Q3 was driving along the quiet country road that led into the village of Langley Park. Dave had found that his journey from Belmont had been relatively quiet for that time of night. Traffic in Durham, for once, had been light so he had made good time getting to the former mining village. As he steered his vehicle into a side street, he could see a tall, brown-haired man, dressed in plain clothes, was waiting for him, as always with two cups of coffee in his hand. He smiled to himself; Andy always liked to make sure his Guv was well prepared.

He noticed his colleagues had cordoned the street off to restrict access. It was a typical street for a village its size: terraced houses ran along both sides of the street with cars parked on either side of the road. Each house had a little fenced off garden at the front, very similar to most of the village streets in that area. Andy was waiting for his superior officer just outside the cordon. Dave climbed out of his car and hurried over to the young detective.

'Alright Guv!' Andy greeted, offering a cup of coffee to Dave, which he took gratefully. Dave quite liked the young Sergeant, although he found he did have a nasty habit of being a bit too eager. But, as he reluctantly admitted to himself, he too had been like that once; young and eager to take on the world.

Detective Sergeant Andrew Jenkins was a modern-day copper. Tall, toned, athletic, who proudly took pride in his appearance: short-cut hair, clean shaven, even admitted to using male grooming products such as moisturiser, something which Dave enjoyed ribbing him about. He also kept in shape by regularly working out. Dave rolled his eyes and chuckled to himself. He did not know how Andy managed it.

'Thanks Andrew.' Dave acknowledged, closing his eyes as he took small sip the coffee. He grimaced at the strong flavour but was grateful for the caffeine boost, 'Have you been here long?' He peered beyond the cordon at the crowd that had gathered – made up mostly of civilians and the odd reporter, who were trying to get a better view of the crime scene.

'Not that long, Guv, just arrived about five minutes before yourself.' Andy admitted, 'SOCO has just set up.' Staring ahead, he pointed to the Scene Of Crime Officers who were getting their equipment ready and were slipping into their protective gear so as not to contaminate the scene. 'From what I can gather the house belongs to Michael and Sally Thorn, they have a son, Tommy. Neighbours raised the alarm when they heard Mrs Thorn screaming.'

Dave moved toward the police cordon with Andy closely following beside him. He gave Andy a questioning look, 'Which officers arrived on scene first?'

Andy gestured toward the two police officers, standing outside the house, talking with a SOCO, 'That would be PC Bates and Cooper, they arrived approximately ten minutes after neighbours raised the alarm.'

They hurried up to the police cordon, Dave flashed his ID at the uniformed officer in front of the cordon, who lifted it, so they were able to get through and walk over to the two uniformed constables.

'Bates, Cooper, I'm DI Barnes and this is DS Jenkins.' Dave said firmly, showing his ID.

The female officer, a tall statuesque twenty-something woman with long red hair tied up at the back, took a small step forward, 'I'm Cooper sir, this is Bates.' she answered, pointing to her the large bulky thirty-something officer who was standing next to her. Dave noted that he appeared pale and shaken, and that Cooper's hands were also shaking as she drank her tea.

'Sorry to ask you both this, but I am sure you understand. Can you tell me what happened when you arrived?' he asked, softly.

The two constables exchanged looks and Bates nodded for his partner to go ahead. Cooper inhaled a deep breath and spoke with a distinct Scottish accent, 'Well sir, at 23:12 Control received a report of a disturbance at this address, shortly after that they requested that we respond. We arrived at the scene at 23:24 where we found several people and neighbours standing outside the front door worried. Some of the neighbours were shouting through the letterbox trying to speak to whoever was inside.' She paused to take a sip from her cup and continued, 'We asked them to move away, so we could take over. We tried knocking on the door and shouting through the letterbox, which was when we heard a woman sobbing loudly. We both decided the best course of action was for us to break in to gain entry. Will here was forced to use his baton to break the glass so that he could reach inside and unlock the door.' Cooper stopped and nodded for Bates to take over.

'As Wendy said sir, I unlocked the door, and we made our way inside.' Bates explained, 'Before making our way upstairs, we had a quick search around downstairs, but nothing was out of the ordinary. We then made our way upstairs, but when we got to the top of the stairs, we found Mrs Thorn sitting in the landing hallway, in what is best described as a foetal position. She was shaking and rocking and was quite hysterical as we knelt beside her. Wendy tried to calm her down so we could find out what happened, but all she could do was point and scream about her son and husband being dead in the bedroom.' Bates closed his eyes, took in a deep breath, and let out a sad sigh, 'While Wendy was trying to console Mrs Thorn, I opened the bedroom door and made my way in, but what I saw just floored me.'

The grim-faced Bates looked at Dave with a haunted expression, tears almost filling his eyes, 'Sorry sir, but I didn't handle it particularly well. I had to run outside and throw up. What I discovered in there, well, it's just something you cannot prepare for. I hope to God, I never see it again. To be honest sir, I don't think I'll ever get it out of my head.' He glanced over to the house and shook his head in disbelief, 'When I got myself together, I radioed into control to let them know of the situation.'

Dave put his hand on Bates's shoulder and gave him a sad thin smile, 'That's okay son, we have all done it, nothing to be ashamed of. I wish I can tell you you'll get used to it.' He shook his head and turned to Cooper, giving her questioning look, 'Where is Mrs Thorn now?'

'She wasn't in a good way, sir.' Cooper replied, 'I eventually guided her downstairs and sat her in the living room. As soon as the paramedics arrived, they gave her something to calm her down, then they carried her into the ambulance. She is on her way to the hospital now.'

Dave looked at the two police officers, he recognised the tired, haunted expression on their faces, 'You both have done a good job, but what you need now is rest. You both can head back now, I know it will be hard, but try to get some rest. Somebody may contact you both to discuss counselling.'

The two sombre-looking constables thanked him and walked slowly back to their patrol car. Cooper then came to stop, turned and looked inquiringly at Dave, 'Sir, I would like to stay involved if it is okay? If you will let me, may I stay on the case with you?' There was an angry, determined look on her face, 'I would really love to catch the bastard who did this!'

Dave could tell Andy was wanting to say something, but he raised his hand as a signal for him to save it for later. He smiled and spoke softly to Cooper, 'Get some rest, Wendy. Afterwards, if you still feel strongly about it then, come visit me and we can talk about it.'

Wendy smiled gravely at him, nodding, 'Thanks, sir.'

Dave watched as Cooper followed her partner to their squad car. He turned and nodded to Andy to follow him over to the SOCO van. A few minutes later, emerging with protective clothing, they entered the house and made their way upstairs. There were already several SOCOs taking photos, making notes, and gathering evidence outside the bedroom. One of the SOCO gave a small nod to the Detective Inspector and waved a hand at the rear bedroom.

As he stood in the doorway and saw the carnage inside the small room, Dave felt the blood drain from his face.

'Jesus help me.' He said in a horrified whisper.

Wendy remained silent as she watched Will bring the patrol car to a stop in the police station car park. They both sat quietly, staring out through the front windscreen. After about a minute, Will cocked his head and stared at her curiously.

'You were quiet on the way back.' he muttered, 'Anything troubling you?'

'No, I was just thinking about that poor family.' She whispered, shaking her head.

Will nodded in understanding, following it up with a small growl of agreement, 'Yeah, that's something I will not forget for a long time. I hope they find the bastard who did it.'

Wendy bobbed her head slightly in silent commiseration. They both opened their car doors and climbed out. She watched as Will headed toward the station entrance before coming to an abrupt stop as he glanced over his shoulder. Wendy was still standing beside the car, staring thoughtfully up into the night sky.

'Are you coming, Wendy?' he asked curiously.

'I will follow you in soon.' Wendy replied, waving her hand dismissively at him, 'I want to get some air and get my thoughts together.'

Will gave a small nod of understanding and silently continued walking toward the station entrance.

Wendy remained silent and watched the doors of the station entrance swing open for her burly colleague to enter. She narrowed her eyes as she quickly scanned the carpark. On seeing there was no-one else around, she pulled out a small mobile phone from a pouch on the front of her jacket. After switching the phone on, she waited ten more seconds for it to fully boot up, before holding her finger over the front button to unlock it. After tapping on the contacts icon, she selected one of the names off the list and dialled the number.

She held the phone to her ear and listened as a female voice answered after a short ring.

'*Northern Electric, what service do you require?*'

Wendy whispered firmly into the handset, 'Cooper security code Tango-Charlie-Gamma-Alpha-One-Six-Beta.'.

'*Stand by.*' the voice replied.

She heard a short beep as her call was transferred and after a short silence a male voice answered.

'*Report.*'

Clasping the phone closer, Wendy replied in a low urgent tone, 'There has been another incident.'

3

**Location: Reality 672, Terra (Counter-Earth)
Pons Aelius, Britannica, Universal Roman Empire**

inety minutes earlier...
'Doctor Claudia, something is coming through the portal.'

Henrietta peered up from her tablet, turned to Theo Andre, the technician who was sitting next to her. She then glanced at the portal in front of her and stared at its shimmering surface. Swiftly rising out of her chair, she adjusted her eyeglasses, and nervously wiped her sweaty hands down the front of her white leather lab coat.

'Is it the synthroid returning?' she asked nervously.

Theo, a short, dark-skinned, bald man, looked down at the holographic display screen on the console, gave a small nod of confirmation just as a black-skinned creature climbed through the portal into the chamber, stopping in front of them.

Henrietta swallowed, trying hide her disgust at the sight of the creature. She had lost count the number of times she had witnessed the synthroid pass through the portal, but still could not help feeling repulsed every time she saw it.

'Were you successful?' she inquired, trying to hide her revulsion.

The creature turned and then peered up at her with its long red eyes. It slowly lifted its long sharp claws, revealing a large grey container held between them. 'Yeesss.' it hissed.

Henrietta turned and motioned to a large powerful looking man standing at the back of the chamber. He was dressed in black and gold leather; the standard for those serving in the military. The soldier marched forward, gave her a small nod of confirmation, before moving toward the creature and taking the container from its claws and handed it to her.

'Escort the synthroid back to its holding pen.' she ordered before turning back to the creature, 'Follow this man, he will take you back to your room.'

She watched the soldier activate a sensor on the wall and there was small hiss of air as the chamber door slid open. Doctor Claudia shivered as she watched the creature step forward and followed the soldier. She stiffened as she watched it come to a stop in the doorway, turn and stare at her briefly. For a second she thought it wanted to say something. However, it remained silent and continued to follow the soldier out of the chamber.

After the chamber door slid to a close, Henrietta exhaled and sunk back down into her chair. She looked at Theo and they both let out a nervous laugh.

'I hate those things.' he whispered, casting a nervous eye at the closed chamber door, 'Gods! When it stared at you, I nearly soiled myself.'

Distracted by her own thoughts, Doctor Claudia lifted her shoulder in a half a shrug as she peered down at the container in her hands. 'You are to take this bio-sample container to medical, immediately.' she ordered, holding out the container to him.

Theo gave a small nod, took the container from her hands and hurried out of the chamber.

After he had gone, Henrietta brought up the holographic screen on her console and pressed on an icon on the display. She waited as the portal shimmered and revealed an image of Tommy Thorn's bedroom. A soft whimpering emerged from the speakers in the chamber, and she shook her head in sympathy as she realised that it was someone sobbing, probably the child's mother. She tried to focus the screen on where the sobbing was coming from, but realised the woman was outside the portal's field of view.

For thirty minutes Doctor Claudia sat in silence as she monitored the portal, making notes on the scene taking place in the child's bedroom. She raised her eyebrow in curious fascination as she watched a uniformed man – she guessed he was a law enforcement officer – enter the room and then swiftly leave to speak to someone outside her field of view. She tried to adjust the volume to determine what they were saying but let out a groan of frustration as she realised that they were just outside of the range of the portal's audio sensors.

She continued to watch through the portal as three people entered the room. From their clothing she concluded it was possible they were forensic crime scene investigators. She regarded them with scientific curiosity as she watched them take pictures and collect samples.

Two men arrived shortly after, also wearing white uniforms, but from their actions, she deduced they were investigating law enforcement officers. However, Henrietta let out a sharp gasp and she felt her eyes grow wide in shock when one of the newly arrived investigators lowered his mask to speak to one of the forensic investigators. She bolted up out of her chair in surprise, lifted her arm up and pressed a button on the device on her wrist. Henrietta swallowed anxiously as a holographic image of a red-haired stern looking woman appeared in front of her.

'Yes, what is it?' The general snapped irritably.

'S … s … sorry general.' Doctor Claudia stammered, 'Something has come up on the portal I think you need to see, immediately.'

'We are on our way.' The transmission ended abruptly as the call was disconnected from the other end. Doctor Claudia sat back down and tapped her fingers anxiously on console's surface as she waited for the general to arrive.

Henrietta turned sharply round on hearing the chamber door slid open and saw a tall statuesque thirty-something woman with short red hair, wearing a black and gold leather uniform walk purposefully into the chamber. She was followed by an older slightly shorter grey-haired man who was also wearing a similar uniform.

'General.' Doctor Claudia acknowledged, jumping to her feet and nervously pointing at the portal.

'Fascinating.' The general murmured curiously, staring at the image on the portal, 'It appears your doppelgänger has entered the game, Colonel Barnes.'

The lean grey-haired Colonel Barnes let out a small grunt in reply. Henrietta watched his steely grey eyes narrow and then the muscles in his face seemed to harden as his eyes followed his counterpart around the bedroom. The colonel walked around the console, leaned close into the portal and his eyes burned with hatred when he saw his counterpart had suddenly stop in front of the portal and appeared to lean in closer.

Henrietta shivered as she felt a chill run down her spine, *Gods! It is as if they are staring into each other's eyes,* she thought to herself. She watched in morbid fascination as Barnes paced back and forth in front of the portal, scrutinising his counterpart. Although they were much alike, she could see there were several differences that separated them physically. Colonel Barnes had a thin scar on the left side of his face and compared to his counterpart, he appeared more leaner and fitter.

Barnes glanced over his shoulder to the general, 'What are we to do with …' His upper lip curled up into a contemptuous sneer, '*him*?'

'Oh, don't worry. We have already planned for this.' The general replied, smiling knowingly.

Barnes lifted an eyebrow and turned away from the portal, taking a step closer to the general, 'Why not kill him now?'

The general let out a small laugh and placed her hand on his shoulder, 'Because my dear Colonel, the High Command have plans for our Inspector Barnes.' Henrietta saw Barnes wince in pain as the general tightened her grip on his shoulder, 'You are not to touch him, do I make myself clear?'

'Yes …' Barnes murmured through clenched teeth, lowering his head.

The general's green eyes narrowed and she slid her hand under the disgruntled man's chin as she glared into his eyes, 'Yes … what?'

'Yes ... I understand, General Cooper.' Barnes replied sullenly.

Henrietta felt a cold a shiver run down her spine as she watched the corners of General Wendy Cooper's mouth slowly lift in a predatory grin. Her steely green eyes glinted with malice as she turned and stared at the portal.

4

Sucking in panting breaths, Detective Sergeant Jenkins ran up the quiet street, the sweat pouring into his eyes. After the previous night's events, he had found it hard to get to sleep when he had eventually arrived back home in the early hours. He had slept poorly; strange dreams had kept waking him; images of being stalked by an unseen animal.

Andy understood why the crime scene affected him like that. He imagined everyone would be affected somehow. But this was the first time a crime scene was responsible for him having bad dreams.

Out of breath, Andy came to stop outside his house, sucked in a lungful of air and pressed his fingers up to his neck to check his pulse. He glanced at his wristwatch, noted his time, and gave a half a shrug. 'Not my best run, but still decent enough.' he muttered to himself.

Normally when he went for a morning run before work, he found it usually helped to set him up for the day ahead by relaxing him. Today, though, he did not feel as if he had felt any benefit from it.

A shower might help to clear my head, Andy thought, peering at his wristwatch, *I still have plenty of time to get cleaned up.*

After unlocking the door and walking into the hall, Andy smiled as a woman's voice with a faint Mackem accent greeted him.

'Morning love! I'm in the kitchen with Alice'. She called out.

Andy strolled into the kitchen and saw his wife, Mary, sitting on a chair at the kitchen counter and their baby girl, Alice, beside her in a highchair. His wife was still wearing her pyjamas as she tried to feed Alice. He chuckled to himself; there was more food on Alice and the highchair than probably in Alice herself.

'Morning pet', Andy whispered, bending down to give her a kiss and then winked at the toddler. 'Good morning spud' Alice peered up at her father, smiling and giggling.

Mary was normally an attractive woman, in her late 20s, tall and slim, although at that moment she was carrying some baby weight, but she had been trying to work that off at the gym. Her long brown hair was scrunched up at the back of her head.

Andy thought back to when he first met his wife. He first bumped into Mary while working out at the gym. She worked as a nurse and one day, on her day off, she had been running on a treadmill and she had reached for her towel to wipe the sweat out of her eyes. Her towel fell down the side of the treadmill and instinctively reached for it. She lost her footing on the treadmill, fell and shot off. At that exact moment Andy had been walking by and was literally bowled by her. Embarrassed and apologetic, Mary had helped the bewildered man back up on his feet. Andy had been lying face down and was just about to get up to say something but stopped as his eyes met Mary's and from that moment it was love at first sight. She asked him out for a coffee as a way of apology, and five years later they got married. A year later, Alice arrived.

Mary turned to look at her husband, her eyes flickering with a hint of concern, 'You got in late last night and then you were up early for a run. Did you get enough sleep last night?'

Andy took a seat beside her, slipped out of his trainers, and glanced at her while waving his hand in a half-hearted fifty-fifty hand gesture, 'Yeah, I got some sleep. Sorry pet, I tried not to wake you, but the case last night really bothered me. I thought an early morning run would help me, but it didn't.'

Mary's forehead creased as she stared at her husband. Andy could tell she was worrying about him. Of course, he knew she was aware she couldn't outright ask him about a case. But he was also confident in the knowledge she would be there for him if he ever needed to get anything off his chest. He smiled as she leaned over and gave him a cuddle.

'Hmmm that's lovely.' he murmured softly, closing his eyes, and smiling as he caught a whiff of the fragrance of her hair; he had always loved the way her hair and neck smelled. He twisted his head to kiss the inside of her neck and grinned wickedly, knowing what it did to her.

Mary gave a shallow moan, squirmed, and then giggled. She raised an eyebrow as Andy's hand moved down to the top button of her pyjama top and began to unbutton it. She slapped his hand playfully, gave him the hairy eyeball and waved a finger at him, 'Ahha none of that, Sergeant Jenkins. You need to get ready for work, and I have Alice to see too.' she pulled away from him and jabbed her finger at the kitchen door, 'Upstairs now, mister!'

Andy rolled his eyes and let out a melodramatic groan, reluctantly got up from the chair and walked upstairs to get changed.

Half-an-hour later he was back downstairs fully showered and changed. While he was getting dressed, Mary had made him some breakfast – bacon, egg, beans, and toast – which he gratefully ate.

'Sorry pet, not sure what time I will get home tonight,' he mumbled with a mouthful of toast as he gave her a kiss on her cheek.

Mary smiled at him as he took a step over to Alice and kissed the top of her head. 'Goodbye Spud, will you be a good girl for mummy?'

Andy smiled as he heard Alice gurgle in reply. He whistled to himself as made his down the hallway to the front door. Life couldn't get any better than this.

Andy arrived at the police station carpark twenty minutes later. He stopped the car at the closed gate and showed his ID to the guard on duty, who gave a small nod and opened the gate. For once he had managed to find a free car parking space without any bother. After climbing out of his car, he noticed a familiar black Audi Q3 was sitting in the parking bay especially reserved for senior officers and wondered if his mentor had spent the night here once again, like he had done many times before. He then hurried into the building and ran up the flight of stairs that led to his office.

Scattered around the office were various desks with flat-screen computers, telephones, and files. A handful of officers and detectives were working in the office, running around, typing, or chatting and raised their heads in acknowledgement to Andy when they saw him walk in. Large whiteboards covered the walls on the far side of the room upon which were various notes and pictures from the previous night's crime scene.

Andy frowned to himself as he noticed the salt-and-pepper-haired man was sitting on a table edge, studying the whiteboards, his fingers tapping on the bottom of his chin thoughtfully.

Walking up to him, Andy stood beside him and greeted him a warm cherry smile, 'Morning Guv.'

As if he was in a world of his own, Dave continued to stare at the whiteboard, barely acknowledging Andy, 'Hmmm, yes.' He mumbled. He appeared too deep in thought to notice that it was Andy standing next to him.

Andy gave a small cough, but when no further response came, he reached forward and gently tapped the pensive man on the shoulder, 'Guv, you okay? You look like you are in a world of your own here.'

Startled, Dave blinked and turned his head, his eyes widening in surprise on realising it was Andy that was standing next to him, 'Oh sorry, Andy. I didn't see you come in there.' He rubbed his chin with his hand and pointed to the photos of the crime scene on the whiteboard, 'Trying to get my head around this case.'

'That's okay, Guv. Have you been here all night?' Andy asked curiously, observing Dave's dishevelled appearance.

The corner of Dave's mouth twitched, and he lifted his shoulder in a small shrug, 'Oh, sort of. When I got back home, I couldn't settle, so I came straight back. Got a bit of kip in my office.' He waved a hand at his office. Andy turned and noticed the blankets and a pillow on the sofa.

'I brought Jenny in with me.' He continued, pointing to the dog lying in her basket, who was silently watching everything going on. Her tail wagged, as if she knew that they were talking about her, 'She has been no bother, and everyone seems to enjoy having her here.'

Dave turned back at the whiteboard and frowned, bringing his attention back on it, 'I cannot place my finger on it, but something just doesn't sit right with me about all this.' he muttered, thoughtfully tapping his chin again, 'Walking around that bedroom, I thought it didn't seem to add up.'

Andy gave a thin smile and nodded in agreement, 'Yeah Guv, something about all this bothers me too. It isn't a break and entry gone wrong because there were no signs of any forced entry. All doors and windows were locked from inside and nothing of any value was taken.'

'Yeah, so why kill, sorry, mutilate, a child and his father?' Dave asked, scratching his head, 'Was it to send a message or something else?'

'We won't learn anything until we get to speak to Mrs Thorn properly.' Andy replied, 'I certainly doubt she did it. From what PC Cooper said, Mrs Thorn doesn't have the build or size to do something like this.'

Andy lapsed into silence and tapped his finger over his mouth, scrutinising the photos on the whiteboard. He nodded himself, he too had sensed something else in the bedroom last night. He had been reluctant to say anything, not wanting to sound like a fool to his superior officer.

Dave cocked his head inquiringly, as if noticing the younger man's hesitation, 'You want to add something, Sergeant?'

Andy inhaled a deep breath, opened his mouth to speak but hesitated slightly, 'Sorry Guv, um ... not sure if this sounds stupid but when we were in the bedroom, as I walked past the mirror, I thought I fe—'

'Like something had walked over your grave?' Dave interjected. He nodded in agreement and gave the hesitant Andy half a smile, 'Yeah, you are not wrong there, son. When I stood in front of that mirror, I got a sense like something.... watching me. To be honest, it creeped me out.' He gestured to the photo on the whiteboard, 'Then there is that.' he sighed, smacking the whiteboard hard with his finger in frustration, 'Three large scratch marks on the dressing table, going from the edge of the table to the edge of the mirror.'

Andy rubbed the back of his neck with hand as he examined the photo in question and wondered out loud, 'Carried out by something moving a heavy object maybe?'

'I don't know Sergeant; I just don't know.' Dave replied uncertainly, shaking his head, 'You could almost say someth—' Before he could finish, a woman's voice with a familiar strong Scottish accent came from behind, interrupting him.

'As if something crawled out and killed Tommy Thorn and his father?'

As Andy turned sharply round to the source of the voice, his eyes widened in surprise on recognising the flame-haired woman who was staring intently at the whiteboard. It was Wendy Cooper. What was she doing here?

'Sorry sir, I apologise for eavesdropping, but I came to ask if I could help you with the case.' Cooper asked hopefully.

Andy gave a small nod agreement, figuring another pair of hands would not hurt and Cooper already knew about the case, but he knew it was not up to him. He cast an eye across to Dave, and he guessed he had been thinking the same thing because he gave him a nod of agreement.

'No Cooper, you weren't eavesdropping,' Dave chuckled and gave her a sly wink, 'You were only being used as a sounding board for our theories. To be honest, an extra pair of eyes and ears could be useful since you already know the case.'

Cooper laughed sheepishly, the relief evident on her face, 'Thank you sir, I won't let you down.'

Dave gave a small nod and then cocked his head inquiringly at her, 'Wendy, sorry I hope you don't mind if I call you by your first name, but I find all this formality leaves me with a headache.' he joked, gesturing back to the whiteboard, 'Continue with what you were saying, please.'

Wendy took a step beside Andy, who smiled warmly and extended his hand in greeting, 'Welcome aboard, Wendy.'

'Thanks sir,' she replied. She frowned thoughtfully, studying the whiteboard, and then shook her head in exasperation, 'To be honest sir, while sitting with Mrs Thorn I just had this sense that something didn't seem right. It is hard to describe, but when I stared into the room, something kept drawing my eyes to the mirror.'

Andy nodded thoughtfully to himself. Deep down, he agreed with everything Wendy had said. It did sound insane, but so far, they had nothing else to go on.

His brow furrowing, Dave looked at Wendy curiously, 'Were you able to get anything out of Mrs Thorn while sitting with her? Anything at all? Even the smallest detail would help.'

The corners of Wendy's eyes creased, and she blew out her cheeks in frustration, 'Sorry sir, by the time we had arrived she was too far gone. Unfortunately, she was just too traumatised for me to get anything out of her, and I didn't want to push her.'

Dave sucked air in through his teeth and pinched the bridge of his nose with his hand. 'I understand Wendy; seeing something like that happen to anybody, let alone your husband and child, will send anyone over the edge.' He lapsed into a thoughtful silence for a couple of seconds before turning back to Andy, 'Andy, I want you and Wendy to go to the hospital and see if Mrs Thorn is in any condition to speak. I will take a trip down to the Medical Examiner and see if she has anything she can tell me.'

Andy bobbed his head to Wendy to follow him and they started walking out. He let out a ragged breath, he was not looking forward to what they needed to do next.

Just as Wendy began to follow her colleague out of the door, she flinched as she felt a small vibration coming from her inner jacket pocket. 'Sorry Sergeant, I just need to answer a call of nature.' she said apologetically, gesturing to the door marked *"Female WC"*.

'No problem, Cooper, I will meet you outside the main entrance.' Andy replied, waving his hand at the stairs ahead of him.

'Thank you, Sergeant.' she replied, smiling.

But as she dashed down the corridor, Wendy cast a surreptitious eye over her shoulder as she came to a stop in front of the female toilet. After confirming the Detective Sergeant was no longer behind her, she opened the door and headed straight into empty toilet cubicle, closing the door behind her. She reached into her jacket and retrieved a mobile phone from her inside pocket.

After unlocking the mobile phone with her thumbprint, Wendy read the text message on the screen.

'Were you successful?' The text read.

'Yes.' Wendy typed back in response, her fingers moving swiftly over the screen.

Ten seconds later, the phone vibrated once again with another text message alert.

'Do they suspect?'

Wendy pressed her lips tightly together, shook her head sadly and typed back a brief message.

'No.'

Her phone vibrated a third time.

'You are to continue as ordered. Proceed with caution.'

5

Wendy sat nervously in the car as it made its way to the hospital. She glanced over to Andy, who was sitting next to her in the driver's seat. He appeared to be deep in thought as he guided the vehicle along the road. She inhaled a deep breath then spoke in a soft anxious tone.

'Sir, I apologise if you think I have overstepped the line by pushing myself onto this case, but I assumed I could be of some use to you during this investigation.' Wendy said quietly.

Andy glanced at her, his eyes widening in mild surprise, 'Cooper, I don't think that, honestly!' he laughed. His mouth broadened into a friendly grin and lifted his shoulder in a half shrug, 'It's like the Guv said; an extra pair of hands will come in useful and also as a bonus, the case already involves you.'

Wendy smiled, feeling herself relax, 'Thanks sir, I hope I don't let either of you down.' she hung her head and let out a deep breath, 'I see how I come across as driven, but I am ambitious, eager to learn, and I hope to make it to Detective like you one day.'

Andy huffed in bemusement, 'Nothing wrong with being driven and ambitious, Cooper.' He gave a small nod of understanding, 'I was a lot like you at your age, eager to succeed, but I still had a lot to learn.' His forehead creased and then he gazed at her thoughtfully, 'I guess the Guv sees that in you too. He likes people who are driven and push themselves. You play fair with him, and he will watch after you and teach you a lot. All he asks is that you observe, learn, and have his back. If you do that, then you cannot go wrong.'

Wendy smiled to herself, feeling the tension ease in her shoulders. She had been anxious when her superiors had contacted her and requested that she had to get herself assigned to Detective Inspector Barnes's team. Initially she had been uncomfortable at being ordered to spy on Barnes and his colleagues, but the more she talked to Andy and the more she listened to him talk about the Detective Inspector, she realised the more she liked them, which left her with the feeling she could learn a lot from them both.

Wendy smiled and bobbed her head in gratitude, 'Thanks sir, I know I will learn a lot from you both.'

'Brown noser!' He answered jokingly, winking, but then held up his hand and gave her a serious looking side eye, 'Please Cooper, when we are alone like this it is okay to call me Andy. I am like the Guv; all this formality gives me a headache.'

'Thanks, Andy.' she replied, 'You can call me Wendy if it is easier.'

Wendy gave her colleague a quick glance. Her first impression of Andy had been that he was friendly and appeared to keep himself in shape. Her eyes drifted to the wedding ring on his finger. He wasn't her type, plus she knew better than to date fellow officers. She liked his easy-going attitude and thought they could work well together. Her jaw tightened, as she comprehended this was the part of the job she hated; being ordered to keep secrets from people she respected.

I hope they will forgive me when they find out the truth, she thought to herself.

They lapsed into a contemplative silence as Andy continued to drive the car along the road. After a few minutes, Wendy turned to her colleague thoughtfully.

'Andy, how do you want to play this when we get to the hospital?' she asked curiously, 'Mrs Thorn may recognise me from last night, so I may have a connection with her.'

Andy frowned thoughtfully and then gave a small nod, 'If you are comfortable to take the lead, go ahead. She may be more willing to speak to another woman. I will keep my distance, observe, and step in if you need me to.'

Five minutes later they arrived at the hospital and drove the car through barrier into the busy visitor carpark, eventually finding a free parking space. As she climbed out of the car, Wendy hurried across the carpark alongside Andy. Approaching the hospital entrance, she silently observed various people walking in and out of the main entrance: patients, possibly making their way to appointments or nipping out for a smoke. Members of staff also came and went, exchanging pleasantries as they passed one another.

The two officers made their way through the hospital into the main reception area. At the reception desk Andy showed his ID card and inquired which ward Mrs Thorn was on. The receptionist glanced at the card and quickly checked her computer. A minute later they made their way to the elevator. Luckily, they arrived just as an elevator door slid open, so they quickly hurried in. Andy pressed a button for floor three and less than a minute later the elevator came to a stop and the doors opened. As they walked out and both turned to get their bearings, Wendy gestured to a floor plan on the wall and after a quick study they were off in the right direction.

As she opened the door leading into the ward, Wendy saw it was a long, narrow corridor lined with doors on either side, leading to individual private hospital rooms, with a nurses' station close to the entrance. But as she took a step into the ward, she could see three nurses were running around the station, busily carrying out their duties. There was a chestnut-haired nurse sitting at the front of the desk, she appeared to be making some notes in a chart and lifted her head as she noticed the couple approaching her. Wendy cast a quick eye over her ID and noted that her name was Monica Walsh.

Wendy remained silent as Andy showed the nurse his ID, 'I am Detective Sergeant Jenkins,' he said, 'and this is Constable Cooper. We are here to speak to Sally Thorn, they admitted her to this ward last night.'

The nurse pursed her lips as she studied ID in her hand and gave a small nod of confirmation, 'Yes, Sergeant Jenkins, we were expecting you.' she handed the ID back and smiled warmly at Andy, 'Your Inspector rang ahead to let us know that you would be coming. Mrs Thorn is in room 5. I'm Sister Walsh, but you can call me Monica, if you would like to follow me, I shall take you down to her.'

Monica walked out from behind her station and motioned for the couple to follow her. As they walked down the corridor she turned and gave them a both a sad look, 'Unfortunately, I am not sure whether Mrs Thorn will be in any condition for you to speak to.' she said gravely, 'She was in such a distressed state when she arrived in Accident & Emergency that they had to sedate her to keep her from harming herself. They transferred her to us a couple of hours ago.'

Andy nodded in understanding and let out a regret filled sigh, 'I understand, but we really need to speak with her. She is a key witness to an ongoing investigation.'

Monica's eyes flickered with sadness and gave a small nod, 'I'll see if she is in any condition for her to answer your questions, but I cannot promise anything.' she leaned in closer to Andy and lowered her voice, 'We understand that her son and husband were brutally killed last night. The rumour is that a wild animal may have been responsible, is that true?'

Wendy felt her jaw tighten and rolled her eyes. She had suspected this would happen – rumours starting to spread. She glanced at Andy and guessed from his expression that he was of the same opinion and had decided it was best not share any information with Monica as she watched him give her a small shake of his head, 'I am sorry, but I cannot comment on an ongoing investigation.'

Monica nodded in understanding, 'I understand.' she muttered, coming to a stop at Room 5, 'If you can wait outside for a minute, I will check to see if Mrs Thorn is in any condition for you to speak to her.'

Without waiting a response, she opened the door and swiftly walked into the room, closing the door behind her. Less than a minute later, the door reopened, and she motioned for them to enter, 'She is awake and calm at the moment.' she whispered, 'She says she is okay to speak to you, but please, try to keep it brief.'

Andy gave a small nod of acknowledgement and glanced at Wendy, inclining his head to her. She gave him a thumbs up in confirmation, she was ready to go ahead with the plan they had discussed earlier.

On entering the room, Wendy noticed it was a typical NHS hospital room. It was compact, a window overlooked the carpark with the blinds half-closed. Beside the window there was a single bed, someone had pulled a small hospital bed table down to the foot of the bed. A small bedside cabinet stood next to the bed. A tiny flat-screen TV was attached to the bed frame on an extending arm and at the bottom of the bed there was a rack which held patient charts. Wendy glanced around the room and noticed there was a door in the room's corner leading to a small bathroom.

Sitting on the bed there was thirty-something pale-faced woman, wearing a white hospital gown. An intravenous tube ran from her hand, leading to a bag of clear fluid that hung on a support hook above the bed. She lay unmoving, staring blankly out of the window, but as Wendy walked into the room, Sally turned her head and stared at her through hollow eyes.

Wendy noted that Sally's eyes were red and puffy, possibly from crying. Her short ginger curly hair was wild and unkempt as if she could not be bothered to comb it. She also looked pale and drawn, having a vacant presence about her. Wendy guessed that it was an effect of the sedative that the hospital had given her to help calm her down. She edged carefully over to the bed, pulled a chair over and sat next to her.

'Sally, do you remember me?' Wendy asked in a soft tone, 'My name is PC Wendy Cooper. I am one of the police officers who came to help you last night.'

Sally's eyes narrowed and she stared back at Wendy with an empty expression, bobbing her head briefly in acknowledgement, 'Yes, I remember you.' she replied in a hushed voice.

Wendy turned and gestured to Andy, who was standing behind her in watchful silence, 'This is Detective Sergeant Andrew Jenkins.' Andy gave a silent nod to Sally as she looked at him. She leaned in closer to Sally as she continued, 'Sally, we are investigating what happened last night and we would like to ask you some questions; is that okay?'

Sally bobbed her head in acknowledgement, 'Yes, that's fine. I'll try to answer anything you ask, but I am still hazy about last night.' she let out a heavy depressed sigh and shook her head sadly, 'Not sure if I can be of any help to you.'

Monica, who was still in the room, touched her shoulder delicately, 'Sally, I will be here with you this whole time. If it becomes too much for you, just say and they will stop.'

Wendy glanced at Monica, gave a small nod in gratitude, and turned her head back to the pale woman, 'Sally, if you don't mind can we start at the beginning?' She reached over and touched her gently on the hand, 'Can you tell me in your own words what happened last night?'

Sally inhaled a ragged breath and closed her eyes, as if reflecting on the events of the previous night, and began to talk in a low melancholic voice, 'I can remember Tommy had gone to bed happy and had been in a good mood. Michael and I were relaxing.' The corners of her mouth turned up in a half a smile, 'We went to bed earlier than usual. As it had been such a long time since we ….' She stopped and her face turned scarlet, her eyes darting surreptitiously over to Andy.

Sensing her discomfort, Wendy leaned forward and held her hand softly, 'It's okay, Sally.'

Sally smiled gratefully and then bobbed her head, 'We had been making love when we heard a scream come from Tommy's bedroom.' She rolled her eyes and shook her head angrily, 'Michael got angry at being interrupted. Tommy has always been afraid of the dark. So, we just assumed it was that.' Wendy could see that the woman's teary eyes were getting wider, 'We had a bit of a disagreement, nothing too major.' she let out a long sad breath as she continued, 'Michael wanted to ignore him, but

I made him get out of bed and check on him. I turned over to go to sleep.' Tears slowly trickled down her cheeks and her breathing started to become heavier. She then squeezed her eyes shut, balled her hands into tight fists and her breathing quickened as her voice began to crack, 'Michael left to check on Tommy, I heard him knock and he asked for him to answer him.'

Whether it was out of concern for her patient's wellbeing, Monica made to reach over to Sally, as if to stop her but Wendy held up her hand, 'Please I realise it's difficult, but we need her to continue.' She pleaded and turned back to the distraught woman and spoke gently to her, trying to encourage her. 'Sally, please keep going Love, you are nearly there.'

'I guess it was a few minutes later I overheard a large thud coming from Tommy's room.' Sally croaked. Her chest started to rise and fall in rapid breaths, 'I shouted for Michael, but he never answered ... I ... I ... got out of bed a ... a ... and ... I ... I ... think I ran into his bedroom ...' Wendy could tell it was all becoming too much for Sally as she watched her eyes widen in shock. Sobbing, Sally shook her head, and then started to pull at her hair, 'I... I... saw their bodies...' Her voice was heavy with anguish as she let out a horrified wail, 'Oh God! Their bodies.'

Monica ran over to the whimpering woman to comfort her, 'It's okay Sally, let it out.' She soothed, looking to Wendy through pleading eyes, 'Please, we really need to stop this now. You can see she cannot take much more.'

Sally waved her hand and shook her head. Wendy could not help admire the woman at the way she was trying to pull herself together and carry on, 'N ... n ... no. I ... I'm fine.' she stammered. Her forehead suddenly creasing, she jerked her head to Wendy and grabbed her wrist, 'I ... it has only just come to me, b ... b ... but ...' She then paused and closed her eyes. Maybe she was trying to build the strength to continue, Wendy wasn't sure, but she reached forward and clasped Mary's hand reassuringly, 'Please Sally, you are doing great.' she whispered, 'Please, anything you can remember, may help us.'

Sally blinked and looked at Wendy uncertainly, 'Y ... y ... you may assume this is nuts or my mind playing tricks on me.' she hesitated, and her forehead furrowed in confusion, 'but when I was standing at the bedroom door.' She cut off, squeezed her eyes shut and shook her head, then inhaled a deep breath and continued. 'For a moment I thought I saw something crawl into the mirror.'

Wendy felt her heart wrench as she watched Sally collapse forward, bury her face into hands and began crying softly to herself. Whether it was because her story was finished, or maybe it had been too much of a strain for her continue, Wendy wouldn't like to guess. She remained silent as she watched Monica gently lay Sally back down and gently stroke her hair.

Wendy turned and glanced at Andy with a stunned expression. The colour draining from his face, he stared back at her in disbelief, as she grimly turned to back to the traumatised woman.

'Thank you, Sally, you have been great.' Wendy whispered.

Andy moved forward and gently tapped Monica on her shoulder, who raised a curious eyebrow as he leaned closer to whisper in her ear.

'I am sure you understand, but I still have to tell you.' he murmured, 'But I would appreciate it if you can keep what you just overheard to yourself. We would be grateful if you didn't discuss it with anyone.'

'Yes, I understand.' she replied glumly, bobbing her head in understanding.

Andy gave Monica a half-smile and wordlessly moved past her. He raised his hand and motioned for Wendy to follow him back through the door into the corridor.

Without making any comment, Wendy got up from her chair and followed her colleague out of the door. Once in the corridor, she leaned against the wall and stared at Andy, shaking her head in disbelief, 'Sir, pardon my French here.' she said incredulously, 'But what the fuck is going on?'

Sombre-faced, Andy lifted his hands and shook his head in frustration, 'I don't know, Wendy. If I hadn't already seen the marks in front of the mirror, I would have put down what she said as hysterics. I don't know about you, but I need a drink and then after that I want to take another look at that bedroom.'

Wendy swallowed and stared at her colleague through narrow eyes, 'Andy, I don't know how to say this, but this is starting to scare me.'

His fingers pinching the bridge of his nose, Andy let out a long heavy sigh, looked up at the ceiling and gave a small nod of agreement, 'Me too pet, me too.'

Wendy shivered to herself as she felt an icy chill pass through her as she made her back out of the corridor. Something in her gut was telling her this was just the tip of the iceberg, and it left her with a stark feeling that things were about to get worse.

Monica quietly closed Sally's door and hurried back to her desk behind the nurses station at the top of the ward. She settled in behind the desk, pulled out a chair and sat down on it. Elaine, who was sitting in the seat in the seat beside Monica, glanced over to her sympathetically.

'We saw you take the police down to speak to Sally Thorn.' she whispered, 'What was it like? Did you find out anything interesting?'

Monica glanced around and leaned in closer to her colleague, 'Sorry Elaine, but I am sure you can understand I cannot really say much. But what I can tell you, if what I learned is true, it was enough to make your skin crawl. I have had to give Sally something to help her sleep, as she was in such a state.'

Elaine gave a small nod of silent understanding and looked sadly down the corridor toward Sally's room.

Back in Sally's room, a cloaked figure stood silently in the room's bathroom and pushed the door open slightly. It watched in silence as Sally turned restlessly in her bed. Undetected by the room's occupant, it pushed bathroom door open, and then glided stealthily into the room, coming to stop bedside Sally's bed. As if sensing someone was standing beside her, Sally opened her eyes and raised her head up and squinted at the shadowy figure standing over her.

'Sorry nurse, I am having trouble sleeping.' she murmured, 'Could you help me sit up?'

Sally smiled as the figure leaned toward her, but then her eyes suddenly widened in alarm as the figure reached out and grabbed her throat with its right hand. Sally opened her mouth to scream, but the figure silenced her cries by covering her mouth and nose with its left hand. Then the silvery hand liquefied and the figure heard Sally gag as the silver liquid flowed into her mouth and nose, choking her.

As the figure watched Sally slowly lose consciousness and her arms drop by her sides, it then leaned forward and held open her eyelids with its right hand. Once it was satisfied that Sally's life was extinguished, it released its grip and watched her body fall limply back on the bed like a rag doll. Its hand solidifying, the figure carefully reached over to the chair beside the bed, picked up the dressing gown that hung over it and carefully unwrapped the gown's cord. With a sense of purpose, it then silently moved to the room's closed door, opened it slightly and peered through the gap. Satisfied that nobody was coming, it gently closed the door and moved back toward the bathroom door.

The figure tied one end of the cord onto the clothes peg on the bathroom side of the door and threw the rest of the cord over the top of the door. After closing the bathroom door, it next carefully picked up the chair beside Sally's bed and placed it in front of the closed door. With defined purpose, the entity silently then took a step toward the bed and, after carefully removing the intravenous tube from Sally's hand, it then picked up her body with extraordinarily little effort and carried her lifeless form over to the bathroom door.

Carefully leaning the woman's dead body on top of the chair, it wrapped the hanging cord around the corpse's neck. Completely satisfied that the cord was tight enough, it knocked the chair away and lay it on its side beneath the hanging body.

Content it had everything perfectly in place, the hooded figure then opened the bathroom door, re-entered the bathroom and closed the door behind it.

6

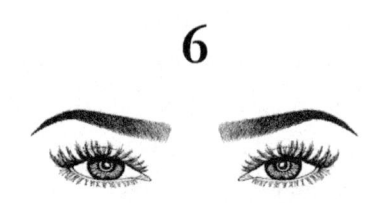

Detective Inspector Dave Barnes hurried through the narrow corridor but came to complete as he spotted the unwelcome figure of Chief Inspector Raymond Thomas lurking in front of him. He rolled his eyes and let out a grumble of annoyance to himself. That was just great! Was asking it too much just to have one day without the conceited windbag trying to interfere with one his cases?

It was not the fact that Thomas was his superior officer – Dave could accept that with no bother. It was because the Chief Inspector was an annoying know-it-all and had a habit of looking down on people, boasting to everyone who would listen he had been educated in a prestigious University. There was just something about the man that really set his teeth on edge, and he was not the only who thought the same way. In fact, the entire station was of the same opinion. The pompous windbag was like a tornado; whenever he appeared people just cleared out of his way.

Dave twisted his head from side to side as he desperately searched for somewhere to hide; anywhere – he didn't care where – so long as it gave him a chance to lay low until the grey-bearded spectre of misfortune had passed him by. Unfortunately, after finding all his escape routes blocked or were already being used by people who had seen the Chief Inspector before him, he was forced to reluctantly concede he had no choice but to take one for the team. He let out a small groan to himself as he realised the man in question had spotted him and was starting to march toward him, arms behind his back, head straight like an army sergeant major.

'Good Morning Barnes.' Thomas greeted brusquely, the tone of his voice had a condescending quality about it, 'How are you today? Feeling good today?' Barely giving his subordinate time to open his mouth to respond, he continued speaking, 'Very good. Very good,' He frowned as he caught sight of a piece of fluff on Dave's shoulder and flicked it away in an absent-minded kind of manner, 'Awful business last night involving that family, just awful. I am right in assuming that you have investigated and already have a suspect in mind?'

Dave's jaw tightened in annoyance, and he felt teeth grind together, but forced himself to relax as he answered in neutral tone of voice, 'Yes sir. It was a horrific scene we came across last night, nothing like we have seen before. But we just started to investigate, so unfortunately it is too early to say that we have a suspect in mind.'

Thomas' grey eyes widened in mild surprise as he stared blankly at Dave, appearing only to be half listening, 'What! No suspect?' he exclaimed, waggling his finger in front of Dave's nose, 'That's not what I heard. In fact, isn't it true we found a suspect at the scene - one who is currently at the hospital? From my experience, in cases like this, it is always a family member responsible.'

There goes my molar, Dave thought to himself as he gritted his teeth more aggressively. He forced a smile and gave the Chief Inspector a small nod, 'Yes sir. Detective Sergeant Jenkins and PC Cooper are interviewing Mrs Thorn in the hospital.' he held up his hands and shook his head, 'But she is not a suspect, in fact she is as much a victim herself. She is being dealt with as a key witness, who I may remind you, *sir,* she did witness the death of her son and husband.'

Thomas let out a pompous grunt and waved his hand dismissively, 'Yes. Yes. I am sure you believe that. I am sure time will tell whether you are right.' His eyes narrowed and he jabbed his finger into the Dave's chest, 'I shouldn't have to remind you the press are already onto this, so I want this dealt with quickly. Understood?'

Without waiting for a response, Thomas turned away from the quietly seething Dave and then began to stare into a window, as if to admire his own reflection. He brought his hand up, brushed his greying beard with his fingers and then straightened his tie before turning back to Dave and gave him the hairy eyeball, 'I don't want to have to tell you, David, that it will not look good for you if *you* don't solve this.' Thomas inclined his head and gave a dismissive flick of his wrist, 'Well carry on, don't let me hold you back.'

Not giving Dave any time to reply, the pompous man turned on his heel and walked swiftly away, leaving the bewildered Detective Inspector to stare at the back of Thomas's head as he hurried down the corridor. Dave rolled his eyes, glanced up at the ceiling and let out a heavy sigh in exasperation. Having dealt with people like that all his life, he had hoped he would have gotten used to it by now, but he was forced to grudgingly accept that the force was all about politics now.

The Chief Inspector flew up the flight of stairs two at a time. As he reached the top of the stairs, he turned and hurried down a short corridor, stopping in front of a door labelled *"Chief Inspector Thomas"*.

Thomas opened the door and walked into a small secretarial office and glanced around. A small desk and filing cabinet stood to the right of him. An open door lay ahead of him, leading to another room. Jayne, a plump middle-aged woman, who was sat behind the desk typing on the keyboard, peered up from her work as the Chief Inspector walked through the door.

'Good Morning Chief Inspector.' she said, smiling.

'Morning Jayne.' Thomas replied gruffly, hurrying toward the open door leading to his office. He stopped half-way through the doorway and snapped back at the woman, without turning around, 'I will be making an important telephone call shortly. I am not to be interrupted. Understood?'

Jayne blinked in surprise and gave a small nod, 'Yes sir, understood.'

Thomas let out a short grunt, stepped into his office and closed the door behind him. He then took off his police uniform jacket and flat peaked police cap, hung them both on the coat hanger beside the door. Next, he strolled over to the desk that was in front of the large oblong window and came to a stop behind it.

Thomas stare thoughtfully out of the window to the carpark below. He frowned as he spotted Barnes dashing towards his car. Brushing his hand over his beard, he watched silently as the vehicle made its way out of the car park and followed it until it was out of his line of sight.

Deep in thought, Thomas pulled out his black office chair and sat down. He reached over, pulled open a drawer and reached into it for his mobile phone. After studying the small device in his hand silently for a minute, he held his finger down on a button and waited patiently for the phone boot up. He next tapped his finger on the phone's screen, brought up a list of contacts and scrolled through it. Once he found who he was looking for, he gently tapped the contact's name and pressed his finger on the green dial icon.

With the phone pressed tightly to his ear, Raymond listened as he heard a male voice answer abruptly after a short ring tone.

'*Yes.*'

'It's me.' Raymond whispered, 'I think we have a problem with DI Barnes.'

'*That is none of your concern. We have already taken steps to deal with Barnes. You are not to interfere ... understood?*'

'Wha ... Wha ... What do you mean?' he stammered, frowning, 'What steps?'

'*That is none of your concern. Do not interfere.*'

Raymond opened his mouth to object, but he quickly realised that his mysterious contact had disconnected the call from their side and lowered the mobile phone from his ear. Deeply troubled, he peered at it silently, swallowed at the heaviness he was feeling in his stomach and wondered, not for the first time, just what he had gotten himself involved in.

Twenty minutes later, after rushing down a long corridor, Dave came to a stop in front of a set of double doors, which was labelled *"Forensic Medical Examiner"*. He pushed open the double doors and strode into a small waiting room. On his right was an open door leading into what appeared to be a changing room, and directly in front of him stood a single closed door. After he took a step forward and gave a firm knock on the closed door, he heard a woman's voice with a strong Cheshire accent, shout out from the other side of the door.

'Come in, but please make sure you change into a gown in the side room before you enter.'

After nipping into the side room and slipping into protective clothing and a mask, Dave walked into a large cold room and saw two medical examination tables with what looked like the remains of bodies on both. In the middle of the two tables stood a large woman wearing a green hospital garment, gloves, and a protective face shield. In one of her gloved hands, she was holding a brain. She turned and beamed at him acknowledgement.

'Hello David.' Karen cried out, lifting her free hand up in the air and holding it over her shielded face in a melodramatic gesture, 'Please tell me today is when you finally come to whisk me away from all this?'

Dave took a step over to her, held up his hands apologetically and grinned, 'Alas my dear Karen, if only I could, but I am here on business rather than pleasure.' Becoming more serious, he gestured to the brain she was holding, 'Is that the murder case from last night? It's actually that I have come to speak to you about.'

Her eyes twinkling mischievously, Karen shook head and laughed, 'See, I knew it was my body you were after.' She twisted her head round and spoke to a young ginger haired man who was standing at the back of the room. He too was wearing a green garment, gloves, and face shield, 'You there, James, is it?' she snapped irritably, clicking her fingers at him, 'Don't just stand there! If you want to make yourself useful, weigh this brain for me.'

James nodded, hurried over to Karen, appearing squeamish as he took the brain from her hands, 'Yes Doctor Logue, I'll do that right away.' he croaked. Dave was almost positive he caught a glint of fear in James eyes as he dashed away from the scowling woman.

Karen gave Dave a bemused side eye and shook her head, 'Don't know where they get these assistants these days.' she whispered, 'Nice boy, but a bit on the slow side.'

Dave chuckled, and then blinked, remembering what he was there for and pointed to the bodies on the tables, 'I am sorry, Karen, but I am on a tight deadline here. Am I right in guessing that these two bodies are the remains from the murder scene last night?'

Karen nodded sadly and peered down at the two tables, 'Yes, I am sorry to say that they are.' She held up her hands apologetically and let out a small unhappy sigh, 'Unfortunately, I cannot tell you much at the moment. Because of the state the two bodies were in when they came to me, it took us both a bit of time to arrange the bodies correctly.'

Dave's eyebrows knitted together as he nodded in understanding, 'I understand. But is there anything you can tell me that may be of use to me now. We are working on the theory that whatever did this wasn't human.'

Karen started and looked at Dave in mild surprise. She cocked her head and waved her hand thoughtfully, 'Well, David, I more or less suspected from the condition of the two bodies that a human couldn't have done this.' She leaned in closer to the remains on the table and pulled a magnifier light over to the torso, 'You see those tear marks; they certainly weren't done by anything human. They also are too ragged to have been done by a weapon. The wounds are quite deep too, they appear to have been done by claws.' She then pulled the light closer, highlighting three tears on the skin, 'The tears are of equal size and spacing on both bodies. I would assume it is something that has three fingers or claws.' She reached forward and held up an arm to Dave, allowing him a closer look. 'Also, you will notice there are no defensive wounds on the arms.'

'So, whatever attacked them, attacked them so fast they didn't have a chance to defend themselves?' Dave murmured in acknowledgement.

Karen nodded in agreement, 'I also noticed that there was some fluid around the wound.' She tilted her head and held up a finger thoughtfully, 'My guess is that it is saliva, and I have taken a swab sample to test for DNA. If I was to guess, I would have to say you are looking for a large animal, but until I get the test results back, I cannot say for definite.'

Dave bobbed his head in understanding and blew out his cheeks in frustration. His eyes narrowing, he glanced over his shoulder to James and leaned closer to Karen. 'This is off the record, but we are working on that theory too.' He stared at her hopefully, 'Can you give me any guess what type of creature could do this?'

Karen lowered her head slightly and her forehead creased as she glanced at the body on the table. 'No, but this may sound crazy. The only thing that makes marks like this is something like a shark, but that would be ridiculous as we are inland, and the victims were indoors.' She took small a step closer to Dave and spoke in a hushed voice, 'I found something else which was strange. There is something off with the weight of the brain, it doesn't feel right.' She jerked her head over shoulder, 'Which is the reason I asked James to weigh it.'

Hearing a cough come from across the room behind him, and Dave spun round and saw James was waving his hand at Karen, 'Dr Logue, can you come here, please? This cannot be right. I have weighed the brain like you asked but the weight is off, I am getting 1100 grams.'

Karen regarded Dave attentively, 'It looks like my hunch was correct.' She frowned and then turned back to the young man, 'James, do me a favour, weigh the other brain and tell me what that is too.'

Dave raised an eyebrow and looked at Karen curiously, 'How much should a brain weigh?'

The woman hung her head and gave Dave a look like that of lecturer teaching a student, 'Well, an adult brain should weigh around 1300 to 1400 grams and if my hunch is right, that child's brain weight will be abnormal too.'

She lapsed into silence and strode over to examine the adult brain. After a few minutes of looking under a microscope, she eventually raised her head and stared at Dave with a look of bewilderment, 'The reason the brain is lighter than it should be is because it is missing the hypothalamus.' There was a tone of disbelief in her voice as she pointed her finger to a section of the brain, 'That is the portion of the brain that releases hormones and controls body temperature.'

James handed the smaller brain over to Karen with a perturbed look on his face, 'This was the same Dr Logue, the weight is off too.'.

Once again, a few more minutes passed, as Karen studied the smaller brain under a microscope. When she was finished, she raised her head up and looked at Dave again with an even more puzzled look on her face, 'This one is the same.' she said incredulously, her voice holding a tone of disbelief, 'It's missing the hypothalamus too!'

A sense of unease building inside him, Dave rubbed the back his neck and looked at Karen through troubled eyes, 'Can you tell me what would need something like that for.'

Karen gave half a shrug and lifted her hands apologetically, 'I am sorry I am at a loss as to why. I will continue my examination and as soon as I get my test results back, I will contact you.'

'Thanks for your help, Karen.' Dave replied and then gave her a wry smile, 'I owe you one.'

After changing, he made his way back out of the changing room, deep in thought. He blew out his cheeks in frustration; just when he thought this case was strange enough, now he had this to consider on top of everything else.

His mind elsewhere, Dave charged through the door, but stopped when he felt it strike something solid. It was then followed by a small yelp of pain of and the sound of a body hitting the floor. Gently reopening the door, he felt his eyes climb up his head in shock at the attractive middle-aged brunette who was laid out on the floor, glasses askew, with a pile of papers scattered around her.

'Oh, I am sorry.' Dave said apologetically, bending down to help her up, 'My fault really, I should have been more careful.'.

He could tell from the way the flustered looking woman was attempting to straighten her glasses, that she was struggling to keep hold of any vestiges of dignity she had left. As he carefully helped her back onto her feet, he noticed the stranger was quite striking, appearing to be of average height; around five foot seven, with long brown hair that was tied up at the back, wearing jeans and a tight-fitting blouse. He also noticed there were the dark circles around her eyes, as if she had not had much sleep.

The embarrassed looking woman shook her head, laughing, as she tried to push all the papers back into a folder, 'Sorry, my fault really, I …' She paused, as if suddenly realising who she was talking to. She placed her hand on her glasses and then squinted at Dave, 'Excuse me, are you DI Barnes?'

'Yes, I am.' he replied, blinking in surprise, 'Do I know you?'

She shook her head and her mouth widened into a warm smile, 'No, but I have been looking for you and your office told me I may find you here.' She extended her hand out to him and gave him a grave look, 'My name is Professor Claire Tulley and I suspect I have important information that may help you with your case. I think I know what may be killing people.'

'James, I just need to nip out for a bit.' Karen barked, 'I want to run these samples down to the lab and I have a meeting to attend, I shouldn't be any more than an hour. If you could continue with what you are doing until I get back.'

James turned away from the table and bobbed his head at the heavyset woman, 'That's fine, Doctor.'

After watching Karen remove her gown and then dash through the double doors, James pressed his lips together and stepped back from the examination table. He then crept over to the double doors and cracked them open slightly and peered out.

Satisfied that he was alone, James moved away from the doors and silently strode across the room, stopping in front of a wall-length mirror. He then rolled up the sleeve of his gown, revealing a long-studded bracelet on his arm and pressed his finger on one stud. With the mirror's surface shimmering like a pool of liquid mercury, James took a couple of steps forward, stretched out his hand and there was faint pop of air as his arm pushed through the barrier. Pushing the rest of his body forward, the silvery surface appeared to envelope the young man, completely covering his body, until there was no trace of him left.

The surface of the mirror continued to shimmer briefly, and then it became still, returning to normal.

7

Abandoned Isolation Hospital, Langley Park, Durham

Zoe laughed bitterly to herself as she threw a stone against a broken window. The corners of her mouth twitched as the sound of broken glass echoed in the deserted reading room. Once, a long time ago, the room served as a place for patients to relax in the ancient isolation hospital but now it was serving as her favourite hiding space.

The ancient building was over a century old, originally built to treat patients suffering from infectious diseases, until it was eventually forced to close. The building was abandoned and left to decay, a sad reminder of the past.

In the summer of 1959, a young child went missing. With the help of local people, the Police searched the area. The remains of the child's body were eventually discovered on the hospital's grounds. The Police's only suspect had been the hospital's caretaker, a young man with a learning disability. The police arrested and charged the poor man. A few weeks later, after a quick trial, they found him guilty and hung him.

The local Council decided they should board the old hospital up and fenced off the surrounding grounds, allowing overgrown bushes and ivy to hide the hospital from view. But as the hospital faded from view, it also faded from the memory of the residents of Langley Park, apart from being used in scary stories or local legend.

When asked for their opinion about Zoe Murray, people would always give the same answer – *"That Zoe Murray was wrong 'un, always up to no good"*. It was true Zoe was a typical rebellious teenager, she even admitted it herself! She enjoyed nothing more than sticking her nose (and sometimes her finger) up at authority at every opportunity. Unfortunately, once again, it had been that rebellious nature that had gotten Zoe into trouble at school. She had arrived late to school that morning in her usual Goth attire with make-up to match. But when she was questioned about her tardiness and clothing, the surly teen answered back in a rude and disrespectful manner. As punishment, her teacher sent her to the head teacher's office for discipline.

However, Zoe had other ideas, deciding she did not want to end up in detention or suspended again. So, the strong willed girl did what she had always done in situations like this; she ran away.

Whenever she got into trouble Zoe would always go to the old derelict hospital to escape. Amongst the other school children of the village, they had learned it was a good hiding spot where they could easily get into mischief without adult interference. Like her, they had grown up hearing the stories and the local legend of the old hospital, but most of them shrugged it off for what it was – scary stories.

Zoe had come to her usual spot in the hospital, that once served as the break room for the hospital staff, but was now a dingy and damp ruin, with the remains of moth-eaten chairs and pieces of broken tables scattered around. Despite its deary appearance, Zoe found the silence appealing; it allowed her to contemplate on her life, while also granting her a temporary reprieve from the pressures of the outside world.

The eerie silence in the small was disturbed by the sound of a buzz coming from a mobile phone. Zoe reached into her back pocket, pulled out the phone and rolled her eyes when she saw her mum's name flash up on the screen. *Nuts to you too,* she thought to herself. Not up to having a shouting match with her mum, Zoe distractedly swiped the phone with her finger. She then slid her phone into the back pocket of her jeans and continued smoking her cigarette.

Suddenly, a strange scratching noise caused Zoe to prairie-dog. Her body straightened in alert pose, her head slowly twisting round, searching for signs danger. Her first thought was the sound was coming from the rats running around the derelict building. She shrugged, brushed her long black hair off her face with her hand, relaxed and continued to smoke her cigarette.

Zoe froze in her seat as she heard the noise once again. She frowned as the noise became louder. There was something different about it, it almost sounded like heavy breathing.

'A dog must be wandering around.' she muttered to herself.

Her curiosity getting the better of her, Zoe slowly stood up and crept across the room to the door, trying not to make any sound. She carefully poked her head around the door, but the corridor appeared empty. Edging into the dark, damp hallway, she slowly made away along, her feet squelching on the moist, moss laden old carpet.

Her heart thundering in her chest, Zoe continued to slink down the corridor. She stopped as her ears picked up on the noise again, this time she thought it sounded like a cracking noise too. She swallowed nervously, realising it was coming from a room just up ahead and edged up to the doorway. Her back pressed against the wall, she poked her head around the corner and peered into the room. However, as her eyes searched the room she froze as she came upon something horrifying on the floor at the other side.

Zoe frowned to herself; her first thought was that it looked like a bear was eating a large dog. But as she continued to stare, she felt the blood drain from her face as it dawned on her that it was even more terrifying than a bear.

The creature was unlike anything she had seen before. It had a long body, its skin was black, covered with shiny, glistening scales. It had four legs with three long, sharp claws on the end of each appendage. Zoe felt her blood run cold when she saw that its front claws were holding its prey in a tight grip. She continued to stare in morbid fascination as the nightmarish beast's claws tore through the body. Its misshapen head looked gruesome; thin and pointed. On either side of its head were small holes, which she assumed were its ears. The animal's eyes were long narrow slits that appeared to be closed as it fed with its long and pointed mouth. She gulped as she made out the beast's sharp, razor-like teeth.

As she watched through wide horrified eyes, the creature continued to tear off the flesh of what it had killed. Tears running down her cheeks, Zoe pulled her head back and pressed her hands over her mouth to stop from herself from screaming. She recognised what the creature was eating – it was Old Bob. Zoe had known him from her occasional visits to the derelict building, bumping into him whenever she came to hide. He was a homeless man, who had always been kind to the young tearaway, letting her sit with him as he told her his stories.

Zoe's mind screamed with terror as she heard a sickly crunch. Wanting so badly to turn and run away, she stubbornly stayed where she was, as if something inside her was telling her she needed to keep watching. Sucking in a lungful air, she poked her head round again and swallowed as she felt the bile rising in her throat at the tableau in front of her. The poor vagrant's rib cage had been torn open, exposing what was left of his heart and lungs, most of which looked it had already been partly consumed by the animal. Appearing to have had its fill, the creature was brutally using its talons to slash open the top of the dead vagrant's head and had started to use its claw-like hands to pry the brain out of the skull. It took all of Zoe's willpower to stop herself from throwing up.

As she leaned against the wall, Zoe held her hand against her mouth and let out a soft sob. Although she was terrified out of her mind, she was acutely aware she had to remain quiet, otherwise the creature would discover her and then she would be dead. Pulling herself together, she closed her eyes, took a deep breath, and carefully began to make her way slowly back down the corridor.

On reaching the edge of the corridor, she twisted her head back in the direction from where she had come and let out a shallow breath of relief. She was going to make it; the creature had not seen her. Zoe glanced round the corridor as she tried to get her bearings. Her usual entry point was through a broken window, which, to her reckoning, was about one hundred metres down the hall at the bottom of the stairs.

'*Shit! Shit! Shit!*' Zoe silently cursed to herself – One hundred metres might as well be one hundred miles. She bit into her bottom lip and squared her shoulders in determination, if she was to have any chance of getting out of there alive, then she was going to be very careful.

With her heart hammering inside her chest like a jackhammer, Zoe carefully tip-toed along the corridor as sweat continued to pour into her eyes. After what seemed like an eternity, she saw her target was in sight, filling her with deep relief and joy; she was going to make it.

Without warning, the quiet corridor was filled with the loud, cacophonous noise of Led Zeppelin's "*Communication Breakdown*". Full of panic, Zoe snatched the phone out of her back pocket and it was then she realised that she must have accidentally changed her phone from silent to ring.

'Nooo! Shit! Shit!' She hissed, cursing at the phone in her hand as she frantically pressed her finger on the red call disconnect icon. With a deep sense of dread, she knew it was too late and that she was in deep trouble. Twisting her head and peering back from where she came, she felt her heart sink in dismay at what she saw - the creature was standing looking down in her direction, snarling.

'Crap!' Zoe screamed.

On seeing the creature charging towards her, Zoe did the first thing that popped into her head; she ran like hell!

Barely making it to the top of the stairs, Zoe cried out in pain as she felt something razor-sharp slice into her calf muscle and she collapsed onto the floor, her momentum carrying her down the stairs. Coming to stop in a heap at the bottom of the stair, her head struck the corner edge on the banister post, stunning her.

With blood pouring into her eyes from the cut on top of her head, she brushed her blood matted hair out of her face, twisted her head and found she was staring directly into the creature's eye. As it stood over her, it leaned and snarled, its mouth centimetres from her face. Zoe squeezed her eyes shut and grimaced as she caught the scent of the creature's bloodstained putrid breath. She did a double take and blinked in surprise. She was not sure whether it was because of the pain or the fear, but was the creature smiling at her?

As she lay on the floor, Zoe caught sight of something on the edges of her peripheral vision – a pointed piece of wood. With all the strength she could muster, she grabbed the wood and stabbed the creature in its side, screaming, 'Eat shit, arsehole!'

The creature howled in pain, and Zoe's head jerked up in surprise as she heard it hiss something to her.

'Arrrrggsssshhh! Youssshh willlsss paysss forsss thatsss.' the creature hissed. It staggered away from Zoe as it desperately clawed at the piece of wood that was stuck in its side.

Adrenaline pumping through her body, Zoe rolled away from the creature and crawled along the floor to the window. Her hands reaching up, she grabbed the edge of the windowsill, pulled herself up and jumped out of the broken window, but let out a gasp of pain as she landed on the ground, hard. With as much strength that she could manage, she stood up, hobbled away from the window, and fell into the hedge at the edge of the grounds. She glanced back at the window and smiled triumphantly on seeing no sign of any pursuit.

Reaching into her pocket, Zoe's triumph quickly changed to alarm as she pulled out her mobile phone and saw the condition it was in. She was dismayed to discover that the screen had shattered, making the phone unusable. It was either caused by the fall down the stairs or her hard landing from her jump out of the window, either way, Zoe was loathed to admit it had not improved her situation.

Zoe crawled awkwardly through the undergrowth, coming upon the gap in the fence she had come through earlier. As she scrambled through it, she let out a gasp of pain as a piece of flesh hanging on her calf snagged on a rusty nail that was sticking on a piece of wood. Her hand instinctively reached her leg, and she screwed up her face as her fingers touched something warm and sticky. It was the first time since the attack that she had the opportunity to examine herself. Her trousers were torn, hanging loose on her right leg. Zoe let out a small grunt of disgust at the sight of the state of her right calf. It was a bloody mess of torn flesh from where the creature's claws had caught her.

As she landed on the concrete path, the exhausted teen collapsed in a heap and let out small sob, unsure what she should do next. A sense of exhaustion began to overwhelm her, which was a sign the adrenalin rush was starting to wear off. All she wanted to do was to lie down and rest, but she knew she dare not linger there; she needed to get as far away as possible. Her subconscious mind screaming at her to move and with the help of her remaining energy reserves, Zoe inhaled a deep breath and pushed herself up.

Suddenly, she jerked back in shock as she felt a hand grab her shoulder. Believing that somehow the creature had managed to track her down and locate her, Zoe let out a weak scream and tried scramble away.

'Easy love! It's okay,' a male voice whispered, 'Jesus, what's happened to you?'

Zoe looked up to see a tall fair-haired man wearing red Royal Mail overall, standing over her with concern etched across his face. He was also trying to put a blanket over her shoulders.

'I was just driving by doing my rounds, love. I saw you fall out of that hole onto the ground. My name is Jack. Can you tell me your name, sweetheart?' Jack asked carefully.

'Zoe' she replied weakly.

'Zoe, you have a cut on your head and a nasty gash on your leg.' Jack said grimly, turning and gesturing to the red Royal Mail van parked at the side of the road, 'I have a First Aid box in my van. I am going to carry you over to it and put a dressing on. Is that okay?'

Giving a weak nod of acknowledgement, Zoe felt her eyes grow wide as saucers as she continued to look frantically around her.

As Jack gently picked her up, Zoe lay her head on his shoulder and let out a small sigh of relief. Carrying her over to his van parked on the side of the road, he slid the van's side door open and gently sat her on the edge with her legs hanging over. After giving Zoe a small tap on her shoulder for reassurance, he opened the front passenger door and grabbed the First Aid box out of the glove compartment.

With the First Aid box gripped tight in his hand, Jack closed the passenger door and knelt in front of Zoe. 'It's okay, lass.' he said in a soft and reassuring tone, tenderly wrapping a dressing around Zoe's leg, 'You are safe now. I will call an ambulance.'

Frantic with terror, Zoe grabbed at his coat and shook her head furiously, 'No, please, you need to get me away from here as quickly as possible.' Half mad with fear, her voice was raw as she pleaded and pointed to the overgrown hedge from which she had just come through, 'I don't know what it is, but I think it is still here. If it finds you, it will kill you too!'

His mouth falling open in disbelief, Jack took a step back from Zoe and stared at her uncertainly, frozen, as if unsure what to do. She could tell from his expression that he was struggling to believing what she was telling him. Jack scratched his head in confusion and he nodded slowly.

'Okay pet, I'll probably get in trouble for this, but I will do what you ask. I'll take you to hospital myself.' he said hesitantly.

After helping the white-faced teen onto her feet, Jack opened the passenger door, and gently eased her into the seat. After making sure the door was secure, he raced around the front of the van and climbed into the driver's side. However, he paused as he heard a howl of rage coming from somewhere in the distance. Feeling a chill run down his spine, he shuddered briefly, gave one last glance to the overgrown hedge, started the van's engine, and drove away.

As the van pulled away, Jack cast an eye up to the rear-view mirror and blinked in surprise as something caught his attention. For a split second he was sure he had seen some sort of animal climb out of the hole where the terrified youngster had come out of. Not wanting to stop to investigate, Jack slammed his foot firmly on the accelerator pedal and felt the van pick up speed. He did not look back again until the van was clear out of the village.

8

The creature hissed in anger.

The synthroid knew it had become too complacent. When it had captured the human male, it had made the mistake of assuming they had been alone.

Its handlers had been allowing the synthroid to use the abandoned isolation hospital as a hunting ground as it was an ideal spot to capture prey and feed. For over seventy years the synthroids had been using the secluded location to gather genetic material of a hormone that the humans from their world lacked so that the Empire could give it to their operatives for them to survive this world's harsh environment.

The synthroid had let its guard down. It thought it had been so clever tracking the lone human male and playing with him; like a cat playing with its prey. It had become so distracted with its own sense of superiority that it had failed to notice it was being watched too.

A loud, awful noise alerted the synthroid that something else was in the building. When it went to investigate, it found a human female trying to sneak away.

The synthroid gave chase, expecting to take it down with ease; but the human did something unexpected, it fought back. With the synthroid wounded and stunned, its prey seized on its chance to escape and fled from the building.

After the synthroid eventually calmed down and let its anger subside, it quickly regained its senses and charged after the human, tracking the female's scent. However, when it climbed through the hole in the fence, the synthroid realised it was too late as it spotted a primitive human land vehicle drive away with its prey.

Irked that its prey had slipped from of its grasp, the synthroid turned and raced back into the abandoned building, back to where the remains of the dead body lay. With careful practice, after extracting the hormone from the corpse's brain, it placed the extracted organic sample into the bio-sample container. Its mission completed, it sprinted down the quiet corridor and up a flight of stairs to a small room.

The synthroid came to a stop in front a large mirror that hung on a wall, and raised its front appendage, activated a device, climbed through the shimmering surface, and vanished.

Location - Portal Chamber, Military Scientific Weapons Research Centre, Pons Aelius

'Something's wrong!' Theo cried out in alarm.

Henrietta frowned and peered up from the tablet she was holding in her hands, turning to look at the shocked man sitting next to her, who was glancing up from the console in stunned surprise. Her eyes widened in alarm as she watched the synthroid emerge through the portal and collapse onto the floor. Quickly realising something had injured the creature, she jumped out of her seat and ran to help it.

'Get a medical team here immediately and get Colonel Barnes, now.' Henrietta snapped. She then turned away from Theo and waved her hand at a burly impassive looking soldier who was standing at the back of the chamber, 'You there, don't just stand there, help me.'

'We'll take this off you.' she whispered as she reached over and took the bio-sample container carefully from the creature's claws.

The soldier dutifully hurried over and knelt beside Henrietta, whose hands were shaking as she handed the container to him. He straightened up, placed he container on the console and then looked gravely at the injured creature on the floor.

Henrietta swallowed as she noticed a piece of wood was sticking out of the creature's side and put her hands carefully over the wound. She jerked back as the creature let out a sharp pain-filled hiss.

'Easy ... easy ...' she said in a soft, soothing tone, while stroking the creature with her hands to calm it.

Five minutes later there was a shushing noise as the chamber door slid open, and the young woman glanced up from the creature to see a grave-looking Colonel Barnes march into the chamber, followed closely by two people wearing white leather uniforms with three blue patches on their arms, indicating they were assigned to the medical sciences. After moving away from the synthroid to allow the two medical personnel to tend to the wounded creature, she took a small step toward the stone-faced man, who was glaring down at the beast.

'What happened?' he growled.

'Sir, I am not sure.' Henrietta replied uncertainly, pointing to the injured creature, 'It arrived through the portal hurt.'

Colonel Barnes let out dissatisfied snort and knelt in front of the synthroid, 'What happened to you? Report!' he snapped. The two medical personnel opened their mouths to object, but an angry look from him soon silenced them.

'Injurdssss, needsss helpssss.' the synthroid hissed weakly in response.

'I said ... *report*.' Barnes barked in a loud uncaring tone. He leaned closer to the injured creature and pressed his hand on the piece of wood sticking out of the beast's side. The synthroid let out a screech of pain.

'Sir, It's wounded!' Henrietta interjected, placing a hand on his shoulder, but snatched her hand away as he shot her a withering stare.

'How dare you touch your superior office in such a way.' Barnes spat, 'I would be very careful in how you handle yourself young lady, unless you would like to be the one held responsible for this fiasco?' His top lip curled up condescendingly, 'Well, do you?'

'N ... n ... no sir.' Henrietta stammered, lowering her head subserviently.

'Report, damn you!' Barnes demanded, turning back round to the beast. He pressed his hand harder on wound and the creature screamed out in pain once again.

'Wasss disssscoveredsss,' the synthroid hissed weakly, 'humansss female, ssshe attacksss.'

'What happened to this female?' Barnes demanded in a harsher tone, his face hardening as he leaned closer to the creature, 'Did you kill her?'

'Nosss, humanssss female essssscapsss. Itsss wasss unesssspectedsss.' the breast replied.

'You mean you were careless!' Barnes scolded, shaking his head in disgust, 'I am terribly disappointed. Not only did you allow that human female to discover you, but you allowed her to escape. Your carelessness could unravel all our years of work. This needs to be fixed now ... now!'

The creature raised its head weakly, 'Yesss masssster.'

'I will give you one more chance.' Barnes sneered, 'We will not accept any more mistakes. You will be punished if you make any further deviations from the plan. We have not spent years painfully and slowly putting our plan into motion for it to come apart now! We are going to have to send in a clean-up squad to remove the body and any lingering traces.' Without waiting for response, he then spun round and snapped his finger at Theo, who swallowed, gave a small nod of acknowledgement, lifted his arm up and pressed a button on his wrist communicator.

'Clean up detail to the portal room!' he said urgently into the wrist device.

Henrietta felt her eyebrows climb up in mild surprise as the synthroid let out a short hiss, twisted its head up to her, and pointed to her. She glanced at the colonel, who wordlessly cocked his head at her but remained silent as she swallowed nervously and knelt closer to the poor creature.

'Sssscannersss … DNA …' it hissed.

Scanner? Did it mean it managed to scan the human before she escaped? Henrietta blinked in realisation, and she gave a small nod in understanding. She carefully unclipped the long metal scanner from the creature's front appendage and stood up. Barnes raised an eyebrow and but remained silent as she held the scanner over a section of the console and brought up a holographic image of the data contained on the device.

Henrietta chewed on her bottom lip as she studied the holographic display in front of her. After a few seconds, she lifted her head triumphantly, turned to Barnes and pointed to the holographic image on the console. 'The synthroid's scanner picked up a reading of the female's DNA during their fight.' she babbled excitedly, 'If she is close by, we will get a lock on her.'

'Excellent work.' Barnes muttered in grudging tone. He glanced back at the two medical personnel next to the synthroid and growled at them, 'Well, what are you waiting for? Take it away for treatment.'

The two medical personnel saluted, quickly helped the injured synthroid onto a hovering stretcher and guided it out of the chamber. As soon as the chamber door had closed, Barnes spun round to face Henrietta and stared at her inquiringly, 'Do you think you can locate the female?'

Henrietta tilted her head and her brows knitted together as she peered at the data on the holographic image and scratched her head. She bobbed her head thoughtfully and waved her hand dismissively, 'Give me a few minutes and I should be able to locate her.'

Henrietta quickly realised she had overstepped the mark as she noticed that a vein was throbbing on the left side of Barnes's neck as the muscles in his jaw tightened. He gave Henrietta a cold stare, nodded, but remained silent with his hands clasped behind his back as she worked at the console. For ten minutes, apart from a faint hum coming from the console and the hiss of the air filtration system there was silence while her hands tapped and swiped on the holographic interface in front of her. Eventually, feeling fully proud of herself, she turned back to Barnes and gestured to the shimmering portal in front of them. Watching the portal focus, Barnes's eyes sparkled with curiosity as he scrutinised the image in front of him. It seemed to be a room, possibly in a hospital, with a teenage girl sitting on a bed.

Her brow furrowed in concentration, Henrietta rose from her seat, stepped closer to the portal and studied the image, while pensively tapping her finger on her chin, 'It appears she was taken to a hospital, and is awaiting treatment.' she murmured, 'I am assuming she is waiting to be assessed by their physicians. Once they have carried that out, they will transfer her to a quieter room, where she will be alone.'

'Could you give me an idea how long that will be?' Barnes asked in a flat tone, impatiently crossing his arms across his chest.

Studying the image in front of her, Henrietta cocked her head, raised an eyebrow, and tapped her finger on her bottom lip thoughtfully, 'We know from the intelligence we have already gathered that their health care system is antiquated, so it could be two, maybe three hours before they transfer her to a private room. Also, I have been able to identify her name.'

Barnes' large grey eyes flickered with contempt as Henrietta spun away from the portal and returned to her seat behind the console. She swiped her hand over the holographic display and leaned back in her chai. Her mouth widened into a triumphant grin as she held up a finger to the image of a teenage girl.

'I have accessed the hospital's computer system, and learned that the female's name is Zoe Murray, a teenager.' she said smugly as she gazed at the holographic display, 'I have also learned they have contacted the local law enforcement.'

'So, we can safely assume we can expect another visit by the colleagues of my counterpart.' Barnes murmured.

Several minutes passed as Henrietta sat in awkward silence, watching Barnes rub his chin thoughtfully as he studied portal's image. She flinched as the quiet hum of the chamber was broken by a loud hand clap followed by his loud barking laugh.

'Excellent! Yes, that will work!' he barked.

'Sir?' Henrietta asked, frowning.

'That will give me plenty of time to find a very special guest to surprise our friends with.' Barnes grinned.

Doctor Claudia watched in astonishment as Barnes spun round and darted out as the chamber, with the door sliding to a close behind him. She turned and glanced at the technician sitting next to her, who returned her gaze with a puzzled expression.

Theo cast an anxious glance over his shoulder and moved closer to his colleague and whispered to her in a low secretive voice, 'You any idea what he was talking about, Henrietta?'

Henrietta gave a wordless shrug and turned back to stare at the holographic image of the young lady. *I can imagine whatever he has planned, it is not going to be good for you,* she thought to herself. Suddenly, her eyebrows snapped together, and the corners of her mouth twitched as an idea slowly began to take shape in her head.

Picking up the tablet that she had been holding earlier, she spun round and handed it to her colleague, 'Theo, I forgot to give this to the medical team when they left with the synthroid.' She said urgently, gesturing to the closed chamber door, 'I need you run it up to them, they may need the data on here to help treat it.'

Theo's eyebrows rose in surprise as he peered at the tablet in his hands. He looked back up at the woman in front of him with a puzzled expression then gave a slight nod of understanding. He stood up from his chair and dashed out of the chamber.

As soon the doors were fully closed, Henrietta raised her left arm and pressed her finger on a button on her wrist communicator. She smiled as a holographic image of General Cooper appeared a few seconds later.

'General, you said you wanted to be kept apprised if anything unusual happened.' she whispered secretively, 'Something has come up which I think you would like to hear about.'

Her mouth curving into a thin smile, General Cooper's holographic image peered back at Henrietta and tilted her head in acknowledgement, 'Thank you, Henrietta. I am pleased I can still rely on you.'

Henrietta bowed her head gratefully, 'My pleasure General, I am happy to serve. Anything I can do for you will be my ...' She paused and gave the image a sly smile, 'sorry, *our* pleasure.'

The corners of her mouth twitching in bemusement, General Cooper's steely green eyes glinted as she lifted an eyebrow, 'Oh, I am sure I can think of something ...' she licked her lips and stared leeringly back at Henrietta, 'I am in my quarters now. I am due for some instruction, and I found our last lesson so informative and ...' she paused, a devilish smile dancing on her lips, 'exhilarating.'

Henrietta felt her cheeks warm, and she grinned back, 'Yes, we both found it quite charging, didn't we, Wendy?'

The image blurred for a second and Henrietta realised Cooper had lifted her arm closer to her face. As the image settled, Henrietta could almost see the burning hunger in the woman's eyes as she spoke in a tone that was filled urgent desire, 'Come to me... *now!*'

Henrietta blinked in surprise as Cooper's image disappeared. She inhaled a lungful of air and let out a long-excited breath, lifted herself out of her chair and quickly exited the chamber. Hurrying down the corridor, she came to stop in front of a door and stabbed her finger repeatedly on the sensor on the wall to summon the transport-pod. Anxiously casting an eye of her shoulder, her fingers tapped impatiently on her leg and silently wished for the transport-pod to hurry up.

Her stomach fluttered as she heard a loud whoosh, followed by a short ping that had signalled the transport-pod's arrival. Without waiting to see if anyone was waiting to exit it, she charged through the doors before they were fully open and barrelled into Theo, whose mouth dropped open in surprise as she barged past him.

'Oh sorry, Theo.' Henrietta panted apologetically, shoving him out of the transport-pod, 'I am urgently needed by General Cooper, and you know how she hates to be kept waiting. The clean-up detail should be along shortly, you know what to do. Hopefully, I shouldn't be too long!'

Two minutes and several levels later, Henrietta could feel her heart racing as she walked out of the turbo-lift doors and made her way down a short corridor. She came to a stop front of the only door in the corridor and placed her hand to the sensor. There was a moment's silence, followed by a female voice that spoke in a hushed tone.

'*Yes?*'

Henrietta leaned in closer to the sensor and whispered, 'Wendy, it is me.'

Henrietta's mouth curved into a knowing smile as the door in front of her slid open and she heard Cooper's seductive voice coming from within, '*You may enter.*'

Henrietta stepped through the open door into the room beyond. The door slid to a close leaving an empty corridor.

9

CLaire sat silence as she drank a cup of tea. She glanced around the small office she was in and saw that it was much like her own: files were scattered over the desk, with notes and messages plastered along edge on the computer screen. She grinned to herself, happy to see she was not the only person whose office was untidy.

She looked through the window into the squad room and caught sight of a tall salt and pepper haired man chatting with other detectives. When she first arrived, the Detective Inspector had led her straight into his office, made her a cup of tea and left to talk to the others. She had caught sight of the whiteboard as she walked through the room, and now as she sat quietly, she found her eyes drawn to it, as if it was pulling her toward it.

Claire was just close enough to study the whiteboard. Her eyes narrowed as she focused on the pictures on it. She started in realisation, recognising they were images of murdered bodies, possibly taken of the crime scene from the previous night.

For several years Claire had been investigating reports of similar attacks and had a programme installed on her computer to scan for certain keywords in the media and social networking websites. Earlier that morning, she had been working in her study when an alert popped up on her computer monitor about the previous night's attack.

Throughout her career the highly resourceful woman had slowly acquired contacts, both in the media and in the police force, who passed on information to her whenever she needed it. As soon as she had finished reading the report, she rang a friend who had owed her a favour for the name of the investigating officer.

As she lived in the area, it had not taken Claire long to get to the police station. Upon arriving, she managed to bluff her way around the Desk Sergeant into giving her the location of Detective Inspector Barnes. Shortly after arriving at the Coroner's Office, she was hurrying down the corridor which had led to the morgue and was making her way through a set of double doors, when a tall man barged through the doors from the other direction, knocking her to the floor. As she lay on the ground, she had laughed to herself that it had been a long time since a man had knocked her off her feet. The stranger then helped her up and after a series of apologetic ramblings, she learned he was the Detective she had been searching for.

After a brief introduction, Claire explained to DI Barnes why she had been searching for him. Curious to know more, he asked that she follow him back to the station so they could talk in a more private location.

Claire brought her attention back to the Detective Inspector and regarded him pensively. He appeared to be in deep discussion with three of his detectives. He looked quite tall and good looking, she thought. On seeing his greying hair, she guessed that he was in his mid-to-late 50s, but she could tell he looked a bit out of shape and quickly put that down to his age. Catching sight of her own her own reflection in the mirror, she let out a small huff and gave a small shrug; she was no spring chicken either!

Suddenly Claire jumped in surprise as she felt something wet touch her hand. She lowered her head and smiled cheerfully at the two sorrowful looking eyes that were staring back at her. She realised she had been so distracted by her own thoughts, that she had failed to see the Cavalier King Charles Spaniel had trotted up to her and put her head on her lap.

'Hello there, aren't you a gorgeous thing!' she laughed, stroking the dog's head, 'Who are you then?'

'That would be Jenny.'

Claire jolted upright as she heard a male voice coming from behind her. She turned round and saw that DI Barnes was standing in the doorway, watching them both. He smiled warmly as he walked over to Jenny and stroked her head. The animal's tail wagged in delight at her master's touch.

'Come on you, back to your bed.' he laughed, pointing at her bed that was lying on the floor in the room's corner, 'Stop bothering the nice woman.' Jenny sheepishly slunk back to where her bed was and crawled into it.

'Oh, she was no bother.' Claire chuckled, 'I love dogs. I don't have one myself because I don't have the time for one.'

'I felt I had to save you from her.' he laughed, waggling his finger, 'If you gave her a biscuit, she would end up owning your soul with those eyes of hers.'

She watched curiously as DI Barnes strode over to his desk and sat down in the chair behind it. He placed his elbows on his desk and made a steeple with his fingers as he regarded her thoughtfully, as if he was sizing her up.

'When we met earlier, you said that you may have an idea on what killed the two people last night.' he said curiously. He inhaled a deep breath and let out a frustrated sigh, 'At the moment I have more questions than answers, so any information you might have would be incredibly helpful.' he waved his hand to the whiteboard in the main office, 'When I came back into my office, you were studying the whiteboard out there, so you already appreciate what we are dealing with.'

Claire bobbed her head in acknowledgement. She was hesitant at how much she should tell him, wary about who to trust. She had learned the hard way about providing too much information, which had come at personal a cost to her, both privately and professionally. However, despite her reservations, she sensed she could trust this man, that there was something about him that she could not place her finger on, but her instincts were telling her she could trust him. He was clearly desperate for any information she could give.

Deciding to take a chance and trust her instincts, Claire closed her eyes, took a deep breath, opened them, and gazed at him curiously, 'Inspector, before I start. Can I ask that you keep an open mind?' She leaned forward, pressed her hands together and held them out in front of her in an almost pleading gesture, 'What I have to say you may find strange, or even delusional, but what I tell is the truth. Please, will you trust me?'

DI Barnes inclined his head and raised an eyebrow at Claire curiously. He gave a small nod and motioned for her to continue, 'Okay, Professor Tulley, I cannot promise to keep an open mind, but I will listen.' He gave her a half smile and extended his hand out, 'Please continue, and you can me Dave by the way.'

'Thank you, Dave, you can also call me by first name if it makes your comfortable, which is Claire.' she said, smiling. She then closed her eyes and took in a deep breath, 'Okay, the first thing I need to say is that this isn't the first unexplained murder like this in this village. There have been a series of murders or disappearances going back, as far as I can tell, for over 80 years. If you search back far enough, you start to recognise a connection.'

Claire opened the file she had been carrying and passed the pages over to Dave, who began to look through them silently as her listened to her continue, 'As you can see, I have done a lot of research.' She pointed to the paper in his hand, 'You see from my notes that Langley Park has been the focal point of some strange events. There have been reports of people dying in strange circumstances or disappearing in strange circumstances.'

Dave's forehead creased as he scrutinised the papers in his hand

and then lifted his head up to Claire, 'Sorry Claire, but as far as I am aware we investigated most of these cases over the years and, for many, we found the person responsible, they were arrested, found guilty and the case closed.'

Her brow furrowed, Claire gave a small shake of her head but continued to speak, 'Yes, the police at the time may have found somebody responsible. But it is my belief in every one of these cases the investigating officers were under pressure from somebody higher up to close the case quickly, quietly and to cover it up.'

Dave's face hardened and shot Claire a cold stare, 'Are you accusing the Police of mass corruption? Are you trying to tell me that officers were ordered to either look the other way or willingly falsify records?' He shook his head, angrily slamming the documents down onto the desk, 'I am sorry, Claire, but I cannot accept. What proof do you have of that?'

Taken aback by the man's anger, Claire jerked back and raised her hand up to him apologetically, 'I understand your anger, but please bear with me. If you can give me time to explain, I can prove it to you.' She reached forward and picked up one of the sheets of paper on his desk, 'On 6th May 1935, Mary Walsh, a twenty-year-old woman, was found on the grounds of the old isolation hospital in Langley Park. Her boyfriend, Adrian Fullerton, was arrested, accused of suffering from delusional insanity, found guilty and hanged.' Pausing to open another folder, she pulled out another sheet of paper and handed to Dave, who hesitantly took it from her, 'You notice that this is a letter from the Home Office, pressuring the Police into finding a suspect.' she explained, indicating the paper in his hand.

Dave frowned at the paper in his hand and shook his head. Claire remained silent as she let him read through the document but as she saw eyes start to slowly widen and his jaw drop open, she knew then he was starting to take in what he was reading. He raised his head and stared back at her in disbelief.

'This implies ...' he said haltingly, as if he was afraid to speak out loud what he was thinking.

Claire didn't have to be a mind reader to guess what was going through his mind. She let out a heavy sigh and nodded sadly, 'If you are trying to ask if they pressured the Coroner into rewriting his report?' She held up hands and acknowledged him with a single nod, 'Yes. He rewrote the report, but with nobody knowing, he kept the original and hid it safely away. I got my hands on the original report detailing the wounds and condition the woman's body was in.'

After reaching into her bag and pulling out another file, she leaned forward and handed the pile papers to Dave, 'These are copies. One is of the Coroner's original report and the other is of a letter from the Home Office to a Chief Inspector. I have the originals stored safely away somewhere.'

Dave peered uncertainly at the copy of the letter in his hand. Claire could tell from his reaction that he had been struggling to accept what she had been telling him so far, she knew if she had any hope of making him a believer, it would have to be down that crucial piece of evidence. She watched his eyes grow wide as saucers as he lifted his head up at her and then back to the whiteboard.

'That's impossible!' he murmured in disbelief, 'They all died the same way! Surely it must be coincidence?'

'Unfortunately, no.' Claire said grimly, shaking her head.

Claire then reached over, picked up another file and handed it over to Dave, who opened the folder, looked at the papers and then back up at Claire, disbelief etched across his face.

'This one is very similar too.' she said sadly, 'In August 1959 the body of a 10-year-old girl, Roisin Stewart, was found on the grounds of the old isolation hospital in Langley Park. The police arrested a man with learning disabilities. Because he had no family to defend him, they quickly brushed it aside. He was found guilty and hanged. Again, the investigating officers were pressured into closing the case quickly and the Coroner's report altered.'

Before Claire could say any more, she cocked her head curiously as Dave pressed his finger against his lips to silence her. He then climbed out of his chair, hurried across the room and closed the door to his office.

'Sorry, but if there is a cover-up involved here, I don't want anybody overhearing our conversation.' Dave said in a hushed whisper, 'I would trust all my officers in that squad room with my life, but I cannot risk any of this getting out yet. To be honest, I have already had a conversation with my Chief Inspector this morning about this case. He more or less implied that closing this case would be in my best interest.'

Claire gave a half a smile and nodded slightly, 'I understand, Inspector.' She relaxed as she felt the tension ease in her body, realising her first instinct to trust him had paid off, 'I have more cases going back years, if you would like me to continue.'

Dave placed his finger over his lips, waved his hand and gathered up the papers on his desk, handing them back to Claire, 'No, it might be best if we continue this conversation later, somewhere less … public.' he whispered, casting an eye through the window into the busy squad room, 'I have two other officers investigating last night's case. May I suggest we all meet up at my place tonight?'

Claire arched her right eyebrow curiously and nodded, 'If you think that is best, Dave. You don't understand how relieved I am that you are taking this seriously.'

A serious cloud covered Dave's face as he gave her a thin smile, 'I take all my cases seriously.'

Dave straightened up and turned to look out of the window. For about a minute, Claire remained silent as she watched Dave gaze thoughtfully of the window with his hands behind his back. He twisted his head back to Claire and cocked his head questioningly at her, 'Sorry Claire, but can I go back to your earlier statement?' He leaned in close to her and lowered his voice, 'You implied you thought you may know what has been killing these people, is that right?'

Claire opened her mouth to reply but hesitated, casting an anxious glance through the window into the squad room. She leaned in closer to him and spoke to him in an urgent whisper, 'I don't know what it is, but what I know is that it is definitely not human. Also, this may sound crazy, but I don't think it is from this Earth.'

Dave's eyes blinked in surprise and stood silence for a few

seconds. However, just as he was about to open his mouth to speak, he was interrupted by a knock on the door. The door opened and a curvy dark-haired woman wearing a navy-blue trouser suit, popped her head in the doorway, 'Sorry to disturb you, Guv, but I thought you need to know straight away. But there has been another murder, but this time we have a witness.'

The colour drained from Dave's face, and he gave the woman a nod of acknowledgement, 'Okay, thanks, Brenda. Any details yet on the witness?'

Brenda looked down at the notepad in her hand and gave a small nod, 'A passing delivery driver discovered a young girl lying on the side of the road. He took her straight to the hospital in Durham.'

Grim-faced, Dave gave a small nod and then leaned in closer to Claire. 'Good, now finally we may get some answers!' he whispered to her. Raising his voice, he turned back to Brenda, 'Sergeant Donnelly contact SOCO, give them the location of the incident, inform them I am on my way. I'll contact Jenkins and Cooper and tell them to get to the hospital to interview the witness.'

Sergeant Donnelly gave a small nod of confirmation, 'I am on it, Guv.' She spun round and hurried out of the office.

As Claire reached over to pack up her notes and belongings, she was suddenly filled a sense of exhilaration. She had been waiting for the chance like this, a chance to actually go to a fresh incident. Hoping to persuade the Dave to allow her to go with him, she turned to him but could tell from his expression that he already had the same idea.

After grabbing his car keys and mobile phone off his desk, Dave turned to Claire thoughtfully, 'Professor Tulley, I know it is a lot to ask. But I think your expertise in investigating these cases could be valuable. I would like you to come with me to this latest incident. Strictly as an observer, of course. Your insight into this may be helpful. I quite understand if you want to refuse.'

Claire crossed her arms over her chest and gave him a hard stare, which was followed by wicked smile as she winked at him, 'Try to stop me!'

Finally, she thought to herself, as she followed the tall man out of his office, *after all these years, I am finally coming to get you. You shiny black bastard!*

Seven miles away in Langley Park, Andy and Wendy were examining the bedroom of Tommy Thorn. The bedroom was still a bloody mess. SOCO had left hours before, but the bedroom still had tape and markers, showing where the bodies had lain. Red blood stains marked the floor, walls, and ceiling.

Wendy tapped her pen on her bottom lip as she studied the bedroom. She lowered her head and read the notepad in her hand while Andy paced around the bedroom, deep in thought as he listened to his colleague.

'Okay, according to Sally Thorn, she said that her husband had checked all doors and windows before they went to bed.' Wendy said, pointing to the bedroom window, 'We can see from the bedroom window that there was no sign of any forced entry.'

Andy strode over to the window, reached his hand up to try the handle on the window and nodded in agreement when it refused to budge, 'This window is locked, and Mrs Thorn said that the downstairs windows and both the front door and back door were locked too.'

Wendy gave a small nod and furrowed her brow in concentration, 'Yes, I can verify part of Mrs Thorn's statement about the front door. When Will and I arrived, we had to force the door open to gain access.' She then turned around and rubbed her chin with her hand as she regarded the bedroom, 'Mrs Thorn said that when she got to the bedroom, she thought she saw something moving on the dressing table.' She muttered, stepping across to the dressing table against the wall. Her eyes narrowed as she scrutinised the bedroom table and realised it was a typical child's dressing table: not that wide with four drawers going down the front, a flat top scattered with various toy figures. Above the dressing table, a large oblong mirror hung on the wall.

Wendy clicked her tongue off the roof of her mouth as she studied the top of the dressing table and spotted three scratch marks on the top. She looked over his shoulder at Andy and waved her at him warily.

'Yeah, I noticed these scratch marks last night.' Andy said, nodding in agreement, pointing to the marks on the wooden surface, 'There was something about them that just bugged me. If you look closely Wendy and tell me, does it appear they are coming from the mirror?'

Wendy leaned forward to examine the scratch marks. Her eyes drew together, and she gave a small nod in agreement, 'It looks that way, Andy. But how is that possible?'

Andy let out a heavy frustrated sigh, ran his fingers through his hair and shook his head, 'I don't know, but I was speaking to the Guv earlier. He had just come from speaking to the medical examiner. He said it was her opinion that a large animal killed Michael and Tommy. Which probably fits with what Sally Thorn had described seeing.'

Wendy scratched her head and looked back at her frustrated partner grimly, 'So what we are saying is …' she paused and shook her head in disbelief, 'We are looking for something that can crawl out of a mirror. Does that sound insane to you?'

Andy nodded sullenly and opened his mouth to answer her, but his mobile phone rang, cutting him off. He quickly pulled out the device from his pocket and Wendy saw him blink in surprise as he stared at the phone's screen, 'It's the Guv.' He pressed his finger on the phone's display and answered the caller, 'Hello Guv, Cooper and I are at the Thorn residence taking another peek at the crime scene …' Wendy noticed that he had stopped talking; she could just make out Dave's voice coming from the phone's speaker.

With a furrowed brow, Andy listened intently to whatever Dave was telling him, 'I see sir … We are already in the village, sir. Is it not best that we … Oh, I see … Understood sir, we'll head straight there now. Goodbye.' After hanging up the call, he turned to Wendy with a puzzled expression, 'He said there has been another murder. Here in the village, up at what used to be the old isolation hospital.'

Wendy turned to leave the bedroom, 'Does he want us to go straight there?'

Andy gave a small shake his head as he followed Wendy through the door. 'No, he's on his way here now along with an observer, whatever that means. There was a witness this time, a young girl. They have taken her to the hospital, and the Guv wants us to head there immediately and interview her.'

Wendy came to a sudden stop, twisted her head and looked at Andy in puzzlement, 'Observer?' she asked, 'What type of observer? And why?'

Andy lifted his shoulder in half a shrug. 'Hell if I know!' His eyes flickered with curiosity as he glanced at Wendy, 'The Guv seemed cagey about it. All he would tell me is that he would explain everything later. He was quite cryptic, but he wants us to meet back at his place this evening, where it is safe and Big Brother is not watching.'

Wendy's finger tapped her chin thoughtfully, 'It is probably best when we go back to the station, if we leave as normal in our own cars. Then we can meet up later at the Guv's.'

'Good idea.' Andy replied, nodding in agreement, 'I will give you directions when we leave.'

Wendy gave him half a smile and nodded slightly. However, as she started to walk downstairs, she could not stop thinking about Dave's warning. She let out a small groan to herself as she realised where it was going and what she may have to do. She stopped walking, closed her eyes, and took a deep breath.

'Sorry Andy, I will meet you back out at the car. I just need to check up on my parents. My mum has not been well, you know how it is?' she lied.

'No worries, Wendy.' Andy replied cheerfully, waving his hand at her in a go-ahead motion, 'Take as long as you need.'

Wendy pretended to smile and waited for her cheerful colleague to walk out of the front door before she moved into the living room and reached into her jacket for the mobile phone. After unlocked the phone, she opened the contacts, selected the only name on the list and pressed on the green phone icon to dial the number.

Holding up the phone to her ear, Wendy listened as a voice answered after a short ring.

'Good morning, Northern Electric, what service do you require?'

'Cooper security code Tango-Charlie-Gamma-Alpha-One-Six-Beta.' She replied firmly.

'*Stand by.*'

Wendy heard a short beep as they transferred her call and after a brief silence a male voice answered in a strong Mancunian accent. She flinched in surprise as she immediately realised that she was now speaking directly to her superior officer – Commander John Payne. What was going on here? Why was she not speaking to her usual handler?

'*Report.*'

Wendy gave a brief report of their visit to the hospital, their interview with Sally Thorn, of their visit to the crime scene and then of Andy's conversation with Barnes. When she was finished, she sucked on her bottom lip as she waited for a reply.

'*You are to proceed as instructed earlier, but this evening as soon as you leave the station, you are to come back to base for further instructions. Understood?*' Payne ordered.

'I understand.' She replied and the call quickly disconnected.

Wendy closed her eyes, raised her head up to the ceiling, took in a deep breath and blew out her cheeks. After lowering the mobile phone away from her ear, she opened her eyes and stared out of the window silently for a minute.

Her forehead creased as she saw that Andy was leaning against the car, smiling, chattering away into his mobile phone. She then hung her head and surveyed the mobile phone in her hand. Her face hardened as she clenched her hand around it.

She did not like where this was going. She did not like it at all.

10

As the vehicle made its way back to the hospital, inside its two passengers sat in contemplative silence, both lost in their own thoughts as they tried to make sense of what they had learned so far. What little information they did have, was troubling and they were finding it difficult to wrap their heads around.

Andy's brow furrowed in deep concentration as he thought back to Dave's phone call and his cryptic message concerning "Big Brother". Working off the assumption that they were being monitored, he wondered had he meant the powers-that-be had started to take a keen interest in this case? Or was it somebody else? The Press, maybe?

He let out a frustrated breath to himself and shook his head as he realised it was just another mystery to add to the ever-growing pile. He cast an eye across to the pensive woman next to him, who was staring out of the car window in silence.

'Penny for your thoughts?' he asked curiously.

From the way Wendy's jerked up in surprise, he guessed she must have been so caught up in her thoughts that his question had startled her. She blinked and turned her head to him, 'Oh, sorry, sir. I was miles away.' She sighed gloomily and waved her hand in frustration, 'Just trying to figure out the Guv's message to you. What it means for us and this case.'

Andy blew out his cheeks and nodded in agreement, 'Something is definitely up; but, until we are told otherwise, we continue to do our jobs. So long as we both have each other's backs, we can face whatever comes our way. My guess is the Chief Inspector is putting pressure on the Guv for a result.'

A few minutes later as he drove the car back into the hospital carpark, Andy stared through the windscreen to the hospital building and shook his head to himself at the unsettling feeling of déjà vu .

'Hard to think we were just here earlier this morning, interviewing Sally Thorn.' he muttered. He turned his head and waggled his eyebrows at Wendy, 'I feel like Bill Murray, in *'Groundhog Day'!*'

Wendy arched her head in bemusement and lifted an eyebrow, 'That must make me Andie MacDowell, then!' She laughed as Andy gave her a sly wink.

Just like they had done earlier that morning, they made their way to the hospital's main reception and up to the main desk. Andy recognised the same receptionist was on the desk again, a forty-something, tall thin golden-haired woman. He searched his memory for her name as she lifted her head up and gave him a warm smile.

'Good afternoon, Patricia. You may remember we spoke briefly earlier this morning.' He said cheerily.

Patricia smiled warmly back at him as a small flash recognition flickered across her face, 'Yes, Sergeant Jenkins, I remember you from this morning. How can I help you now?'

Andy frowned as he pulled out his notepad and glanced at it, 'Someone brought in a young girl, we are here to speak to her. I believe her name is Zoe Murray.'

Patricia's forehead furrowed as she peered down at her computer monitor, her fingers flying as they typed away on the keyboard. After less than a minute, she raised her head back to the watching Sergeant and gave him half a smile, 'Yes, it looks like she is in Accident and Emergency.'

Andy thanked the woman and turned back to Wendy, who pointed to the map on the wall. They hurried down the corridor and came to a set of double doors labelled *"Accident and Emergency"*. They walked through the double doors and entered a busy waiting area full of people with various injuries waiting for treatment. The pair then walked up to the reception desk and after a few minutes of waiting they spoke to a receptionist. After flashing his ID, Andy quickly explained the reason they were there.

The woman smiled politely, spun round on her seat, gazed at the whiteboard behind her and gave a small nod of confirmation, 'Yes, Miss Murray has been assessed, and they took her straight up to the surgical ward. I understand her mother arrived just a few minutes before you and is already up there with her.'

After receiving directions from the helpful woman, Andy turned back to his colleague and frowned as he suddenly realised that she was no longer standing next to him. He looked over his shoulder and saw that she was already waiting by the elevator doors. He dashed over to her and stood beside her and waited for the elevator to arrive. The elevator arrived a few seconds later and the two police officers entered the elevator only to find a few people were already standing in it.

Eventually reaching their destination, the impatient pair quickly exited the elevator as soon as the doors were open and found themselves in a long corridor. After a short walk, they came to a stop in front of a set of doors signposted *"Surgical Ward"*.

Walking through double doors, Andy approached the nurses station, and introduced himself to the nurse on duty.

'Yes, she's being examined by the consultant.' The weary looking brunette said, leaning over the desk and pointing to a room down the corridor, 'Her right leg was quite badly torn up. When she was assessed in A & E, they felt she may need immediate surgery to repair the muscle tissue. Poor girl may need plastic surgery.' She gestured to the large woman sitting outside the room, 'Her mother is sitting outside if you would like to speak to her.'

Andy bobbed his head, thanked her, turned, and hurried down the corridor. They slowed as they approached a woman who was sitting on a chair outside a hospital room. She was a large, forty-something, overweight woman with short black hair wearing a large green jacket over a T-shirt that was obviously too small for her with a pair of loose-fitting jogging bottoms.

'Excuse me, Mrs Murray, is it?' Andy asked as the woman lifted her double chin in acknowledgment and scowled at him through deeply suspicious eyes, 'My name is Detective Sergeant Jenkins, and this is PC Cooper. We are here to speak to your daughter about her accident this morning.'

Mrs Murray rolled her eyes and let out a huff of annoyance, 'Humph! I telt 'er one of these days.' she moaned with a thick Geordie accent, 'If she carries on the way she is ganning, somebody will attack her. Did she listen? Oh, no, she's just like her fatha!' She let out a snort, her face screwing up in apparent disdain, 'He was worthless too. Well, I hope ye' arrest 'er and throw the book at 'er. That will teach the disobedient little bitch a lesson. 'Av had to lose a day of work because of this!'

Andy could feel his jaw tighten as he listened to the woman's tirade of abuse. He took a deep breath and mentally gave a slow countdown from ten. He glanced across to Wendy for help, but she suddenly appeared to be engrossed in something on her mobile phone.

'Errr, yes Ma'am.' Andy replied slowly, giving her a pretend smile, 'Unfortunately, we are just here to have a chat with Zoe. Since she may be the victim, it's important we find out what happened to her.'

Mrs Murray folded her thick arms across her chest and gave Andy a dirty look, 'Humph! Ye' lot are a waste of time!' she moaned as she lifted her hand and waved her thick finger in front of his face, 'In my day a copper could give 'ah insolent kid a good hiding and that would teach 'em a lesson. Ye' cannae dae that today, can ya? Useless the lot of ya!' Then, without waiting for a response, she stood up out of her chair and threw her hands up in the air, 'Ye' can dae what ye' want with 'er! I've washed ma hands with 'er!' she snapped and gestured with her thumb to the double doors from where he had just come in through, 'I'm ganning for a fag.'

To his disbelief, Andy watched as the deeply unpleasant woman waddled down the corridor, eventually storming out of the ward through the doors. He turned to Wendy and shook his head in dismay.

'I cannot understand why people like that have children!' he said, trying to hide the contempt he was feeling in his voice without much success.

Wendy opened her mouth to say something but was stopped when the door to Zoe's room opened, revealing a tall Indian man. He was wearing a long white hospital coat and had a stethoscope hanging loose over his neck. Andy noticed the ID badge on his jacket read *"Dr Jabeel Shinglata"*. He was muttering to himself, as he continued to write on the clipboard he was holding.

'I don't know what is going down there, but why on earth was she sent up here?' he grumbled to himself.

Andy took one step forward and gave a small-but-polite cough. The startled consultant raised his head up from his clipboard, stopped writing and glowered at Andy.

'Excuse me, Doctor?' Andy asked.

'Yes? Can I help you?' Doctor Shinglata replied, irritably.

'Sorry to bother you, but we are investigating the attack on Miss Murray.' Andy said, flashing his ID and gesturing to the room from which the doctor had come out of, 'We want to ask her a few questions. Could you tell us whether she is in any condition to answer some questions?'

Doctor Shinglata eyes narrowed as he stared back at Andy with a touch of irritation. Andy could tell there was a hint of bewilderment and annoyance on his face.

'Yes, I would say she is perfectly able to answer questions.' Shinglata snapped, 'In fact, I would have to say there is nothing wrong with her! For the life of me, I cannot understand why Accident & Emergency sent her up to me. Somebody must be playing silly buggers down there. Life-threatening injury indeed! Apart from a scratch on her leg, she's perfectly fine.'

Andy frowned and glanced at Wendy with a look of puzzlement, 'I am sorry, Doctor, but we were told that she had been attacked. But you are telling me that isn't actually the case?'

Shinglata let out an exasperated laugh, 'Hah! I think this girl is playing a joke on you Detective. If I were you, I would arrest her for wasting police time.' He straightened his shoulders and fixed Andy with a harsh stare, 'Now if you excuse me, I have actual patients who *do* need my help.' Without waiting for a response, he turned and walked away from the two police officers.

Andy rolled his eyes, let out a small snort frustration and turned back to Wendy, who appeared to be just as equally puzzled, 'Wendy, I want you to interview her. I'll stand back and study her reactions. Is that okay with you?'

Wendy bobbed her head in understanding as she followed him into the hospital room. They opened the door and walked in to find a pale skinned teenage girl sitting on the bed. Andy could see she was quite toned and athletic looking, her shaved head emphasising her thin face. She was sitting on the bed playing with a mobile phone, ignoring the two officers as they entered the room.

Andy leaned against the wall and watched silently as Wendy took a small step over to the bed, 'Hi Zoe.' She smiled warmly, extending her hand to the distracted teen, 'My name is PC Cooper. I would like to talk about what happened to you earlier.'

Without raising her head, the sullen teen crinkled her crooked nose and grunted in acknowledgement but continued to play with her mobile phone. Her smile slowly fading, Wendy continued to press the ignorant girl, 'Zoe, I really need you for you to look at me. Don't you know it's rude to ignore somebody when they are trying to talk to you.'

This time Zoe gave a loud tut and rolled her eyes but continued to play with her mobile phone. Wendy's eyes narrowed in annoyance as she reached over and swiped the mobile phone out of the girl's hands.

Zoe angrily jerked her head up to Wendy and was about to open her mouth to object but stopped short. Andy noticed her emerald eyes suddenly grew wide as saucers as she stared up at Wendy for the first time. Her brows appeared to knit together in confusion as a hint recognition flashed on her face. For a brief second, he picked up on something else as he watched the colour drain from her face. Was it fear? Before he could react, it disappeared as the teenager appeared to regain her composure.

'Hey! That's mine.' she shouted, 'You cannot take that!'

Wendy waved her hand as she held up the mobile phone up and handed it to Andy, 'Don't worry, you will get it back. But we really need to speak to you. This is serious, Zoe.'

Andy took the phone from Wendy and frowned as he scrutinised it. The device seemed to be brand-new with barely a scratch on it. Something in the back of his mind was telling him something did not feel right, but he ignored it and brought his attention back to the young girl on the bed. He paced around the room and listened intently as Wendy continued to question her.

Zoe rolled her eyes and let out an impatient snort, 'Fine, I'll answer your stupid questions!'

'Thank you. We heard that something attacked you.' Wendy asked, 'Is that right?'

Zoe grunted, shook her head, and held her hands up, 'Durr! Does it look like something attacked me?' She lifted her shoulder in a half shrug and smirked, 'I was messing about in the old, abandoned hospital. I fell and scratched myself, alright!' She let out grunt disgust, 'Tore my good jeans too.' She lay back on the bed, folded her arms across her chest and let out a long heavy sigh, 'I lied because I would have got into trouble for being there.'

From the way the tendons in Wendy's neck were tightening, Andy could tell Wendy was getting annoyed with Zoe's insolent attitude. She looked over her shoulder at Andy, but he waved his hand for her to continue. She gave a small nod, turned, and fixed Zoe with questioning look, 'Zoe, the nurse told us when you first came in that your right leg was badly injured, but now we can see that's not the case. Care to explain why she would say that?'

Zoe stuck out her bottom lip, pouted and answered in a surly tone, 'Maybe she's bored?'

As Andy paced around the room, he cocked his head as he listened to Zoe speak. He frowned, there was something in her accent he found troubling, but he wasn't sure what it was. However, before he had a chance to give it any more thought he came to a stop as he caught sight of something on the floor in the doorway leading into the bathroom. Pretending to tie his shoelace, he knelt for a closer look and felt his eyes widen in surprise as he saw several small droplets of blood. He felt his body stiffen as an alarm bell rang in his head.

Something is not right here, he thought to himself.

Slowly straightening up, trying not to make it obvious to Zoe, Andy coughed and made a retching noise. Wendy turned and gave him a look of concern.

'Sorry Ma'am, I need to use the toilet.' he wheezed. With his right hand pressed over his mouth, he held up his left hand and jerked his thumb toward the bathroom, 'I think it might have been something that I ate with Inspector *Watson* this morning.'

Andy caught a glint of understanding in Wendy's eyes. He could tell she had discerned that her wheezing colleague may have noticed something irregular and did not want to alert Zoe of his suspicions. Wendy gave a brief nod in understanding, 'That's okay Constable, do what you need to do.' She turned back to the frowning teen and shrugged her shoulders, holding up a finger to her mouth as she whispered, 'Ignore him, he's still a trainee not used to the job yet.'

Pretending he was about to throw up, Andy covered his hand over his mouth, bounded into the bathroom, slammed the door shut and made several loud retching noises. He waited a minute and flushed the toilet, then turned on the faucet and filled the wash basin as he made splashing noises to sound like he was washing his hands. He inspected the bathroom and noticed several small blood spots on the floor with a trail that led up to the wash basin. Understanding dawning on him, his mind immediately started to put two-and-two together. The hairs on the back of his tingled as he realised, they had to get out, quick.

Trying not to make it obvious to Zoe, Andy walked unsteadily back into the room and groaned at Wendy, 'Sorry Ma'am, but I think we really need to go as I am not feeling well. I am sure Zoe here understands and won't mind if she comes to the Station for you to finish your chat with her?'

There was a small flicker of comprehension in Wendy's eyes as she gave Andy a nod in understanding and smiled, 'That's okay. I am sure you won't mind Zoe, if we finish this off later?'

If she was suspicious, Zoe did not show it as she gave a small curt nod, 'Sure, whatever.'

After following Andy out of the room, Wendy grabbed his arm as they hurried down the corridor, 'Sorry Sir, but what was that all about?'

Andy placed his fingers over his lips and shook his head while whispering, 'Not here.'

As they reached the end of the corridor, Andy suddenly had an idea and came to a stop at the nurses station, 'Sorry, hope you don't mind my asking?' he asked curiously, 'But has someone been with Zoe Murray the whole time since she arrived?'

The dark-haired nurse frowned and gave a small nod, 'Yes, somebody ha—' She cut herself off and clicked her fingers, 'Oh hang on, she was alone for about ten minutes while we had to deal with an emergency on the ward.'

Andy bobbed his head gratefully and turned away from her. Wendy raised an eyebrow and opened her mouth as if to say something but stopped herself when Andy waved his hand and shook his head. They quickly departed the ward and hurried down the corridor.

As they rushed down the corridor, Andy's felt his eyebrows knit together as he spotted a uniformed police officer just ahead of them. He appeared to be standing outside a ward they had been in earlier that morning. He gave Wendy a side-eye and pointed to the officer in front of them.

'Wendy wasn't that the ward where we spoke to Sally Thorn this morning?' he asked curiously.

Wendy frowned in puzzlement as she stared ahead of her and gave a small nod of acknowledgement. But as they got closer to the ward, recognition crossed over her face when she realised who was standing in front of the door and as soon as she was close enough, she came to a stop and lightly tapped him on the shoulder. She smiled as the startled Constable

Bates wheeled around and blinked at her in surprise.

'Wendy!' Bates blurted out, 'When I reported for work, this morning, they told me you had been reassigned to Barnes' team.'

Wendy gave a small shrug and grinned, 'Yeah, I wanted to help with that case from last night.'

'Yeah, I guessed that.' he answered grimly, glancing at Andy.

Wendy must have seen Bates's curious look as she stepped to one side to introduce Andy, 'This is Detective Sergeant Jenkins. Andy, I'm sure you will remember Constable Will Bates from last night.'

'I would be careful with this one.' Will laughed, winking as he gave Andy small nudge with his elbow, 'She will probably make Detective Inspector next year.'

'Oh, I wouldn't be surprised if she did.' Andy chuckled, but then coughed as he noticed the withering look Wendy was giving him. To change the subject, he pointed at the ward Will was standing in front of, 'What's happened here?'

Will shook his head sadly as he cast his eye over his shoulder and motioned for them both to follow him into the ward.

'A patient committed suicide.' Will whispered sadly once they were inside the ward and out of earshot of the busy corridor, 'Sally Thorn. A nurse found her hanging in her room when she went to check on her.'

Stunned, Andy exchanged a shocked look with Wendy. He stared back the sombre constable in disbelief, not believing what had just heard.

'We interviewed her this morning.' Andy said gravely and gestured to far end of the corridor, 'Do you mind if I take a look?'

'Go ahead, sir.' Will replied, shrugging his shoulders, 'One of your lot will be along shortly anyway.'

'I will stay and get some details off the nurses.' Wendy murmured to Andy.

Andy gave a small nod and then Wendy watched as he zipped down the corridor. After Will returned to his post in front of the entrance to the ward, Wendy took a step closer to the nurses station to speak to the familiar looking nurse that was sat behind the desk.

'Monica?' Wendy whispered.

'Constable Cooper, I remember you from this morning.' Monica replied gravely, 'You interviewed Sally Thorn.'

'Yes. I just learned what happened.' she said, pointing to the room Andy was entering.

Monica nodded sadly and stood up from her chair. She moved a step closer to Wendy and arched her head toward the room behind the nurses' station. Wendy quickly followed Monica through the door into the small staff room, who closed the door behind her.

'Sorry Officer, I didn't want to say anything out there. I was the one that discovered Sally when I went to check up on her.' Monica said. Wendy could tell she was trying to hide the distress in her voice and she noticed there was a haunted look in her eyes.

'That must have been awful.' Wendy said soothingly, holding out her hand and touching Monica's shoulder in sympathy.

'Yes.' Monica sighed. She straightened and her eyes flickered with uncertainty, as if she was struggling to deal with something, and looked over shoulder at the closed door, 'You may think I am mad, but I don't think Sally committed suicide. Was she upset after speaking to you this morning? Yes, but I would not say she was upset enough to kill herself. After you had left, I gave something to help her sleep, to relax her.'

'Did you see anybody else go into the room?' Wendy asked. Deep down, she felt a sense of dread build up inside her as she guessed what the woman's answer would be.

'No.' Monica answered bitterly, shaking her head angrily. She rubbed the back of her neck and stared at Wendy in bewilderment, 'But that is what's strange. She would not have had the strength to kill herself the way she did!'

Wendy swallowed, glanced over her shoulder to the closed door and placed her hand on Monica's shoulder, 'We are investigating it. But can I ask that you don't repeat what you just told me to anyone?' She paused to reach into her pocket for her card which had her contract details on and handed it to her, 'This is my number. If you remember anything else, contact me; nobody else. Do you understand?'

Monica looked at the card in her hand and gave a sombre nod in understanding. Without making any comment, she turned and opened to the door to leave the room, with Wendy following her out through the door. As Monica scurried back to her seat behind the nurses' station, Wendy scooted back to her place in front of the desk.

Less than a minute later, a solemn-looking Andy came back up the corridor and motioned for Wendy to follow him out. Wendy opened her mouth to speak, but he waved his hand to cut her off.

'Not here, wait until we are outside.' He whispered, just low enough so that only she was the only that could hear.

As they made their way out through the main entrance, Andy pursed his lips as he caught sight of a familiar, unfriendly looking woman, who appeared to be in deep conversation with another gentleman; a tall bleach blond haired man wearing a Royal Mail delivery uniform, holding one of those leak proof collapsible coffee mugs in his hand.

Andy nudged Wendy and pointed to the couple, 'Isn't that Zoe's mother standing over there? Who is she talking to.'

Wendy gave a small nod and followed Andy as they headed over to the two people, coming to a stop in front of them.

'Hello Mrs Murray, again.' Andy smiled and bobbed his head at the hospital building behind hm, 'We have finished speaking to Zoe for now, but we may need to speak to again when she gets home.'

Mrs Murray let out bark of disgust and gave a dismissive wave of her hand, 'Humph! If ye ask me, they should lock 'er up, and the key be thrown away for wasting ye time.' Then, not waiting for the two police officers to respond, she stood up and waddled away.

The tall gentleman that had been chatting with her turned to Andy and shook his head in disbelief, 'What a charming woman!' There was a hint of sarcasm in his voice.

Andy gave him half a smile and showed him his ID, 'Mind if I ask sir, who are you and your reason for talking to Mrs Murray?'

The tall gentleman blinked in surprise and shook his head. 'No, I don't mind.' He held out his hand to the curious Andy, 'In fact, I hoped that you would want to speak to me. My name is Jack, Jack Wood. I was the one who found Zoe and brought her to the hospital.'

Andy gave small nod in understanding and shook Jack's hand, 'I'm Detective Sergeant Jenkins, and this is PC Cooper.' He waved his hand over to spot where car was parked, 'Do you mind if we have a private chat in our car where we can ask you some questions?'

Jack lifted his hand and signalled for them to lead the way, 'No I don't mind, ask away.' He smiled as he followed the two officers to their parked car.

Wendy opened the rear passenger door for Jack, who climbed in a took a seat in the back of the car. She then opened the front passenger door and climbed in, while at the same time, Andy quickly opened the driver's side door and situated himself in the driver's seat.

Andy stared curiously at Jack, who was sitting uncomfortably on the back seat, 'Sorry about this, thought it would be best if we could sit here, where it's more private. You wouldn't mind telling us how and where you came across Zoe?'

'No bother!' He replied, bobbing his head in acknowledgement.

Andy watched as Jack leaned back in the seat and took a sip from his coffee cup. He closed his eyes as if he was trying to reorganise his thoughts, then took a deep breath and exhaled slowly, 'It was around 11.30 this morning. I work as a delivery driver and was in the middle of doing my rounds in Langley Park. I just so happened to be driving by the remains of the old isolation hospital, when I saw the young Zoe fall onto the pavement through a hole in the fence.' he shook his head gravely, 'She looked like she was in awful shape, so I knew I had no choice but to stop and help her.'

'What condition was she in when you came across her?' Andy asked. He looked across to Wendy and noticed she was making a transcript of their conversation in her notebook.

'Well, I stopped the van and got out to see if she was okay.' he said with a touch of sadness. He let out a heavy breath and continued, 'I could tell from the way she was lying on the ground and the state she was in that she was badly injured. Her right leg was in a hell of a mess.' His face darkened and fixed Andy with an intense stare, 'It wasn't half a bloody mess, I can tell you that. She had a nasty cut on the top of her head too. I bent down to help her, which was when she started screaming at me. After I eventually calmed her down, I picked her up and carried her over to my van.'

'What did you do next?' Andy prodded gently. He could see Wendy was continuing to write furiously in shorthand on her notepad.

'I didn't like the way her leg looked and the cut on her head was really bleeding.' Jack replied in a matter-fact tone. He took a sip of coffee from his cup and continued, 'I got the First Aid box out of the front of the van, and I dressed her leg and patched up the cut on her head.' He shook his head and let out small mirthless laugh, 'She's lucky I know First Aid. I was going to ring for an ambulance, but she got so upset, screaming that something was trying to kill her. I had no choice but to bring her to the hospital myself.' He paused as he held up the coffee cup to his mouth, and he took another sip, Andy noticed his hands were shaking.

'Did she say anything to you while you were driving here?' Andy asked carefully, trying to avoid upsetting the man any further, 'Did she tell you what hurt her?'

Jack's brown eyes widened, and he nodded furiously, 'Yes. Yes. She was pretty much out of it, tired really.' He shook his head in disbelief, 'But she told this awful story about seeing an animal attack this homeless guy in the hospital and when she tried to sneak out, she said that's when it attacked her, which probably explains the wound on her leg and the cut on her head.' He drew back, stared up at the car's ceiling and let out a horrified laugh, 'If I hadn't seen it for myself, I wouldn't have believed her!'

What did he just say? Gobsmacked, Andy did a double take at Wendy then stared back at Jack, blurting out, 'Sorry, but you saw it?'

Jack recoiled slightly in surprise. He hung his head, tightened his hands into fists, closed his eyes and nodded hesitantly, 'Yes … sort of. As I was driving away, I saw something jump out from the hole in the fence that Zoe had fallen out of. It was too big to be a dog, but it looked mean and nasty.' He opened his eyes and fixed Andy with a cold stare, 'I mean seriously nasty, not something you would want to mess with. I decided not to hang around to see what it was, so I put my foot down to get away as fast as I could.' He shuddered slightly, 'There is something else, something I've just remembered. Just after I placed her in the passenger seat, I was walking round to the other side of the van, when I thought I heard what sounded like an animal howl, coming from the somewhere close to me.'

Andy stared at the shaken man silently for a moment as he slowly considered what to say next, 'Jack, thank you for telling us this, you have been a big help.' He spoke in a hushed tone and leaned in closer, 'But I need to ask you that you don't speak about this to anyone. I don't want to alarm you, but Zoe has denied everything that has happened to her. I don't know what is going on, if somebody has got to her, but you may put yourself in danger if you tell anybody about what happened. Do you understand?'

Jack stiffened, then looked at Andy and gave him a small hesitant nod, 'Uh, yes! I think so. What do I tell my work? They will want to know where I have been and why I haven't finished my deliveries?'

Andy scratched his head as he thought for a second, 'Tell them you witnessed a terrible traffic accident, and you had to come to the station while we interviewed you.' He handed him a small thin oblong card, 'This is my number, tell them to give that a ring and I will confirm your story. But it is important that you say nothing. If anybody other than Wendy or myself contacts you to ask questions or if anything strange happens, you ring me. Understand?'

The shaken man nodded in understanding. Andy could see his eyes were growing wide with fear, 'I understand … well really, I don't. But I will do what you ask.' He swallowed and pointed to the car door, 'Is it okay if I go now?'

Andy nodded to Wendy, who gave a small nod He watched as she opened her door and climbed out of the vehicle. She then opened the rear passenger door to let Jack out. She then gave him a hug and he caught her slipping her card into his pocket, and whisper something in his ear. He couldn't make out what she was saying, but he guessed she was telling him that Jack could use that if he couldn't get a hold of Andy. Wendy then smiled and gave him an encouraging tap on his shoulder, released the frowning man from her hug and raised then her voice, 'I am sorry for your loss, sir.'

Andy could tell Jack was taken aback by her behaviour as he frowned in confusion. He then gave her a knowing smile, followed by a sly understanding wink, 'Thank you, Officer.' He said a bit too loudly as he turned round and hurried away.

Wendy then climbed back into the car. She glanced at Andy, who was scrubbing his face with his hands.

Wendy out a heavy despond sigh, 'Sir, just what the hell is going on?' She shook her in bewilderment and gestured to the hospital building, 'What the heck happened in there?'

Andy stared forlornly out of the car window for a minute and nodded to himself. He turned back to Wendy and fixed her with a sobering look, 'While you were talking to Zoe, there were a few things which weren't making sense. One of them was her mobile phone. It looked brand new, and I mean brand new, like it had just come out of the box.' He waved his hand, putting that thought to one side and then shook his head, 'The other was her story. I also noticed drops of blood leading into the bathroom. They looked like they were leading to the mirror and then I noticed marks that were very similar to the scratches we saw in the Thorn's bedroom.'

A look of horror covered Wendy's face as her eyebrows shot up in realisation, 'You mean something was trying to attack Zoe? But why not kill her when it had the chance.'

Andy narrowed his eyes and he waved his hand, 'No, it didn't want to kill Zoe. Think about it Wendy. Why would she change her story? Why does she not have any wounds, even though the nurse told us before we went in that she may need surgery?'

'No! That's not possible!' Wendy gasped with a tremulous voice, her eyes widening in fear.

Andy nodded grimly, 'Yes, don't ask me how or why or even if it is possible.' He waved his hand at the hospital building in front of them,

'But the Zoe Murray that had been attacked this morning is not the same Zoe Murray in that hospital bedroom right now. They have replaced her. By what, I don't know. Which was the reason I wanted to get out of there as quick as possible. This may sound stupid, but I got a sense we were being watched!'

Wendy's face hardened and she nodded in understanding, 'And you didn't want to let on who that person impersonating Zoe Murray or whoever may be watching that you knew.' She blinked as if struck by a sudden realisation and she slapped her palm across her brow, 'Ahh! Of course. Why did I not see it before?' she moaned, 'I didn't think about it until now, but I just remembered the young girl in there was speaking with a strange accent, it was English, but her accent was strange, like she wasn't local.' She then shot Andy with a questioning look, 'Did you pick up on it too?'

'Yeah, now that I think about it, I heard it too!' Andy answered hesitantly. He shook his head, let out a harsh breath and ran his hand down his face, 'Sally Thorn's suicide makes little sense either. There was something about it that just didn't seem to add up. The chair she supposedly used to stand on before knocking it away just looked too neat, as if they had carefully placed it. Did you get anything from the nurse?'

'No.' Wendy answered quickly, 'She left Sally alone in her room to get her something to help her sleep but had been held up by an emergency. When she finally got back to her, she found her dead. She doesn't think anybody else is involved.' She then tilted her head and looked at Andy expectantly, 'Do we let the Guv know?'

'To be honest, Wendy, I don't know!' Andy replied, trying to hide the frustration in his voice, 'But I have a hunch that when the Guv gets to the isolation hospital, he will find nothing.'

They sat in silence for a few minutes, locked in their own troubled thoughts. Eventually Wendy spoke, 'Sergeant, I don't know about you, but this is scaring me.'

Andy did not answer, all he could do was nod in agreement.

Back in the hospital, Zoiè Vulso sat and smiled at the nurse, who was talking away to her, 'You will be pleased to hear the Doctor has said it's okay for you to go home.' she was saying enthusiastically, 'I will be back in a few minutes with your discharge papers.'

However, as the nurse turned to leave, she paused and gave Zoiè a double take, her eyebrows knitting together in apparent confusion.

Did she notice there was something different about her? Zoiè wondered. Maybe she could tell she was a doppelgänger? Was she going to have to deal with her before she could raise the alarm?

Slipping her hand beneath her sheet to the small laser pistol she had hidden beneath the sheet, Zoiè held her breath and waited for the nurse to raise alarm. But she quickly realised she didn't need to worry as she watched the nurse give a dismissive wave of her hand, turn and swiftly leave the room.

As soon as the door was closed, Zoiè felt herself relax as she pulled her hand out from beneath the sheet and gave the door a stern look. She quickly climbed off the bed, opened the drawer on the bedside cabinet and pulled out a long metal wrist band. After clipping the band to her arm, she next carried the chair over to the bedroom door and jammed it under the door's handle. She then stealthily made her way into the bathroom. Coming to stop in front of the wash basin, she pressed her finger on a button on her wrist band and watched as the mirror shimmered briefly.

There was a cold tone to her voice as she stared into the shimmering portal and addressed someone on the other side using her accent.

'We may have a problem.'

11

Location: Pons Aelius, Britannica, Universal Roman Empire

After dreaming of falling endlessly into a black void, Zoe left out a soft moan and opened her eyes. At first she felt relieved at waking from what she thought had been a horrible nightmare. But then she found her vision was all blurred – almost as if there was a thin film covering her eyes. She then grimaced as she noticed a chemical taste in her mouth, along with the dull ache that was coming from the back of her head.

'We may have a problem.'

Zoe blinked to clear her vision and for a moment she could not determine whether she was standing, sitting, or lying down. Also, she could have sworn she had just heard herself talking.

But as the fog started to lift from her mind, Zoe shivered and she discovered that she was not only lying on her back but she was also on a cold hard floor. Twisting her head round to see where she was, she could see she was in a brightly lit room.

The last thing Zoe could remember was being in the hospital, lying on a hospital bed. She remembered a nurse had been talking to her and then had left her room to fetch the doctor. She closed her eyes and let out a tired groan as she struggled to recall what had happened after that.

Her hand gingerly touched her forehead, and she winced in pain. It was starting to come back to her, she had hurt her head when she had fallen earlier that day.

No, that is wrong, she thought to herself, *I got hurt when something attacked me.*

Zoe inhaled a sharp breath as the mind fog suddenly began to clear and her memory came flooding back to her. She had been alone, lying on the hospital bed, waiting for the nurse to come back, when she overheard a noise from the bathroom and had turned to investigate. The last thing she saw was someone attacking her as they sprayed something sweet tasting into her face and then everything went black.

Carefully raising up to see where she was, Zoe could see she was lying in a corner in a brightly lit chamber. In the middle of the chamber was a rectangular console of some sort, with two people standing behind it. They appeared to be looking at a large wall-length mirror. No wait, not a mirror. It was … She shook her head and frowned in confusion; she wasn't sure it was.

Zoe stiffened as she saw the two strangers were looking at somebody in the mirror-thing, but what she found even more disturbing was the figure in the mirror looked just like her! Wait? What? She rubbed her eyes in disbelief, not believing what she was witnessing.

One of the strangers, a short dark-haired woman, wearing a strange white leather bodysuit with thin red lines going down the length of each arm, was speaking in English, but with a strange accent. Zoe frowned to herself as she thought there was something oddly familiar about her accent, was it Italian?

'It appears we may have to deal with Sergeant Jenkins sooner rather than later. We may have to kill him.' The dark-haired stranger was saying.

The other stranger, a tall powerful looking woman with short red-hair and dressed in a black and gold leather uniform, turned to the shorter woman, and laughed malevolently. Because of her impressive height and build, Zoe was immediately reminded of an Amazonian from the film *Wonder Woman*. She also noticed the intimidating looking woman's accent was strange too as she listened to her reply to the woman in the white leather jumpsuit.

'Oh, I have a better idea on how to deal with Sergeant Jenkins. If we kill him now, that will raise suspicion.' The flame-haired stranger said menacingly, 'He just needs the right push. We just need to send him a message that he will ... understand.'

The shorter woman gave a small nod of understanding and tapped on something on the console. The image on the mirror-thing blurred and changed to that of an older-looking brown-haired woman. Curious, Zoe lifted herself up to get a better view and saw the image was now that of a woman standing in front of them, staring back at them, singing to herself as she combed her hair. Zoe did a double take as she realised the woman on the other side of the weird window device must have been standing in front of a mirror.

'The loss of a wife can do strange things to man.' The sinister woman chuckled malevolently.

I need to get away. Zoe thought to herself and slowly lifted herself up off the cool floor. She screwed up her face as she felt a stab of pain from the wound on her leg and let out a small grunt.

To Zoe's dismay, her gasp of pain must have alerted the two figures as she saw them they spin sharply round. Now the focus of their attention, Zoe swallowed as the Amazon woman slowly strode over and knelt beside her. Zoe tried to scramble away, but a wall kept her from going any further.

'Please don't kill me.' Zoe pleaded, her voice wobbling.

The sinister looking woman's mouth curved into a wicked smile and she leaned in closer to Zoe. 'Ah, I see you can understand what we are saying, so I must assume the translator chip that we inserted into your cerebral cortex is working perfectly' She extended her hand and stroked Zoe's head as she spoke in a soothing whisper, 'Shush! My dear. We have no intention of killing a lovely young specimen like yourself. Why, that would be such a waste. After all, why destroy so much... potential?'

Zoe's eyes narrowed in confusion, 'Wha— what are you talking about?'

The shorter woman moved closer to the intimidating red head, lifted an eyebrow, and cocked her inquiringly, 'Found yourself a new plaything already, Wendy?' she chuckled. The woman called Wendy glared at the woman sternly, who dropped her head in a subservient manner, 'Sorry, General Cooper, I meant no disrespect. I just assumed as this was Colonel Barnes' idea, shouldn't he be the one here dealing with her?'

Rolling her eyes, Cooper gave a small dismissive wave of her hand and continued to study Zoe as her top lip curled up in a sadistic grin, 'Oh, we are going to be such great friends.' she laughed menacingly as she continued to stroke Zoe's long black hair, 'You are to be my personal slave.'

What the crap? How dare she call me slave? Infuriated, Zoe slapped Cooper's hand away, 'Listen, you evil bitch!' she snapped incredulously, 'No way am I going to be a slave. Last time I checked, I was underage, and anyway slavery is illegal in United Kingdom.'

With all the strength she could muster, Zoe leaned forward and spat in Cooper's face. She watched in satisfaction as a glob of spit flew through the air and struck the woman in the eye.

'So, screw you!' Zoe screamed defiantly.

Cooper's head jerked back, wiped her face with her hand and then scowled at Zoe. After a period of silence, she pulled her head back and let out a bark of laughter.

'What's so funny, Queen Bitchiness?' Zoe grinned. She secretly hoped her false bravado would hide the uncertainty in her voice.

Zoe suddenly felt an icy chill go down her spine as she saw Cooper's mouth widen into a sadistic grin and then looked down at her with cold menacing eyes. 'Oh, my dear Zoe.' Cooper sighed dramatically, 'For one thing, you are not in the United Kingdom anymore, you are in Britannica, which is part of the Universal Roman Empire and the other thing ...' She suddenly paused, knelt, and then Zoe screamed out in as she felt Cooper's hand squeeze her wounded leg. 'You now belong to us, and we can do whatever we want.' Cooper hissed sadistically, 'Oh, I am going to have so much fun breaking you in.'

Zoe's head exploded in a blinding whiteness as she felt a searing pain shoot up her leg with stomach churning intensity. She squeezed her eyes shut and collapsed back on the floor. Forcing herself not to cry, she bit into her bottom lip, twisted her head away from the sadistic woman and moaned something inaudible under her breath.

'Sorry, what was that dear?' She heard Cooper curiously as she felt her move closer to her.

'I said break this!' Zoe screamed back in reply.

With every bit of defiance that she could gather, Zoe lunged at the surprised woman and head-butted her in the face. She listened in satisfaction as she heard something crack in Cooper's nose and watched in delight as blood spurted down her mouth and chin.

Shocked, Cooper stumbled backwards holding her nose and collapsed onto the floor. Zoe let out a loud laugh as Cooper, moaning in pain, sat on the floor, her hands pressed tightly against her bloodied nose.

'Who's laughing now, bitch!' Zoe snapped, her tone taunting, 'There is one thing you need to know about me, Queen Bitchiness. I hate bullies and people who think they can order me around. I didn't like my teachers telling me what to do. So, you think I am going to let some cosplayer on a power trip tell me what to do, I don't think so, you red-haired witch.'

She could tell Cooper was struggling to blink away the tears streaming from her eyes as she spun round and glared up at a shocked looking black woman at the other side of the room. It was then Zoe realised she had failed to see the black and gold armoured soldier when she first opened her eyes and she guessed from the style of her uniform, that she must be a military guard of some sort.

'Donf sust dant her fase sher sto ar schel.' Cooper moaned incoherently.

'Ma'am?' The soldier replied, confusion etched across her face.

Despite the precarious situation she found herself in, Zoe could not help but laugh hysterically as she pointed at the red-faced Cooper, taunting her.

'Take her to a cell … Now!' The furious woman roared.

Her face a mask of indignant fury, Cooper wheeled round and kicked out at the taunting girl's head. Zoe gasped in pain as Cooper's boot struck the side of her head, stunning her.

The chamber door then slid open to reveal a male soldier, wearing similar black and gold armour. Zoe assumed he must have entered the chamber to help his colleague pick her up and carry her out.

Feigning unconsciousness, the stunned girl felt herself being carried down the corridor. Zoe blinked away the tears to help refocus her vision and was surprised that she recognised some insignias and badges on the various soldiers walking by.

It slowly dawned on Zoe that she had seen those emblems before. She remembered seeing them in books during history lesson at school, when they had been teaching about the Roman Empire. On the wall in front of her there was a plaque with an eagle symbol, underneath which was inscribed with the words '*Ad Honorem Et Victoriam*'. Zoe's grandmother had been Catholic and from her time spent with her she had learned enough to know that plaque was in Latin and that it translated as '*For Honour and Victory*'.

The two soldiers hurried down the corridor, coming to stop at a closed door, marked *Transport-Pod 3* One of the soldiers put their right hand on a sensor and less than a minute later the door slid open, and they walked in. Zoe waited anxiously as she heard the door shush to a close behind them, which was followed by a small jolt, and then a faint mechanical hum as the transport-pod began its ascent.

Zoe let out a loud groan as she pretended to regain consciousness. The two soldiers glanced down at her briefly, as they waited for the pod to come to a stop.

'It looks like she is coming round.' The male guard muttered to his female colleague, 'Surprised she is not still out, Cooper gave her a pretty hard kick.'

The female soldier gave a small nod and grunted, 'Did you see Cooper's face?' She spoke in a hushed guarded tone and pointed to their charge, 'This one was responsible. I guess our illustrious leader got more than she bargained for!'

'Wish I could have seen that.' he chuckled. The corner of his mouth lifted, and he let out a bitter laugh, 'It was bound to happen sooner rather than later. I would have loved to have been in the room just to see that arrogant smile get wiped off her face.'

The female guard's eyes darted around the pod's cabin in concern, then gave her colleague a hard stare and shook her head, 'You better not let her catch you repeating that, Julius.' she scolded him in a hushed tone, casting an anxious look up to the ceiling, 'She has ears everywhere. I am going to pretend you didn't say that and if you value your life or your family's lives, you need to be more careful in future.'

'Hah! What's she going to do?' Julius scoffed and lifted his shoulder in a shrug, 'She doesn't scare me. You worry too much, Brida!'

'You are a fool if you believe that.' Brida hissed and gave him a cold stare, 'She is a general for a reason. Rumour is, you piss her off then Gods help you! I heard a rumour that the last person who made that mistake, ended up in a re-education pod for a month and when he was eventually let out, he was a vegetable.'

'But that's all it was, wasn't it? A rumour?' There was a hint of uncertainty in Julius' voice as he gave Brida a fearful side eye. Out of the corner of her eye, Zoe saw his hand instinctively reach up and touch the thin metallic collar around his neck.

Brida swallowed nervously and shot Julius a strange look. Zoe recognised that there was a hint of fear in her eyes as she snarled at him through clenched teeth, 'In Hera's name, do you want to find out? Just be careful, friend. Rumour is they are getting ready for a big mobilisation soon.'

They lapsed into silence and then Zoe felt a faint jolt as the transport-pod came to an abrupt stop. The doors slid open, and they moved out of the pod into a long corridor. Two official looking officers who were standing in front of doors as the trio exited the transport-pod, barely glanced at the two soldiers as they barged their way past them into the waiting pod. When they were far enough away Brida gave a fleeting look back over her shoulder. Zoe wondered whether she was checking to make sure the transport-pod's door. Was she afraid that she would be overheard?

'They say fifty legions are to be used in the first wave. Big invasion, I have learned. My advice, friend, is to be extremely careful what you say at the moment.' she whispered to her colleague, 'You may suddenly find yourself on the front line.'

'I picked up the same rumour too.' Julius replied, nodding in understanding, 'I have also heard the resistance is causing colossal problems too. Rumour is they were behind the assassination of a prominent ranking Senator. I have also heard a rumour that we are being pushed back by the Greater China Republic too!'

Her eyes suddenly blazing in anger, Brida twisted her head, looked round the corridor and then squinted back at colleague, 'Quiet you fool.' she snarled, 'Are you trying to get us caught? Expressing something like that will end with you up in front of a military tribunal and then sent to a re-education centre!'

They continued to walk down the corridor in silence. They came stop at a closed door and Julius placed his right hand on a sensor on the wall, and there was slight hissing noise as the door slid open. Zoe let out a surprised gasp as she found being lifted up and was then unceremoniously thrown into the room. Zoe cried out in pain as she landed hard on the floor. Indignant at the way she was being treated, she spun round and shot her captors a hate-filled stare.

Zoe was positive she saw a flicker of sadness in Brida's eyes as she glanced down at her from the doorway, 'You best prepare yourself for a long stay, child.' she said sympathetically, 'You are going to be here for a long time. You better make peace with whatever gods you worship. When General Cooper is finished with you, you will wish for death. Gods have mercy on your soul.'

'You can stick your advice where the sun doesn't shine.' Zoe hissed, making no effort to hide the defiance in her tone.

There was a puzzled expression on Brida's face as she peered down at Zoe, 'I don't know what that means, girl, but you are going to need that fighting spirit if you are to survive here. Rest up for now, somebody will be along shortly to tend to your wounds.'

Zoe shrank back as the door slid to a close with a quiet hiss. After a few seconds, she inhaled a deep breath, painfully straightened and then slowly spun around in a circle to study the room she now found herself in.

The cell was small, square, and brightly lit. There was a small single bed on one side, with a sink and a toilet beside it. The floor and walls were all white and bare, apart from an air vent up in the corner, from which she could pick up the small hiss of recycled air that was being fed into the small cell. She looked around and realised that there was no window, the only light available was coming from a collection of light panels that covered the ceiling. Zoe carefully limped over to the cell door to examine it and was dismayed to discover it appeared to be airtight.

Grimacing in pain from her aching leg, Zoe hobbled over to the small bed and perched herself on the edge of the mattress. She looked down at herself and realised that she was still wearing the hospital gown she had been wearing when they had taken her from her Earth. She let out a small bitter laugh and shook her head to herself; If anybody had told her that one day, she would find herself her trapped on a parallel Earth – she probably would have laughed in their face.

Slowly pulling up her gown, Zoe carefully examined the dressing on her right leg. She huffed in disgust when she saw that it had become soaked through from the blood oozing out from the wound.

'That bitch, Cooper, made it worse when she squeezed it.' she grumbled bitterly to herself.

As she reached down to gently remove the dressing around her leg, Zoe let out a small of scream of pain. The gauze had become so soaked through in her blood; it had stuck to the skin around wound. Her eyes filling with tears, she gritted her teeth and carefully pulled the remaining fabric off. Sucking in a lungful of air, she let loose with a series of pain-filled F-bombs as she continued to pull at the blood-soaked bandage, until eventually all the dressing had completely come away. She examined the wound and blanched at the sight of the torn flesh on her leg. She was then filled with overwhelming sense of nausea as she caught sight of the blood that was seeping out between the gaps of ragged flesh.

Zoe's eyebrows knitted together as a distant memory flashed in her mind, from the time when had taken a basic First Aid class at school – something about trying to keep the wounds clean. In a slow purposeful movement, she reached down and lifted her up gown and tore off a long strip of fabric, collecting it into a tidy ball. Then, in slow methodical movements, she carefully wrapped the fabric around the wound on her leg, until she was happy that could she no longer see blood seeping through.

Once she was completely finished making sure her make-shift bandage was wrapped securely around her leg, Zoe lay back on the bed, let out a sob to herself and gently pulled her legs up to chest. Overcome with exhaustion, she let out a soft whimper cried as she drifted off to sleep.

A short time later, Zoe woke to the sensation of something cold and hard on her skin. Startled, she opened her eyes and saw Cooper was leaning over her – but not only that, she appeared to be locking something around her neck. Zoe scrambled back and instinctively grabbed at her neck, only to discover there was a thin metallic collar fastened securely around it.

'What the hell!' she exclaimed.

Cooper gave the stunned teen an icy stare and her mouth curved into a smile as she took a step away from her. Zoe noted with deep satisfaction that there was a puffiness around her eyes and her nose appeared slightly swollen.

'Ah, I see you are awake.' Cooper smirked with a tone that held a touch of malice, 'I thought it would be nice to continue our brief chat from this morning, my dear.'

Zoe leaned forward and gave Cooper the best defiant stare she could manage, 'Sure. It would be nice to knock a few teeth out this time.'

However, before Zoe could launch herself at Cooper, her vision suddenly went white as an agonising pain sent her crashing onto her knees. Writhing in agony, Zoe screamed from the unbearable pain that was tearing through every fibre in her body. Her chest heaved as she gulped for air and slammed her fist on the floor. It was unlike anything she had experienced before; it was as if all the nerves in her body were suddenly on fire.

Her expression hardening, Cooper knelt closer to Zoe and gave her a lopsided grin, 'What's wrong, my dear. Lost for words, are we, hmm?' Her mouth curved into a wicked smile as she pointed to the collar around Zoe's neck, 'That, my dear, is an obedience collar.' she paused and licked her lips in obvious perverse pleasure, 'Something especially designed to ensure obedience.'

Desperately fighting back the tears, Zoe scowled up at Cooper and saw that she was holding a small control pad in her hand. It reminded her of a very small mobile phone. She frowned as she noticed Cooper was wearing a similar collar around her neck too.

'You get out of line or do anything I don't like … ZAP!' Cooper pressed her finger down on the pad.

Zoe screamed and writhed in agony on the floor as the searing pain once again enveloped her body.

'You stare at me the wrong way … ZAP!'

Zoe shrieked in agony.

'You do anything at all I find offensive …. ZAP!'

Zoe's shrieks turned into desperate squeals as the pain in her body increased in agonising intensity. Between bouts of pain, Zoe gasped and twisted her head to look up at Cooper, 'St … st … stop.' Her chest rising and falling, she closed eyes and sucked in deep agonising breaths, 'N … no … m … more.'

Cooper pursed her lips, pressed her finger on the pad again and then laughed sadistically as Zoe let out another howl of pain and then began to writhe on floor in agony, 'Hah-hah-hah, sorry, I missed that. Do you want me to stop?' she tilted her head and held her hand to her ear, her face hardening, 'All you have to say is *Please Stop Mistress Cooper*, say that and I will stop.'

Her face damp with sweat, Zoe sucked in a lungful air, closed her eyes as she tried concentrate on blocking out the pain. Then, with all the strength she could manage, she raised her head and stared insolently at Cooper, 'Please … stop …' She squeezed her eyes together, gritted her teeth and spat the last words out, 'Queen Bitchiness.'

Cooper tutted to herself, shook her head, rolled her eyes, and waggled her index finger. Even though she had a fair idea what was going to happen next, Zoe still tried to steel herself for what was about to come. Zoe shrieked in agony as Cooper smashed her foot down onto her injured leg. Then, as if she was almost revelling in the misery she had just inflicted, Cooper stood back and smirked at Zoe, as she writhed on the floor, crying in pain.

'Oh, my dear.' she drawled, 'I am going to so enjoy breaking you. It has been a long time since I have had somebody with such … spirit.' She leaned over, grabbed Zoe's face with her hand and sneered at her, 'You will find there are worse things than me on this world.' she chuckled menacingly, 'Oh yes, there are people on this world … of the degenerate persuasion … that enjoy, if you know what I mean, young girls of your age.'

Cooper then released her grip, pulled her hand away from Zoe's face, straightened up and then moved away from her. She peered down at Zoe's injured leg and waved her finger in disgust, 'But first we need to get you fixed up. I need you to be fully fit if we are to continue your … education.' But before Zoe had time to dwell on that foreboding comment, Cooper wheeled swiftly round and shouted toward the direction of the doorway, 'Send him in!'

On hearing the cell door open, Zoe twisted her head and saw an elderly Indian man, wearing an all-in-one white leather bodysuit, walk into her cell, carrying a small medicine bag. He was a short, overweight man, dark brown skin, and brown eyes, with a greying moustache on his top lip and had a mop of greying brown hair covering his head. She noticed that he was wearing an obedience collar too. He glanced down at Zoe in sympathy and then gave Cooper a questioning look.

'You look like shit!' he said in a matter of fact but softly spoken tone, 'What's wrong, you forget to turn on the light and walk into a wall?'

At first Cooper just stared and shot daggers at the elderly man. Then her mouth curved into a smile as she spoke to him in a dangerous tone, 'I would be careful with your tone, doctor,' she smirked and pointed to the collar around his neck, 'You practice medicine at our discretion. Your leash is only as long as we deem fit. It would be *shame* if anything were to happen to you because of a slip of your tongue.'

The grey-haired doctor's eyes flickered with hatred as he gave Cooper a challenging stare, 'I am old, your threats no longer scare me. There is nothing you can do to me you haven't already done.'

'Is that so?' Cooper chuckled. She cocked her head and lifted an eyebrow as she waved her finger at him, 'You still have a son, Jeevan, I believe. A doctor too, isn't he? It would be a shame if something were to happen to him.' She let out long dramatic sigh and shook her head sadly, 'Imagine the shame if it came out that he mistreated a patient, especially a child. No, I can imagine that would make things tough for him.'

The elderly man's face clouded with anger as he crossed his arms over his chest and silently gave Cooper an icy stare. To Zoe, it looked like a battle of wills, as Cooper also locked her eyes onto his; neither willing to give in. But finally, the grey-haired physician lowered his eyes and turned away from Cooper to focus his attention on Zoe and tutted to himself in disgust.

'That leg does not look very good, and I will need to be alone with her while I examine her.' he mumbled, 'I am sure you can understand?'

'Fine! Make it quick.' Cooper snapped, giving a dismissive wave of her hand as she stormed over to the doorway. She twisted her head back at Zoe and winked, 'See you soon, my dear.'

After the door had closed, the elderly man ambled over to Zoe, carefully helped her up and gently eased her back to the bed. As Zoe gazed up at him to thank him, she noticed his eyes held a sad kindness.

'Thank you, Doctor.' she said softly.

'People call me Doctor Jayaprakash.' he said sadly, extending his hand to Zoe, 'But you can call me Prakash, young one.'

'My name is Zoe, Zoe Murray.' Zoe replied, hesitantly, taking Prakash's hand and shaking it, 'You probably won't believe me, but I am not from this world.'

'You are not the first person I have had to treat who has said that.' he replied grimly, nodding in understanding, 'They have taken many people from your world.'

As she watched him lean in closer to her, Zoe frowned as she saw him put his finger to his lips. She could just barely make him out as he lowered his voice to speak to her, 'Be careful what you say, they are listening.' He then shook his head, and raised his voice, 'Oh dear, oh dear. That leg is not very good at all. We cannot have that, can we? If I don't treat that straight away it will become infected.'

Feeling a bit apprehensive, Zoe swallowed and gave a small wordless nod as the strange enigmatic man continued to stare thoughtfully at her injured leg. She watched curiously as he reached into his bag and pulled out an injection, along with a small square electronic device. He pursed his lips and gave her a small shrug of his shoulders.

'Sorry, but this will hurt.' Prakash said apologetically.

Zoe screwed up her face and gasped as he jabbed the needle point into her thigh. She then watched in fascination as Prakash held a small device over her wound and stared in wide-eyed in amazement as the skin began to slowly knit together. When he was finished, he put the device to one side and carefully re-dressed her leg.

After he was finished re-dressing her leg, Zoe lowered her head back on the bed and let out a deep sigh of relief. She frowned on hearing a small cough and saw Prakash was waggling his index finger at her. Her eyebrows shot up as he once again reached into his bag and pulled out what appeared to be an advanced auriscope.

'I just need to check your ears.' he said in a matter-of-fact tone. She nodded slightly in understanding as she saw give a slight wink as he leaned in closer to her.

As he examined her ears, Prakash lowered his voice to the point Zoe could barely him, 'I work for the resistance. It will take time, but we will get you out. I injected a tracker into you so they can keep track of you.' He put his hand on her shoulder and gave it a reassuring squeeze, 'You need to hold on and don't give in. Be patient. Rumour has it, the General likes her girls young because of her unusual appetite.'

Zoe felt her eyebrows dart up in shock and opened her mouth to speak but held her tongue when she heard the hiss of the door opening. Prakash placed his finger to her lips and shook his head slightly as she heard Cooper's heavy footsteps coming from behind her.

'Well!' she snapped, 'Is she okay? Will she be able to handle re-education?'

With his back still facing Cooper, Zoe gave a small nod as she watched Prakash discretely tap the bottom of his nose with his finger before bending down to pick up his bag and ambling over to the sour-faced woman.

'I am sorry General Cooper, but she is in quite a terrible state.' he said with a tone of authority, 'Her leg was already badly injured, which was made worse by your … manhandling. I have had to give her an antibiotic to fight the infection, but you won't be able to move her for …' he gave a small pause and coughed apologetically, '*three weeks* until she heals.'

Cooper scowled turned scowled at Zoe and grunted in frustration. She stood in silence for a minute, before letting out a loud, menacing laugh. 'Fine! I can wait until then. I prefer my *students* to be at full strength when I educate them.' The corners of her mouth quirked up and she stared leeringly at Zoe, 'I am hoping it will give you something to look forward to, having my *special* attention.'

A chill ran down Zoe's spine as she saw Cooper lick her lips and then wink at her knowingly. Doctor Prakash gave Zoe an understanding look of sympathy as he turned and ambled out of her cell.

Zoe stared at Cooper with a sense of unease as she sauntered over to her and stroked a hand down her face. She cringed as the woman leaned forward to kiss her cheek. Feeling like her skin was crawling, Zoe pulled herself away and shot Cooper a disgusted-filled-stare.

'Such spirit!' Cooper smirked, 'Oh, my dear, I will enjoy breaking you.'

Zoe continued to give a spunky stare as Cooper spun on her heel and strode out of the cell. As soon as the door silently slid to a close, an exhausted Zoe lay back on her bed and massaged her temples with her fingers. She squeezed her eyes shut as she tried to remember Doctor Prakash's hidden message.

What was it he said? Three weeks, yes, that was it. The resistance will rescue me in three weeks, so I must hold out for three more weeks. Zoe thought to herself and then slammed her hand down obstinately on the bed, *Yes. I can do it! I can handle anything they throw at me until then.* Fatigue wearing heavily on her, Zoe pulled her legs up to her chest and let out a small whimper. She buried her face into the pillow and shook her head adamantly. *No! I refuse to let them see me cry again. When I get out, I am going to make these people, especially that bitch Cooper, this Roman Empire and even this world, regret they ever messed with me. By God, if my teachers thought I was a pain in the arse, then these people haven't seen anything yet!*

Her eyes getting heavier, Zoe slowly drifted off to sleep. As she slept, her mind began to dream of escape and revenge.

12

As the vehicle drove through the busy Durham streets, it passed the heavy afternoon traffic, which were carrying various types of people going about their daily business. The morning rain had cleared up, and the sun was trying to make its presence felt through the clouds.

The Audi Q3 approached a set of traffic light and slowed as they changed from green to red. Inside the vehicle, Dave pressed his foot down on the brake pedal, bringing the vehicle to complete stop. As he sat, waiting for the light to change, he peered over to the Claire who was sat in the passenger seat beside him. He could see she was silently scribbling notes in her notepad.

'I am sure you will have guessed, but I did a bit of research on you, Claire.' Dave said, 'I am sure you can understand. I usually like to know who I am working with.'

Claire lifted her head from her scribbling and looked across to him. The corner of her mouth turned up into a knowing smile as she raised a curious eyebrow, 'I would have been surprised if you hadn't. Perfectly understandable really. I would have done the same if the situation had been reversed.'

'If I was a betting man, I would bet that you had already done the same on me before we even met.' Dave grinned, tilting his head to her as he gave the woman a sly wink.

Claire cocked her head as she gave him the side eye and let out a small laugh, 'I think you probably would have lost that bet. Come on, Dave, what did you find out. What secrets have you uncovered?'

Dave laughed and opened his mouth to say something but stopped as he spotted the traffic light had changed to green, he then gently released his foot off the brake and pressed down on the accelerator. He shrugged and pursed his lips together, 'Nothing Earth shattering, my dear. You were born on 23rd June 1967 in Dryburn Hospital in Durham. You never married but went to Cambridge University and studied history. Eventually you got your degree and qualified as a history professor. You taught at various schools around the world, but approximately 15 years ago you took up a post as a professor in history at Durham University.'

'Oh, but you forgot the most important bit of information.' Claire answered cryptically, waggling her finger as she gave him a knowing wink, 'That I was born and bred in Langley Park!'

Dave scrunched his face up and shook his head, 'I didn't forget.' he replied, giving Claire a speculative glance, 'I wanted to see if you would tell me. But the interesting question is, why would a History Professor be investigating cases involving murder or disappearances?'

'It's ... complicated.' Claire replied hesitantly. Her eyes flickered with sadness and her smile slowly faded as she turned her head to gaze out the window.

After a moment of silence, Dave reached over and touched the sombre woman's hand briefly, 'Does it have anything to do with your twin sister's death?' he asked gently.

Claire lowered her head and peered at Dave's hand. She inhaled a deep breath and let out a ragged sigh, tears filling her eyes as she pressed her lips together. 'I don't want to talk about it just now.' she whispered, there was a tone of mourning in her voice, 'Please David, let it be for now. But I will tell you everything you want to know, when we meet back at your place this evening.'

Dave gazed at the oncoming traffic in silence and nodded slowly, 'Okay, Claire' he said softly, 'We'll leave it for now.'

After spending the rest of the journey in contemplative silence, a short time later they approached the outskirts of the village. Dave bobbed his head to Claire and pointed his finger at the village head of them.

'How long has it been for you since you were last home?' he asked curiously.

Claire nibbled on her bottom lip as she surveyed the oncoming village. As the village got closer her face hardened and she spoke in a subdued tone, 'To be honest, I try to visit as often as I can. It seems like I have never left, as if a part of me is still here.'

Dave gave a wordless nod of understanding as he stared out of the windscreen to the village ahead of him that was situated in a green grassy valley. As they drove into the village, they passed a working men's club and a row of Victorian stone buildings along the front street.

'It still appears the same.' Claire murmured, 'They try to modernise or change it, but deep down there is still that sense of something sinister lurking deep in the bowels of the village. When you have lived here for such a long time, you get used to it and slowly the darkness consumes you. It is like a cancer slowly eating away. Eventually you accept it, and it becomes part of you. It is only when you move away that you recognise it and then feel free ...' She lapsed into a silence but continued to stare ahead with a faraway expression as the car turned a corner and continued up the familiar looking high street. There was a tone of hopelessness in her soft voice as she shook her head to herself, 'But you never escape from it, really. Eventually it will find a way to drag you back kicking and screaming.'

Claire blinked as if she suddenly noticed that the car had stopped. Dave sat silently as he eyed her with heavy concern. She lifted her head heavenward and let out a bitter groan, 'Oh God! I really need a stiff drink. This place always gets to me.'

Dave opened his mouth to say something, but Claire held her hand up to him to stop him. Their eyes locked together, and they both bobbed their heads in silent understanding.

His cheeks warming, Dave gave a small, embarrassed cough and pointed his finger to something in front of him, 'Ahem, we are here.'

As he climbed out of the car, he could see other police cars and vans were parked along the side of the road. With the aid of a set of large industrial bolt cutters, two officers were trying to cut through the lock and chain that was wrapped around the large, rusted gates, while a group of uniformed officers were watching on, standing just outside the gate. Some of them were holding the leashes of police tracker dogs, who were barking excitedly.

As Dave approached them, they all turned and stood at attention, awaiting instructions. He stopped in front of them and raised his hand to the derelict building in front of them. 'Okay, we have little information to go on here.' he said in a loud but firm tone, 'All we have been told is that somebody has been killed and their body may be in the old building. I shouldn't have to say it, but I am going to; be careful. We don't know what is in there or if the attacker is in there too.'

All the officers murmured in acknowledgement as they got ready to enter the grounds. There was a small cheer when they saw that their two comrades had successfully unlocked the rusted gates and were in the middle of pushing them open when the air was filled with a loud squealing noise, as if the aged barrier was protesting about being opened.

'Okay ladies and gentlemen.' Dave ordered, 'We do this by the book. Canine units will go first, and then we will follow behind. I want you all to fan out and inspect every inch of this ground.'

There were more murmurs of acknowledgement as the officers got into position. Dave spun round and looked back to Claire, who was still standing beside the car. She arched her head curiously as he strode over to her.

'It is probably best, for your own safety, that you stay here until we have searched the area and made it safe.' He said gravely, gesturing to two constables standing in front of the opened gates, 'I will leave two officers outside to guard the entrance. If you need me for anything, they will contact me.'

Claire gave a small nod understanding and opened her mouth to say something but stopped when another constable hurried up to them and motioned to something further down the road.

'Sir, we have come across something. I think you need to see this.' The sandy-haired man said, frowning.

Dave lifted his chin and motioned for his colleague to lead the way. He followed him onto the footpath and after following the fence that marked the boundary of the old hospital's grounds, they eventually came to a stop at a gap in a fence. He pursed his lips as he knelt to study the red stained patches marking the grey footpath. He frowned as he lifted his head up to his colleague and pointed to the footpath and to the hole in the fence, 'The dispatcher who took the call this morning reported that a gentleman had witnessed a girl falling through a hole in the fence at this location and she was lying on the ground bleeding.' He scratched his chin thoughtfully as he peered through the hole, 'Well, looks like we can safely say this is the spot she came through.'

He then straightened up and took a step closer to the hole. But as he knelt to examine the area, Dave inhaled a sharp intake of breath as he caught sight of something on the edge of the hole. He glanced back to the constable standing behind him, 'Tell me Paul, does that look like a piece of skin to you?' he asked curiously and watched as Paul knelt for a closer look and gave a slight bob of his head in acknowledgement. Dave tapped him on the shoulder and gestured in the direction from where they had come, 'Run back to the van and get me an evidence bag, will you? Ask one of the dog handlers to come back with you too.'

Paul straightened up and gave a small nod of acknowledgement, 'Yes, sir!' He spun sharply round and ran back up to the main gate.

Dave reached into his pocket and pulled out a pack of disposable gloves, along with a tiny case that held a set of tweezers. He gently leaned closer and carefully lifted the piece of skin off the nail. As he was doing this, he turned his head as he heard footsteps coming from behind him and saw that Paul had returned. He was also being followed by Constable Lisa

Dawson, who was holding leash that had a German shepherd attached to it.

Dave stood up and smiled gratefully as Paul handed the evidence over to him. 'Thank you, Paul.' He then looked at the dog handler and gestured to the dog beside her, 'Lisa, do you think she'll be able to get a scent off this piece of skin?' he asked curiously, 'I would like to see if she can lead to where the girl was in the building.'

Lisa tilted her head curiously, looked down at her canine companion and smiled knowingly, 'I am sure Sasha can do that, Sir.'

After carefully handing the tweezers with the piece of skin over to her, Dave watched as Lisa knelt beside Sasha and gently placed the piece of skin in front of the dog's nose. The dog sniffed at it and then began to bark excitedly. She handed the tweezers back to Dave, who carefully slipped the piece of skin into an evidence bag. He then raised an eyebrow and cocked his head at Lisa quizzically, who was bobbing her head in acknowledgement.

'Well Sir, it looks like Sasha has picked up the scent.' she said proudly and gave him a questioning look, 'Do you want me to let her off now?'

Shaking his head, Dave raised his hand in front of him, 'No, wait until I give you the order to release her.' He twisted round and waved a hand in the direction from where she had just come, 'I am going back to the main gate and walk round to the other side of that hole. Lisa, when I tell you to, I want you to release her.' He then wheeled round to Paul, 'Paul, you stay here, please. Place markers on these blood stains and then place tape across this hole.'

Without waiting for him to respond, Dave raced back up to the main gate to where the group of officers were gathered. After giving the order for them to proceed, he stood back and watched as the canine units went in first, followed closely by the rest of his colleagues, who slowly began fanning out as they entered through the gates.

After dashing through the main gate, Dave followed the bush boundary marking the edge of the hospital's grounds. He came to a stop as he heard a dog barking from the other side of undergrowth. Then, with his hands held up on either side his of his mouth, he craned his head back and shouted in the direction from where the barking was coming from, 'Lisa, is that you?' He smiled as he heard a woman's faint reply, 'Okay, let Sasha go and then you run back to the main gate and head this way too.'

Dave cocked his head and listened to Lisa issue a command to her canine companion. Less than a minute later the dog appeared through the undergrowth, barking, and sniffing excitedly. He grabbed onto her collar, patted her back and praised her for a job well done, 'Good girl.'

Two minutes later Dave spun sharply round as he heard loud heavy footsteps coming from behind him. Lisa bobbed her head gratefully as she put Sasha back on her lead. He motioned for them to continue and watched in silence as Lisa knelt closer to the dog and gave her a command.

'Seek! Sasha, Seek!' She said firmly.

Dave watched in interest as Sasha barked excitedly as she led her trainer toward the old hospital building. A short time later, the dog came to a stop in front of brick wall, beneath a broken window. However, before Lisa could praise her canine companion on a job well done, the dog suddenly let out a small whine and then tried to cower behind her startled handler.

Lisa looked at Dave with a puzzled expression, 'She has never done that before!' There was a concerned tone in her voice and as she knelt to comfort the scared dog, 'Easy, it's okay, girl.'

On bending down to examine the ground, Dave's eyebrows drew together as he noticed the dirt around the bottom of the wall was stained with black patches of what he assumed to be dried blood. He rubbed at his chin as he examined the soil. He could tell from the shape of shoeprints, that they could possibly have been made by a pair of trainers. But then his eyes narrowed as he noticed a set of unusual tracks pressed into the dirt next to the shoeprints. He swallowed anxiously as Sasha let out a fearful whine as she gave the strange tracks another sniff. It left him no double that whatever had made them was not of human origin.

Dave looked up at Lisa and pointed to the fearful dog, 'I think it's best if you take her away now. She has done a brilliant job, Lisa. Thank you.'

Lisa nodded in agreement and led her canine companion back

toward the main gate. Dave continued to examine the area but paused as he noticed a broken window approximately two metres up from the ground. He cocked his head speculatively and realised that it must have been from where the girl had gotten in and out of the old building.

Twenty minutes later, alongside a group of his fellow officers, Dave stood at the main entrance of the old hospital and watched as they forced the entrance open so they could get inside. As he stood chatting with some of some his colleagues, he twisted round to see DS Donnelly racing up toward him.

'Sir, we've carried out an extensive search of the building.' Brenda said sadly, waving her hands at the building's entrance, 'Unfortunately, apart from mice and a lot of scared birds, there isn't anything out of the ordinary, apart from a dead dog. I think somebody has been wasting our time here.'

Dave shook his head, gave her half a smile, and let out a grunt of frustration, 'Thank you, Sergeant. I would have to agree with you. You and the others head back to the Station, I will follow you shortly. I am going to take another search around with Professor Tulley. I'll contact the local council for them to come out and make the main gates secure again.'

Brenda lifted her chin in acknowledgement and raised her hand to signal her colleagues to follow her. Dave scratched his head as he stared thoughtfully up at the empty building, scrutinising every bit of its decaying structure. There was something about the place that set his teeth on edge, but he was desperate to take another peek around. He spun sharply round, made his way out of the gates, and dashed over to his car. He then spotted Claire was still sitting in the vehicle reading her notes.

Claire opened the car door and climbed out of the vehicle. She opened her mouth to speak, but a ringtone from Dave's mobile phone cut her off. He took the phone out of pocket and his eyebrows perked up as he recognised the name on the caller display.

'It's Sergeant Jenkins. I had sent them to the hospital to interview the young girl found injured here.' Dave said curiously. He held his finger on the green icon on the phone's screen and pressed the phone to his ear, 'Andy, please tell me you have something good to report.' He became silent as he listened to Andy's summary of the events at the hospital.

After Andy was finished, Dave ran his free hand down his face and groaned in frustration, 'Andy, I would have done the same thing if I had been in your shoes. Professor Tulley and I will take another look around here. In the meantime, you and Wendy get a bite to eat, and we will meet back at my place at around seven this evening. We've got a lot to talk about and I would prefer to do it somewhere private.'

After listening to his colleague's acknowledgement, Dave lowered the phone and disconnected the call. He looked up at the heavens and let out an enormous snarl of frustration.

Claire cocked her head and listened with a raised eyebrow as Dave gave her an account of the phone call had just had with his concerned colleague. After he had finished, Dave bobbed his head in sympathy when he saw the shock and confusion that was etched on the woman's face.

'So, what do we do next?' Claire whispered, there was a hint of uncertainty in her voice.

Dave stood silently with his hands clasped behind his back and studied the old hospital in front of him. Just what was going on here? What had they gotten themselves involved in? He blinked as he felt Claire's hand touch his shoulder, breaking him out of his reverie. He glanced at her and scratched his head in irritation.

'We are going to have to tread carefully here. Something is definitely not right. Somebody is playing with us, and I don't like it.' he grumbled.

'You can see now, what I have been telling you is true.' Claire replied grimly, 'Whatever is happening, has been going on for years and may extend all the way to the top. How high ...' Her voice trailed off, and she stared into Dave's eyes as if realising the implications of what she had just said.

Dave frowned as he looked at the old building thoughtfully and turned to Claire, waving his in front of him, 'I would still like to take another look in there.' he muttered, 'There are a couple of things I found that you may find interesting. One of them may be from our mysterious beastie friend.'

Claire's eyes flickered with curiosity as she gave him a lop-sided grin and laughed, 'Oh, you know all the right things to say to a woman!' She then jerked her head in the direction of the old building, 'Lead on, my good man.'

They both laughed at one another as they walked toward the decaying building.

A cloaked figure was standing watching from a window that was situated on the abandoned hospital's top floor. It silently observed the two people as they slowly walked toward the building.

Only after Dave and Claire had moved out of its field of view did it then move away and strode over to a dirty, narrow mirror that was resting against a wall.

The hooded figure came to an abrupt stop in front of it, raised its arm over the mirror and watched as the reflective surface began to shimmer like the surface of water on a bright summer's day. The figure then stepped forward and disappeared into the glistening surface.

Seven miles south-west of Langley Park, Karen Logue was sat all alone in the morgue staring open-mouthed at her computer monitor. She leaned back in chair and shook head, not believing what she was reading. On the screen were supposed to be the results of the samples that she had taken earlier that day from the bodies of Tommy and Michael Thorn, but the more she looked at the results, the less sense they made to her.

'That's impossible. I don't believe it!' Karen huffed to herself as she continued to stare at her screen in utter bewilderment.

Karen reached over to pick up the mobile phone that was lying beside her keyboard and brought up her contact list. As she was doing that, she frowned as she heard a strange sound coming from somewhere behind her. She was positive it almost sounded like gas escaping from oxygen cylinder.

Her attention focused on her phone, Karen's eyebrows knitted together as she heard someone give a small cough behind her. 'James, is that you? Where have you been?' she asked irritably, 'You won't believe what I have found, my boy.' On receiving no to reply to her answer, she screwed up her face in annoyance, let out an exasperated grunt and then spun sharply round, 'James, what are you doi—' The words died in her as she instantly recognised the figure standing before her.

Completely taken aback, Karen was lost for words as she gazed at Detective Inspector Barnes. But he appeared to be staring back at her with an odd look on his face. She started to ask what he was doing there but stopped as she suddenly sensed something did not feel right.

The phone slipping out of her hand and onto the floor, Karen climbed out of her chair to get a better look at the man standing before her. She cocked her head and lifted an eyebrow as she suddenly noticed he was wearing a long black leather jacket with black leather trousers, giving off a sinister militaristic vibe which reminded her of a German Gestapo officer from World War II.

She felt her heart miss a beat as she watched him move toward her, his mouth widening into a cold malevolent-like grin. She let out a sharp gasp when she finally noticed the thin scar on the left side of his face that went up his cheek, stopping and then continuing above his left eye.

With every fibre of her being screaming at her, telling her something was wrong, Karen swallowed and looked at him warily, 'David, are you okay?' She croaked, as she raised her trembling hand, and pointed to the uniform he was wearing, 'Why are you dressed like that?'

'Oh, I see you already know my counterpart on this world.' Barnes chuckled as he held up a finger and nodded. Karen's felt her mouth go dry on hearing the man's strange Italian-like accent. His mouth broadened into a wicked smile, and he took a step closer to her, 'A shame… a real shame.'

Terrified beyond belief, Karen tried to back away from the menacing looking man but found her escape route blocked by her desk. A small whimper escaped her lips as Barnes extended his hand and gently stroked her face. Then, as if to put further strain on her already fragile mental state, she watched in slack-jawed astonishment as the mirror on the wall opposite her started to shimmer like a pool of liquid mercury. She stared in wide-eyed wonder as three more people climbed out of it. It was then she noticed that two of newcomers were soldiers, dressed in a strange black and gold armour. She frowned as she thought there was something oddly familiar to their uniforms.

Karen then focused her attention on the third person and felt her blood freeze. Fearing her mind was starting to unravel, she did a double take, but she still could not believe what she was seeing. Unfortunately, as much as she wanted to not believe her eyes, there was no denying it - the woman standing before her was an exact duplicate of herself. Sensing her sanity slip away, Karen opened and closed her mouth in disbelief as she watched her doppelgänger click her heels together and then bow her head to Barnes.

'Colonel Barnes! I am here to serve.' she barked. Despite her own fear, Karen could not help noticing her double was also speaking in a strange heavily accented English.

Barnes' mouth opened in a wide toothy grin, and he tilted his head in acknowledgement, 'Excellent Logue. You know your duty. Do not fail me.'

Karen became overwhelmed with terror as Barnes made a move towards her. She collapsed onto the floor and pressed her hands to chest as she pleaded at him, 'Pl … pl … please don't.' she sobbed, 'Please d … d … don't kill me I … I … w … w … will do anything you w … w … want.'

Karen recoiled in revulsion as Barnes leaned closer to her and kissed her on the forehead. She squeezed her eyes shut and groaned when she felt his hand trail down her chin and neck as he whispered to her.

'Oh, my dear. You are going to wish you hadn't said that.' Barnes hissed, his mouth twisting as he leered at her, 'I have such plans for you. After I am through with you, you are going to wish for death. Yes, we are going to have such… fun.' He spun abruptly round to the two soldiers stood beside him, who straightened and clicked their heels together in salute, 'Follow me and bring this one too.' he ordered, pointing to the cowering woman on the floor.

As she watched Barnes climb through the portal and vanish, Logue grinned as she turned and watched her doppelgänger convulse with fear as the two soldiers unceremoniously heaved her up off the floor and dragged her through the portal, screaming.

Laughing to herself, Logue bent down and picked up her counterpart's mobile phone off the floor. She studied it and played with its functions before setting it one side. She then let out a malevolent cruel laugh, as she sat down in front of her doppelgänger's computer. Logue chuckled as she reached over to another chair, pulled it closer and placed her feet on it. She then picked up the mouse her counterpart had been using and gave it a bemused look.

'A mouse. How quaint!' she scoffed derisively.

Dropping the mouse down, she then began to sing to herself as she guided the pointer on the display monitor and purposely deleted the sample results on the screen.

13

After investigating the old hospital building and grounds thoroughly with Claire, Dave realised that there was nothing useful could find that would be of any help to them. He reluctantly decided it was best that they go back to the police station.

Dave sat in silence on the journey back, lost in his own thoughts. Claire had said very little too. Even though he hadn't known her long, he could tell their pointless search had left her frustrated.

As Dave guided the vehicle into the station carpark Claire gave him a sidelong glance, 'It might be a good idea if I go home to freshen up before meeting with you later this evening.'

He gave her a wordless nod as he manoeuvred the car into a parking bay. After Dave had brought the car to come to a stop, Claire unfastened her seatbelt and opened the car door, but before she could get out of the car, Dave leaned over and handed her a piece of paper.

'This is my address.' He said helpfully.

Claire took the piece of paper from him, peered at it thoughtfully, smiled and climbed out of the car. Dave tapped his hand on the steering wheel as he watched her walk up to her own car, an apple green Nissan Juke. After a few seconds, he frowned as he saw her stop and then she appeared to think about something, before spinning round, and hurrying back to him. Puzzled, Dave got out of his car and then he felt his eyes widen in surprise as she continued to walk back over to him.

'Claire, what's wrong? Have you forgotten something' he asked worriedly.

'Yes, this.' Claire answered cryptically, her mouth curving into a mischievous smile. Dave became lost for words as she leaned in close, kissed him on the cheek and then him a sly grin as she pulled away from him, 'Hope you are not planning on doing anything stupid while I am away. I still owe you an explanation.' She then winked, clicked her tongue, and pointed her index finger at him, 'Catch you later.'

Completely dumbfounded, Dave didn't know how to react as he watched as Claire turn on her heel and saunter away from him. He raised a hand to touch his cheek and stared at her as she made her way back to her car. He found his eyes were suddenly drawn to her slender legs and for the first time he became aware how tight her jeans were, especially around her bottom.

Dave blinked and shook his head as he tried to bring his attention back to something else. Unfortunately for him, it was at that point Claire glanced back over her shoulder and the corners of her quirked up in amusement. She stared directly at him and teasingly waggled her finger, mouthing, '*later*'. She pulled her head back, laughed, opened her car door, and climbed into the small vehicle.

From the slow warmth building on his face, Dave was suddenly conscious that he was blushing and shook his head to himself in disapproval. 'Stop being a fool for God's sake.' He muttered to himself, 'You're an adult, stop acting like a teenager!'

He gave an embarrassed wave and watched Claire drive her vehicle out of the parking space, his eyes following the Juke as it sped out of the car park. He frowned as he heard laughing coming from behind him, turned and saw that three young officers had been watching his awkward exchange with much amusement.

Dave coughed and gave them an embarrassed smile, 'Ahem, yes, carry on now.'

He turned sharply away from the trio, only to walk directly into a lamp post. A roar of laughter came from the bemused men. Dave shot them an angry, cutting their laughter short.

'Have you lot got anything else better to do?' he snapped as he straightened himself and clasped his hands behind his back, 'I am sure I can find some volunteers for Chief Inspector Thomas' next lecture!'

The sheepish trio lowered their eyes and turned swiftly away. Apparently they must have realised they *did* have somewhere else to be. Dave's mouth twitched as he silently watched the departing group of red-faced men hurry away from him. He lowered his head, glanced at his watch, and dashed through the station entrance as he made his way back up to his office to collect Jenny.

Five minutes later, Dave opened the passenger door of his car, allowing Jenny to jump eagerly in. He then strode around to the other side of the car, climbed inside, and stared thoughtfully across the quiet carpark.

'I think it may be a good idea if we drop by the morgue on our way home to see if Doctor Logue has learned anything new.' he murmured to himself, then cocked his head and shot the dog an inquiring look, 'What do you think?'

He chuckled as Jenny gave a little bark in response.

Twenty minutes later Dave dashed down a long corridor and slowed as he approached a set of double doors that led to the morgue. After he stepped through the double doors, he arched his right eyebrow as he heard singing coming from behind the door that led into the examination room. Dave frowned and walked into the side room, put on protective clothing and then knocked on the door.

The singing stopped and Dave's eyebrows knitted together as he heard what he thought was Karen, answering in an angry tone, 'Yes? What is it? Don't you simpletons realise I am busy?'

Startled, Dave took a step in back in surprise. He had been friends with Karen for a long time, but there was something in the tone of her voice that unsettled him. He coughed and knocked on the door again, 'Karen, sorry it is me, Dave, can I come in?'

Dave cocked his head and raised an eyebrow in amusement as he heard what he thought sounded like a loud clatter, followed closely by an angry tirade of expletives. He felt his stomach churn with anxiety – in all the years he had known her, he had never heard her swear like that.

'Yes! Yes! Come in by all means.' He heard Karen shout.

Dave frowned to himself as he tried to discern the tone of her voice. He wasn't sure, but he was positive she sounded - excited?

Tentatively opening the door, Dave walked warily into the chilly room and saw Karen was standing in front of the examination table, smiling at him. But as he walked over to her, he was suddenly aware that she was looking at him strangely, as if she was scrutinising him. For some reason he started to have a great sense of unease at the way she was acting; it was if she was seeing him for the first time and was studying him.

It is probably the morgue playing tricks on my mind. We have known each other professionally for at least twenty years, he thought to himself.

'Hello, Detective Inspector.' Karen greeted. Dave frowned as he thought he recognised something in her tone, was it anticipation? She extended her hand to him and smiled warmly, 'What a pleasure to see you. I was really hoping that we would finally meet.'

What did she just say? Dave's eyebrows drew together and he gazed at Karen in confusion, 'Uh, Karen, we saw each other this morning. Don't you remember?' he said with a concerned tone, 'Are you feeling okay?'

Karen's eyelids fluttered and her mouth curved into a smile. Dave flinched in shock as, without warning, she tilted her head back and let out a loud laugh, the sound of her laugh reverberating around the silent room. 'Oh, of course we have my dear boy. I am just pulling your leg.' she said gleefully. Her large round grey eyes glinted as she gave Dave an impish wink, 'I'm perfectly fine. You know how it is? One gets so busy. One just loses track of time.'

A sense of unease screamed at Dave from the back of his

mind. His gut was telling him that something was wrong, but he could not place his finger on the reason. Trying to compose himself, he brushed the thought aside and pulled himself back to the reason he had come to see Karen.

'O ... o ... okay ... s ... s ... sure.' he stammered, 'I ... I ... just thought I would drop by to see if you have found out anything new since my visit this morning.'

The corners of Karen mouth lifted and she nodded slowly. She then turned away from Dave and pointed to the computer monitor on top of the workstation, 'Yes ... yes ... I think you might like this. I have something wonderful to show you.' She gestured to a chair in front of the computer terminal, 'Take a seat, please.'

Dave haltingly walked over to the workstation, lowered himself into the chair in front of the computer monitor and placed his hand on the mouse to clear the screen saver. He drew his eyebrows together in puzzlement as he studied the blank screen in front of him.

'What am I supposed to be looking at?' Dave asked, pointing curiously to the blank screen. He shifted uncomfortably in the seat as he suddenly became aware that Karen was standing uncomfortably close to him.

Dave's stiffened in surprise as Logue leaned across him provocatively and he felt her hair brush his face. He closed his eyes as he caught the overpowering scent of her perfume and felt his Adam's apple jump up and down as he swallowed anxiously. He squeezed his eyes shut in concentration as he tried to think about something to distract him from Karen's close proximity.

'Oh dear, is it not on the screen?" he heard Karen sigh in frustration, "Let me see if I can enlighten you.'

His eyes still closed, Dave silently counted to ten and shivered as he felt her warm breath on the back of his neck. His hands tightened into fists as he desperately thought to himself, *'Good thoughts, think good thoughts.'* Despite his anxiety, he sensed he was starting to become aroused and shuddered to himself as he felt a cold bead of sweat trickle down the back of his neck.

He let out a breath of surprise as he felt Karen's hands sliding in-between his leg and grab at his crotch. His mouth falling open in shock, Dave opened his eyes and saw that Karen was grinning menacingly at him as he felt her hand reach for the zipper on his trousers.

'Oh ... my! Aren't we a naughty boy.' she moaned seductively, 'Does he want to come out to play ... hmmm?'

Startled, Dave jumped up out of the chair and tried to back away from Karen, but he was dismayed to discover she had him trapped against the desk. He suddenly noticed that she was not wearing her protective shirt and she had unbuttoned the top of her blouse. Sweating profusely and with an increasing sense of panic and confusion, Dave struggled to back away.

Her eyes flickering with malice, Karen licked her lips as she peered down at Dave and her mouth twisted into a smile. He felt helpless as he watched her lean even closer into him and grab his hand with malicious intent.

'Oh come now, David. Don't be shy. Deep down, you know you have been wanting to do me for years.' she hissed through clenched teeth, 'Admit it! All this time you have come to see me here; you have fantasized bending me over this table.'

Paralysed with fear, Dave felt powerless as she forced his hand down the front of her open blouse and was surprised to find she was not wearing anything underneath. She then roughly placed his hand on her exposed breast and let out a moan of pleasure.

'No!' Dave roared and then with all his strength, he shoved the moaning woman off him, the force of his push throwing her across the room. He placed his hand over his mouth in alarm as he watched her collide with the examination table and collapse onto her knees.

For a brief second, concerned that he had pushed her too hard and fearing she had hurt herself, Dave took a step closer to her. Against his better judgement, he bent down to help Karen up.

As he helped her to her feet, Dave smiled warmly as he felt Logue's hand touch his right cheek. But his smile quickly vanished as he watched Karen mouth widen into a maniacal grin and he let out an exclamation of pain as he felt her long, sharp nails dig into the flesh of his cheek, scratching him. Caught by surprise, he slapped Logue away with his hand, unintentionally striking her in the face. He felt the inside of his mouth turn dry as he caught sight of blood trickling from the corner of her mouth.

Tormented with guilt, Dave leaned forward apologetically and extended his hands to the woman, 'I am sorry, Karen. I didn't mean to hit you like that.'

Karen glared at Dave in wide-eyed surprise and raised her hand to wipe her mouth. She peered at the blood on the back of her hand and then back at Dave. Her eyes radiated with hatred as she sneered at him, 'That's the David I know. So, you do like to play rough too.'

Dave shook his head in confusion as he backed slowly away, a sense of desperation building inside him as he pleaded at her, 'Karen, s … s … stop this. This is not you. What's wrong with you? We have been friends for years.'

Karen hung her head and pouted, 'Oh spoilsport!' she let out a snort of disgust, rolled her eyes and gave a dismissive wave of her hand, 'You are no fun, not like … *him*'

Filled with a mixture of dread and confusion, Dave barged past the grinning woman and raced out of the morgue through the door. Her manic laugh echoing in his head, he charged down the corridor and did not stop until he was outside.

Dave stopped at his car and, after fumbling for his car keys, he climbed inside, and collapsed into the seat. He placed his hands on his steering wheel, rested his head against them and sucked in several deep breaths, desperate to calm his pounding heart.

Startled, he jumped as he felt something nudge his arm. He lowered his head down and saw Jenny was trying to rest her head on his lap. She was staring up at her master with concern filled eyes as he slowly reached down to stroke her head.

'It's okay, girl. It's okay.' Dave whispered in a soft soothing tone, 'Just your dad going insane, that's all.'

Back in the crypt like room, Logue cackled to herself as she carefully refastened the buttons her blouse. She raised her eyes to the ceiling and let out a frustrated sigh, 'The men on this world are so boring.' she pouted and shook her head sadly, 'I just wanted a bit of fun. Poor, poor David. You will see soon. In fact, everybody on this backwater world will all see soon.'

Without warning, she collapsed onto the floor, and screamed in pain. It felt like her heard to trying to explode from the inside.

'*You were warned about misbehaving!*' she heard a female voice hiss sharply inside her head, '*I warned you before coming to this world. If you continued with your deviant behaviour, there would be consequences!*'

'P … p … please, I … I … I … am sorry.' Logue pleaded as tears ran down her cheeks from the pain, 'It w … w … won't happen again. F … f … forgive me. G … g … give … m … m … me … a … a … a … another chance.'

Collapsing onto the floor, Logue's chest rose and fell in rapid breaths as she felt the pain in her head ease.

'*I will give you one more chance to prove yourself.*' the disembodied voice hissed again, '*One more infraction and I will submit you for … re-education, along with your family. They will disappear and it will be like nobody will have ever heard of you or them … Cooper, Barnes, nobody … understood!!*'

Panting, Logue stretched her legs out in front of her and leaned back against the desk. Frantic with fear, she squeezed her eyes shut and nodded as a low whimper came out of her mouth.

'Yes … I understand.' she whimpered.

'*I have plans for Detective Inspector Barnes.*' the voice hissed. Logue jerked back in surprise at the mention of Barnes' name, '*You jeopardise them again …*'

Logue took a deep breath, reached up to the desk and pulled herself up off the floor. She hobbled over to the mirror, raised her hand to fix her hair and brushed her hand down her blouse. Her face ashen, she placed her hands behind her back and lifted her chin. She stared into the mirror through wide scared eyes and bowed her head slightly. Her voice was numb as she forced the words out of her fear gripped throat.

'I will comply.' she rasped.

Filled with anxiety, his heart hammering away inside his chest, Dave inhaled a deep ragged breath to help regain his composure. He felt Jenny lick his hand and he glanced down at her, smiled sadly and stroked her head.

His hands were shaking as he reached over and pressed the engine start button and flinched as he heard the vehicle's engine rumble to life. Dave pressed his foot on the accelerator pedal and felt the car pull away. An alarm startled him, and he cursed himself when it dawned on him, he had forgotten to put his seat belt on. He frantically pulled at the seat belt, and after two attempts, he clicked the seat belt into place.

After a nerve-wracking drive, Dave drove his car into his driveway and brought it to complete stop. He switched off the car engine and sat for about five minutes, his was mind racing as he stared at the house in front of him. He took a deep ragged breath, opened the car door, and climbed out of the vehicle. Half-way up to his front door, he came to a sudden stop and smacked his forehead with the palm of his hand. How could he be so stupid – he'd forgotten Jenny. Sprinting back to the parked vehicle, he opened the vehicle's passenger door and gave Jenny a sheepish half-smile as the dog gave him an accusatory glance as she jumped past him. After making sure he had locked the car, he turned and continued to walk back to his front door, his hands trembling as he fumbled for his house key.

Just as he was about to unlock his front door, Dave froze as he was overcome with a sudden sense of paranoia and he stepped back from his front door to gaze along the empty street. He shook his head and let out a snort of disgust with himself as he continued to open the door and enter his house.

After closing the door behind him, Dave wearily threw his car fob and house key into a bowl on top of a small table in the hall's corner. As jenny trotted into the kitchen, Dave followed close behind and picked up a bottle of whisky from the wine rack near to the kitchen door. Grabbing an empty glass from the kitchen bench, with his hands still shaking, he poured out a small measure and downed it in one go.

Dave screwed up his face as the whisky hit the back of his throat and poured out another measure into the empty glass. Still carrying the whisky bottle and the glass, he stumbled into the living room and collapsed into a chair. Jenny followed him and lay herself down next to his feet but continued to look up at her master through worried eyes.

He downed the whisky in one go again and poured himself another small measure. Carefully placing the whisky bottle on the table beside him, Dave leaned back in the chair and, still comforting the glass in his hands, he closed his eyes and slowly dropped off to sleep.

Dave groaned as he heard a loud knocking, along with the barking of a dog. Disorientated and confused, he opened his eyes and jumped up out of his chair, spilling the contents of the glass over him. Dave blinked in surprise as he glanced at his watch saw that it was 6.30pm; he had been asleep for over an hour.

As the knocking and barking continued, Dave became aware that Jenny was barking at somebody knocking on the door. Stumbling into the kitchen, he grabbed a tea-towel that was hanging on the oven door handle to wipe himself down. He gingerly staggered out to the hall and saw Jenny was standing at the front door barking.

'Jenny, come!' he snapped irritably. He frowned as he took step closer to the door, 'Sorry who is it?'

Claire's muffled voice was heard coming from the other side of the door, 'Sorry, Dave? Is that you? It's me Claire, sorry Professor Tulley. You remember you said we should meet back up this evening?'

Dave scrubbed his face with hands as his muffled brain synapsis started to fire and a memory drifted through the fog in his brain about asking everybody to meet back up at his place. He quickly opened the front door and was relieved to see Claire was standing in front of him, wearing jeans and a plain white blouse. *Looks like she has come prepared.* he thought to himself as he noticed that she was holding a bottle of wine in one hand and

Double Jeopardy

a takeaway bag in the other.

'Oh, sorry Claire,' Dave yawned, wiping the sleep out of eyes, 'I must have fallen asleep and hadn't realised the time. Come in, please.'

The corner of Claire's mouth twitched in amusement as she walked through the doorway. She stopped in front of him and gave him a look of concern, 'Jesus! What happened to you? You look like shit.'

Dave looked down at himself and shrugged, 'Oh, this. I fell asleep with a glass of whisky in my hand and spilt it over me when your knocking and Jenny's barking woke me up.'

Claire took a step closer to Dave and frowned. Dave wondered for a moment why she was staring at his face. She pursed her lips, bent down, put the takeaway bag on the floor and raised her hand to touch his face.

'Dave, what happened to your face?' she asked, her voice heavy with concern.

Dave blinked and winced in pain as he felt her fingers touch his face. Having forgotten Karen had scratched him earlier that evening, he gave Claire a half shrug and waved his hand in front of him, 'That is a long and weird story!'

Giving him a stern side eye, Claire gently took Dave's hand and led him into the kitchen, 'It looks nasty and needs to be treated.' She frowned as she gazed around the kitchen, 'Do you have a First Aid box? You can fill me in while I treat it.'

Dave jerked his head toward a kitchen cupboard on the wall and watched as Claire, after putting the wine and food on top of the kitchen counter, walked over to the cupboard, and pulled out a First Aid box.

'You don't have to do this, Claire.' he protested, 'I am perfectly capable of doing this myself!'

With the First Aid box held firmly in her hands, Claire eased over Dave and forced him to sit on the kitchen stool. He rolled his eyes as she opened the First Aid box and pulled out a pack of cotton wool.

'Shush!' She admonished, glaring sternly at him, 'For once, do as you are told. Didn't I warn you earlier about not doing anything stupid?'

Dave cocked his head and chuckled as he watched Claire pour a small amount of disinfectant onto a piece of cotton wool. As she dabbed the cotton wool onto his face, Dave hissed sharply as he felt the disinfectant touch the exposed part of the wound.

'Stop being a baby!' she said with a firm tone as she put a hand on his shoulders to stop him from squirming, 'Sit still and do as you are told Barnes!'

Dave opened his mouth to protest but stopped as Claire hung her head and shot him a disapproving look over the top of her glasses. For a moment he felt like he was a child again; being told off by a strict teacher.

As she carefully continued to treat the wound, Dave regaled Claire of his visit to the morgue and of his strange encounter with Karen. When he was finished, she closed the First Aid box and shook her head in disbelief.

'Just another mystery to add onto the ever-growing pile.' she said sadly.

Dave gave a small nod of agreement and glanced at his watch, 'Andy and Wendy will arrive shortly. We have a lot to discuss.'

Claire bobbed her head and placed the First Aid back from where she had gotten it from. As she took Dave's hand to help him off the kitchen stool, she screwed up her face and waved her hand in front of her, 'Christ, you smell like a distillery!' she moaned, 'You need to get freshened up and change your clothes.'

Dave snorted and gave a dismissive wave of his hand, 'I'm fine, really. They will arrive shortly, and I need to give you a hand with the food you brought.'

Claire shot him a disapproving look and shook her head, 'I can handle things down here. For once do as you are told and get your backside upstairs, Now!' She ordered firmly, indicating that it was not up for discussion as she pointed her hand to the stairs.

Dave rolled his eyes in protest as Claire pushed him into the direction of the stairs and slapped him on the bottom playfully. He stuck his tongue out at her and ducked as she threw a tea-towel at him. He grinned to himself as he walked upstairs to get changed.

He strode into his bedroom and sat on the edge of the large

double bed. After taking off his whisky stained trousers and blood-stained shirt, he threw them onto the bedroom floor and dashed into the bathroom, where he turned on the taps to pour some water into the bathroom wash basin. As he waited for the basin to fill up with water, he glanced into the bathroom mirror to examine his scratched face. He gave a small throaty groan when he noticed there were three nasty deep lacerations on the right side of his check from where Karen's fingernails had scratched him.

As he stared into the mirror, Dave narrowed his eyes as he began to feel an overwhelming sense of paranoia as if someone was watching him. But as he moved slowly away from the bathroom sink, he felt his stomach tighten as he thought of the day's events and began to put the pieces of the clues together.

Quickly regaining his composure, Dave finished cleaning himself up and then, to make sure not to alert whoever was watching him, he carefully moved back into the bedroom and closed the bathroom door after him. After slipping into a pair of jeans, T-shirt, and trainers, he scratched his head and pretended to search around the bedroom for something as he discretely moved over to the square mirror on the wall. Flattening himself against the wall beside the mirror, he reached over and gently nuzzled the frame off the wall with one hand. With his other hand gripped tightly to the bottom of the frame, he slid it down the wall until the edge was touching the floor, and then lay it flat onto the floor with the reflective side lying face down.

Dave jumped as he heard a firm knock come from downstairs. On realising it was coming from the front door, he rushed to the top of the stairs and opened his mouth to shout down to Claire to be careful. But as he heard the front door open, he realised he was too late. However, a surge of relief passed through him as he recognised the distinctive tones of Andy and Wendy coming from the hallway.

Dave raced down the stairs and found the three people had ventured into the kitchen. As he raced through the kitchen door, he was greeted with the cheery smiles from his two colleagues.

'Hi Guv! We were just introducing ourselves to Claire here.' Andy said, smiling warmly as he nodded to Claire.

Their cheery smiles quickly vanished, replaced by looks of confusion as Dave shook his head and held his finger to his lips. Claire opened her mouth to say something but was stopped by Wendy, who had placed her hand on her arm. Andy's and Wendy's eyes grew wide, and they nodded in understanding as Dave mouthed silently to them, *They may be watching.*

Dave snapped his fingers at his two colleagues, pointed to the mirror on the wall in the hall and then to the one in the living room. Andy acknowledged him with a thumbs up as he followed him into the living room. Wendy gestured with her thumb to Claire, who appeared to be confused but acknowledged the younger woman with a tilt of her head as she followed her into the hall.

The two men both carefully eased the living room mirror off the wall, carried it outside and gently lay it on the ground with the reflective side facing down. As they turned to walk back into the house, they met the two women in the doorway as they carried the hall mirror outside too. Dave motioned to where he wanted them to lay it and they placed it next to the one that had been in the living room, also with the reflective side facing down.

After rushing back into the kitchen, Claire panted for breath as she turned to Dave with a confused expression, 'Sorry, but do you mind telling me what was that about? I like party games like the best of them, but what the hell?'

Dave looked apologetically at the bewildered looking Claire and placed his hand on her shoulder, 'Sorry Claire, but I just want to be careful.' he said gravely, jerking his thumb to the ceiling, 'While I was upstairs standing in front of the bathroom mirror, a theory formed in my head. I remembered Andy's phone conversation from earlier after he had tried to interview Zoe Murray and he said something which didn't seem right. He then told me about the blood leading to the mirror.'

Andy lifted his hand, waved his finger, and nodded in understanding, 'I guess you have the same thought too, whatever *it* is, it's not only taking people by using a mirror but somehow it's leaving a copy.'

'No, not leaving a copy.' Dave replied gloomily. He shook his head thoughtfully as he rubbed his chin with his hand, 'I think *it*, or *they*, are replacing people with doppelgängers. I went to visit Dr Karen Logue, you know the Forensic Medical Examiner, in the morgue. When I got there, she was acting all weird, as if we were meeting for the first time. She attacked me and when I pushed her away, she got all upset and started moaning something about I wasn't any fun, not like *him*. That's when it hit me upstairs. Not only could they be using the mirrors to take people, but …'

'They could be using them to watch us!' Claire blurted out, her mouth falling open in shock. As he watched Andy and Wendy exchange worried glances, Dave could tell that his news had shaken them.

Andy took a deep breath and gave a small grim nod, 'Well, if that theory is right, that could explain the strange scratch marks at the crime scene last night.'

'Okay, that may explain the how.' Wendy asked, there was a hint of uncertainty in her voice as she shifted awkwardly on her feet, 'But what about the why? Also, surely this cannot be the first time something like this has happened?'

Dave cocked his head at Claire with a raised eyebrow, who acknowledged him with a silent nod. He picked a glass and plate from the kitchen counter and motioned to the living room. 'Well, I think it's best if we go into the living room and take a seat.' he said, gesturing to Claire, 'I invited Claire tonight as she has a lot of evidence which suggests, not only has this been going on for years but they covered it up with orders from above. I suggest we grab a plate of food and head into the living room. It's going to be a long night.'

Wendy coughed and raised her hand. Surprised, Dave stared at her questioningly.

'Guv, can I tell you something?' she grumbled sourly.

Dave swallowed and then looked worriedly at Wendy, 'Sure Wendy.'

Wendy inhaled a deep breath and let out a long melodramatic sigh, 'Is it too late to say I was joking about wanting to help with the case?'

Dave lifted his head back and let out a loud laugh, 'Sorry Cooper, but you are too late. We are up to our eyes in shit now and we are sinking!'

Andy nudged his unhappy colleague and winked, 'Come on Wendy! Surely you don't want to leave now, just as it is getting interesting?'

Wendy lifted her hands up the ceiling, rolled her eyes and let out a snort of disgust, 'I really hate you two!'

Dave pressed his hands to his cheeks in mock horror, 'Now my dear, that's no way to talk to a superior officer.'

Wendy gave him a cold look of disapproval and waved her hand melodramatically. She then reached over for the bottle of wine off the kitchen counter. 'Screw it.' she grunted, 'I really need a stiff drink.'

14

The four people sat round the coffee table in the living room. Claire and Dave were sitting on the sofa, with Andy sat in a chair on one side and Wendy sat in the other chair across from him.

Wendy picked up the bottle of wine to fill up Claire's glass while Andy picked at his food with his fork, Dave guessed that he was not in the mood to eat, much like himself.

After the disturbing events of today, who can blame him! he thought to himself.

Claire gave the helpful young woman a shy smile as she filled up her glass, then held up her hand to stop. Wendy offered the bottle to the brooding Andy, who waved his hand indicating that he had enough in his glass. She lowered herself back into her chair, sat back and regarded the middle-aged woman with a curious expression.

'The Guv had told us you may have some information that might help explain things.' Wendy said guardedly as she studied the older woman,

'Is that true?'

Claire glanced across to Dave, who lifted his hand up and gestured for her to continue, 'Go ahead. Tell them what you found out.'

Claire pushed her glasses up on the bridge of her nose with her finger nervously as the corners of her mouth lift in a half-smile, 'Well, I wouldn't say it will help to explain things. But I've spent years looking into this. Researching previous cases of strange disappearances or murders that occurred in Langley Park or the surrounding area. If you read carefully enough, you see a pattern.'

Andy frowned and peered across to Claire with a puzzled expression, 'Why you?' He held up his hands apologetically, 'Sorry that came out the wrong way. I mean, why are you investigating cases involving murders and disappearances? You are only a History Professor, no offense intended.'

Clare lifted an eyebrow, and the corner of her mouth turned up in a bemused smirk, 'None taken. I am sure Dave here has told you I am originally from Langley Park.'

Andy nodded slowly, 'Yes, but that still doesn't explain the why?'

'Careful Andy.' Dave scolded and gave him a dirty look, 'Give her time.'

Claire smiled at Dave, waving her hand, 'No, it's fine. I really need to tell him.'

She picked up her glass and sipped at her wine, not so much as if she was savouring it, but as if she was delaying her response in order to think. She eventually lowered her glass and placed her hands on her knees. She swallowed as she lowered her head and closed her eyes as she spoke in a soft calm tone, 'As you may have learned, I originally came from Langley Park. My parents both came from the area. My dad, he was a coal miner, worked in the mine in the village. My mother worked as a teacher in the village's junior school.' she inhaled deep breath and let out a heavy forlorn sigh, 'What you probably don't realise is that I am, or was, a twin. I had a sister, Emma. She died when I was eight years old, killed by our dog.'

Wendy's shook her head as she raised her hand to her mouth in shock, 'Oh Claire, I am so sorry!'

Claire smiled thinly and gave a dismissive wave of her hand as she stood up and paced slowly back and forth in front of the fireplace, 'That's the story we were told, but that's a lie.' she sneered as she glanced up at the ceiling and shook her head, 'Our dog, Sandy, wouldn't hurt a fly. She was a lovely, kind dog and loved us both. She was very protective of us both, especially Emma. They used the dog as an excuse to cover up what really happened. I know because it is the same thing that has been killing people for years. Because …' Her eyes began to fill with tears and she let out a shallow breath, turned and sank back down onto the coach with her head in her hands.

Dave gave a nod of understanding and then spoke with a grave heavy tone, 'Because you saw what killed her.'

Her hands still covering face, Claire gave a small nod in silent confirmation. Wendy quietly rose from her seat, went over to the distressed woman, and sat beside her, placed her arm over her shoulder and whispered softly to her, 'It's okay if you don't want to continue.'

Claire sniffed and lifted her chin up at Wendy. Tears glistened in her eyes as she gave her a sad smile and tapped her hand, 'No, it's fine, Wendy.' She sucked in a deep breath and let out a heavy sigh, 'It's the first time I've told anyone this, so please bear with me.'

Dave reached over for the bottle of whisky on the table beside him and poured a measure into Claire's empty glass and offered it to her, 'Here, this may help.'

Claire took the glass and then, to Dave's surprise, she downed contents of the glass in one go. Her eyes watering, Claire blinked and coughed. 'Thanks, Dave.' There was a hoarseness to her voice as she croaked, 'That helps.' Her eyes lowered to the empty glass in her hands and gazed into it in silence. Sadness clouded her features as she swallowed and continued, 'We had been trying to get to sleep, but we were both excited as Mum and Dad were taking us away for an exciting trip the next day to Butlins. You remember how it was as a child, being excited knowing you are going somewhere, but too excited to sleep. Emma was buzzing, while I was too tired and shouted at her to get into bed, but she was adamant that she was too excited to sleep.'

Claire lifted her head and gave a mournful smile as she held up her empty glass to Dave, who refilled it without comment. She knocked her head back, gulped down the contents of the glass, scrunched her face up and continued.

'Anyway, I was getting fed up with her jumping around.' She shook her head slightly and let out a small laugh, 'If you have a brother or sister, especially a twin, then you appreciate how sometimes they know how to push the right button. I picked up my pillow and threw it at her, telling her I hated her and wished she was dead. She got upset with me and said she hated me too and she was going to sleep with Sandy downstairs and that was the last time I saw her alive.' She let out bitter laugh and then stared tearfully up at the ceiling, 'Do you realise what it is like? To tell someone you love that you hate them, then knowing that would be the last thing you ever say to them.'

Dave leaned across to tearful woman and held her hand, 'You were kids, you didn't realise what you were saying.' he whispered gently, 'Children can say mean things, but really, they don't mean it. As children, we have all said awful things to people we love, but we never meant it. I am sure Emma felt you loved her.'

Claire smiled thinly at Dave as she placed her hand on his and nodded slowly, 'Yeah, I keep telling myself that and one day I may accept it.' Her shoulders sagged and she let out a heavy despondent sigh, 'Anyway, I was lying in my bed angry at myself for being a jerk. After half an hour Emma hadn't come back up to bed and I just assumed she was doing it to annoy me, so I decided that I would apologise. I got up and I can remember standing at the top of the stairs - I could hear Sandy whining. I was trying not to wake my mum and dad, so I crept down the stairs and as I got to the bottom, I noticed that the kitchen door was ajar, and I could hear Sandy was still whining. I opened the kitchen door and slowly walked in, and then that's when I saw it.' She paused to take another gulp from her glass, grimaced at the taste, took a deep breath and lifted her eyes up to the ceiling, 'At first I am not sure what I am looking at.' her began voice trembling but she pressed on with her story, 'At first, I thought it was a bear. Then I realised it was something else. It was large, its skin was black and shiny. It had claws on its hands and feet.' Dave noticed her breathing becoming faster and that was she starting to twist and wring her hands together, 'I watched as it looked like it was eating something on the floor. It was then I realised the body on the floor was Emma. I can remember screaming as the beast looked up at me. It had this awful thin, long head and when it hissed at me, it was then I saw it had sharp pointed teeth. Suddenly, I spun round to run, but that was when I felt something sharp scratch at me and then everything went black.' She paused and dropped her left hand to her right side, pulling her blouse up to reveal three old scars on the right side of her back, 'I was not sure how long I had been out for, but when I eventually regained consciousness, it was like I was in a daze. All I can is remember standing next to my parents' bed. At first my dad was angry at being woken, then my mum screamed when she saw the blood on me. They jumped out of the bed and started shouting at me asking me what happened, where Emma was, but they could not get any sense from me.' she stared up at the ceiling and shook her head sadly, 'While my mum was comforting me, my Dad went downstairs to see what had happened. The next thing I remember was hearing my dad's horrified scream coming from kitchen. My dad wrongly guessed Sandy was responsible because I can remember him angrily shout her name, followed by the noise of the back door slamming as he carried her out into the yard. I am not sure who rang the police. By this time our neighbours, on hearing all the noise, ran in. It is all a blur after that. I can remember somebody, a neighbour, taking me in their house.'

Claire paused again as she took another drink out of her glass and continued with her story, 'I tried to tell everybody what I saw, but nobody believed me. Later the police told my parents that the dog had been responsible, and they had to put her down.' She frowned and gave the other people in the room a questioning look, 'This is the thing I found strange after all these years. At first my parents believed me about what I saw; they didn't accept Sandy would hurt my sister or me. I can remember they were visited by people wearing black suits and not long after they told everybody the dog had killed Emma.'

'So, you assume the government pressured your parents?' Dave said carefully, trying not to push too hard.

Claire laughed bitterly and gave him a hard stare, 'Oh, I am certain they did! Not sure if they were from the government or some unofficial department.' she waved her in a dismissive manner and continued, 'Anyway, after that day my parents refused to talk about it. Even as I got older, they would never speak of it.' Her face contorted with anger as she looked at the faces in the room. Dave could tell she was fighting back the tears as she slammed her hand on the table in front of him, 'I never stopped accepting what I remember seeing was real. I swore to myself that I wouldn't stop until I uncovered the truth.' She stabbed her finger into her chest and hissed defiantly, 'I owe it to Emma's memory to find whatever killed her and make it pay.'

Andy leaned over to touch Claire's trembling hand sympathetically and nodded in understanding, 'Which is why you began investigating murders or disappearances that occurred in or around Langley Park.' His forehead creased as he pointed to himself and Dave, 'Surely we, I mean the police, would have spotted any pattern?'

Claire's eyebrows knitted together in annoyance, and she let out a snort of disgust, 'Oh, yes they did, but I found anybody who started investigating were pressured to drop their investigation by a superior officer or they suddenly found them reassigned.'

The shock evident on Andy's face, he twisted his head round and stared at Dave in disbelief, 'Sorry Guv, I don't know about you, but I am finding it hard to accept that fellow officers would cover up something as large as this.'

Dave shook his as he held up both his hands and let out a small grunt of frustration, 'Unfortunately Andy, I believe Claire what she is saying. We appreciate that there is a history of corruption in the police force. We are aware they've accused the force of various cover-ups over the years.'

Andy rose out of his chair and angrily paced around, throwing his hands up in the air, 'Sure I realise that, but we are talking of a cover-up that has been going on, what, over forty years!'

Claire coughed and Andy's eyes widened in surprise as he spun round to her, 'Sorry Andy, but I think it has been going on longer than that.'

Staring at Claire in open-mouthed disbelief, Andy twisted his head round to Dave, who gave a small nod confirmation, 'She is right, Andy.' he said gravely, 'She has proof.'

Andy threw his hands up in disbelief and shook his head. He looked at Wendy with a bewildered expression, 'You have been quiet during all this. Surely you don't accept this too?'

Wendy lifted her head up at him and bobbed her head slowly, 'I think we need to listen to what Claire has to say. Andy, after today we both realise something strange is going on.' Her eyes narrowed as she jabbed a finger in his direction, 'You, yourself, said to me earlier something didn't seem right. Remember, you were the one that suggested something was off while we were interviewing Zoe Murray.'

Andy blinked at her and rubbed his forehead with the palm of his hand. He let out a frustrated groan, sat back down in his chair and nodded reluctantly, 'Yeah, your right.' He turned back to Claire and gave her an apologetic smile, 'Sorry Claire, not really having a go at you.'

Claire shrugged her shoulders and gave Andy a lopsided grin, 'It's okay, Andy. It is a lot to take in but remember I have been looking into this for a long time, so I can understand your frustration. All I ask is that you keep an open mind, please.'

As his two colleagues each gave a small nod in agreement, Dave inhaled a deep breath and let out an enormous sigh, 'Go ahead Claire. Continue, please.'

He watched as Claire reached over to her bag, pulled out some files and began passing them around, 'Okay, Dave has already read some of these. I started researching this about fifteen years ago, just after I got my post at Durham University. I have been able to use their resources to gain access to some confidential information. From what I have been able to uncover, my best estimate is that this has been going on for at least ninety years, if not longer. We learned they built the isolation hospital in Langley Park in 1895 to help treat people with infectious diseases.'

Dave frowned as he gave a small nod of acknowledgement, 'Sure, that is common knowledge.'

Claire reached into her bag, pulled out another folder and withdrew a handful of papers, 'Well, *this* wasn't common knowledge.' she continued, indicating to the sheets of paper in her hand, 'These are memos and letters which hint at the government's concern at the rise of the Nazi party in Germany. In 1932 the Government, concerned that the country was not equipped for another war, wanted to get a step ahead of Nazi Germany in developing new weapon technology.' She paused as she handed the papers over to Dave, who glanced at them and passed them onto his two curious colleagues. 'A German scientist, Dr Allen Selyab, was researching matter transference.' She continued and pointed to the papers they were reading, 'He believed they could transport a person over an enormous distance in a blink of an eye.'

The corners of Wendy's eyes creased as she peered at the papers in front of her and lifted her head to Claire with a stunned expression, 'Hang on, are we talking about teleportation like in *Star Trek* or *Blake's 7*?'

Andy pulled his head back and let out a loud laugh, 'Hey Guv, looks like Wendy is a nerd.' His face reddened as his two annoyed colleagues shot him a disapproving look. He shifted in his sheepishly and dropped his head.

Appearing to ignore Andy's comment, Claire rolled her eyes as she gave Wendy a nod of agreement and continued, 'Yes, but probably not in the same way. The British government feared what Germany could do if they got their hands on that technology.' She shook her head and stared up at the ceiling in wonder, 'Imagine it: large armies, or even spies, being able to travel in a blink of an eye. Well, that must have really worried the British government, because they were so desperate to be ones to have that technology first. They learned Dr Selyab, who was Jewish and feared the rise of a Nazi government, wanted to defect. On 23rd June 1930 MI6 they snuck him out of Germany by faking his death in a car accident.'

Dave inhaled a sharp intake of breath and lifted his head up in shock from the papers he was reading. 'This sounds like the plot of a bad James Bond film!' he exclaimed, 'Surely we would have heard about this if the government had been using advanced technology during the war?'

Claire gave a small nod in agreement and pointed to the papers in front of them, 'Yes, I agree, but that would probably have been true if it had been successful. But from what I have been able to learn, a year later, the government set Dr Selyab up in a secluded location to conduct his experiments.'

Dave raised an eyebrow as he regarded the woman thoughtfully, 'Let me guess.' He tapped his finger on his chin as realisation slowly crept into him, 'That secluded location was the isolation hospital in a quiet mining village in the northeast of England?'

Claire mouth widened into a triumphant smile, and she snapped her fingers at him, 'Spot on! My guess is the government set up his lab under a Victorian Hospital with modern technology, modern technology for the 1930s that is.' She frowned and scratched her head as she waved a hand at the papers scattered over the table, 'This is where it gets fuzzy, though. The records only go as far back as 12th September 1932. I have a letter from the ministry of defence to the then prime minister -- Ramsay MacDonald. It mentions a visit to Dr Selyab's lab by the home secretary on that date.' She paused, reached into the folder, and pulled another document, 'The letter reports of an accident, killing Dr Selyab and his team. The home secretary states in his letter that the experiment was a failure.' She leaned over and handed a copy of the letter to Dave, who glanced curiously at it.

A line appeared between Andy's brows as he turned to Dave and Claire with a confused expression, 'Hang on a minute, Guv! Surely if there had been some secret lab in that hospital, then surely it would have been discovered after all these years or you would have seen signs of it when you searched the grounds today?'

Dave rubbed his chin thoughtfully, shook his head, and pointed to the papers on the table, 'Not necessarily Andy. The lab may have been under the hospital. We now know that in the 1930s and 1940s they placed a few weapons research centres or secret intelligence headquarters under unassuming buildings such as hospitals or even large stores. The entrance might have been well hidden.' He cocked his head and held up a finger to the bewildered-looking Andy, 'Remember, it has been Ninety-odd years, plenty of time for mother nature to cover up any evidence.'

Wendy taped her bottom lip with her finger and nodded in agreement, murmuring thoughtfully, 'I agree, Guv. If it's okay with you, I would like to take a drive out to it tomorrow and scrutinise the ground, fresh eyes, and all that.'

Taken completely surprise by Wendy's comment, Dave cocked his head at the younger woman and gave her a look of concern, 'I don't want you to go by yourself Wendy, take Andy with you.'

Andy nodded in agreement, but before he could open his to say something he was interrupted by Wendy, 'That's okay, Guv.' she said carefully, 'I can manage. I live closer and so I can get there early enough and report back to you quickly if I find anything.'

Dave was silent for a second as he considered Wendy's request. He had at uncanny ability at being able to read people and there was something in her body language that told him she was trying to hide something. He let out a tired sigh and massaged his temples. Reluctantly putting his paranoia down to tiredness, he quickly decided to give her the benefit of doubt and nodded in agreement, 'Okay, Wendy, go ahead. But the first sign of any trouble or if something doesn't look right, I want you out of there.'

Wendy shot him a lopsided grin and gave him a firm nod of confirmation. Andy raised an eyebrow as he gave him a questioning look. Dave responded with a slight shake of his head and small wave of his hand.

Dave brought his focus back to Claire as she continued to speak, 'Well, we know something must have happened in the lab that day. Because a year later there is a report of a death in the isolation hospital, a nurse was found dead in unusual circumstances. They found the door to her room had been locked from the inside. The police at the time had ruled it as unexplained and quickly closed the case.' She pulled out a sheet of paper from a folder and handed it to Dave, 'I got a hold of a copy of the coroner's report. See something interesting?'

Dave's forehead furrowed as he examined the paper in front of him and his eyes grew wide in astonishment. As he handed it over to his curious colleagues to read, Wendy bobbed her head to herself, but Andy lifted his head up at Claire aghast.

'Bloody hell!' he blurted out, 'The wounds are exactly the same as to those found on Michael and Tommy Thorn!'

Claire gave a faint nod and pulled out other pages from her folder, 'I showed Dave this earlier, but just over a year later, on the 6th of May 1935, Mary Walsh, a twenty-year-old woman, was found on the grounds of the old isolation hospital. Her boyfriend was arrested, and they said he was suffering from delusional insanity. He was found guilty and hanged.' She indicated to the document in her hand, 'This letter from the Home Office shows they pressured the police into finding a suspect. The coroner was also pressured into rewriting his report. Like I told Dave earlier, I got my hands on the original coroner's report detailing the wounds and condition the woman's body was in.' She paused as she reached into her folder, pulled out another set of papers, and handed over them to Andy and Wendy, while continuing to speak, 'In August 1959 a 10-year-old girl, Roisin Stewart. Her body was found on the grounds of the abandoned isolation hospital in Langley Park. Again, the police were pressured into arresting a man, this time with learning disabilities. He also was quickly found guilty and hanged. The coroner, again, was pressured into altering his report.'

Andy read the papers in his hand and shook his head in consternation. He handed the papers to Wendy, who read them silently. Andy then stood up and began to pace around the room. He stopped in front of the fireplace and rested his hands on the mantelpiece, took a deep breath, and let out a throaty yell of frustration.

Dave studied the pensive red headed woman curiously, who had just placed the papers back on the table, her face oddly neutral. He guessed he must have been staring at Wendy for too as long because she appeared to alter her demeanour slightly and then gave him a lopsided grin.

'I am fine Guv, honestly.' Wendy said, smiling.

Dave realised there was something about her attitude that worried him. But as he opened his mouth to question her, he was distracted as he heard raised voices coming from Andy and Claire.

'Okay, we have three suspicious murders, sorry four, if we are to include your sister.' Andy argued, 'But surely there has to be more if we are talking about some science experiment gone bad, which is being covered up?' He slammed his fist down on the mantelpiece in frustration and winced in pain from the impact.

Claire gave him a small nod of agreement, 'Yes, there were probably murders that occurred during the war years that may not have been reported or explained in another way.' She crossed her arms across her chest and gave Andy a determined look, 'I also believe by this stage whoever was covering up strange deaths was getting good at it as the years went on. I have also found that there were some strange reports of people going missing and then suddenly turning up later, all fine but later relatives reporting that they were acting strangely, not like themselves.'

Dave cocked his head at Claire and waved his hand at her, 'It's not that strange for people to disappear and suddenly turn up years later. It is common for people to change, you know.'

Claire threw back her head and let out a huff of annoyance, while giving a dismissive wave of her hand, 'Not like this. These people go missing for days. When they are eventually found, they appear slightly different, colder, more intelligent, and ambitious. They then sever all ties with their families and gain important and respected positions across the globe.' She stood up, inhaled a ragged breath, and began pacing around the living room. She placed her hands on her hips as she lifted her head up to the ceiling and let out a shaky breath, 'My investigations have come with a personal cost.' she said miserably while looking back down to the people in the room, 'Remember the prime minister's disappearance three years ago? Well, I didn't believe the official story of her going away for a few days to a retreat for stress. I must have rattled somebody's cage, as I received death threats. When they realised that would not stop me digging, I found myself suspended by the university and my research grant taken away from me.'

Claire sat back down, reached for her glass of wine from the coffee table and took large gulp out of the glass. She grimaced and then let out a bitter laugh, 'Their reason for suspending me - sexual misconduct with a student!' she scoffed and shook her head disgust, 'Unofficially? The government pressured them into suspending me, but that is....'

Without warning, Claire was interrupted as Wendy let out a loud mirthless laugh. Claire's eyes to blazed with anger as Wendy then shot her a bemused look. 'Oh, come on now Claire, her disappearance was just explained away as fake news at the time!' Wendy scoffed, 'I think you are trying to look for shadows when there aren't any!'

Taken aback by Wendy's disrespectful outburst, Dave exchanged a worried with Andy. He opened his mouth to say something but realised he was too late as Claire, her face crimson with rage, bolted up from her seat and stood directly above the younger woman as she glared at her angrily.

'You want to know why it was fake news? Do you?' Claire screamed tearfully as she vehemently waved her hands around, 'Because Thomas Chawson controls the press. The same kind and generous Thomas Chawson who disappeared for days. The same man, who turned up a week later, safe and sound but completely changed, becoming cold, hostile, and reclusive.' Collapsing on to her knees, she placed her hands over her face and her body shook with long, racking sobs, 'When I investigated him and others like him,' Her voice trembled with emotion as she forced herself to speak in between sobbing gasps, 'I received threats and then the allegations at the university arose. When I refused to back down, I received a visit from some unpleasant people, and they threatened if I continued to push it. My parents would, in their words, meet with an unfortunate accident.'

Dave quickly jumped out of his seat and rushed over to distraught woman. He knelt in front of her, gently lifted her up and placed his hands on her shoulders. He blinked in astonishment as she suddenly buried her head into his shoulder and sobbed. Wendy sheepishly averted her eyes as Dave gave her a dirty look.

'I am sorry, Claire.' Wendy mumbled, 'I didn't mean to upset you, but I am sure you can understand why I had to do it.'

The embarrassed looking woman pulled away from Dave, who gave her a concerned look. Claire gave a small grateful nod while giving him a half-smile. He pulled out a clean handkerchief from his pocket and offered it to her. She let out a small, embarrassed laugh and took it off him and dabbed her eyes. She then sat down next to Wendy, who slowly reached over and placed her hand on her shoulder. Claire smiled sadly at the younger woman and leaned in closer as they hugged each other. Dave nudged Andy and they both turned away, suddenly becoming more interested in a crack in the ceiling.

'You don't need to apologise Wendy, it's part of your police training to be sceptical. I know you were trying to get me angry to see if I would make a mistake.' Claire said and nodded in understanding and then pulled away from Wendy, 'I am sorry for making a fool of myself getting upset.'

Wendy tapped Claire's hands compassionately, 'Don't be silly, Claire. I cannot imagine the stress that you have been under. You have nearly spent all your life investigating this, while we only began to investigate this today. So, I am sure you can understand it is a lot to take in all at once.'

Claire let out a harsh breath and gave a small nod. She lifted her chin and peered at the people in the room, 'Don't worry, I can understand your reluctance to accept what I am telling you. But I am glad you have given me the chance to show you what proof I have.' She groaned and massaged her temples with her fingers. She then inhaled a deep breath and let out a small anxiety-filled sigh, 'After they threatened my parents, I was on the verge of giving up, but then I sat down with them and spoke to them, and they convinced me to carry on. They told me to keep digging, no matter the cost, not for them but for Emma. They admitted to me somebody pressured them into keeping quiet about Emma's death and were ashamed they had kept quiet about it for so long, but all they want now, before they die, is to know the truth.' Her eyes suddenly filling defiance, she twisted her head at the other people in the room, 'Even if it kills me, I am going to continue digging and continue pissing people off. Even if I must do it all by myself, by God, people will discover the truth!'

Dave moved closer to Claire, gently picked her hand up and placed his hand on top of hers. He glanced across to his grim-faced colleagues, who both stood up and put their hands on top of Claire's too.

'That will not happen Claire, you are no longer alone in this.' Dave said, his voice holding a tone of defiance, 'We have your back. No matter the cost. Tonight, we draw a line in the sand. The lies stop now!'

With tears rolling down her cheeks, Claire jumped up from her seat and hugged the three people, 'Thank you. You don't realise how much that means to me.' she said joyfully.

Andy spun round to face Dave and looked at him questioningly. 'So, what now Guv?' he asked worriedly.

Dave moved away and was silent for a minute as he paced pensively around the living room. He glanced at his watch and gave a small nod to himself. 'I suggest we call it a night. Go home and get some rest.' he said firmly, 'I will see you all early in the morning and then tomorrow we help Claire in uncovering the truth. I will not sugar-coat this, but I can imagine we are in for a fight, especially if what she says is true, that it goes all the way to the top.'

Andy bobbed his head in agreement and let out a mirthless laugh, 'Goodnight Guv. I better head home quick before Mary and Alice forget what I look like!'

Dave gave a tight smile, and he patted the younger man on the shoulder. Andy gave Claire a hug, before he turned and strode out of the living room but stopped in the doorway to glance back to Wendy, who acknowledged him with a wave. He held up his hand to his head as he turned and continued towards the front door. They heard the front door open and close as he left.

Wendy shrugged and gave Dave a sad smile, 'I suppose that's my cue to leave too. I am sorry if I overstepped earlier Guv. I hope I can still be of use to you?'

Dave lifted his shoulder in a half shrug and waved his hand at her, 'It's already forgotten about Wendy. You've apologised to Claire, which is the important thing. You just let your frustration get the better of you. I am guessing even if I wanted you to, you are too involved in this case now to walk away.'

Wendy cocked her head with an arched eyebrow and let out a small laugh. She turned to Claire, who smiled affectionately at her. She gave the Claire a hug and then spoke to her in a low whisper, 'The Guv has my number if you want to have a chat later. If you feel you need to talk.'

Claire blinked in amazement and gave a wordless nod.

After closing the front door behind her, Wendy shivered slightly in the cool October night air, pulled the zipper on her jacket up to her neck and marched down the driveway to where she had parked her car earlier.

Wendy tilted her head, and she frowned as she noticed a large black car, a Land Rover Defender was parked further down the road. She climbed into her car, a four-year-old blue KIA Niro, and started the engine. Her right hand slid across the steering wheel and lightly tapped the lever beside it. The indicator icon on the dashboard flashed and cast a green light over her face while she prepared to drive away. She heard the automatic handbrake release and felt the car move away. She gave the parked black vehicle a brief glance as she drove past it. Looking in her rear-view mirror, she watched as the vehicle pulled away from the curb and began following her.

Five minutes later Wendy drove her vehicle into a deserted car park, brought it a stop and watched the black car pull up behind her. She then reached into her glove compartment, pulled out a small pistol and, after gently slipping the pistol into her jacket pocket, she unfastened her seatbelt and got out of the vehicle. As she marched up to the black car, she raised her left eyebrow as the left rear passenger door opened and then saw Lieutenant Kendra Goynes climb out. Wendy glided past her, their hands briefly touching one another, and she acknowledged Kendra with a tight smile before climbing into the car.

Inside the darkened vehicle, she could just make out the figure of a man sat in the left rear passenger set. Wendy stiffened slightly as she realised it was Commander John Payne. She swallowed as she felt a growing sense of unease growing inside her. Before now she had always met Payne back at their complex. So, for them to meet here – outside – was highly irregular.

'You were right, sir.' Wendy said sadly to the figure sat next her, 'Tulley knows too much and thanks to her, Barnes now knows too.'

Payne was silent for a minute and then let out a sigh of resignation, 'Unfortunate, but not unexpected Cooper.' he said wistfully, 'I think it's time I had a chat with them. I will arrange for Alpha Squad to pick them up first thing tomorrow. You are to join them to make sure things go smoothly. I would rather DI Barnes came quietly, but if he gives you any bother, then you are to take care of the situation, understood?'

Wendy nodded sadly, 'Yes, sir.' She cocked her head and looked him curiously, 'Is it true what Tulley has said? About the murders and disappearances all being covered up?'

There was an uneasy silence for several minutes as she watched Payne peer thoughtfully out of the car window. He then gave a small shake of his head and exhaled a heavy sigh, 'Cooper, I am afraid it goes even deeper than some murders or people disappearing. You will learn the truth tomorrow, along with Barnes and Tulley. When you do, I am sorry to say, it will shatter your perception of the world as you know it.'

15

Dave sat in silence as he watched Claire pack up the copies of letters and other documents, slotting them into their folders. As she swivelled her head to him and gave him a wry smile, he suddenly realised at how tired she looked. He also noticed something else, as if he was seeing it for the first time, there was a warmth and kindness contained in those eyes that seemed to bore deep into his soul.

I would gladly lose myself in those eyes, he thought to himself, as his gaze followed the bridge of her nose, noticing how her glasses sat on her face. He followed the line of nose, noticing the fullness of her lips and the curve of her chin, and her slender neck.

Dave blinked and tried to avert his eyes but realised he had been staring at her too long as he saw her lean in front of him. Claire chuckled and waved her hand in front of him.

'Hello! Earth to Inspector Barnes, are we receiving?' Claire said with a touch of bemusement.

Embarrassed at being caught out, Dave blinked and coughed. He bolted up and spun away from Claire, trying desperately to distract her from his obvious faux pas. He felt his cheeks flush as he backed away from the bemused-looking Claire and held up his hands in front of his chest apologetically.

'O ... o ... oh, s ... s ... sorry Claire,' Dave stammered. He imagined his inner voice was screaming at him, saying something along the lines of *Say something, you fool!* Then, in an act of desperation to save himself from crashing and burning any further, he burst out with the only thing he could think of. 'Err I ... I ... was wondering if you fancied something?' He squeezed his eyes shut and cringed to himself as soon as he heard the words leave his mouth. *Oh yeah. That was better. Idiot!*

Claire's mouth dropped open, and she pressed her hands to her cheeks, her eyes widening in alarm, 'Oh, my, whatever do you mean, Inspector Barnes!' she exclaimed and then her demeanour changed as an impish glint appeared in her eyes and then the corners of mouth twitched as she burst out laughing.

Dave felt his cheeks flush even more as he watched Claire grin wickedly at him. He could tell she was revelling in his discomfort as he became even more flustered.

'S ... s ... sorry I ... I ... meant if you fancied, sorry, would you like a cup of tea or coffee?' he stammered. He closed his eyes and smacked his forehead with his hand. *Nice try, Moron!*

'Tea would be great thanks. Are you sure I am not keeping you from anything?' She giggled and gave him a warm smile.

Dave gave her a lopsided grin and waved his hand at her, 'No, you are fine. I'll just nip into the kitchen to make it. Be right back.'

Claire lifted her head in acknowledgement as she watched Dave sheepishly bend down to pick up the tray of empty plates. She kept her face neutral as she watched him make a hasty retreat out of the living room. A few seconds later she laughed as she heard a bang, closely followed by the clatter of plates coming from the kitchen, which was then shortly followed by a loud curse.

Shaking her head, Claire placed her hands on her hips as she lifted her head up to the ceiling. She could not help teasing him, but there was something about him she found attractive. There was definitely a spark between them, and she was sure he sensed it too. She found she simply enjoyed teasing him. It made her feel happy, which was something she had not experienced for a long time.

As she walked slowly around the living room, the corners of her mouth twitched as she listened to the sounds that came from the kitchen, the rattle of cups followed by nervous muttering. She smiled as she stopped in front of the sideboard and saw a photo of a young handsome brown-haired man dressed impeccably in a formal suit, standing next to a woman in a white dress. Her curiosity piqued, Claire lifted the picture frame, and she raised an eyebrow as she realised it was a photo of a much younger Dave and his wife that had been taken on their wedding day. Her smile vanishing, she placed the frame back down.

I did not realise that he was married! Claire thought to herself as she stood in silence and pressed her lips together as she scrutinised the photo in front of her. She jumped as she heard a shout come from the kitchen, breaking her out of reverie.

'Do you take milk and sugar?' she heard Dave shout.

'Just milk, thanks.' Claire replied.

Crestfallen at the realisation that Dave was married, Claire hurried back over to the couch and thumped back down onto it. She lowered her head into her hands, shook her head, sucked in a deep breath, and exhaled. 'Stupid woman!' she whispered miserably, 'Of course he's married.'

Sensing movement, Claire flinched as she felt something wet touch her arm. She peered down and gave a half smile as Jenny's eyes stared back up at her. As the dog rested her head on her lap, she gave Claire a sad-eyed-puppy-type stare and whined. Did she understand what Claire was thinking?

Claire gave the worried canine a sad smile as she lowered her hand and stroked her head, 'It's okay, girl.' she whispered, 'It's just my heart breaking.'

Dave whistled to himself as he headed back out of the kitchen of the carrying a tray with two cups of tea. But as he stepped through the doorway into the living he frowned as he thought he saw Claire quickly wipe her face with her hand. Had she been crying? He shook his head, believing it was just his eyes playing tricks on him. Dave then gave her a broad smile as he caught sight of her stroking Jenny.

'Oh, I will have to be careful now.' he chuckled, 'I can see she is becoming fond of you. She is an excellent judge in character.' He grinned and gave a cheeky wink, 'I better take care, otherwise I will have two women ganging up on me.'

As he carefully placed the tray on the coffee table in front of them and picked up a cup from the tray, he smiled warmly as he handed the cup over to Claire, 'Here's your tea. Sorry it took so long, had to wait for the kettle to boil.'

Claire bobbed her head and gave him a strained half-smile as she took the cup from his hands silently. Dave raised an eyebrow, noticing the change in her demeanour.

'It's fine, thank you.' Claire said brusquely, taking the cup from his hands.

Dave gave a small nod and frowned, sensing a wall had suddenly appeared between them. He looked at her through the corner of his eye as they drank their tea in silence. Puzzled at her sudden change in attitude, he lifted his chin to Claire awkwardly. He paused as he realised that he wasn't sure at what he should say. If he pressed her, would it push her further away?

After a few minutes of silence, Claire let out a small shallow breath, placed her cup down and rose from her seat, 'I think it is best that I leave.' she muttered sadly, while reaching for her bag.

Had he done something wrong? Feeling like a wedge had suddenly come between them, Dave watched in silence as an unhappy looking Claire gathered up her belongings. 'Claire, what's wrong?' he asked, with a tone that was mixed with confusion and fear, 'Have I upset you?'

Her eyes flickering with emotion, Claire twisted her head and shot Dave a hurt look, 'You didn't tell me you are married.' she said flatly and gestured to the sideboard, 'I saw your wedding photo over there.'

'Ah, I see.' Dave replied. He closed his eyes and nodded in understanding. He gave Claire a reassuring smile as he placed his cup down on the tray and reached up to take her hand, 'Don't go, please.' he whispered gently, 'If you sit down, I can explain.'

Claire cocked her head and gave Dave a curious side eye as she appraised him silently for several minutes. Without saying a word, she sat back down and gave a furtive smile as Jenny placed her head on her lap again, and she lowered her hand to stroke the animal's head.

Realising he could no longer put it off, Dave lifted his head, let out a deep shallow breath and pointed to the picture on the sideboard, 'We got married when we were young, too young probably. I had just left police training college. Linda, she worked as a receptionist. At first everything was great.' he shook his head and smiled wistfully, 'Sure it was a struggle, both of us weren't earning much, but you know how it is when you are young, you assume love can see you through.' He stared across to the picture on the sideboard thoughtfully and exhaled, 'Then, as we got older, we became more distant with one another. I became more and more of a workaholic trying to provide for us both. I was too fixated on trying to make detective, that I lost focus on what was in front of me until it was too late.'

Realisation dawned on Claire's face as she slowly edged herself closer to Dave. The corner of his mouth lifted as she took his hand in hers but remained silent as he continued with his story, 'My fault really, because of my short-sightedness, I pushed her away into the arms of another man. I don't blame her, really. I was hardly home, and when I was home, I was too distracted with this case or that case to give her the attention she needed.' He glanced up at the ceiling and blew out a slow regret-filled breath, 'I didn't know until I got home one day and found her sitting with her cases packed. She told me she had been having an affair for over a year and she was leaving me for him. Deep down I knew it had been my fault, so I did the only thing I could do, I let her go.'

'You shouldn't blame yourself.' Claire interrupted. Tears shimmered in her eyes as she gave him nod of understanding, 'Remember, there are two people in a marriage and you both have to work at it.'

Dave lowered his head and tapped Claire's hand with his hand. He gave a small shake of his head and let out a bitter laugh, 'No, I am afraid if I hadn't been working so hard, I would have been able to give her the attention she wanted.' he groaned, rubbed his forehead with his hand and he lifted his shoulder in a half shrug, 'It wasn't all bad though, we had been married ten years, and we had some good times, but not enough I am afraid. I still blame myself if I am being honest. I realised the best I could do for her was grant her a clean divorce so she could have the happiness she deserved.' He glanced once again at the wedding photo on the sideboard, hung his head and let out a small melancholic sigh, 'I received an email from her seven years ago. She had invited me to her wedding, but I expected it would be too painful, so I never went. I don't know why I still hold on to that photo; perhaps it is time I put it away and stop punishing myself.'

Claire pursed her lips as she regarded Dave pensively. Her eyes glistened as she leaned closer to him. Dave's eyebrows perked up in astonishment as she kissed him on his cheek and then rested her head on his shoulder.

'You have a big heart, Dave. Any woman would be lucky to have you.' she murmured softly.

Dave gave her a warm smile as he turned his head and kissed her on the top of her head. She smiled back, pulled her legs up onto the couch and snuggled closer into him. He sat in silence, his eyes following the flames as they danced in the fireplace.

'What about yourself?' Dave asked in a slow careful tone, 'Is there anybody you are close to; is there a Mr Tulley?'

'Oh, I am sure you already know the answer to that.' Claire laughed as she tilted her head gave him a knowing a look. She poked her finger into his ribs and grinned as he squirmed, 'Isn't that right, Detective Inspector Barnes?'

Dave cocked his head, shrugged, and then gave her a devilish smile, 'Well, I said to you earlier that I had investigated you. So, I know that you aren't married. Apart from that, there wasn't much else to tell me about you personally.'

Claire gazed into the fire with a sad vacant look. She sat in silence for several minutes. As Dave watched her stare into the blazing fire, he caught something in her eyes. Had she become lost in the past and was thinking about her dead sister? But before he could say anything, Claire looked awaye from the blazing fire and inhaled a long breath, 'You are right, I am single.' There was a regretful hushed tone in her voice, 'Any relationship I've had never lasted because I was so wrapped up in what I was doing. Partly because I was too busy and another because I was afraid of letting anybody close, afraid that they wouldn't understand my …' she paused and shifted uncomfortably in her seat, 'obsession.'

'Don't put yourself down, Claire.' Dave replied softly and tapped his hand on her knee, 'I would say it is your sister's death that drives you, but obsessed, no. It has driven you all these years to uncover the truth. A quality I admire, really. We are much alike, you and I, both of us driven to learn the truth but sadly learning the truth sometimes comes at a personal cost.'

Claire's forehead creased as she gave a small nod of agreement, and her mouth curved into a smile as Dave slid his arm across her shoulders, pulling her close to him. They both sat in silence, listening to the sound from the ticking clock on the wall and the crackling of the gas fire. They both were unwilling wanting to move in case it spoiled the moment.

After several minutes, Claire raised her head and glanced at her wristwatch. She wrinkled her nose as she pulled her legs out from beneath her and stretched them out in front of her. She stumbled as she straightened up and bent down to massage the muscles in her legs with her hands.

'I guess it is best I head off now.' She said reluctantly, tilting her head and gesturing to the doorway, 'Can I use your bathroom before I go?'

Dave gave a small nod of acknowledgement, and his eyes followed the woman as she left the room. He cocked his head as he listened to her climb the stairs. Jenny trotted over to him and jumped onto the couch with him, placing her head on his lap. As he began to absent-mindedly stroke her head, his mind drifted through the past as his eyes followed the flames on the gas fire as they continued their mesmerising dance in front of him.

Jenny was filled with contentment as her master's hand continued to stroke the back of her neck. She loved those moments with Dave and wished they would never end. She turned her head and licked at his hand. Yes, it was those moments that made her life worthwhile.

But then she stiffened as she picked up a familiar scent coming from direction of the doorway. She wagged her tail excitedly. Dave's friend had returned. She liked Claire, she smelt nice. She lifted her head and saw Claire was standing in doorway, bare legged, dressed in one of Dave's tops. Jenny cocked her in puzzlement. Dave was quite fond of that item of clothing, he wore it whenever he sat down in front of the strange box that had tiny people inside of it. She didn't know what the game was called, but she knew Dave always got really excited whenever he watched those tiny people throw the odd-shaped ball around.

As Jenny stared at Claire, she titled her from side to side as she noticed there was something strange about the human. An aura surrounded Claire. That wasn't strange because every human had one, but this one different – it seemed unnatural. But then she felt her hackles rise as she noticed the ghostly figure standing beside Claire. It appeared to be an elderly white-haired human and it looked like he was whispering in Claire's ear. Was he manipulating her? If so, why?

Jenny narrowed her eyes and let out a small growl as a warning to the apparition. Then, to her astonishment, it turned toward her, raised his finger and shushed her. What? How dare he shush her!

She jumped off the couch and turned to Dave. She needed to warn her master. She gave a loud bark, hoping to break him out of his dream-like state. But Dave just sat there, ignoring her as he continued to gaze into the fire. However, he blinked in surprise as he heard a small cough coming from behind him and turned his head. Jenny wagged her tail happily. Yes, Master Dave would save her now.

But Jenny could only watch in dismay as Dave's mouth dropped open and he then gazed at Claire in wide-eyed astonishment. She nudged him in the leg and whined at him. What's wrong with him? Why was he acting like this? Yes, Mistress Claire didn't have much clothing on, but that didn't mean his brain had to go to mush. She rolled her eyes in disgust. Humans!

Realising she was going to have to save Claire herself, Jenny turned back to the door. However, she paused as she realised that Claire was now by herself. Where had the stranger gone to? She looked up at Dave and whined at him.

'Calm down Jenny, it's only Claire.' Dave snapped irritably, as he stared wide-eyed at the woman in front of him. His eyes blinked furiously, and he inhaled a deep breath, stammering, 'Claire, I … I … I …'

'Three I's in one breath, come on Dave spit it out.' Claire gave him a bemused look as she waggled her finger.

Jenny shook her head and let out a small huff of disgust as she watched Dave's face turn a shade of scarlet. He then lowered his head and peered down at Jenny. She cocked her head up at him and scowled back at him, *Seriously! Do I have to explain it to you?*

From the way he was acting all flustered, Jenny could tell the sudden shift in the evening's direction had unsettled her human. She could make out the uncertainly that was etched across Dave's face as he slowly rose from the couch and stared at the woman in the doorway. Jenny nuzzled him in his leg and whined, *Do you need a hint!*

Composing himself, Dave closed his eyes, took in a lungful of air, and then slowly opened them. He gave Claire a half-smile and held up his hands in front of him, 'Claire, I am flattered really.' he said hesitantly.

Claire stood in patient silence and continued to gaze at him from the doorway. Dave awkwardly shifted from one foot to the other. 'B … B … but we have just met each other today.' he babbled, 'Um, is this not going a bit too quick?'

Claire smiled knowingly and moved closer Dave, offering her

hand to him, 'Dave, we are both grown adults. We both know there is something between us.' There was a touch of longing in her voice as she edged closer to him. 'All I know is I don't want to be alone tonight, and I would rather spend it with you. We both know something is coming and we may not get a chance at happiness soon and I aim to grab it when I can before time runs out on us both.' She pressed her hands together and smiled warmly at him, 'Please, all I want is for you to hold me and for once feel like a woman who has a normal life. Is that too much to ask for?'

Dave gave a small nod understanding and inched closer to Claire. He reached up and touched her face with his hand and kissed her delicately on the lips. She beamed as she reached down and took his hand in hers. Dave's mouth curved into a smile as she jerked her head toward the stairs and guided him toward them.

Jenny watched from the doorway as they climbed the stairs. She spun round and trotted back to her basket in the living room's corner, lay down and closed her eyes. She opened her eyes as she heard a strange sound coming from a little square shaped box that was lying on top of the table beside her.

She peered at it curiously as the irritating noise played for several more seconds before it stopped, and everything went silent again. Jenny lowered her head, closed her eyes and drifted off to sleep.

16

Thirty Minutes earlier....

The vehicle continued along the road at a leisurely pace, while inside its passenger's thoughts were distracted by the events of the day, the ongoing investigation, the troubling interview with Zoe Murray, along with Claire's revelation and her proof of a conspiracy.

As he guided his car onto his driveway, Andy pressed his foot on the brake pedal and brought the vehicle to a stop behind his wife's silver Ford Focus. He sat with both of hands on the steering wheel for several minutes while he distractedly listened to the radio. He grunted to himself as he lowered his hand, turned the car's ignition key, and listened to the vehicle's engine go silent.

Andy unfastened his seatbelt but remained in his seat as he stared out of the front windscreen and surveyed the house in front of him. The bedroom and living room lights were shining partially through the closed curtains. He closed his eyes and his thoughts drifted to Mary as he tried to imagine how he was going to explain the events of the day to her.

'She is going to love this.' Andy muttered to himself as he looked into the rear-view mirror and let out a bitter laugh, 'She's been telling you for years a secret group, made up of the heads of the world's major corporations, has been controlling the world's governments. That they have been responsible for some major events in the twentieth and twenty-first century.' He sneered at his reflection and waved his hand in disgust, 'Aye all this time you have just rolled your eyes and secretly laughed at her. What do you do? You uncover evidence that proves her right ... great job dickhead!'

It was then an icy chill ran down his spine, and he shivered as he thought about Claire's theory of police corruption going all the way up to higher levels of authority. He let out a small moan to himself as he realised his wife had been right all along. Andy pinched the bridge of his nose and shook his head as he considered the ramifications. If there was a conspiracy of silence, then the less his wife knew, the better. The muscles in his face tightened as he suddenly became conscious of the fact that if he was to protect his wife and child, then he needed to remain silent for now.

Andy inhaled a deep breath, opened his car door, climbed out of the car, and then absent-mindedly pressed the key fob to lock the car as he morosely strolled up the drive to the front door. He stuck his front door key into the front door to unlock it. However, just as he was about to fully open the door, he froze as he felt the hairs on the back of his neck rise and he cast a nervous eye over his shoulder. Believing that the day's events had made him paranoid; he gave a small of his head and stepped through the doorway into the hallway.

But as he entered the house, Andy frowned as he was greeted to the sound of Alice's loud cries coming from upstairs. His brow heavy with concern, he arched his head and called out, 'Mary, it's me, Andy. Is everything okay pet?'

On hearing no response, Andy's stomach churned as he raced into the living room. Apart from the TV being on, a movie playing away to nobody, the room was empty. He did a quick search around the kitchen and he was starting to become increasingly concerned when he found nobody was there either. Feeling his heart flutter in his chest, he rushed up the stairs and came to a stop in front of the first bedroom door on the landing. As he peered into the doorway, he felt a sense of relief wash over him when he spotted baby Alice was standing in her cot, crying.

Andy rushed over to his child and lifted her up, 'What's wrong, Spud?' he asked in a soothing tone that was supposed to help calm her, 'Is naughty mummy being a nasty girl and ignoring you?'

Andy bent down, picked up Alice's pacifier and placed it into her mouth, easing her cries. She beamed up at her daddy as he settled her back into her cot and gently stroked her head. His eyes narrowed as he felt a slow sense of panic starting to build inside him.

'I am just going to check on mummy, Spud.' he whispered. 'I won't be far away.' He felt like his heart was going to melt as Alice gurgled back at him in reply.

After slowly creeping out of Alice's bedroom, Andy carefully made his way along the landing, opened the front bedroom door, and carefully popped his head through the doorway into the bedroom. However, he became even more concerned as he noticed the broken glass on the floor and then he inhaled a sharp intake of air as he spotted a small patch of blood on the carpet. His heart beating away in his chest, he took several slow methodical steps into the seemingly empty bedroom.

'Mary, is everything okay?' Andy croaked, his voice catching in his throat as his mouth became suddenly dry.

His concern increasing by the minute, he reached into his jacket and pulled out his police issue taser from its holster but froze as he heard a noise coming from the ensuite bathroom. Andy automatically altered his posture, brought up the weapon in front of him and edged toward the bathroom's doorway. His hand trembling, he carefully reached for the door handle, but jerked back as he watched the handle turn. He raised the taser and pointed it at the door as it slowly began to open.

Her eyes widening in astonishment, Mary jerked back in shock at the taser pointed at her, 'Hell's teeth!' she snapped irritably, 'You scared the shit out of me. What in the shitting hell do you think you are you doing?'

For several long seconds, Andy could do nothing but stare open-mouthed at the annoyed woman. He had rarely heard his wife swear in front of him; she had always been shy at swearing and was usually quick to tell her husband off whenever she heard him utter any curse words. He blinked and shook his head angrily as he realised that he had probably scared Mary to death by pointing the taser at her.

Quickly holstering his taser, Andy held up his hand apologetically and took a step forward, 'Sorry love, the baby was crying. She was alone, and you were nowhere to be seen. When I shouted your name and didn't get a reply, I was worried something had happened to you.'

Mary's face hardened as she gave Andy a dirty look, 'I didn't hear you, okay!' she snapped with a tone that was as cold as ice, 'I knocked over a glass and when I was cleaning up, I cut myself. So, I was dressing the wound in the bathroom and the water was probably running, so I never heard you shout.'

Andy raised both of his hands up in front of him as he pleaded at her, 'Listen pet, I am sorry for scaring you. I have just been on edge. It has been a tough day at work, I am sure you can understand?'

Deeply ashamed for the upset he caused, Andy took a slow step toward Mary and leaned in to kiss her on the cheek. He raised an eyebrow surprise as he watched her turn her head away from him and then pushed past him. 'Fine! Whatever!' she snapped tersely, 'Just because work destroyed your day, no need to bring it up home!'

Andy swallowed and then he gave his wife a questioning look. His gut was telling him something was wrong, that his wife was not normally like that. He gave a small shake of his head and pushed the thought to one side, *You are just being stupid and paranoid, you fool, h*e thought angrily to himself, *she is probably just freaked out and scared after I pointed my taser at her!*

Andy gave a small nod and let out a small, short sigh as he strode over to the bed. He took his jacket off, unfastened his holster and placed it on the bedside cabinet. But as he sat down on the bed and bent down to take off his shoes, he felt his eyebrows knit together as he watched Mary bend down to pick up the broken glass from the floor and noticed that she was wearing a T-shirt and black jogging bottoms. He cocked his head and frowned as he started to become aware of something else about Mary –

there was something about her physically that didn't look right. She appeared to be more toned and muscular and the T-shirt she was wearing seemed to be far too tight on her. He pressed his lips together as he also noticed that her hair seemed different from that the last time he saw her that morning; it was no longer shoulder length – but was now shaved short at the back and along the sides.

Andy scrunched his face up as he shook his head to himself dismissively, *She told me she was trying to lose the baby weight and was trying to work out. She must have finally got her hair cut short too.* His brow furrowed as he continued to study the woman in front of him, *Strange, she always said she would never get her hair cut short.*

As his eyes followed her hair line, Andy's gaze wandered down to the bottom of her neck. It was when he noticed the strange eagle tattoo on the back of her neck. Feeling like someone had punched him stomach, he stiffened as he remembered something Mary once told him.

'*I hate tattoos and I wouldn't be seen dead wearing one!*'

As his mind raced back to the events of the day, Andy shivered to himself as he felt a cold bead of sweat trickle down his back. He inhaled sharply as he was hit by a sudden frightening realisation – that was not his wife.

His hands slowly tightening into fists, Andy thought back to Zoe's Murray's behaviour during the interview and remembered Claire's warning of people who had disappeared only for them to resurface appearing to have changed in character. He swallowed as he thought back to Wendy's comment about Zoe's strange accent.

As his mind started to put two and two together, Andy felt his heart jump up into his throat as he twisted his head and slowly examined the bedroom. He felt his blood run cold as he noticed a small faint trail of blood leading to the tall mirror in the bedroom's corner.

His mind screaming at him to do something, Andy swallowed as he felt his throat constrict from the increasing feeling of panic rising within him. He closed his eyes and took in a long deep breath as he tried desperately to think a course of action.

Trying to keep his tone neutral, he lowered his head down and gave Mary a pretend smile, 'How was Jenny today, was she a good girl?' he asked innocently. He crossed his fingers and secretly prayed to himself that he was wrong, that she would pick up on his mistake and correct him.

'Sure, she was a wonderful girl. We had a lot of fun today.' Mary answered, her back still facing Andy.

That was all the confirmation he needed. Andy felt his heart sink as stared at the back of Mary's head. His anxiety increasing even more, he became nauseated and tried to force the rising bile in his throat. What should he do? He couldn't leave without finding out if Mary – the real Mary – was alive.

'Are you okay sweetheart? You've gone quiet there?" Mary asked.

Andy inhaled a sharp intake of breath as he suddenly realised something – there was no trace of his wife's normal accent in the woman's voice. Why had he not noticed it before?

Slowly rising from the bed, Andy scanned the bedroom as he desperately tried to think of a way getting out of there safely that did not involve having a confrontation with a muscular powerhouse of woman. From the corner of his eye, he could see the bedside cabinet where he had placed his taser moments earlier and a nucleus of a plan began to form in his head. He quickly realised his best option was to distract the woman, grab his taser, stun her, get Alice, and get the hell out of there. Yeah, sure, as easy as that.

Carefully inching his way along the edge of the bed, Andy came to a sudden stop as he glanced back down at the woman on the floor. He felt his heart skip as he caught sight of Mary's hand moving. The movement had been so slight, but if it hadn't been for his heightened terrified state, he would have missed it. He was positive he had seen her grab a piece of broken with her right hand. Andy's heart began to race faster as he watched the muscles in her arms tense up. Was she getting to read to attack him? He swallowed and quickly cast an eye to the taser on the bedside cabinet. Dare he risk it?

Without warning, a cry from Alice was heard coming from her bedroom, breaking Andy's concentration. His chance gone, Andy sat helplessly as he watched Mary pounce up off the floor and turn to look at him with her hands touching the sides of her face in mock concern.

'Oh dear, something must have upset her again. I'll see to her.' Mary said with heavy concern.

Desperate to put some distance between them, Andy inched closer to the doorway and smiled nervously. 'N ... no. It's okay, I can go to her.' Fear creeping up his spine, he tried to keep his voice calm and flat as he lied to the woman in front of him.

Mary gave Andy a concerning look and placed her on hand on his shoulder. An unbidden image popped into Andy's head as he pictured those hands hurting his wife and he felt himself recoil. It is then he realised that he had just made a huge mistake as he watched Mary's eyes tighten with suspicion.

'What's wrong, honey?' she asked curiously.

Andy gave the woman a half-smile, shrugged, inhaled a deep breath, and let out a yawn, 'Nothing pet. I am tired, that's all.' he gave her a pretend friendly smile, secretly hoping he was sounding convincing, 'I just assumed you are already busy cleaning up that glass and you could probably do with a break from her too.'

Several seconds passed as Mary gazed at him silently. Andy wondered what was going through her mind. Was she getting ready to kill him or did she have something else in mind? He held his breath as he watched her cock her head, give him a lopsided grin and then spoke in a sweetly innocent tone, 'It's no bother, honey. You rest yourself. I will go to her.'

As Mary moved closer to him and kissed him on the cheek, Andy steeled him and smiled. It took every bit of his willpower not to cringe as he felt her lips touch his skin. He wanted nothing more than to grab the scheming woman by the neck and strangle the life out of her, but he held back as he thought of the real Mary and Alice and how much they were relying on him.

Andy held his breath as he watched Mary wheel round and dash out of the bedroom. Then, as soon as she was out of the room, he let out a harsh breath as his heart continued to hammer away in his chest. He then reached into the pocket and pulled out his mobile phone, his hands trembling as he brought up Dave's number and pressed the green phone icon for it to ring. He closed his eyes and prayed to himself as he listened to the ring tone and let out a small curse as the call was diverted to voicemail.

'Guv, please if you get this, I need you. Get over to my place quickly!' He said desperately.

Nearly at his wit's end, Andy twisted his head to the bedroom doorway to check if the coast was still clear and then glanced at his phone again. His hands feeling cold and clammy, he selected Wendy's number and again pressed the green button to dial. He listened to the dial tone and lifted his head up to the ceiling in relief when he heard her distinctive Scottish accent.

'*Andy? Is something wrong?*' She asked worriedly.

'Wendy, I ne—'

Andy stopped talking as he sensed movement from behind. He spun around and he felt the blood drain from his face as he came face-to-face with Mary; her face was a picture of steely rage as she barrelled toward him.

Unfortunately, he was too slow to react and could not avoid the woman's charge into him. The force of her impact knocked the phone out of his hand, sending it flying through air, eventually landing on top of the bed. Andy was not as lucky, however. The force of the enraged woman's impact knocked the wind out of him, sending him crashing into the bedroom mirror. He groaned in pain from the pieces of broken shards that were stabbing into his back, and gasped as he felt Mary's powerful hands grab his shirt, slamming him once more against the shattered reflective surface.

'You tiresome little gnat!' she hissed, 'You assume I didn't suspect that you knew. It's a shame really, your wife put up much more of a fight. It's true what they say, the men of this world are weak and soft.' A cruel smile formed across her lips as she leaned forward and whispered into his ear, 'I am going to enjoy killing you, but first I want my fun.'

Andy gasped as the woman's hand right hand shot up and took hold of his throat in a vice-like grip. He had seen this move carried out before during close combat self-defence training exercises. It was a move that was designed to collapse a person's larynx in seconds. He knew full well that Mary had the advantage and that he only had seconds left before he blacked out.

The pain in his throat was intense, Andy could feel the pressure increasing on the various cartilages in his larynx as they started to collapse, forcing his voice-box into his trachea. His eyes widened in shock; he had never known a grip like it.

Andy squeezed his eyes shut as he realised, he had very little time left and had no choice but to fight for his life. His mind racing back to his self-defence training, his body's muscle memory took over as it relaxed, and he let his hands slip from Mary's shoulders. With all the strength he could muster, he karate chopped them into either side of her neck.

Horrified, Andy's eyes grew wide as he watched Mary smile at him menacingly. Her grip did not slacken at all, not even a millimetre. Her neck was like a steel cable. It felt as if he was trying to karate chop a lamp post.

As his vision began to turn white, Andy head swam as he started to black out. He blinked furiously, suddenly remembering the broken silver shards of glass that were lying beside him. Flailing desperately, he grabbed hold of one of the pieces and plunged it into Mary's extended arm. Unfortunately, all it did was give him an extra second as he sensed her grip momentarily slacken. Mary's lips drew back into a snarl as her silver eyes flickered with annoyance from his feeble attack.

But that extra moment was all he needed. Andy quickly raised the broken mirror shard again, but this time he stabbed it into the direction of her right eye. Unfortunately, he was too slow. Glimpsing the broken piece of mirror closing in on her eye, Mary shifted her head at the last moment, causing the sharp piece of glass to scrape across the side of her skull, cutting into her earlobe.

Andy felt her grip slacken as the shocked Mary released her hand and instinctively reached up to touch the side of her head. He collapsed onto the floor, coughing, as he desperately fought to get his breath back.

Mary pulled her hand back from the side of her face and inspected the blood on her fingers. Andy's eyes widened in panic as she peered down at him, and instead of being angry, she actually smiled at him! To his disgust, Andy watched her lick the blood off her fingers as she laughed maniacally at him.

'Oh, that's more like it!' Her lips curled into a sneer as she moved towards him, 'Maybe the men of this world are not a total loss. Maybe I will get to have my fun with you after all. I hope the men of this world are better at pleasuring a woman than fighting, otherwise I am really going to be pissed off.'

Gasping for air, his voice rasping from the damage done to his larynx by Mary's vice-like grip, Andy shook his head and laughed weakly, 'Well you are seriously in for a disappointment, bitch!' he rasped painfully, 'To be honest I would sooner stick my dick in a blender.'

Her eyes widening with fury, the doppelgänger's face contorted with rage as she charged into Andy. But that was what he was hoping for. With all his remaining strength he jumped up and slammed his head into Mary's stomach, knocking the wind out of her. He quickly pushed his head into the bottom of her chin and slammed her head back. Their momentum carried them across the room as they both crashed onto the bed and bounced off it onto the floor. Andy just missed striking the bedside cabinet with his head. However, Mary was not so lucky; her head caught the corner of the bedside cabinet, stunning her. Disorientated, Andy lay on the floor, staring up at the ceiling and shook his head to clear his vision. As he twisted his head, he managed to catch sight of Mary from out of the corner of his eye. He could tell she was equally dazed, but was also trying to recover her senses.

Not giving her a chance to recover, Andy pounced onto the stunned woman and started to pound her with his fists. He winced painfully as he screamed at her with his damaged throat in between blows, 'You monster! What have you done to my wife?'

Her teeth clenched together, Mary squeezed her eyes shut and raised her arms up to shield herself from Andy's pummelling fists. Her top lip curled into a snarl as his ineffective blows landed on her thick muscled arms. He heard her let out of small grunt of contempt as he felt his punches strike her solid abdomen.

A cry from Alice gave Andy pause and he cast concerned glance over his shoulder to the doorway. It was then Andy realised he had just had terrible mistake as he detected movement out of the corner of his eye. He saw Mary's hands shooting towards his throat, but he instinctively managed to block the shot. Unfortunately, the force of the blow caused him to lurch to his feet, but he was still able to get in a solid kick to Mary's head, stunning her. He then wheeled away from her in an effort to scramble out of the bedroom to rescue Alice.

The stunned woman blinked, shook her head, and watched as her quarry staggered out of the doorway onto the landing. Becoming aware of a metallic taste in her mouth, she twisted her head and angrily spat out blood. Her body quivering with indignation, she let out a guttural cry of rage as she leapt to her feet and charged after him.

On hearing the primal roar, Andy wheeled around and was paralysed with fear when he saw the look of pure rage on Mary's face as she smashed into him, sending them both crashing down the stairs. Their bodies became an oddly shaped ball of arms and legs as they careened down the stairs, knocking the wind out of them when they landed unceremoniously on the hallway floor.

His head ringing, Andy blinked and shook his head in an effort to recover his senses. He pressed his hand down and touched something firm and soft. His eyes widened in surprise as he realised that he was lying on top of Mary's body. He lifted his head and his eyes locked with a pair of eyes burning with hatred.

'Sorry!' he rasped apologetically and proceeded to punch her in the jaw.

After managing to separate himself, Andy scrambled across the floor to the bookcase in the hallway. He leapt up and grabbed the baseball bat, a gift from their honeymoon in Toronto, off the trophy stand and swung around with it grasped firmly in his hands. He swung the bat with all his strength with the hope it would connect with woman's head.

Andy guessed Mary must have sensed what was coming as he watched her roll away at the last minute. The bat just missing its target, it struck empty space and Andy's face scrunched up in pain as he felt the bat smash into the wooden floor. He released the bat as felt the impact reverberate up his arms.

Still on the floor and with her back to Andy, Mary kicked her leg out and caught him in the stomach, forcing him back as the wind was knocked out of him. Winded, he staggered back into the kitchen as he desperately tried to put some distance between him and the deadly woman.

His clothes soaked with sweat, Andy panted as he scanned the kitchen looking for anything to help give him an edge. He had always proudly considered himself a fairly decent fighter, being able to hold his own on any given day against any normal opponent. But he knew this was not any given day and this woman, whoever she was, was not a normal opponent. From his experience with her upstairs, he was acutely aware that she was obviously a trained killer and could probably kill him in a variety of different ways, if she was given the chance.

Andy knew if he had any chance of surviving, then he must try and hold her off long enough for Wendy to arrive with help. He prayed she had heard enough of the struggle on the phone before it was cut off and was on her way with backup, otherwise he was well and truly screwed!

As he spun round, Andy felt his chest tighten with fear as he saw Mary storm in the kitchen, her eyes blazing with anger. Out of the corner of his eye he spotted a knife block on top of the kitchen counter and lunged over, grabbing a knife out of the block. Without looking to see what knife he was holding; he wheeled round and pointed the knife defiantly at the advancing the woman.

Then, much to Andy's surprise, Mary suddenly stopped her advance and cocked her head in bemusement. Andy frowned and then glanced down to the knife in his hand, but was dismayed to see, in his haste, he had grabbed a small cheese knife. He lifted his head up to the bemused looking Mary, who tilted her head at him and from the contemptuous look on her face he guessed she was saying, '*Seriously!*'

Andy lifted his shoulder in a half shrug, threw the small knife at Mary and lunged over to the knife block, this time making sure to pull out a large, pointed meat knife. He wheeled round and held it protectively in front of him in his right hand, with his left hand raised up in front of him in a fighting stance. Mary wiped away the blood from the corner of her mouth and her mouth curved into a smile as she looked at the knife in Andy's hand with a glint in her eye. He suddenly realised with astonishment from the look on her face and the steely glint in her eye, she was actually enjoying this. He clenched his jaw as he watched her back away from him but stopped and then looked at something over her shoulder.

His first thought had been she had spotted a knife or some other type of weapon. It slowly dawned on Andy what she was doing as he watched her reach over and grab two thick magazines off the kitchen table. Rolling them up together tightly, she bent forward and slowly edged towards Andy with the rolled-up magazines held up in front of her. There was a broad grin on her face as she raised her empty left hand and wiggled her fingers tauntingly at Andy, as if to say, '*Come at me.*'

They both circled each other, and Andy watched warily as Mary edged toward him and he reluctantly thrusted his knife out at her. Andy realised he had just made a serious error as he realised that was what she was waiting for. As soon as he lunged at her, Mary feinted to her left and repeatedly struck the rolled-up magazine onto his right elbow, hitting the ulna nerve, causing his hand to spasm, releasing the knife. His right hand numb, Andy held his right arm protectively as he tried to edge away.

Sensing her opportunity, Mary pressed her attack and began striking her target repeatedly across his head and body with the makeshift rolled up magazine weapon. Andy teetered back from the repeated blinding blows on the sides of his head and body. Dazed, he began to feel the numbness leave his right hand and held his arms up in front of him. He desperately threw a punch, but Mary was able to dodge his feeble attack with ease. She then released the rolled-up magazine, straightened her fingers, and jabbed her right hand into his armpit. Andy let out a scream of pain as he felt his right arm drop numbly to side.

His legs starting to buckle, Andy began to sway and reeled back in pain as Mary continued her advance. She viciously jabbed repeatedly at his chest, and he cried out in pain as he felt his one of his ribs break and coughed, feeling something warm and metallic in his mouth. The corners of Mary's lips turned up into a cruel smile as she dropped to her knees and slammed her fist into Andy's groin.

His vision going white with pain, Andy's face scrunched up in pure agony as he felt his legs turn into jelly and collapsed onto the floor. Eyes watering, he lifted his head and opened them just in time to see Mary lift her right leg up and bring her foot down hard onto his leg, striking it just below his knee. Andy shrieked in pain as he felt his leg break. Mary stepped over him and her eyes bore into him as she watched his chest rise and fall with each painful gasp of air. She cocked her head and her mouth twitched as she lowered herself down and sat on his stomach, forcing the remaining air out of his lungs. She gave him a malicious smile as she leaned forward and licked the side of his face with her tongue.

'It's such a shame you had to ruin such a perfect moment, honey.' she purred, 'If you hadn't gone and been such an idiot and act like a detective, we could have had the perfect marriage.'

Andy squeezed his eyes shut and tried to fight back the tears. He opened his eyes and tried to give Mary the best defiant stare he could manage. He wheezed as he tried to force the words out of his mouth, 'Okay ... then ... pet. Can ... I ... ask ... a ... favour?' He swallowed a gulp of air and let out a harsh chesty cough.

Mary lifted an eyebrow and cocked her head at him, 'Sure, baby! What is it?'

Eyes watering with pain, his chest rising and falling in rapid breaths, Andy pressed his lips together into a grim smile, 'Can ... I ... have ... a ... divorce?'

Mary's back stiffened, lifted her eyes up to the ceiling and gave her head a small shake. She hung her head and pouted sadly, 'Oh baby, you shouldn't have said that!'

Suddenly her fist slammed into the side of Andy's head, and he watched as his vision faded. Darkness enveloping him, his last thought was of his wife as his consciousness ebbed away.

'Mary, honey, I'll be with you soon.'

17

Claire opened her eyes, stretched her arms out in front of her and yawned. Suddenly sensing movement next to her, she stiffened and shot straight up. Her heart racing, she looked around the unfamiliar room with wide confused eyes. Eventually her sleepy brain stirred, and the memories of the previous night started to flood back to her.

She twisted her head around and stared at the sleeping body lying next to her. Claire lay back down and then turned onto her left side, resting her head on her left arm. As she silently studied Dave as he lay sleeping, she began to think about what she had done.

Her mind drifted back to the previous night and the corners of her mouth curled up as she thought back to the moment she had led him upstairs. They had not made love when they had climbed into bed. Instead, with his arms wrapped around her, she lay with her back to him while they continued talking, eventually falling asleep in each other's arms.

Claire tapped her finger on her chin thoughtfully. It had been a long time since she had a good night's sleep. Since Emma's death, she had never seemed secure, her mind not switching off to allow her a full night's sleep. But last night was different, being held in Dave's arms while she nodded off. She had felt something that she had not enjoyed for such a long time, a sense of security. For the first time in a long while she had fallen asleep knowing that it was safe to do so.

But she was also deeply troubled at what she had done. It had been so out of character for her. She had one rule – never to sleep with anyone she had only just met. Up until now, it was a rule she had strictly adhered to. So why had she broken it? Had David slipped something into her tea? No, that wasn't it, because she clearly remembered acting on her own free will. Anyway, David didn't seem to be that kind of person.

Claire lay back down onto her back and wondered whether she should make a quick exit. That seemed like the most logical choice to her, because she felt it would cut out any awkwardness. She reached over and looked at her phone; the time was 06:12. Gently, so as not to wake the slumbering Dave, she eased up and swung her legs over her side of the bed. She leaned over and carefully grabbed her glasses off the bedside table, unfolded them and placed them on the bridge of her nose. Trying to not disturb the man next to her, she quietly straightened up and peered down at herself. On realising that she was still wearing Dave's rugby shirt, she made the decision that she would snatch up her clothes and get changed downstairs. She could easily get a shower once she got back home.

However, just as she was about to creep out of the bedroom she came to a stop. *Don't go. You need to stay.* She blinked and then turned back to look at Dave. What was she doing? Why was she going to leave? *You weren't going to leave. You were just on your way downstairs to make some breakfast. Isn't that right?*

'Yes, that's right, I was going to make some breakfast.' Claire murmured as she edged away from the side of the bed. *It would be nice to surprise Dave if you brought it up to him.* She nodded to herself, 'Yes, that sounded lovely, he would like that.'

Carefully tiptoeing around the bed, Claire stopped at her pile of clothes that she had carefully folded and placed on the chair in the bedroom's corner the night before. She bent down and picked up her panties and carefully slid them on then quietly slipped out of the bedroom onto the landing at the top of the stairs, where she next delicately moved into the bathroom.

A few minutes later, Claire was standing in the kitchen and opened the fridge door to check what food was available. She pressed her lips together and tutted to herself as she realised the fridge held little to work with. Her finger was tapping thoughtfully on her chin, gazing into the fridge, as she suddenly sensed something soft brushing against legs.

Claire's heart skipped a beat as she felt something wet nuzzle into her leg. She lowered her head and touched her chest in relief as she was it was only Jenny, looking up at her, tail wagging.

'Good morning, girl.' Claire greeted, smiling warmly, 'What do you want?'

She frowned as she watched the dog trot over to the patio doors, twist her head back and gave her a small whine. Immediately guessing the dog was wanting to go outside, she opened the two doors wide and watched her take an anxious look into the garden. She laughed when she heard the dog let out another small whine.

'It's okay. You can go out.' Claire said softly, pointing to the garden reassuringly.

Jenny slowly stepped outside and trotted onto the lawn, she paced round in a circle and then cocked her head back to Claire. Claire let out an amused laugh, turned her back to the dog and marched back into the kitchen but froze when she heard a loud yelp coming from behind her.

What was that? Startled by the noise, Claire spun around and rushed into the garden to discover Jenny was lying on the grass. Deeply concerned, Claire ran over to her, and shivered as the chilly morning breeze blew against her bare legs. A sense of dread hit her as she noticed a tranquiliser dart was sticking out of the dog's right flank.

Her chest tightening with fear, Claire spun sharply round and made to run back into the house. But she let out a small scream of pain as she felt something sharp strike the side of her neck. As her hand reached up to probe her neck, her mouth formed an 'O' of surprise as her fingers came across a dart embedded in the side her neck.

With her heart pounding in her chest, Claire pressed her lips together and screwed up her face as she pulled it out and scrutinised the object in her hand. It appeared to be a small tranquiliser dart. Claire shook her head in confusion. Surely this had to be a mistake?

It was then her vision started to blur and she quickly realised that she was starting to feel the effects of the sedative. Claire shook her head and took a step forward, only to collapse onto the grass as she lost all sensation in her legs. She tried to crawl weakly toward the house, but her body collapsed fully onto the ground as darkness began to envelope her and she lost consciousness.

Dave woke up with a start. He opened his eyes and, after adjusting to the darkness, twisted his head around only to discover he was still in his bedroom. He was not sure what it was, but he had been positive a noise had woken him up, and he could have sworn it was a woman's scream.

Suddenly remembering that he had gone to sleep with Claire lying next to him, he glanced over to the other side of the bed. A sense of disappointment filled him as he stared at the empty space beside him. He leaned over, clicked on the bedside light, and looked around the bedroom.

After noticing Claire's glasses were no longer lying on the bedside table, Dave peered across to the chair in the bedroom's corner and smiled cheerfully to himself when he saw her clothes were still lying on it, neatly folded.

She must have gotten up to make breakfast. His mood lightened and he smiled knowingly to himself.

Gently swinging his legs over the side of the bed, Dave straightened up and then moved over to the wardrobe, reaching in, and grabbing a T-shirt and training bottoms. He sat down on the edge of the bed, slipped into the bottoms, pulled the T-shirt over his head while awkwardly guiding his arms into the sleeves.

Five minutes later, after a brief pit-stop in the bathroom, Dave arrived downstairs and strode into the kitchen, scratching at his head as he muttered to himself.

'Claire, I guessed you must have got up to make breakfa—' He froze as he saw there was no sign of the woman and shouted toward the direction of the living room, 'Claire? Are you there?' He frowned when he received no reply. His brow furrowed even deeper as he noticed that Jenny had not ran up to greet him like she usually did.

It was then he noticed the cool breeze on his bare arms and he spun sharply round to see the patio doors were wide open to the garden.

Claire must have taken Jenny outside to the garden, he thought to himself and moved toward the open patio doors.

After taking a hesitant step through the open doors onto the patio, Dave's eyes narrowed as he scanned the garden. At first, he thought it seemed empty, apart from what seemed to be a small black lump at the far end of the garden. But as he edged closer, he inhaled sharply as he realised the black lump was Jenny.

His heart lurching in his chest, Dave ran over to her and knelt beside her. His first thought was that she had hurt herself, or worse. He let out a sigh of relief when he saw her stomach was rising and falling from her breathing. He then gently placed his hands on her to check if she had any injuries.

'Hey girl, what happened to you?' His tone was soothing as his hands moved over her. He knew it was stupid to ask a dog a question, expecting her to answer, but he could not help it. He lifted his head and scanned the area around him, muttering, 'Also, where the hell is Claire?'

As he opened his mouth to shout for the missing woman, his voice caught in his throat as his hand came across something unusual - a dart of some type was sticking into Jenny's right flank. Dave gulped and he shivered as he felt trickle of fear run down his spine. He then felt a knot form in his stomach as it slowly hit him the reason why there was no sign of Claire.

With adrenaline pumping through his body, his eyes began to search around the garden for any sign of intruders. Believing he was now in extreme danger, Dave straightened and made to run back to the door but froze as he detected movement coming from behind him. He spun sharply round to the movement's direction but stopped and exclaimed in pain as he felt something sharp strike his neck.

His hand jerking up to site of the pain, Dave's eyebrows knitted together as his fingers came across something embedded into his neck and immediately pulled it out. He stared down at the object in his hand and felt the colour drain from his face as he realised it was a tranquiliser dart.

His legs becoming heavy and leaden, Dave stumbled back and collapsed onto the ground. He shook his head desperately and through sheer willpower pushed himself off the ground, forcing his legs to move toward the house. Suddenly, he cried out in pian as once again he felt another sharp pain in the side of his neck. His legs folding from under him, Dave desperately clawed at the grass with his hands and tried to drag his body to safety. His breathing becoming more laboured, he felt the strength drain out of his arms and he sunk onto the grass. As he rapidly began to lose consciousness, he lifted his head off the ground and just as he was enveloped in darkness, he caught a glimpse of three blurred shadows as they edged toward him.

'Put him with Professor Tulley and bring them back to base. Command would like to speak to them when they wake up.' He heard Wendy say sadly before he eventually succumbed to the darkness.

Dave opens his eyes and blinks as he lets his vision slowly adjust to the dimly lit room. He realises he is back in his bedroom. But as he lifts his head and searches his the room, he sees that is now alone. There is no sign of Claire, her clothes are no longer on the chair in the bedroom's corner.

Swiftly jumping out of bed, He looks down at himself and is astonished to see he is wearing the suit he normally wears for work. As he creeps towards the bedroom door, he freezes as he catches movement coming from the tall mirror in the bedroom's corner. His forehead furrows as he remembers he has never owned a mirror like that. He anxiously moves over to it and wordlessly examines it, but finds nothing unusual in it, it is just a mirror.

He then hears a loud moaning coming from outside the

bedroom. But as he is about to walk over to the bedroom door, he freezes as he notices his reflection in the mirror – it is smiling at him! Dave feels the blood in his veins freeze as suddenly the surface of the mirror begins to shimmer and the reflection's head pushes through the membrane-like-surface. It is like a scene from a horror movie, where the pulsating creatures forces itself out a gelatinous incubation sack.

The head twists and grins malevolently at Dave, 'Hello Dave. I thought it's about time I introduced myself. I am you, that is the one you keep hidden from yourself. You know who I mean, your dark side!'

Shaking his head, terrified beyond belief, Dave slowly backs away from the mirror, until he feels his back hit the bedroom door. With his eyes still locked on his reflection, his fingers fidget for the door handle, and he gingerly opens the door.

'Oh, come on Dave, don't be a spoilsport.' Mirror-Dave snarls, its lips lifting above its teeth in a nightmarish-like sneer, 'We only want to play with you!'

Dave hesitates as he opens the door and stares at his other self, puzzled, 'We? What you mean, we?'

Mirror-Dave laughs menacingly and then points Dave. He suddenly realises it is not pointing at him, but to something behind him - the bedroom door.

'Go on, look out, you will see what I mean. We only want to play.' it cackles.

His heart hammering in his chest, Dave opens the bedroom door fully and steps out and becomes frozen on the spot at what he sees. The hairs on the back of his neck stand up as the reality of what is ahead hits him.

The door should have led into the hallway at the top of his stairs, but now Dave is standing in a long hallway that appears to go on forever in both directions. Along the side of the walls are mirrors of varying sizes, in each mirror there is a distorted reflection of him staring malevolently back at him; all waving, laughing, and pointing at him.

Dave spins round to go back into the bedroom, but the door is no longer there. In its place stands another large mirror. He lets out a horrified

Double Jeopardy

gasp as he sees another odious reflection staring back at him, cackling menacingly.

To his horror, the reflection's arm reaches out from inside the mirror and its hand grabs at Dave's neck, squeezing hard. Dave screams and smashes at the hand with his fist, causing it to release its grip. As he massages his sore neck, Dave spins round and rushes down the corridor.

As he runs down the corridor, he shakes his head in denial, screaming, not believing what he is seeing. The corridor twists and turns into a maze. No matter what direction he runs, mirrors are facing him, with his reflection staring back at him from inside each one, laughing maniacally as they wave and point to him.

Dave screams and smashes his fists on the mirror closest to him. The surface shatters, and the broken shards lay on the ground around him, with his face laughing menacingly at him from the inside each one.

'You cannot escape us, Dave!' they all taunt at him, 'Join us. You know you want to!'

Frantic and scared out of his wits, Dave pulls at his hair and opens his mouth in a silent scream. His eyes are wild with terror as he spins round and runs. He twists his head back over his shoulder and a nameless dread engulfs him as he sees that the broken mirror shards are starting to liquify and reform in the shape of another large mirror – his own face and body cackling maniacally at him from within.

Dave feels his bones turn to jelly as he tries to turn and run, but another large mirror suddenly appears in front of him, stopping him in his tracks. But this one is different – it holds an image of Claire within. He can see her hands banging furiously on the surface, she is screaming but he cannot hear her.

Dave's voice is shrill with fear as he pounds his fists on the surface of the mirror, 'Claire! Claire!'

Dread gnawing at his inside, he watches helplessly as Claire stops pounding the mirror and shrinks back in fear. He can see she is shouting his name. Her eyes are round and wild as she spots something terrifying and points frantically to something behind him. Dave spins around and fear chokes him as he watches the scene unfold in front of him.

Panic surges through him as mirrors lay all around him, each one holding an evil replica of himself. The eyes of each face glow red and their evil grinning mouths widen showing their black pointed teeth, black drool pouring from all their mouths. They all point and laugh malevolently at him.

Dave's body trembles in fear as each figure crawls out of their mirror with a sickening slurping noise, their long-pointed fingernails pointing in his direction. The colour drains from his face as they slowly crawl along the floor towards him.

He can feel nothing but blind terror as he watches all their hands grab at him, tearing at his own flesh. He tries to twist his head to see Claire, but his mouth opens in a silent scream as he is made to witness her fragile form being torn apart by a shadowy figure. With his panic fuelling him, Dave pushes and fights his way through the melee as he tries desperately to reach Claire.

'No! Claire!' his voice is thick with fear as he screams, 'Claire!'

As he let out a horrified scream, Dave was suddenly aware of someone's hands grabbing at him. He tried to shake them away but could still feel them tugging at him. Overcome with panic, he opened his eyes but all he could see was darkness.

'Claire!' he screamed. His heart hammering in his chest, he shrank back in fear as he once again felt someone's hands on him.

'Dave! Dave! Easy, you were dreaming.' Claire's soothing voice came from out of the darkness.

Suddenly the darkness vanished and is replaced by bright light, blinding Dave. He blinked as his vision adjusted to the light, and he twisted his head in confusion. A great sense of relief washed over him as he caught sight of Claire standing beside the bed, her hand on the light switch.

Concern etched across her face, Claire sat back down beside Dave, placing her hand on his shoulder, 'Jesus! You had me worried there.' she said worriedly, 'They brought you in just after me. Sounds like you were having a bad dream. You were tossing and turning and screaming my name.'

Dave collapsed back onto the bed, his chest heaving as he let out a harsh breath, scrubbing his face with the palms of his hands. His heart feeling like it was wanting to burst out of his chest, he closed his eyes and slowed his breathing to help bring his pulse rate down.

'Holy shit!' His voice was edged with fear as he swallowed and tried to not throw up, 'What a nightmare. I dreamt I was surrounded by all these mirrors, and I tried to run away. I saw you too, but I couldn't help you, as I watched helplessly as they tore you apart.'

Claire peered down at him with a raised eyebrow and gave a gentle laugh, 'So you were dreaming about me, from the sounds of it, I'm not sure whether I should be flattered.'

Dave opened one eye at the bemused looking Claire, gave her a cheeky grin and winked. As he opened both eyes, his forehead creased as the events from that morning flooded back to him.

'Hang on!' he gasped, 'The last thing I remember I was in the garden looking for you and saw Jenny lying on the ground, tranquilised.' He felt his panic start to rise as he gave a small shake of his head, 'Then the next thing I know, a dart hits me, I black out and then I wake up here.'

Fearing for their safety, Dave bolted up but cried out in pain as he felt his head strike something above him. He looked up and saw he was lying on the bottom bed of a bunk bed. As he massaged his forehead with his hand, he glanced around the room and noticed they were in a small room, very similar to a prison cell. On the adjacent wall there was a small metal wardrobe. Next to it was a table and two single chairs. The room had no windows, just three fluorescent ceiling lights, that lit up the small room with a bright warm glow.

He cocked his head at Claire who was sat next to him. She appeared to be wearing a black military style overall. She gave a small nod as she looked down at herself and raised her shoulders in a small shrug.

'They grabbed me just before you.' She said, as if answering his unspoken question, 'They woke me up an hour ago, but they must have really given you a real potent dose as they had a hard time trying to wake you, they felt it was best just to leave you and wake you up gradually. I was still wearing your rugby shirt and not much else when they brought us in.'

Claire's cheeks then turn a deep shade of crimson as she waved a hand down the front of her body, 'I am not sure who was embarrassed more, me or them.' she chucked, 'Once they found out my size, a female soldier kindly loaned me this overall, along with some underwear.'

Dave gave a faint nod and looked at his watch; two hours had passed since they had tranquilised him. He stood up and groaned as he tried to get his stiff joints to work. As he paced around the compact room, he lowered his voice and pointed at the door.

'Have they given you any explanation who they are or why they took us?' he asked warily.

'No, I know they look like military personnel. Which branch of the military, I don't know.' Claire murmured, her eyes darting over to the closed door. She tapped her chin with her finger as if contemplating their dilemma, 'I can guess why they took us. Over the years I have pissed many people off, so I guess they were keeping tabs on me, and somebody mustn't have been too happy that you were speaking to me.'

Dave pressed his lips together and continued to pace around the cell thoughtfully, 'That's my hunch too. I am guessing they only wanted you and me, otherwise they could have stormed in and taken us all last night. I am hoping they haven't grabbed Andy and Wendy too. I am hoping once Andy learns I haven't arrived at work, he will realise something is wrong when he cannot contact me.'

Unless they grabbed him too. If they did, then we are screwed, he thought to himself, *but probably best if I keep that to myself, Claire has enough to worry about without adding that to the mix.*

Dave stretched his arms and gave a loud yawn, 'Well, no time like the present, I suppose!' He spun round and raised his voice, 'Let's get this show on the road.' Straightening his shoulders, he marched over to the door, held up his right hand and banged it hard on the door, 'Hey! Numbnuts!' he shouted impatiently, 'Can you tell your boss we are ready for the pleasure of his company!'

There was a small click from the other side of the door and Dave watched as it slowly opened and a soldier wearing black uniform appeared and glowered at him.

'Somebody will be along to see you soon, sir.' he growled.

Dave lifted his finger to his head in a small mock salute and the soldier gave him a stern look as he closed the door. He raised an eyebrow in surprise as he noticed the soldier had kept it unlocked. He twisted his head back to Claire and gave her a cheeky grin.

'Oh good. Somebody will see to us soon.' he said sarcastically.

From the way Claire was lowering her head and glaring sternly at him over her glasses, Dave got the distinct impression she wasn't amused. 'You, play nice!' she said firmly, pointing her at him.

Dave gave her a innocent wide eyed look, held up his hands up to chest and opened his mouth as he wordlessly mimed – *Who me?*

Claire let out a small groan of disgust and planted her face into her hands.

Five minutes later the door opened, and a tall broad shouldered black woman, with a lean boyish face, short cropped black hair, wearing a tight-fitting black bodysuit strode purposefully into the small room. Dave guessed she that she must be in her early-thirties and from the way she was carrying herself it was safe for him to assume she knew how to handle herself.

'Detective Inspector Barnes. Professor Tulley.' she said brusquely, from her accent he guessed she was from the south of England, possibly the London area. She held open the door and pointed to the hallway, 'My name is Lieutenant Kendra Goynes, and I am this facility's Chief Of Security. If you would like to follow me, please.'

With Claire following close behind, Dave followed Kendra out of the door. They moved into a long, dark corridor, busy with various people, rushing around in the middle of their various tasks. The two newcomers were given brief glances as they were escorted down the corridor. From their attire Dave assumed they were a mixture of soldiers and civilians.

As they were escorted down the corridor, Dave glanced at Kendra and tapped her on the shoulder, 'I am guessing this is a military bunker of some sort.' he asked curiously, 'I guess that some of these people are agents too. I'm guessing MI6 or something?'

Kendra turned her head slightly to Dave as they continued to hurry down the corridor and nodded briefly, 'Yes, some of us are MI6, some, like you guessed, are military and others from other branches. But that's all I may say for now.' She held her hand as he opened his mouth to ask another question, 'I know you have a lot of questions, but please be patient our … leader … will explain everything shortly.'

Dave cocked his head at Claire who was walking next to him. She raised her eyebrows questioningly and gave him a small shrug as they continued to follow Kendra down the corridor.

Five minutes later they watched in interest as Lieutenant Goynes stopped in front of a large door. She gave a small knock, pushed the door open and jerked her head in the direction of the open door.

'If you would like to go in, they are waiting for you.' she said cryptically.

Dave took a hesitant step forward as Kendra moved back to allow him entry. He blinked to let his eyes adjust to the brightly lit room. It was quite a large room, resembling a study. Shelves lined the walls, with various books filling each shelf. Three tables stood in each corner of the room, with a leather sofa pushed against one wall. At the far side of the room stood a desk, with a computer monitor sat on top of it. Various folders and papers were scattered untidily across the desk's surface. Behind the desk a woman sat with their back to him, she appeared to be chatting on the phone. In front of the desk, a familiar-looking red-haired woman was standing with her back facing Dave. Dave's eyebrows knitted together as he thought she looked oddly familiar.

As she turned to face them and smiled warmly at him, Dave felt his jaw drop open in disbelief as he realised it was Wendy. He did a double take and shook his head in disbelief, there was no doubt about it, the woman standing before him was Wendy Cooper.

Dave glanced over his shoulder at Claire. He could tell from the stunned expression on her face she was just as equally shocked. Then it was as if somebody flicked a switch and her face suddenly changed in front of him. Her face became a deep shade of red as her top lip curled up over her teeth and her features morphed into a mixture of hurt and hate.

To Dave it felt like everything was moving in slow motion. He blinked and he realised Claire was no longer standing in front of him. As he turned slowly, he saw she was moving past him and was charging toward Wendy.

Her eyes were filled with blazing fury as she let out a primal roar, 'You bitch, I'm going to kill you!'

18

Location: Pons Aelius, Britannica, Universal Roman Empire

Colonel Barnes jumped back as the general slammed her fist down angrily on the console. He watched as a cup bounced off the console, crash onto the floor and then shatter into pieces.

'What did you say?' General Cooper hissed; her steely green eyes burning with anger as she stared back at the people in the room.

Barnes glanced at Doctor Claudia, who was standing beside him. She lowered her head and shifted uncomfortably on her feet. Realising it looked like it was up to him to say something, Barnes cocked his head, coughed, and gave her a slight smile.

'Sorry general, I apologise if you could not hear.' he answered regretfully, 'It appears we have lost contact with the operative we sent in to replace Mary Jenkins.'

Cooper then marched over to Barnes and stood face to face with him, barely centimetres apart. Barnes shuffled his feet uncomfortably at the invasion of his personal space.

'Oh, I heard you the first time, Colonel!' she snapped. Barnes blinked as he felt the spittle from her mouth hit him in the face, 'Care to explain how we could lose contact with someone who, in your own words, was *being monitored closely*?' She folded her arms across her chest and shot him a withering look, 'Well, I am all ears!'

Barnes gave a sidelong glance to the two people standing on either side of him. Doctor Claudia was standing to his right, but Lieutenant Akinjide, a tall black muscular man dressed in a standard black military uniform was standing in silence to his left. He had hoped Doctor Claudia would have stepped forward and said something, but he could see he was going to get no help from her.

'Don't look at them! Look at me when I ask you a question.' Cooper hissed.

Barnes lifted his head and gave Cooper a small smile as he stared into her eyes, 'Yes General. As you know, we had sent Specialist Mann to Counter-Terra to immobilise and then replace her doppelgänger.' he gave a small indifferent shrug of his shoulders, 'Her assignment was to assume the role of Mary Jenkins and keep a close eye on her husband. I ordered her to blend in, so she could get close to …' His top curled up in disdain as he forced the last word out, '*him*.'

'You mean your counterpart?' There was a hint of bemusement in Cooper's voice as she smirked at him.

'Yes … my counterpart.' The colonel grunted unhappily, gritting his teeth as he continued, 'Her mission was, when the moment was right, to kill Detective Inspector Barnes.'

Cooper tilted her head and gave him an icy stare, 'And who gave you the order to have him killed?'

Barnes furrowed his brow as he looked at Cooper in bewilderment, 'I … I … did.' he stammered, 'I … I … thought my counterpart posed a threat.' He straightened and arched his head in arrogant determination, 'In my judgement, I considered the risk he posed was too great and needed to be taken care of.'

Cooper let out a long breath as her hand casually reached up and touched Barnes's face. She then squeezed his cheeks together and pulled his face towards her. Barnes gasped in pain as he felt her sharp fingernails dig into his skin.

'Let me say this, slowly, so you can understand.' she whispered calmy, 'We do not pay you to think. We pay you to do what I tell you, nothing else.' her eyes narrowed as she stared intently into his eyes, 'You are to leave your counterpart alone. Do you understand?'

Barnes stared back at Cooper and shook his head in confusion, 'N … n… no, General. I don't understand. Why don't we take care of him now?'

Cooper rolled her eyes and blew out a harsh breath. Barnes sensed her hand loosen as she pulled her hand away from his face, 'No, I suppose your feeble little brain wouldn't.' Cooper's lip rose slightly into a contemptuous sneer. He flinched as she patted him on his face, 'Your fragile ego has put decades of work and planning put at risk. Plans were set in motion decades ago and soon, remarkably soon in fact, we will see them come to fruition. We have plans for your counterpart. High command believes Dave Barnes has an important role to play in the events to come, that's all you need to know.'

Barnes took a small step back from the general and rubbed his face with his hand. He bowed his head and clicked his heels in salute, 'Yes, General. I will not fail you again.' he said with a soft respectful tone. Inwardly he was thinking, *Touch me again like that you bitch!*

Cooper waved her hand dismissively at Banes. He remained silent as he watched her turn away from him, appearing to focus her attention on Doctor Claudia. Up until this point, she had been so silent, Barnes would have hardly guessed she had been in the same as room him.

'Now, can somebody tell me how we lost contact with operative?' Cooper snapped, spinning round and clicking her fingers at the smaller woman, 'You, Doctor Claudia is it? You were supposed to be on monitor duty. Explain to me, why is it, with all our advanced technology, we lost contact with one of own people?'

Henrietta inhaled a deep sigh and moved forward anxiously, with a computer tablet held tightly against her chest. She glanced over to Barnes, but he did not return her gaze.

'Everything was going as planned, General.' she answered. Barnes noticed that her fingers were nervously touching the obedience collar around her neck, 'We sent Specialist Mann through the portal and, as expected, she immobilised the target easily. We sent in a clean-up crew to retrieve the unconscious Mary Jenkins. Everything went like clockwork. The operative changed into the clothes that Jenkins wore, granted they were a tight fit, but we thought we could get away with it and we hoped Sergeant Jenkins wouldn't detect the difference.'

Understanding dawned on Cooper's face as she held up her hand with her finger extended and glowered at Doctor Claudia, 'I am guessing something went wrong, and he did?'

Henrietta dabbed the sweat off her brow with her sleeve and gave a nervous cough, 'Ahem, yes. Well, we watched as Sergeant Jenkins arrived home and everything seemed to go fine until the baby started crying and he was going to check on her, but Specialist Mann persuaded him that she would do it.' she inhaled a heavy despondent sigh and shook her head, 'That is when it all went wrong. As soon as she left the room, the sergeant used his mobile phone device. Mann discovered Jenkins calling for help and she attacked him. During the fight they smashed the mirror, which is when we lost contact.'

Cooper gave a small nod and turned away from the anxious woman. Barnes watched as she wordlessly paced around the console, her hand trailing along the console's surface. She then came to a sudden stop and raised her hand absent-mindedly, as if to inspect her fingers and mumbled, 'What is the baby's name?'

Henrietta opened her mouth and stared at Cooper uncomprehendingly, confusion etched across her face, 'Sorry, General, but I don't understand?'

Cooper spun round, her eyes ablaze with anger as she snarled at Henrietta, 'What name did Jenkins say when he said he was going to check on the baby?'

Henrietta stared at Cooper uneasily, blinked, and gave a slight shake of her head, 'I … I … I …' she stammered, 'think he called her Jenny?'

Cooper gave a wry smile, folded her arms behind her back, and gave Henrietta a speculative glance as she continued to pace around the room. 'And you know that for certain? I am sure we have a record of the baby's name?' She flicked her hand and pointed at the tablet in woman's hands, 'Go on, I can wait.'

With Cooper watching on, Henrietta turned away and typed furiously into her tablet. Barnes noticed her back stiffen, and as she slowly turned back, he saw that the colour had drained from her face.

'A … A … A …' Henrietta choked back her response, swallowed and then rasped, 'Alice.'

Cooper stormed over to the trembling ashen-faced woman and came to sudden stop, their faces almost touching as she snarled at her, 'I didn't hear you.' She turned her head and pressed her ear close to Henrietta's mouth and hissed, 'Say that again!'

'H … h … her n … n … name is Alice.' Henrietta stammered, trying not to look into Cooper's eyes.

Cooper moved away from Henrietta and nodded in understanding, 'I see.' She pressed her lips together and paced around the room silently. After a minute of uneasy silence, she stopped and cocked her head at Barnes, 'Have we had any contact at all from Specialist Mann?'

'Unfortunately, no, general.' Barnes answered with a touch of resignation, 'We have received no communication from Mann on any channel since we re-established a portal.'

Henrietta held up her index finger and gave an anxious cough. Barnes and Cooper both turned to look at the woman in mild surprise as she whispered to them, 'We may have another problem.'

'Another problem!?' Cooper replied incredulously.

Henrietta gave a nervous nod and then began to type into her tablet furiously, 'W… w… w… we...' she babbled nervously. her voice was thick with trepidation as she tried to get the words out, 'We have lost contact with Detective Inspector Barnes, Professor Tulley and Constable Cooper. Normally, it wouldn't be strange to lose our surveillance on one person, but to lose contact with three is definitely unusual.' she exhaled a deep sigh and hung her head, mumbling, 'For reasons unknown to us, we cannot track them.'

Cooper twisted her head at Barnes and stared at him in disbelief. Taken completely surprise by this news, Barnes took a step back and crossed his arms, 'This is the first time I am hearing this too.'

Cooper's eyes narrowed as she shot Henrietta with a cold stare and hissed at her through clenched teeth, 'How long?'

Henrietta's forehead creased as she stared at Cooper in confusion and gave her a small unknowing shake of her head, 'Pardon General?'

'How long has it been since we lost contact?' Cooper roared with such ferocity it took Barnes by surprise. He had never seen Cooper act like that before. Although he had heard rumours of her vicious temper, up until now he had never actually witnessed it.

Barnes could see the panic in Henrietta's eyes as she shrank away from Cooper. Her hands kept touching the obedience collar around her neck as she answered Cooper in an anxious whisper, 'Twe … twelve hours.'

'Twelve hours.' Cooper said incredulously with wide-eyed disbelief, 'You mean to tell me we have been out of contact with Specialist Mann for twelve hours?'

Henrietta shuffled awkwardly and shook her head gravely, muttering, 'No, General. It is coming up to twelve hours now since we lost track of Barnes and Tulley. We also lost track of Sergeant Jenkins for a brief period, but we located him again when he arrived at his home, but that was just before we lost contact with Specialist Mann and Sergeant Jenkins when she attacked him.'

Cooper waved her hand in disgust and spun round to Colonel Barnes. He eyed Henrietta with disdain. He couldn't understand how someone as incompetent as her ended up on a project like this. Now, because of her incompetence, Cooper was probably looking to land the blame of his fiasco on his shoulders. Barnes held his tongue as he watched Cooper let out a snort of frustration as she strolled purposely around the chamber. He shuddered as Cooper's fingernails made a scratching noise along the surface of the console.

After a few seconds, her anger visibly building, Cooper slowly turned and glared angrily at Henrietta. 'So, you lost contact twelve hours ago,' she said with a slow measured tone of voice, 'and you are only telling me this now, is that right?'

Henrietta lowered her eyes away from the intense glare of Cooper's gaze and gave a small silent nod in acknowledgement. Cooper then pulled her head back and let out a loud hysterical laugh. Barnes watched with uncertainly as she continued to pace around the chamber. Cooper then stopped, turned back to the smaller woman, and held up her hands above her head.

'Well, we are waiting in anticipation.' she laughed, 'We cannot wait for you to tell us. I for one could do with a good laugh! Please tell me.'

Henrietta shuffled her feet uncomfortably, twisted her head to Barnes. Was she hoping that he would help her? Barnes refused to look her in the eye by pretending to inspect his fingernails. Oh no, this was her mess, let her clean it up. She shrank back in fear as Cooper angrily stormed across and stood directly in front of her, nose to nose.

'Well! Tell me! What was so important that it kept you from informing your superior officer as soon as you realised something was wrong?' Cooper snarled. Henrietta blanched and Barnes could almost see the fear in her eyes as he listened to Cooper's voice slowly increase in volume, 'Were you dying? Were you ill? Did you come down with exploding diarrhoea?' she roared, with such ferocity her eyes were bulging, almost as if they were about to burst of her head, 'Well, tell me! What was so bloody important that it stopped you doing from your duty?'

Henrietta visibly shrank back from the woman's fury. She dabbed at the sweat on her forehead with her sleeve and bowed her head, 'I ... I ... thought it was system glitch.' Her voice trembled as her small hazel eyes glistened with tears, 'I apologise General, but I sincerely believed that I could locate them, but when it became apparent that something was wrong. I ... I ... panicked.'

Her emerald eyes narrowing, Cooper gave Henrietta a piercing stare but remained silent for a minute. She then gave a small smile, 'You panicked.' She laughed warmly and raised her hand to stroke Henrietta's pale face, 'I understand my dear.'

As Cooper dropped her hand and moved away, Henrietta beamed and let out a tremendous sigh of relief. Barnes felt a cold shiver run down as his spine as he watched the warm smile disappear from Cooper's face, turning into a cold sneer. He could almost see the blood drain from Henrietta's face as he watched Cooper lean in toward her.

'Yes, I finally understand that it was a mistake to put my faith in you.' Cooper growled, cocking her head as she waggled her finger at the terrified-looking Henrietta, 'I realise now, you are working for the resistance and are plotting against me.'

Henrietta's eyes widened in shock, 'N … n … no general, that's not true!' she cried and dropped to her knees, begging, 'P … p … please I beg you. I have always been a loyal servant to the Empire. You know I have served you faithfully.'

With her emerald eyes staring coldly down at the pleading woman below her, Cooper's demeanour unexpectedly changed as she let out a small chuckle and knelt closer to her, 'Yes. You are right.' Her tone was soft as she reached out and stroked Henrietta's brown hair, 'You were a faithful and loyal servant, which is why I will be lenient.'

The relief evident on Henrietta's tear-stained face, she gazed up to Cooper with hope-filled eyes, 'Tha … tha … thank you, general.'

The corner of Cooper's mouth twitched as she straightened up and then marched over to Lieutenant Akinjide. Barnes had forgotten about him, he had been standing impassively in the corner, back straight and rigid to attention.

'Shoot her.' Cooper ordered firmly, pointing her finger at the kneeling Henrietta.

Lieutenant Akinjide blinked and stared at Cooper in confusion, 'General?'

Fearing things were starting to get out of control, Barnes took a step closer to Cooper and gave her a questioning look, 'General Cooper, are you sure about this?' he said warily, gesturing to the ashen faced Henrietta, 'Yes, Doctor Claudia has made a mistake and needs to be punished, but wouldn't it be wiser t—' A withering expression on Cooper's stern face stopped him from finishing the sentence and he quickly dropped his eyes away.

Cooper let out a small, frustrated breath and gave a small reluctant nod. Henrietta continued to cower as the stone-faced Cooper took a step closer to her and placed her hand tenderly on her shoulder.

'Yes, you are right. It would be a mistake to shoot you.' Cooper whispered and her mouth lifted in a half smile as her hand gently stroked the Henrietta's pale face. There was a faint glimpse of hope in Henrietta's eyes as she gave a small nod in gratitude.

'Thank you.' Henrietta breathed in relief.

Barnes saw Cooper's face harden and then he heard Henrietta let out a gasp in pain. He swallowed as he realised Cooper had tightened her grip on Henrietta's shoulder.

'I have just had a better idea.' Cooper grinned. She then reached into her jacket pocket and pulled out a small control pad.

Henrietta drew back, her eyes widened in alarm and shook her head as she recognised the small control pad, 'P ... p ... please, n ... n ... no. I... I ... I am s ... s ... sorry!' Barnes could almost hear the desperation in her voice as she clasped her hands and began to plead at Cooper. 'I ... I ... did as you instructed me! P ... p ... please, I promise I won't say anything.'

What did she just say? Barnes cocked his head curiously. Was there something else going on here? He narrowed his eyes and stared at the back of Cooper's head. Just what game was Cooper playing at here? Desperate to know the truth, Barnes took a step toward Cooper to intervene. However, before he could so he felt a firm hand grab his arm, stopping him. He spun sharply around and was surprised to see Lieutenant Akinjide was standing next to him with his hand clasped tightly his arm. He opened his mouth to order the lieutenant to release him, but the burly soldier looked at him sadly and wordlessly shook his head; Barnes gave a small nod of understanding as he realised it was too late to do anything. All he could do was to stay silent and witness the events play out in front of him, powerless to act.

Barnes stood in a resigned silence as Cooper, who was staring down at the quaking Henrietta icily, held the small control pad in her left hand. She then pressed her right index finger onto the pad firmly.

Henrietta's face contorted as the collar around her neck lit up and shrieked as electricity ripped through her body. Barnes could almost see the enjoyment on Cooper's face as the unfortunate woman writhed around in agony on the floor, shrieking in pain, while trying desperately to grasp at the collar around her neck. Licking her lips in sadistic pleasure, Cooper increased her pressure on the pad and the chamber was filled with agonising wails as the poor woman's pain intensified.

Deciding he had seen enough, Barnes loosened himself from the lieutenant's grip, rushed over to Cooper and grabbed her shoulder, 'That's enough general!' he shouted as he spun her around, 'Can't you see you killing her. Please, general … Wendy, stop!'

There was a flash of indignation in Cooper's eyes as she looked down at the hand that was on her shoulder and her nostrils flared with rage as she spun her head round. On seeing her rage filled stare, Barnes quickly let go and stepped back.

'I will decide when she has had enough!' she sneered and increased the pressure on the pad.

Henrietta suddenly rose off the floor, her eyes grew wide as without warning her screams cut off. To Barnes it seemed like time had suddenly slowed down, as the collar around the poor woman's neck lit up, pulsed a steady red, and was followed by a dull pop that seemed to come from inside her head.

The top of Henrietta's skull appeared to expand size and remained that shape for one second until it was at that point where the natural law of pressure took over and it was released in an explosion of organic matter, covering the walls, console, and the people in the room.

As the poor woman's headless body collapsed onto the floor, Cooper's lips turned up in disgust and she looked down at her blood-stained uniform. Barnes felt the contents of his stomach shift as he noticed that her hair and face were all covered with blood and organic matter. He looked down at himself and was disgusted to see that there were pieces of brain plastered over his uniform too. Cooper's face screwed up as she carefully reached up and picked pieces of skull out of her hair. She then looked up at the ceiling and shook her head in disgust, before turning her gaze back to the lifeless body that lay on the floor.

'You see what you made me do? You made me make a mess!' she screamed. Her eyes were full of rage as she kicked out at the headless corpse.

Fighting back the urge to vomit, Barnes could only stand and watch as Cooper continued to scream violently like a mad woman. He sensed she was starting to lose it as she repeatedly lashed out at the corpse on the floor.

'You ... know ... how ... I ... hate ... mess!' Cooper snarled, her chest heaving as she continued to kick at the headless corpse.

Not believing what he was seeing, Barnes watched in astonishment as Cooper then dropped to her knees and began pounding at the body with her fists. *By the Gods!* he thought to himself, *she's insane. We need to do something.*

Barnes turned to Lieutenant Akinjide, who returned his gaze with a look of confusion as he gestured in the general's direction. To his amazement, the lieutenant nodded in agreement. He watched as Akinjide moved closer to the raging Cooper and tapped her on her shoulder as he spoke gently at her, 'General, please. You need to sto—'

Unfortunately, Lieutenant Akinjide never got the chance to finish the sentence as without warning Cooper's head snapped round and gave him a look that would curdle milk. Barnes's eyes widened in alarm as he watched Cooper, her eyes full of rage, bellowed and then lunged at the unfortunate lieutenant, pushing him against the wall, with both of her hands clenched tightly around his neck.

'How dare you!' Her voice was full of fury as she raged at the poor man, 'How dare you touch your superior officer in such a way!' she snarled vehemently, 'You are pond scum, you do not touch me, ever! I will make your life a living hell for touching me in such an intimate way.'

Cooper grinned maniacally as Akinjide struggled in her grasp, gasping for air. Barnes could tell he was starting to black out as he watched Cooper's fingers tighten around his neck, 'I think a month in a re-education pod should teach you a lesson.' she licked her lips in sadistic pleasure, 'I'm going to enjoy listening to you suffer.'

Believing he had to intervene, Barnes reluctantly took one small step forward and coughed. Cooper turned to face him, blinked, turned back to the lieutenant and then back to Barnes.

'General, sorry but you are killing him, and high command frowns upon wasting excellent resources unnecessarily.' he said gravely, gesturing to the unfortunate soldier in her clutches.

Cooper's eyes glowered at Barnes, and he instinctively placed his hand on the thin collar around his neck. It was in that moment Barnes thought he going to die as he imagined he would be next to receive her wrath. But to his surprise Cooper let out a small bitter laugh, released her grip around the poor Lieutenant's throat, dropped her hands, and moved away from him.

'Yes, you are right.' Cooper sighed as she gave a small nod of reluctant agreement, 'These Gondwanian men make such magnificent warriors, it would be such a waste to dispose of such a necessary resource, especially since the Empire has put a lot of time and money into training them.'

Barnes watched as Lieutenant Akinjide slid down the wall, and collapse onto the floor, coughing. He lifted his head up to Barnes and gave him a grateful thin smile.

Cooper turned in a circle as she examined the blood-stained chamber and the headless body on the floor. She let out a heavy bitter sigh and shook head, 'What a mess!' She placed left hand on hip and a give small flick of her right hand at Barnes, 'Arrange for someone to clean this place up and then get yourself cleaned up too. It is so unfortunate that we got into this mess. Before you get yourself cleaned up, make sure Lieutenant Akinjide receives treatment.'

Without waiting for any acknowledgement, Cooper spun on her heel and marched toward the door. She activated the sensor beside the door and watched as it slid open. She paused and without turning back to the two men in the room, spoke firmly to them.

'There shall be no further mention of this incident, understood?' she said coolly and then without waiting for a reply, she continued to stride through the doorway.

As she exited the chamber and barrelled down the corridor, Cooper ignored the questioning glances that her bloodied appearance was receiving. Cooper smiled to herself. Her underlings knew better than to question her, because it was common knowledge to those who served near her - if they valued their lives, and that of their families, it was best to continue with what they were doing and act like nothing was out of the ordinary.

As she came to stop in front of a transport-pod door, she pressed her hand on the sensor on the wall and waited. Thirty seconds later, the transport-pod's doors opened, and she strode into the waiting pod. Suddenly, she became aware that two women were already standing inside. They glanced at her uncomfortably as her eyes bore into them and shot them a hard fixed stare.

One of the women smiled anxiously, coughed, and pointed to the open doorway, 'Ahem, sorry General. You can have this one, we'll get the next one.' Without waiting for confirmation, she dragged her protesting colleague with her as the doors slid to a close behind them.

Cooper placed her hand on a sensor as she spoke in a firm voice, 'Level 2. No stops. Security clearance Cooper Beta Omega One Nine Four Six.' She lowered her hand from the sensor and felt a slight shudder, followed by a faint hum as the pod began its ascent.

Less than a minute later the pod arrived at its destination and Cooper exited the doors into a small corridor which had a lone single door at the end. She rushed down the corridor and came to a stop at the door and placed her hand on the sensor on the wall. The sensor lit up and her head inched closer to the device as she spoke out loud.

'Cooper, Wendy.'.

There was a beep and the door in front of her slid open and she strode through the door into a long hall. Along each side of the hall, decorating the walls, hung various framed photos, medals, and commendations, showing her various conquests and achievements throughout her career.

The hall then opened out into an enormous living room. Gold-coloured tiles covered the living room floor. On the floor lay several large rugs, some were trophies of animals she had hunted and killed. A large black leather couch stood in the centre of the room. On each side of the couch stood two ornate tables, on the top of each was a bronze bust of her likeness. A large holographic fire stood at the base of the right wall opposite the couch, with a large, simulated fire blazing away. An enormous window made up the rear wall, in front of which stood a large ivory dining table. In the centre of the ceiling hung an enormous diamond encrusted chandelier, the sun's rays shone through the window onto the diamonds, casting a rainbow of colours on the wall. To the left hung a set of ornate doors leading to her bedroom.

'A glass of red wine, chilled.' she said out loud.

She watched as the food replicator hummed and a glass of red wine appeared. She strode over to the device, picked up the glass, took a small sip and smiled knowingly to herself.

A holographic image of a woman's featureless face appeared in front of Cooper and gave her a warm smile.

'How are we today, General?' she asked in a soft tone.

Cooper pursed her lips and cocked her head toward a small luminescent box on the dining table, 'I am good, Oracle.'

As she moved toward the large ornate bedroom doors, Cooper flung them open to reveal an enormous bedroom. Gold tiles covered the floor and in the centre of the room lay a large circular bed, with a large polar bear skin rug decorating the floor just in front of it. On the far wall, hung a large diamond encrusted mirror. To the right stood a door that led into a large walk-in wardrobe. A door leading to an ensuite bathroom was to her left.

'Did everything go as planned, Wendy?' Oracle asked in a curious tone.

'Yes, Oracle. You did well, thank you.' Cooper smiled knowingly.

'You're welcome.'

The corner of Cooper's mouth quirked as she listened to Oracle's reply and chuckled, 'Oracle, you have been my greatest achievement.'

Oracle; a sophisticated artificial intelligence, was designed in secret by Cooper, to act as a brain rather than a computer. Its vast sentient intellect used a predictive algorithm, allowing it to predict the future. It was Oracle that had aided the young ambitious officer throughout her career, assisting her in her quest for more power.

Carefully removing her blood-stained clothes, Cooper stood in front of the large mirror and tilted her head as she inspected her naked muscular body. She guided her hands down her firm breasts and over her muscular abdomen; her fingers following the various scars over her body.

As she next turned and slowly walked into her ensuite bathroom, a circular chamber opened in front of her, and she stood into the centre of the chamber as it closed around her.

'Oracle send a message to Lieutenant Akinjide.' she said quietly, 'Tell him I wish to see him in ten minutes.'

Oracle's image appeared in front of Cooper and beamed at her, 'Affirmative Wendy.'

Oracle's eyes sparkled as she sent a signal to activate the sonic shower. There was a faint hum from the chamber and Cooper let out a moan of pleasure at the sonic vibrations pulsing through her body, that began to slowly increase in rhythm.

Five minutes later, feeling more refreshed and invigorated, Cooper stepped out of the bathroom, picked up her robe and wrapped it around herself.

'Did you enjoy that, Wendy?' Oracle's eyes appeared to glow as she gave Cooper a warm smile.

'Yes, my darling.' Cooper moaned and gave a small satisfactory nod, 'You know me so well.' Becoming more serious she shot the hologram a stern look, 'Lieutenant Akinjide will arrive any minute. Whatever happens, you are to remain silent. Understood?'

'I understand.' Oracle said in compliance.

Oracle's image disappeared and, carrying her wine glass, Cooper sauntered back into the living room and sat on her couch. She raised her arm up, placed her elbow on the arm and rested her head on her hand as she gazed out through the window, deep in thought.

Cooper's reverie was broken by a beeping noise coming from the direction of the door.

'Yes, who is it?' A smile danced on Cooper's lips as she heard a male voice on her intercom.

'*General. It is I, Lieutenant Akinjide. I received a message. You asked to see me.*'

Cooper gave a half-smile and pressed a button on her wrist communicator, and heard the door slid open. She cocked her head as she heard heavy footsteps coming from the hall and twisted her head to see Lieutenant Akinjide marching into the living room.

'General.' he greeted, clicking his heels together in salute.

'At ease.' Cooper commanded, waving her hand as she slowly rose from her seat and sauntered over to him, beaming.

Akinjide cocked his head at Cooper and gave her a lopsided grin, 'Did I do well, General?'

Cooper paused in front of him, gave him a brief nod and her hand touched his face, as she leaned in close to him, and kissed his thick lips, 'Your performance was remarkable, Kalifa.' she breathed heavily, 'I guess Colonel Barnes never suspected a thing.'

Kalifa grinned, pulled his head back and let out a loud laugh, 'No General. He appeared to be clueless.'

As she pulled him forward and kissed him passionately on the lips, Cooper's heart skittered as she felt Kalifa's firm hands reach into her gown and touch her breasts. She gave him a hard slap on the face and smiled as she watched his nostrils flare in annoyance. He then moved back, his face a mixture of shock and surprise.

As Cooper let her gaze wander over Kalifa's rugged face, she smiled as she noticed that the veins on his neck were throbbing. He wanted her. No, he didn't just want her, she could tell he was craving her. She shook her head and grinned. She was going to torture him, make him work for it. As she moved into the bedroom, she deliberately let her rob slip off her body. Pausing in the bedroom doorway, she glanced over her shoulder and waggled her finger teasingly. She smiled as she watched Kalifa lick his hips and then move slowly over to her.

As he gently reached forward to touch her breasts with his hands,

Cooper slapped them away. She then strolled over to the bed, lay herself down on top of it and gave him a piercing stare as she pointed her finger at him.

'Take your clothes off.' she whispered in a tone that was both firm and playful as she pointed to the rug on the floor, 'Then I want you to lie on the rug.'

After he had slowly removed his clothes with inviting purpose, Cooper's breath quickened with desire as the light shone off his toned muscular black body and thick arms. Then, as he lay himself on the rug, he lifted his head, let out a small seductive snarl. Standing directly over him, Cooper licked her lips as she watched his body come to attention and felt her heart slam against the inside of chest in desperate need. She then slowly lowered herself down on him.

His face scrunched up in orgasmic pleasure, Kalifa collapsed onto the top Cooper's glistening body and buried his face into the side of her neck. They lay entwined in one another for a few minutes, before he rolled himself off and lay on his back, his chest rising and falling.

Her body sleek with sweat, Cooper twisted onto her side and rested her head beside Kalifa's as she nibbled his ear. 'Does anybody else know?' she asked breathlessly.

His eyes still closed, Kalifa shook his head and gave her a knowing smile, 'No, General. I told no-one.'

Cooper's eyebrows joined together as the corners of her mouth lifted in a tiny malevolent smile. She then kissed Kalifa passionately as she playfully ran her fingers over his thin obedience collar and then led them down his chiselled body. A smile danced on her lips as her fingers came to his still erect manhood. She grinned as she plucked at his pubic hair and listened to his squeal of pain. She lifted her head up to him and grinned coyly at him.

'Does he still want to play?' she whispered excitedly.

Kalifa wordlessly nodded and smiled as Cooper climbed on top of him. She bit her bottom lip as she felt him enter her once again. As she leaned over him, she deliberately pushed her breasts into his face, and then let out a moan of pleasure as she felt his teeth bite one of her nipples. She stretched her arms out, touched the head of the rug and slid her fingers inside the open mouth, wrapping them around the knife that she had kept hidden inside. She then pulled her arm back, straightened her back and then in one fluid motion she sliced through Kalifa's neck, severing his carotid artery.

She watched as Kalifa's eyes grew wide with astonishment. His hands reached up to his neck and then he looked at Cooper in confusion as blood continued to seep through his fingers. With the small scalpel still clutched tightly in her hand, she stared down at Kalifa through cold eyes down as he gasped for air. She could see the panic in his eyes as she felt his blood covered hands scratch at her body.

Not done with him yet, Cooper grabbed Kalifa's hands and held them down as his body writhed desperately beneath her. His warm blood continued to spray out over her, covering her body in a crimson like body-paint. She squeezed her eyes shut and moaned in pleasure as she felt the dying man writhe beneath her. Her lips curled up in morbid pleasure as she gyrated against the manhood that was still inside her. Then Kalifa's body became deathly still and the life in his eyes faded. Cooper leaned forward, kissed the dead man's handsome face, and slowly got up.

'Oracle, please dispose of the body.' she commanded.

'Yes, my love.' Oracle replied.

Still naked and covered in blood, Cooper gingerly strolled into the living room. She paused in front of the window as her left hand reached up and lingered over her bloodied pain collar and tapped her fingers on it pensively. She lowered her left arm and pressed a button on her wrist communicator. A holographic image of Barnes, kneeling in front of a synthroid, appeared in front of her.

Cooper lips formed a contemptuous sneer as she listened to him speak to the creature.

'*Hello old friend. I have a job for you; one I think you might enjoy.*'

Her lips pressed together into an evil smile, Cooper tapped her finger on a button on the wrist communicator and the image of Barnes disappeared.

'It had been a shame to waste such a delicious specimen like Lieutenant Akinjide.' she sighed to herself in bemusement, 'He played his part well, but he had served his purpose and had become a loose end that needed taken care of.' She smiled malevolently to herself as she tapped a button on her wrist communicator and stared at the image of Henrietta, 'It had been fun seducing Henrietta, gaining her trust and manipulating her into making a *mistake.*' she chuckled out loud to Oracle, 'She had been so easy to play with, not that it wasn't fun. I knew well beforehand of Henrietta's pain fetish. It was during our violent lovemaking, using an obedience collar, that we came up with the idea to torture poor her in front of Colonel Barnes. The silly woman even came up with the whole scenario!' She pulled her head back and let out a loud maniacal laugh, 'The poor woman was so infatuated with me, she had failed to see that she was being used until it was too late. Kalifa and Henrietta had both played their parts well in pushing Colonel Barnes in the direction that will lead to his downfall.'

Cooper lapsed into silence as she gazed out through the window into city below. She turned her slightly as Oracle's image appeared behind her.

'Everything is going to plan, Oracle.' She smiled and let out a small contemptuous snort, 'Barnes is weak and so easy to manipulate. He believes he is so clever, but the fool doesn't realise he is just a pawn in a long game.' She tilted her inquiringly at the holographic image, 'Are we still proceeding on schedule?'

Oracle nodded her holographic head in confirmation, 'Yes, my love. Project Mors is proceeding on schedule. In one year, we will initiate the Mors Protocol, as planned.'

Cooper smiled to herself and stared down at the city below her. The setting sun cast an eerily red glow as the city's lights started to shine in the twilight.

'High Command are weak.' she growled, her voice thick with contempt, 'They see Counter-Terra as a resource to be used in their war against the Greater Chinese Republic.' She paused as a holographic image of Counter-Terra appeared before her. Her cold emerald eyes narrowed as she stretched out hands over her head and sneered at the rotating sphere, 'I see it as a world to rule as my own. In one year, I shall burn this world and from the ashes I will arise, Empress Cooper, ruler of Counter-Terra!'

As the holographic Counter-Terra continued to spin above her, Cooper reached up and gently touched the moving image with her hand as her evil laugh continued to reverberate around the room.

19

Forty minutes earlier…..

Barnes watched as the door slid down behind the General and let out a harsh breath, shaking his head, sadly, as he thought to himself, *that woman terrifies me.* He knew Cooper was ambitious and, from his experience, anybody who stood in her way usually ended up regretting it.

Inhaling a deep breath, his fingers massaged his forehead as he closed his eyes and contemplated how he had reached that point in his life.

David Barnes had spent his life serving the Empire faithfully, his military career spanning forty years. Like most who served the Empire, they had taken him from his family at a young age. He had been eight years old when his family had sold him into service. The children of the Empire were given a choice; serve in the military or become a slave. From early childhood, the young Barnes had developed a natural survival instinct and when it came his time came to choose, his instinct told him to choose the military. He was quickly placed into a military academy, as was the standard for children who had opted to serve.

Life in the Empire's military academy was harsh, and the instructors were tough, drilling students morning, noon and night, and punishment for failure was severe. Only the fittest survived.

It was during his time at the academy where he had learned the most important lesson – survival.

While most the students yearned to be the top dog and fought for leadership, the young Barnes instinctively observed from the shadows, unnoticed, while others placed themselves forward, becoming a target for other ambitious children.

The scheming Barnes learned the best way to survive was through deception and manipulation. He quickly learned how to become close to those in leadership and whisper in their ear from the shadows. He was happy to stand back while others took the credit.

As he became older, his actions attracted the attention of a visiting general who had witnessed the young rascal from a distance and took a keen interest in the teenager. So as soon as Barnes turned eighteen years of age the general bought him out of the academy and took him under his wing.

General Trialus was a kind man and had treated his protégé like a son, teaching him valuable lessons in military strategy and deception. It was here where he had also learned another important lesson: that knowledge was power.

From the shadows Barnes learned with keen interest at how his mentor had manipulated people for his own gain. He taught him how to get close to people, how to hack into their systems to learn their secrets and when the time was right, to use it against them.

As the years passed, with his proud mentor watching, the young apprentice became more proficient in the art of manipulation, deception and intelligence gathering. Eventually it developed into a competition between them both, with each one trying to outdo the other.

Then one day it was Trialus's pride that led to his downfall. He had taught his apprentice so well that he failed to see his protégé's deadly nature until it was too late. In his eyes, Barnes acknowledged that his mentor had become too small for his own ambition and if he was to rise further in the ranks, then he needed to be with somebody whose ambition for power rivalled his own.

Barnes came up with a scheme to frame Trialus by placing an encrypted file on his personal mainframe, indicating that he had been working for the resistance. Then, it was a simple matter of contacting the security division and feigning deep concern that he was worried his master was working against the Empire's interests. The security officer had been a simple man, arrogant, easy to manipulate and deceive. Barnes even made it look like the arrogant fool had found the information himself. The obnoxious oaf had been so easy to manipulate that he even believed he had found the evidence all by himself.

From the shadows Barnes watched as they placed Trialus in electro chains and led him away to the security shuttle. As the shuttle door closed, Barnes stepped out into the light and caught Trialus's attention. As they stared at each other briefly, Trialus gave a knowing smile and bowed his head in silent acknowledgement as he realised the student had become the master.

Barnes later learned his former mentor had been taken to the lunar prison, as was the standard for those charged of treason within the Empire, where they held him without trial and found him immediately guilty. In the Empire, those found guilty of treason are brutally executed by spacing.

Spacing is a slow and painful way to die. The terrified elderly man had his clothes stripped off him and was forced to stand naked in an airlock as they ejected him into space. As Trialus's body drifted into space, the oxygen in his body would have expanded. His body would have ballooned up to twice his normal size, but his body would not have exploded, as human skin is elastic, it would have held his body together. Trialus would not have died immediately: all the liquid in his body would have vaporised. The surface of his tongue and eyes would have boiled and because there would have been no air in his lungs, there would have been

Double Jeopardy

no oxygen going to his brain. Ninety seconds after being ejected into space Trialus would then have died from asphyxiation and then his body would have drifted for eternity, frozen solid.

The young Lieutenant Barnes did not suffer from any remorse after he learned what happened to his elderly mentor. To him, he had been a means to an end.

For his part, in the arrest of a high-profile traitor, the investigating officer was quickly promoted and, to show his appreciation, offered the scheming lieutenant a place in his team. Through time, using his skill in deceit and manipulation, Barnes carefully rose in rank.

After eventually learning of a rising young officer, who had gained a fierce reputation in the ongoing conflict with the Greater China Republic, earning her the admiration of the High Command. Desperate to be noticed, Barnes expertly placed himself within the young officer's circle and within minutes of meeting her, he knew Colonel Cooper's ambition rivalled his own and secretly helped the ambitious woman achieve the rank of general.

Soon after the High Command had promoted Cooper to general, and with the help of Barnes' manipulation, she was appointed as commander of the portal project. However, as their work with the project increased, the colonel's concerns deepened while he watched Cooper's ambitions rise to dangerous levels.

Barnes opened his eyes, squared his shoulders, and blew out a long breath. *I think the time has come*, he thought to himself. His hands rubbed at his temples in resignation as he thought about the difficult decision he had been forced to reach, *I need to take care of her before she takes me down with her, but I cannot do it alone.*

He peered down at Lieutenant Akinjide, who was sitting on the floor with his back against the wall panting, massaging his neck with his hands.

'Are you okay, lieutenant?' Barnes asked with a sympathetic tone as he extended his hand to Akinjide, 'Get up son, I'll take you to medical to get examined and cleaned up.'

The lieutenant gave a grateful nod as he took Barnes's hand and stood up. 'Thank you, sir.' His voice was hoarse as he leaned against the older man, 'The General gets ... excitable, doesn't she?'

Barnes scowled and gave a small grunt as he helped the unsteady soldier over to the console. After making sure Akinjide could stand unaided, Barnes pressed his finger on a button on the bracelet on his left wrist. The device gave a small beep and lit up as a small holographic image of a woman's face appeared.

'I need a clean-up crew in the portal chamber, immediately.' Barnes barked, his face hardening as he gave the woman a frosty look, 'The General needs this done efficiently and quietly. Nobody is to discuss what they see here, understood?'

The olive-skinned woman nodded grimly, 'Roger that!'.

Without making any further comment, Barnes pressed a button on the communicator and the image blinked off.

Barnes then guided Lieutenant Akinjide over to the doorway and moved back as the door whooshed open. They both stepped out into the busy corridor.

As he moved into the corridor, Barnes could tell he was receiving curious glances from people that were passing, but nobody stopped and commented, at least openly. Of course, Barnes was aware of the reason for this – those who served in the Empire knew better than to stop and ask questions when they saw something unusual.

Barnes turned gestured at the two soldiers who were standing on guard duty outside the portal chamber door, 'This man needs to go to medical now.' he ordered, clicking his fingers at nearest soldier, 'You! Take him quickly, now, and then return to your post as soon as it has been done.'

The broad-shouldered soldier stepped forward, snapped his heels in salute, and then assisted Lieutenant Akinjide down the corridor into an open transport-pod door.

As he stood in the corridor, Barnes gradually became aware of the curious glances he was receiving from people as they moved past him. Suddenly remembering he was still covered in blood, he quickly dashed down to the corridor, stopped at the transport-pod door, and slapped his hand on the sensor on the wall.

Thirty seconds later the pod's doors opened and as he was about to walk in but he became aware that somebody was behind him. He spun sharply round and let out a small *oomph* as a distracted technician, a short curly-haired blond woman smacked into him. The annoyed technician peered up from her tablet and opened her mouth as if to hurl indignant abuse at the person responsible but suddenly found herself lost for words. The colour drained from her thin face and her eyes widened in horror as she recognised the blood covered man in front of her.

'You get the next one!' Barnes snapped in a tone that indicated it was not up for discussion.

The petite woman opened her mouth to protest but a withering look from Barnes made her to take a large gulp of air as she promptly re-evaluated her choices.

Whether it was because she realised who she had bumped into, or because of Barnes's bloodied appearance, the poor woman gave a wry smile, lifted her finger and dropped her head. Barnes watched as she wordlessly took a step back and the pod's doors closed in front of her.

As soon as the doors closed, Barnes put his hand on the sensor and spoke in a firm tone, 'Level 3, no stops. Security Clearance Alpha Gemini Taurus One Six Draco!'

The pod shuddered briefly, and Barnes heard a small hum as it sped down the shaft.

Less than a minute later the transport-pod came to a stop, and the doors slid open, allowing Barnes to exit. After casting a swift glance down the empty corridor, he dashed toward his quarters and came to a stop in front of a sensor panel on the wall. As he reached forward and placed his hand on the scanner, it lit up and gave a small beep.

'Barnes, David.' Barnes said in a soft but clear tone.

As the door swished open, there was a small welcoming chime followed by a synthetic female voice coming from out of the scanner's speaker, 'Hand print recognised. Voice print recognised. Welcome home, David.'

Barnes let out a small grunt of acknowledgement as he strode into his quarters and the door slid to a close behind him.

'Lights, fifty percent.' He barked.

As he walked further into his quarters he blinked as the lights came on, giving the room a warm glow. His head turned as he inspected his quarters. It was a fairly spacious living room. There was a small window on the far wall. In the middle of the living room, stood a small leather sofa. On a wall in front of the sofa, hung a large flat-screen monitor. On the opposite wall, a holographic fireplace simulated a raging fire. On the wall beside him there was a small dining table, with a food replicator fixed into the wall above it. A door to the right of him led to a small bedroom.

After placing his wrist communicator and sidearm on the table, Barnes marched into the bedroom and removed his clothes, dropping them into a laundry hatch on the wall. He then entered the ensuite bathroom, stood in front of a circular chamber and heard a faint hum as the sonic shower activated. As he rested his arms on the chamber wall and hung his head, he let out a small, relieved sigh as he felt the sonic vibrations pulse through his body, removing the blood and dirt from his skin and hair.

Barnes closed his eyes and relaxed his shoulders as he felt the therapeutic vibrations massaging his entire body. As he stood waiting for the sonic shower to finish, his hand brushed up against the obedience collar around his neck distractedly. His mouth then curved into a wicked smile as an idea slowly formed in his head.

Twenty minutes later, a clean and fully clothed Barnes marched back into his living room. After picked up his sidearm and communicator off the table, he slotted the weapon in his side holster and clicked the communicator into place around his wrist.

Barnes moved toward the food replicator and ordered a pre-programmed meal. A plate, consisting of meat, vegetables and potatoes, and a cup of hot coffee materialised in front of him. He picked up the plate and cup, carried them over to the table. As he ate, his brow furrowed in thoughtful contemplation while he ran through his idea in his head.

Ten minutes later, after putting the empty plate and cup on the replicator, Barnes spun around and moved toward the main door.

'Open.' he barked and watched as the door whooshed open. He paused in the doorway as he twisted his head over his shoulder and called out, 'Lights off.'

As the doors slid to close behind him, Barnes turned and rushed down the corridor toward the turbo-lift doors, stopping in front of the sensor on the wall so he could summon it.

Thirty seconds later the turbo-lift door slid open as the pod arrived. Amazed to find it was empty, Barnes called out in a loud authoritative voice, 'Level 15. No stops. Security Clearance Alpha Gemini Taurus One Six Draco!'

Again, the small pod shuddered briefly, followed by a faint hum as it sped to its destination. There was small jolt as it braked and came to stop, followed by the doors sliding open to reveal a dimly lit corridor.

As Barnes moved out in the corridor and approached a door marked with the words "*Caution*". He paused, placed his hand on the sensor and watched as the door slid open.

Taking a careful step forward, Barnes squinted as his eyes adjusted to the gloomy chamber. Hearing a hiss come from beside him, he turned his head and saw a thin blue energy barrier, with a black shiny skinned creature pacing on the other side of it.

His upper lip curled as he held up his right hand and there was cackle of electricity as the energy barrier shimmered in response. The synthroid cocked its head inquiringly and hissed.

Initially, the synthroids were engineered by the Empire for the sole purpose of being foot soldiers in their war against the Greater China Republic, but the Empire found the creatures were too uncontrollable on the battlefield. However, despite their volatile nature, it was discovered the creatures had one redeeming quality – they were excellent trackers. From that moment on, the synthroids had been breed for one specific purpose: to hunt.

When the portal to Counter-Terra was discovered, the Empire was surprised to discover the creatures could survive that world's hostile environment. It was not longer after that they decided that they would send the creatures to Counter-Terra, to not only gather intelligence and but also collect samples of the hormone that would allow people from their world to travel to Counter-Terra and survive.

The synthroid bowed its head and hissed, 'Baaarrnness.'

After he had deactivated the containment barrier, Barnes knelt in front of the creature and the corners of his eyes creased as a smile danced on his lips. 'Hello old friend.' He whispered in a soothing tone, extending his hand and scratching the synthroid's head, 'I have a job for you, I think you might enjoy.'

The synthroid let out a small hiss of pleasure.

20

Secret Command Centre Known As The Castle – Location Unknown

*Y*ou bitch, I'm going to kill you!'

Dave felt powerless as he watched Claire, her face a picture of pure rage, charge at Wendy. From the wide-eyed look of disbelief that was on Wendy's face, he didn't have be genius to see she hadn't been expecting that reaction. He tried to reach out to stop her, but to his surprise he realised she was too fast for him as she shot by him.

Wendy's round face was a mixture of shock and confusion as Claire hurtled toward her, arms outstretched. There was no doubt in Dave's mind what Claire's intent was. However, Wendy towered over Claire by a good six inches, and he guessed she must outweigh her by a good stone at least, so he knew Wendy wasn't in any real danger.

He wasn't sure if was her training, or if she was acting on instinct, but as Dave watched Wendy grab hold of Claire's wrist, he knew what was coming next – because he'd seen the same move performed plenty of times during self-defence training. The idea was simple, a person could use their attacker's momentum against them and swing them over their shoulder. Wendy performed the manoeuvre flawlessly, sending Claire the crashing to the floor. She followed it up by pressing her knee into Claire's back.

'You bitch.' Her glasses askew, Claire's large sky-blue eyes burned with rage as she screamed up at Wendy. She grimaced as she tried to pull herself up, 'Let go of me.'

'Claire, calm down.' Wendy's tone was gentle but firm as she struggled with the angry Claire, 'The more you struggle, the more it will hurt, and I don't want to hurt you.'

'Yeah, well, I really want to hurt you!' Claire screamed back indignantly.

Dave took a small step closer and placed his hand on Wendy's shoulder. 'Let her go, Wendy.' His tone was firm but also held a touch of anger.

Wendy glanced at Dave and gave him a small nod of acknowledgement. He guessed she must have realised from his tone that it was not a request as she he watched quickly release her grip. As she stood up and moved away, Claire spun over onto her back and gave Wendy a look that could kill.

As Dave held out his hand and helped her up from the floor, Claire's face contorted in fury, and she tried to charge Wendy. But this time Dave was quick enough as his hand shot out and grabbed her arm, stopping her. She twisted her head at and scowled at him.

'Calm down, Claire.' Dave said in a gentle but firm voice.

Claire exhaled in resignation, relaxed, and slowly turned away from Wendy, who let out a deep sigh of relief and smiled in gratitude at Dave.

'Thank you, Guv.' she said as she put her hand on his arm gratefully.

But Dave wasn't having any of it. He angrily snapped his arm away from Wendy, 'Oh, I didn't do it for you.' His nostrils flared as he took a step forward and lifted his fist up to her threateningly, 'To be honest Cooper, I am ready to knock you on your arse. I don't know whether I am angry or disappointed. How could you betray us like this? I trusted you!'

The hurt and shock evident in her eyes, Wendy moved back Dave and stared silently at him for a second, before shaking her head and letting out a despondent sigh, 'Sorry Gov, but I was under orders. I couldn't tell you.' She held up hands against her chest and looked at him pleadingly, 'Please sir, the last thing I wanted to do was to hurt you, especially you Claire, but I had no choice.'

'Ordered by who?' Dave snapped. The centre of his eyebrows met together as he stared at Wendy through suspicious eyes.

'That would be me?'

Dave spun round on hearing an authoritative sounding woman's voice coming from him. He frowned as he thought odd Cambridgeshire accent sounded familiar and he had forgotten there been somebody else in the room when they first walked in. As he turned to look at who was speaking, he felt his jaw drop open in shock. He did a double take then glanced at Claire and saw she was just as equally stunned as him. He shook his head in disbelief. No it couldn't be her?

The attractive black woman stood up from her chair and smiled warmly at the couple. She was a middle-aged, tall, and slender woman with long shoulder length black hair and was wearing dark trousers, a dark open jacket with a white blouse. She raised an eyebrow as Dave continued to stare at her with open-mouthed shock, and then let out small a small laugh, 'You realise, there are many people who would want to pay a lot of money to see two women wrestle.' she said jokingly, winking.

Dave opened his mouth to speak but was lost for words, he swallowed as he tried to regain his composure, but all he could do was stammer, 'S … s… sorry. I … I …'

'What's wrong? Have I got something on me?' The woman asked curiously. She lowered her head to peer down at herself and chuckled, her hazel eyes twinkling in mischief. She then moved from behind the desk and stepped closer to the speechless couple and offered her hand.

'Let's start again.' she said in a bemused tone. Her piercing white teeth gleamed as she grabbed Dave's hand and shook it firmly, 'Hi, I am Sophia Collins, Prime Minister.'

'Yes, ma'am. I recognised you.' Dave replied and gave a small nod while he shook her hand, 'I'm Detective Inspector Dave Barnes.'

'Yes, I know.' Sophia answered cryptically, the corners of mouth curling up knowingly. She then turned to Claire and offered her hand, 'Professor Claire Tulley, I presume. It is good to finally meet you.'

Claire's eyes widened in surprise as she shook the prime minister's hand, 'Thank you, Prime Minister. Forgive my surprise, but I didn't realise you were aware of me.'

Sophia gave a brief nod, smiled, and tapped Claire's hand sadly, 'Yes, we are aware of you. We've been monitoring you for some time. Your tenacity at getting to the truth during your investigation into your sister's death has impressed many people here.' She exhaled a long sigh and shook her head sadly, 'Unfortunately, as you've discovered, it has come at a cost.'

Claire's glared icily at Sophia through narrow eyes and her top lip curled up in a sneer, 'Yes. I am sure you are perfectly aware of the cost.'

The smile faded from Sophia's face as she detected the change in the Claire's tone, stepped back and raised her hands apologetically, 'Please forgive me, but that was not my doing and beyond my control.'

'Forgive me, Prime Minister.' Dave interjected, trying to change the subject, 'But aren't you supposed to be in the United States at the moment?'

Sophia twisted her head and for a moment Dave could swear there was a hint of sadness in her eyes. For the first time, he noticed there was a tired weariness emanating from her. 'That is …' she paused as she gave a wry smile to Claire, 'complicated, but I suspect Professor Tulley already knows the answer though. I know you all have questions. Don't worry, we will explain everything shortly.'

Without waiting for a response, Sophia motioned to Wendy, who had been standing patiently beside her, 'Inspector Barnes, Professor Tulley. Please don't be too mad at PC Cooper.' she said apologetically and held her hand up to her chest, 'She was only following my orders. Please, as a favour to me, go easy on her. Also, please accept my apologies in the way they brought you in. We had to do it quickly with nobody seeing.' she raised her arm and placed it on Wendy's arm, 'Now if you excuse me a minute. I just need to speak to Cooper privately for a second.'

Dave gave a polite nod as he watched Sophia wrap her right arm around Wendy's left arm and then guided her to the other side of the room. He tapped his chin thoughtfully as he wondered what they were discussing. There seemed to be a lot going on here and Sophia's presence only made him even more curious. He blinked as he felt Claire's hand touch his arm and he looked at her questioningly.

'You any idea what's on going on here?' She asked in a hushed whisper.

'Damned if I know.' he answered, shrugging his shoulders, 'but I'm sure we will find out soon enough.'

Claire frowned and he could tell she was desperate to know more. But as she opened her to mouth ask him something, Dave raised his finger to lips to shush her as he noticed the two women had stopped speaking and were making their back over. He gave Sophia a polite nod as she came to stop in front of him.

'Now, Detective Inspector Barnes and Professor Tulley,' Sophia said cheerfully, clapping her hands together, 'please excuse me, I've an urgent matter to deal with.' She waved a hand to Wendy, 'I am sure there are things you need to discuss with Cooper. I will be in the conference room when you are ready.'

Without waiting for a response, Sophia spun on her heel and marched with purpose out of the room. Dave exchanged an uncomfortable look with Claire and then to Wendy. He shifted on feet uncomfortably, unwilling to make the first move. After about a minute, Wendy coughed and then smiled anxiously at him.

'Well, I suppose I better start before Claire gets the idea to charge me again.' she grinned. Her smile disappeared as Claire answered with a snort of disgust.

'Yeah, as much as I enjoyed seeing a cat fight, it was definitely one sided.' Dave laughed and scratched his head as he felt tension in the room ease slightly.

Claire folded her arms across her chest, shook her head, and let out a long breath, but continued to glower angrily at Wendy. 'I don't know whether I can forgive you just yet.' Her tone was flat as she shot Wendy a long hard stare and gave her a small shrug, 'But go ahead, you talk, and I will listen. After that, I cannot promise anything.'

'Fair enough.' Wendy replied as she gave a small understanding nod and motioned to the chairs around the small conference table, 'Please sit. I can tell you what I know. The Prime Minister kindly arranged for some food for you to eat, since you probably didn't get the chance to eat breakfast before they brought you here.'

Suddenly realising he had not eaten, Dave's hand touched his stomach in surprise as he felt it rumble. As he looked over to the food on the table, he was suddenly aware at how hungry he felt. Surprised to see a continental style buffet had been set out ready for them, he glanced across to Claire, who just shrugged and gave him an indifferent nod. They walked over to the chairs and sat down to eat. Wendy pulled up a chair and but remained silent as Dave and Claire ate.

After he had enough to eat, Dave pushed his plate to one side, placed his elbows on the table, and steepled his fingers together as he stared at Claire thoughtfully. Wendy lifted her head up to him, met his eyes and she bit her bottom lip as she dropped her eyes sheepishly. He could tell he probably needed to break the uncomfortable silence and spoke first.

'So ...' Dave asked hesitantly, 'who are you working for, Wendy? Are you really a police officer?' The muscles in his face tightened as he looked closer at her, 'And more importantly, why were you spying on me?'

'Guv, I am a real police officer!' Wendy snapped. Her face quickly turned the colour of scarlet and she raised her hands up in front her, 'Sorry, didn't mean to snap at you, but I am sure you can imagine it has been quite stressful for me. Anyway, I wasn't sent to spy on you. I attended police training college, just like you. Unlike you, MI6 approached me when I graduated. They told me that I had impressed them during my training and told me they were interested in recruiting me, but I would still work for the police force. They would choose my placement, all they asked was that I keep an eye out for anything unusual. They also told me that somebody would contact me if they needed me for an assignment.'

Dave gave a small nod of understanding and held up his right hand with his index finger pointing up, 'Let me guess, they placed you in

Durham Constabulary.'

Wendy gave a slight nod of acknowledgement and let out a long breath as she held up her hands in front of her, 'Well, I am sure you can imagine. When you are a young graduate, to be recruited by MI6 is a dream come true. I grabbed at the chance. For three years I served and nothing unusual happened.' She paused as she lifted her head and stared up at the ceiling with a look of sadness, 'That was until the other night, when I investigated a noise disturbance in Langley Park. At the time I just assumed it was a routine murder case, but that changed for me after talking to you.'

Dave closed his eyes and bobbed his head in realisation as he began to put it all together in his head. 'Let me guess.' he asked speculatively, 'MI6 contacted you.'

'Sort of Guv.' Wendy answered, waving her hand in a vague gesture. She took in a long breath and slowly blew out her cheeks, 'During my working hours my time is spent at the station, but I spend most of my off-duty hours here at this facility, so I am always in contact with them in some way. But it wasn't until the other night where I was summoned to see the senior staff. It was then that I was informed they wanted me to get assigned to the case with you, and to report anything unusual back to them.' She straightened up in her chair, placed her hands on the table and leaned to Dave, 'I am sorry if you assume I was spying on you both.' she leaned back and held out her hands in front of her. She then scoffed, squeezed her hands into fists and threw her hands up in the air in frustration, 'I was just doing what they ordered me to – to investigate the case with you. At no time was I ordered to do anything else, believe me. To be honest, I am as much in the dark as you.'

Dave rubbed his hands through his hair and pressed his lips together. Would he have done any different if their situations were reversed? He reluctantly conceded to himself that he was being too hard on Wendy, that she was only doing her duty. He then stood up and strode over to Wendy and offered his hand to her. 'I perfectly understand the pressure you were under, Wendy.' He winked and punched her playfully in the shoulder, 'Sorry if I gave you a hard time there. No hard feelings?'

Wendy beamed as she rubbed her shoulder and took his hand,

'None taken Guv. I hope I haven't lost your trust?'

Dave gave her a wry smile and shrugged, 'To be honest Wendy, it proves to me what type of person you are and, if you don't mind, when this is over, I would like to make your transfer permanent.' The corners of his mouth quirked up as he gave her a sly wink, 'So long as I have your *handler's* permission.' He pulled his head back and let out a loud laugh as Wendy's face turned crimson with embarrassment.

'Ahem!'

On hearing an annoyed sounding cough coming from behind him, Dave cocked his head to Claire. To his shame he had forgotten all about her. As he stared at her expressionless face, he wondered what was going that mind of hers. He swallowed nervously as he watched her slowly rise of her seat and take several purposely small steps up to Wendy, stopping in front of her. There was a noticeable height distance between the women, with the imposing younger woman's six-foot-three athletic body giving her the advantage over the smaller woman's five-foot-seven curvy body, but Claire's piercing stare was still enough to make Wendy shift on her feet uncomfortably.

Wendy blinked at Claire uncomfortably, lowered her head and then turned away from her, 'Claire … I …'

Claire remained silent as she gave a small shake of her head and took Wendy's hands in hers and then smiled warmly as she pulled her close to hug her. Then, much to Dave's surprise, he watched as she carefully reached up and placed her hands on either side of Wendy's face, stood on her tip toes and then kissed her on the cheek.

'I am sorry for attacking you earlier.' Claire murmured softly, 'I've been so angry over what has been happening to me lately. The thought you had betrayed us was the last straw. Please forgive me.'

Wendy shook her head furiously and pointed her finger to herself, 'No, I should be the one apologising. I hope I didn't hurt you when I tried to restrain you. Sorry, I just acted on instinct.'

Claire pulled her head back and let out a small laugh as she rubbed her shoulder with her hand, 'I will probably have a bruise to show for that later.' There was small audible gasp from Wendy as she punched her in the shoulder, grinning, 'Let's call it even.'

Dave coughed and groaned impatiently, 'Oh, for God's sake!' The two women turned and gave him a questioning look, 'Are we finished with this over display of emotion?' He asked impatiently and jerked his thumb toward the closed door. 'Do you remember there is a small matter of trying to find out why we are here. Also, I am sure the squad room are probably wondering where I am.' He frowned and scratched his head thoughtfully, 'That reminds me, we need to bring Andy in on this. I am surprised you didn't bring him in too?'

Wendy cocked her head at Dave, raised her hand and pointed to the ceiling above them, 'Well, we are in an abandoned complex under Durham Castle. The Prime Minister will explain to us what this place is when we meet back up with her.' She lifted her shoulder in a small shrug, 'I got a message through to the office and told them we were investigating a lead.' She paused and the smile disappeared from her face as she stared at Dave unhappily, 'Guv, there is something you need to know about Andy … he … sir …'

'Cooper, what's happened? Is he okay?' Dave interrupted with heavy concern. He felt his stomach wrench as he thought he saw something in Wendy's tears-filled eyes.

'I think it is best I show you, Guv.' she whispered gravely.

Feeling the blood drain from his face, Dave staggered back from Wendy. Claire moved up beside him and placed her hand in his. He glanced at her and smiled sadly, then his eyes narrowed as he gave Wendy a pained look.

'Show me… now.' he asked in a tone that was almost pleading.

Wendy sighed and nodded sadly, 'This way.'

As Dave followed Wendy out through the doors, he watched as she lowered her voice and then said something to a barrel-chested soldier who standing on guard outside the room. Without saying a word, the burly soldier escorted the trio down the corridor that they had just come down minutes earlier and then continued up a flight of stairs, coming to stop outside a set of double doors. Dave felt his heart jump up into his throat as he noticed on the wall beside the door there was a sign marked "I*nfirmary*".

Wendy pushed open the double doors and went through them, with Dave and Claire following close behind. As he passed through the doors, Dave found himself standing inside what appeared to be a hospital ward, comprised of twelve hospital beds, six on each side, with a small office at the far end of the room. Most of the beds looked like they were empty apart from one at the far end of the room, which had the curtains closed around it. Going off what he had seen so far of the building architecture and the style of the beds on the ward, Dave guessed the facility they were in must have been built in sometime during 1960s.

Three army nurses walked around the ward doing various jobs. A bald white man wearing a white medical coat spotted the three people as they entered and hurried up to them. He was short, fifty-something, and wore small circular glasses. He smiled warmly at Wendy as she walked up to him.

'Doctor Porter.' Wendy said in greeting, turned and then introduced the two people beside her, 'This is Detective Inspector Barnes and Professor Tulley. We are here to see Sergeant Jenkins.'

Doctor Porter's lips turned up in a sad knowing smile and gave them a small nod as he motioned for them to follow him, 'If you would like to come with me, I can take you to him.'

Dave felt his heart pound in his chest as he followed Doctor Porter down the ward and watched as he came to stop in front of the bed. It was the one which had the curtains closed around it.

As the curtain was pulled back to reveal a gravely injured familiar looking brown-haired man, Dave felt like the air had been punched out of him as he felt his eyes grow wide in shock. He then heard a loud horrified gasp come from behind him and turned to see Claire had her hand over her mouth in shock.

Dave stared uncomprehendingly at the figure in front of them. He felt his heart wrench at the state of Andy's badly bruised face. His left eye was completely swollen shut and there was a large black bruise along the front of his neck. He could see that his right leg was in a plaster cast and it was elevated at a forty-five-degree angle. A butterfly needle was sticking in his left hand, attached to a long thin clear tube that led to a bag full of clear fluid that hung over him. A small tube that was attached to a ventilator was split into two small tubes that ran up his nostrils, feeding oxygen in him, while an ECG machine beeped steadily next to him.

Dave swallowed as he felt his throat tighten and turned to Doctor Porter, 'I... is he ...' he coughed and cleared his throat, 'Is he okay?'

Doctor Porter looked at Dave grimly and gave a slow nod, 'He is stable.' he gestured to Andy's plastered leg, 'His right leg was broken in two places, we were able to reset the break, we had to carry out some surgery to fix the bone in place using a plate, screws, and a rod. Once the swelling subsides, we will get a better idea of how it is healing. He also has two broken ribs, which thankfully didn't puncture his lung. His left eye socket is fractured, but it should heal once the swelling subsides. It appears whoever attacked him tried to crush his windpipe, his larynx is badly bruised so it will be painful for him to talk.' He exhaled and shook his head in disbelief, 'To be honest, he was lucky. If Constable Cooper had arrived a minute later, it may have been much worse.'

Dave reached over and touched Andy's hand gently and then lifted his head up to the doctor, 'Can we talk to him?' he asked hopefully.

'He will still be groggy from the anaesthetic.' Doctor Porter said reluctantly, pausing to place a compassionate hand on Dave's arm, 'But I must warn you, he may not be particularly lucid as he is on powerful painkillers to help with the pain. If you need to talk to him, try to keep it brief so you don't tire him out.' He waved a hand to the closed curtains, 'I will give you some privacy, but I will not be far if you need me.'

Dave smiled and gave a small nod of gratitude as he watched Doctor Porter leave. He looked over his shoulder to Wend. She had remained silent the whole time, standing behind Claire.

'What happened?' Dave asked through gritted teeth as he fought to keep his emotions in check.

Wendy took a step forward and gave a small shake of her head, 'To be honest, Guv. I am not sure what happened.' She closed her eyes and inhaled a deep breath, 'After I left you last night, I met up with three people from this facility, they wanted me to brief them on what we had learned. I was in the middle of doing that when I received a call from Andy's mobile. He started to talk but something cut him off, and then the next thing I heard was someone screaming followed by a crashing noise, like two people fighting. Luckily the guys I was with knew where he lived and we weren't that far from him, so we were able to get to him quickly.' She edged closer to Andy, placed her hand on his bed and looked down sadly at him, 'When we broke our way into his house, we could hear a baby crying from upstairs and the sound of people struggling coming from the back of the house. We raced in, we could see Andy lying on the floor in a bad way. A woman was sitting on him, punching him hard. Two of the guys charged her and were able to get her off him.' Struggling to contain her anger, she paused, placed her hands on her hips and looked at Dave incredulously, 'Jesus, Guv! If I hadn't seen it myself, I wouldn't have believed it! Whoever this woman was, she was strong. The two guys who tried to restrain her are ex-marines, so you can imagine they are tough, but she literally threw them aside like they were paper. Hard to believe, but the four of us struggled to even slow her down. Impossible as it may sound it took two tasers to just bring her to her knees. I had to use a baseball bat across the back of her head to put her down.'

Dave's face hardened as he gave Wendy a look that would curdle milk, 'Is she still alive?'

Wendy gave a small nod of acknowledgement, 'Yes.' She gave him a tight smile, 'But she may be suffering from a major headache when she wakes up.'

Dave's upper lip curled as he sneered at her, 'Good!' He then raised a curious eyebrow at her, 'Any idea who she is?'

Wendy lifted her shoulder in a half shrug, 'No idea, Guv.' She glanced over her shoulder and gestured to the double doors at the end of the ward, 'I believe she is being held on the detention level. I suspect they may know who she is, but they are not saying.'

Dave sniffed and pressed his lips together, 'Well, I want to speak with our mystery woman.' He suddenly felt surge of defiance build inside of him as he crossed his arms over his chest, 'If they want to stop me, I would like to see them try.'

Wendy's mouth twitched as she gave him a frosty look, 'Don't worry, Guv.' There was a hint of affection in her eyes as she looked at the figure in the bed, 'I want answers too. Let them try to stop us both.'

Dave let out a bitter laugh but stopped and blinked as he suddenly remembered Andy's wife and child, 'Andy has a wife, Mary, and a baby, Alice. What happened to them?'

Wendy held up her hands as her mouth curved into a smile, 'Well, we found the baby in her cot crying. She's being looked after here by the base personnel. As for Andy's wife.' She paused and there was a tone of uncertainty in her voice as she continued, 'There was no sign of her in the house. Guv, I suspect our mystery woman may be responsible for her disappearance.'

Dave's brow furrowed in deep concentration as he chewed on his bottom lip. He started to wonder if the people who had abducted Karen were responsible for Mary's sudden disappearance too. But before he could open his mouth to voice his theory, a groan from Andy interrupted him. He looked down to see Andy had opened his eyes and was staring bleary-eyed up at the three people standing around him.

'What the hell does someone have to do to get some sleep here?' Andy woozily groaned.

Delighted his friend colleague was awake, Dave looked across to the two women and beamed at them. Wendy ran over to the doctor, who hurried back over to them.

As he leaned in closer to the woozy man, Dave whispered to him softly, 'Andy, it's me, Dave.'

'Hey Guv! Why are you in my bedroom?' Andy croaked. He blinked and then stared at people standing around the bed in confusion, 'Am I dreaming? Guv.' He held up his hand to his head and groaned, 'Ugh! I need to tell you about this awful nightmare I had.'

Dave glanced anxiously across to Doctor Porter, who stepped forward and gently examined the disorientated man. He touched Andy's face with his hand and used a penlight to shine a light into his eyes. Andy waved irritably waved his hand to brush the penlight away from his eyes.

'The confusion is probably coming from the painkillers and the anaesthetic.' Doctor Porter said in a hushed tone and took a step back from Andy, 'Try to keep it brief and let him rest.'

Dave gave a small nod of acknowledgement and knelt closer to his friend, 'Andy, Wendy and Claire are here too.' He smiled and gently placed his hand on the bed-ridden man's arm, 'You are in a hospital bed. Can you remember what happened to you?'

Andy waved his hand and closed his eyes, but continued to mumble, 'Sorry Guv, I don't think I will be well enough to come to work today. I've a real sore throat and a headache. I am probably coming down with something.' He let out a pain-filled groan, touched his head with his hand and yawned, 'Nice of you to come to visit me.'

Wendy took a step closer to the bed and gently touched Andy's hand, 'Andy, it's me, Wendy.' She blinked furiously to clear away the tears in her eyes, 'Can you remember what happened to you?'

Without opening his eyes, the corner of Andy's mouth twitched as he tapped Wendy's hand, 'Hey Wendy, nice of you to come too.' He gave a small cough and groaned, 'Ugh! I had this awful dream. I was at home, and I thought I was talking to Mary, but it wasn't Mary, just somebody who looked like her and we had a fight. Jesus, it was awful. She was like a Terminator, just kept coming at me.'

Stunned, Dave spun round to face Claire, whose eyes widened in shock and she shook her head in disbelief, 'They replaced her!' she whispered incredulously.

Andy coughed out a painful groan and yawned, 'Sorry guys, but if you don't mind, I am tired. Let yourselves out and lock the door after you.' He smiled and waved his hand at them sleepily.

Doctor Porter took a small step closer to Dave and put a hand on his shoulder, 'I think it's best if you leave him now.' His firm tone indicated that it was not up for discussion, 'He really needs to rest. If there is any change, I will let you know.'

Dave nodded reluctantly and slowly stepped away from the bed, walking back to the double doors. Dave paused and gave the two women a frosty look.

'I don't know about you.' he snarled, his face hardening as his mouth set in a hard line, 'But I just about had enough of this. I think it's about time we got some answers about what is going on.' Dave struggled to contain his anger as he waved his across his chest, 'If they want to cover things up, fine. But when they come at us through our friends and family, like you Claire and now Andy, that is just not on!'

Wendy's nostrils flared as her eyes blazed with anger and nodded in agreement, 'I am with you, Guv. Wherever this takes us, I am with you.'

Dave turned to Claire in expectation as she looked at him thoughtfully, 'You realise.' She whispered, casting an eye over her shoulder and then lowering her voice, 'If we continue to do this, they will come at us harder.'

Dave scowled and waved his hand in front of him angrily, 'Screw them, let them try!' He closed his eyes and sucked in a deep breath as he tried to regain control of his emotions, 'I think it is about time we had a chat with the prime minister.'

Wendy's mouth curved into a small smile and gave a small nod of agreement. She edged closer to Dave and spoke in a hushed voice, 'I am with you, Guv. I don't think I should be telling you this, sir, but when I was talking to her earlier, the prime minister ordered me to bring you to see Andy. I think she is counting on your reaction so that you will be open to what she has to tell you.'

Dave rubbed his chin thoughtfully for a minute and exhaled a heavy resigned sigh, 'To be honest, if it had been the other way around, I probably would do the same thing. We've done it ourselves many times to get the reaction we need from people during interrogation.' As if to steel himself for what was to come next, he straightened his shoulders, spun round, and pushed open the doors. He then cast an expectant eye over his shoulder at the two women, 'Time to get the show on the road.' After giving them a mischievous wink, he forced his way through the doors.

As he pushed through the doors, the soldier who had guided him earlier, straightened to attention and looked at Dave with a startled expression, 'Sir, if you would like to follow me.' he said sharply, 'I've been ordered to escort you to the Prime Minister as soon as you are done here.'

Dave looked closer at the soldier, bobbed his head, gave him a tight smile and then motioned to the corridor ahead of him, 'Lead the way, my good man.'

The frowning soldier cocked his head, nodded slightly, and marched down the corridor, with Dave following close on his heels. As he hurried down the corridor, Dave leaned in closer to Wendy and lowered his voice.

'Wendy, do you know what happened to Jenny after they took me?' he asked worriedly, 'When I last saw her in the garden, and it looked like she had been tranquilised.'

'Don't worry, Guv. She's fine.' Wendy smiled warmly, 'Alpha Squad, the guys who took you, are really sorry for having to tranquillise her, as they are all dog lovers. They brought her here too.' She shook her head and laughed, 'In fact, she is with them now. They have become quite attached to her. She was a bit … annoyed … at first, but after a few treats she settled down.'

'That's Jenny, you give her a treat and affection and she's your friend for life.' Dave chortled.

As he stared at the soldier in front of him, who was leading them through a maze of corridors. He lapsed into an uneasy silence as he made a mental note to himself of the various signposts along the corridor, in an attempt to memorise their route. *Just in case we need to get out of here quickly*, he thought to himself grimly.

21

As the unusual looking trio followed the soldier through a maze of corridors and up a flight of stairs, they passed several people who stared at them but gave no comment. Coming to a stop in front of a large metal door, the burly man looked up to the camera that was above it and pressed his finger on a button on the wall. Seconds later, they heard a small buzz, followed by a loud click as the door swung open.

Dave glanced at Wendy curiously, who held up her hand up and gestured to the open door, 'The Prime Minister is expecting us.' she said, as if answering his unspoken question, 'We can go in.'

Dave gave a small nod in acknowledgement, took a deep breath, and walked through the door. He looked over his shoulder and noted the two women were following close behind him.

He strode through the door into a large circular room. In the middle of the room there was an enormous desk with two flat computer screens sitting on top, at the end of the room there was a medium-sized square window. On coming to an abrupt stop in front of the window,

Dave felt his jaw drop open in amazement as he caught sight of the impressive area below. He gave Claire a sidelong glance and could tell from her awed reaction that she was just as equally impressed.

As he stared through the window into the room below, he could make out various computer workstations. On the front wall hung four large flat screen monitors displaying various images.

Dave leaned closer to Claire and whispered in her ear, 'It reminds me of a military command station, like I've seen in films of the American NORAD bunker.' There was a tone of admiration in his voice.

In the chamber below, a variety of people, some in military uniform and some in plain clothing, were sitting at computer workstations or hurrying around the centre involved in various tasks.

'Impressive, isn't it?'

As the quiet voice brought his attention back to the room he was in, Dave turned from the window and blinked in surprised. When he had first stepped through door, he quickly realised that he had been so distracted by the scene below, he had failed to see the other people that were already in the room.

Dave moved forward and looked closely at the three people in front of him. He noticed that Wendy had walked straight over to Sophia Collins as soon as they walked in. He could tell she was struggling to hold in her laugh at his obvious embarrassment.

Dave coughed with embarrassment and gave Sophia a lopsided grin as he gestured to the room below them, 'Yes, ma'am, very impressive' He held up his hands in front of his chest in an apologetic manner, 'I must apologise for my ignorance, I didn't see you there.'

Sophia waved her hand and let out a small chuckle, 'No need to apologise, Detective Inspector.' The corners of her mouth turned up as she cocked her head to the command centre below. 'In fact, I had a similar reaction when I was first shown this.' She arched her head inquiringly at him, 'I guess Cooper brought you up to speed?'

Dave raised an eyebrow and tilted his head at Wendy, who hung her head, as if embarrassed by the attention. 'Yes … she did.' He replied carefully, trying to hide the anger in his voice.

Sophia took a small step toward Dave and took hold of his hand, 'Please, Dave. Is it okay if I call you Dave?' Her voice was thick with compassion as she tapped his hand, 'I can understand what you are thinking now, but we need you on this with us. To understand the seriousness, I needed you to see your friend first.' She held up her hand, as if to wave away an unspoken question, 'Don't worry, he is in excellent hands and being taken great care of. I am sorry if you assume you are being manipulated, but we don't have time to sugar-coat things.'

Dave moved away from Sophia and was silent for a minute. He cocked his head at Claire, who was standing next to him. She reached for his hand and gave a small nod in understanding. He placed his hands on his hips, closed his eyes, lifted his head up to the ceiling, and pinched the bridge of his nose, letting out a long heavy breath.

'I quite understand, ma'am.' je said with a reluctant tone, 'Desperate times call for desperate measures, I suppose. Seeing Andy like that is hard. I've worked so closely with him, I rely on him, in fact he is like a son to me.' He grimaced as he lowered his head, placed his hands over face and groaned, 'Oh God, please don't tell him I said that.'

The corners of her mouth twitching in bemusement, Sophia patted Dave on the shoulder and gave him a sly wink, 'Don't worry, your secret is safe with us.'

'Thank you.' Dave laughed. He straightened his shoulders and gave a Sophia a serious look, 'Ma'am I need to ask. Sergeant Jenkins has a baby girl, Alice. Is she okay?'

Sophia smiled wistfully at him, 'Alice is fine, considering. We brought her here along with her father. She is being well taken care of, although missing her father and mother.'

Relieved at the news that his colleague's baby girl was safe, Dave gazed around the room and pointed at the window to the command centre below, 'Care to tell me where we are and what this is?' he asked curiously.

Sophia let out a long breath, gave a small nod and waved her hands above her head, 'Well, *this* is a long story.' She turned and introduced the two people stood behind her, 'First let me introduce Commander John Payne from MI6 and Doctor Sharon Fisher, our chief scientist and reluctant scientific advisor.'

Dave studied the tall man stood behind her. He could see he was about an inch taller than him, at six feet tall and appeared to be in his early forties, with a square rugged face, sharp piercing blue eyes, clean shaven with short dark hair. He guessed from the suit he was wearing that he took pride in his appearance.

John moved forward and offered his hand to Dave, 'Detective Inspector Barnes, good to meet you.' he said warmly, 'I've read a lot about you.'

Dave took John's hand and shook it. He could tell from the solid, firm handshake that he worked out and from the way he was scrutinizing him, that he was sizing him up; wondering whether to trust him.

'Oh, don't believe everything you've read.' Dave laughed as he pulled his hand away and tried to shake the feeling back into it.

'Oh, I don't. I prefer to rely on my instincts.' John winked and Dave let out a small grunt as he gave him a playful smack on the shoulder. 'Much like yourself.'

Dave nodded in acknowledgement and gave John an inquiring look, 'Very true.' He held up his index finger and frowned at him, 'Am I wrong, but do I do detect a Mancunian accent in your voice?'

John grinned and gave Dave nod of admiration, 'Very good.' he smiled and straightened his head proudly, 'Yes, Manchester born and proud of it.'

Noticing the golden-haired woman hanging on the end of the rugged man's arm, Dave watched as she fingered her glasses anxiously while she smiled shyly at him. She was an attractive looking twenty-something woman, very petite, slightly smaller in height than Claire, and was wearing a white lab coat. He could see there was a significant degree of intelligence behind her blinking chestnut eyes as he watched her jump forward to grab Claire's hand and shook it furiously.

'Professor Tulley, what a pleasure it is to meet you!' Sharon beamed as she breathed hard in excitement, 'I've been following your work and you cannot believe what a thrill it is to meet you. I've read all your theories and would love to ask you some questions?'

Double Jeopardy

Dave covered his hand with his mouth as he tried to keep in his laugh at the look of astonishment and surprise that had suddenly appeared on Claire's face. She opened her mouth wordlessly as the excitable Sharon continued to fire question after question at her, not giving her time to answer. There was a hint of panic in her widening eyes, and he guessed from her pleading look at him she was saying, *Help me!*

It was at that moment Sophia stepped forward, took a hold of Sharon hand, forcing her to release her grip on poor Claire.

'All in good time, Doctor.' Sophia said firmly and gave Claire a bemused look, 'I am sure Professor Tulley is tired and we don't want to tire her out even more. I am sure she will be more than willing to answer your questions later?'

'Oh … oh … yes … yes.' Sharon stammered excitedly, glancing over to Claire and pointed her finger at her own chest, 'We can talk later … yes … that will be good … talk later!'

As he watched as the excitable young woman, who was still muttering to herself, walk to the other side of the room, and place herself in front of a computer screen, Dave lowered his voice and leaned in closer to Claire, who was trying not to laugh, 'Oh, look! You've made a friend on your first day at school.'

His mouth widened in a childish grin as he watched Claire's face turn a deep shade of red. She rolled her eyes and nudged him in the ribs, 'Oh, shush you.'

Sophia held up her hand apologetically as she leaned in to speak to Claire in a hushed voice, 'Forgive Doctor Fisher. She can be a bit …' she paused and gave a small wave of her hand, 'excitable. But she means well.'

Grinning impishly, John leaned in closer to Dave, winked at him and lowered his voice, 'We call her the Energizer Bunny. We have a pool running to see what type of batteries she uses, we—oww!'

Dave had seen Sophia glide stealthily up behind John, but he released he didn't have time to warn to warn him as he watched her smack him across the back of his head with the palm of her hand. Her eyes continuing to bore into the back of the John's head, her face hardened as she snapped back at him in a hushed tone, 'Please, tell everybody that is not funny, and they are to stop that now. Tell them that this order has come straight from me!'

Like a naughty schoolboy caught by a strict schoolteacher, John lowered his head and murmured a sullen reply, 'Yes, ma'am.'

Without further comment, Sophia turned and motioned to the chairs around the table, 'Please sit. You've a lot of questions. I think it's time we answered them.'

Dave, Claire, and Wendy each took a seat around the table, with John taking a seat beside Sharon. Dave noticed a small smile pass between them. Their eyes appeared to lock briefly, just before Sharon dropped her eyes shyly and her face turned a bright shade of red. He wondered from their body language that maybe John and Sharon were in a romantic relationship? However, as he turned his head he caught Sophia's eye, she gave him a silent nod of acknowledgement to his unanswered question.

Smiling warmly, Sophia rose from her chair and placed her hands behind her back, 'Okay now where to begin. What would you like to learn first?'

Dave looked over his shoulder and pointed at the chamber through the window, 'Well, I am sure Claire would agree with me here.' he asked, raising a curious eyebrow, 'Where are we and what is this place?'

Sophia gave a small smile and gestured to John, 'I will let Commander Payne explain that to you.'

John bobbed his head and rose from his chair, 'You are in a nuclear bunker.' He walked over to the window and gestured to the chamber below, 'They first built this place in the 1960s, during the height of the Cold War. At the start, MI6 understood they needed a secure place in the event of a nuclear war. The thought was the farthest away from London the better, so they built a complex under Durham Castle.'

Claire's eyes widened and she blurted out in astonishment, 'What! You are telling us we are actually beneath Durham Castle?'

John gave a knowing smile and pointed up to the ceiling above them, 'Well, not only are we under the Castle, because of the size of the complex, we are under Durham Cathedral too.' He turned and nodded to Sharon who typed on the keyboard in front of her and then picked up a computer tablet beside her. She stood up from her chair and walked over to the front of the monitor on the wall. As she tapped on the tablet a schematic appeared on the monitor. John stared up at the monitor proudly, 'We are about one thousand meters down. They hid the construction during the re-development of Durham in the 1960s. Anybody noticing large equipment being moved around would have been none the wiser because of the re-development going on. They constructed an access point a mile away, just outside county hall. From the outside it looks like a large storehouse, but inside there is a lift that can take vehicles or people down to a transport hub, which leads here.' He waved his hand at the ceiling above him, 'There is a smaller entrance in Durham Cathedral, which is supposed to be used for emergencies, but it is useful for quick trips out, say we need to go up above to clear our heads or take a little trip into the city centre. We have a good relationship with the clergy in the Cathedral, sort of a symbiotic relationship if you will.' He paused as the schematic on the monitor moved out, revealing more detail of the complex, 'The complex is comprised of 15 levels, each level housing separate specialities, armoury, research, living quarters, etc.' There was a hint of pride in his voice as he continued to speak, 'Two levels are designed specifically for growing our own food and crops. Our air recycling and water filtration is run by a system so advanced NASA would sell their souls to have it. The complex is powered by geothermal energy, from a reactor about a mile below us, syphoning power from the Earth's geothermal reserves.'

Dave blinked and shook his head in amazement, 'Unbelievable!'

John smiled wryly at him and nodded proudly in agreement, 'Only a select few were aware of this complex.' He waved a hand up to the window, at the Command Centre below, 'They kept it off the books. Not even the Government knows about it. They understood it was best to keep something like this a secret until it was necessary to reveal it. It had been unused for a few years. That is until the early 1980s, when MI6 discovered something disturbing. So, we use this as the base of operations, and we only select the best and brightest to work here.'

Claire's eyes widened in awe as she cocked her head at John, confusion etched across her face. Her mouth opened and closed like a dying fish as she tried to get the words out. She then closed her eyes and held up her hands, as if to gather her thoughts, 'Hold on! I am sure something this big would show up. Running something this large would create a paper trail.' She shook her head and stared centre below in bewilderment, 'I cannot imagine the budget required to run something like this, but surely that would leave red flags?'

Dave raised an eyebrow and gave Claire a speculative look, 'Oh, come on, Claire. You've not seen the movies? Money diverted in secret to a clandestine government organisation. It would be easy enough to alter the books, say one hundred thousand pounds for an extra toilet seat here or a hundred thousand pounds for a brand-new cappuccino machine there.'

John waggled his finger at Dave and let out a small laugh as he gave a small shake of his head, 'Well, that isn't too far from the truth. Thanks to some …' he paused and waved his hands in an evasive gesture, 'Shall we say, creative book-keeping, we've been able to make this place one of the most advanced equipped centres in the United Kingdom.'

Dave inhaled a long breath and let it out in a long-ragged sigh as he stood up and pointed to the complex below, 'But what about the people? How is something this large able to run in secret?'

John's eyes flickered briefly as he stood in silence for a minute and glanced at Sophia and Sharon, who stared back at him with bleak expressions. He let out a long shallow breath and stared at Dave grimly, 'Everybody who works here knows the threat we face.' There was a hint of sadness in his voice, 'We've all, in some way, been affected or aware of somebody who has suffered. We are all prepared to sacrifice ourselves, if need be, to protect this place.'

He took a small step toward Sharon and placed his hand tenderly on her shoulder. She lifted her head up at him and gave him a small sad smile. Dave noticed that her eyes contained a deep sadness.

Puffing out his cheeks and running his hands through his hair, Dave turned his head to John and looked at him questioningly, 'Okay that explains where we are.' The centre of his eyebrows bunched together as he lifted his hands up in the air, 'But what about the *why*? Is this anything to do with the case we are investigating and what has happened to Sergeant

Jenkins?'

John and Sharon exchanged a strange look, and the sombre faced woman gave a small nod in acknowledgement. He turned back to Dave and bobbed his head to him.

'Yes.' he replied and paused as he looked at him speculatively, 'Let me ask you a question. During your investigation, did you notice something irregular? That things were not adding up, or people appeared to be behaving in an unusual manner?'

Dave cocked his head to Clare and they both nodded in agreement. John tapped his fingers on his chin as he turned to Claire thoughtfully, 'Professor Tulley, I believe you stumbled across the truth during your investigations.'

The startled woman blinked, let out a nervous laugh and waved her hands in denial. She laughed nervously and shook her head, 'Me? I only have theories and copies of papers about an abandoned experiment.'

'Yes!'

Dave jumped as Sharon suddenly let out a squeal of delight as she leapt out of her chair in excitement. She then darted up to Claire, her face beaming, and began to to jabber at her excitedly, 'Don't you see? Your theories are right, they abandoned the experiment for a reason.' she then stared up at the ceiling and shook her head to herself, 'Can you imagine trying to carry out quantum entanglement with 1930s technology? It is no wonder it failed. Imagine the power needed to transmit quantum information.'

Dave scratched his head and blinked in confusion as Sharon continued to babble excitedly. After a few seconds, he rubbed his hand over his face and let out a frustrated sigh as he tried to, unsuccessfully, make sense of what he was listening to. He waved his hand to John, who took a small step toward him and cocked his head as Dave lowered his voice.

'Do you understand any of this?' Dave asked carefully.

John laughed weakly and lifted his shoulder in a half a shrug, 'I find it is just best if I nod my head. She will come up for air soon.' He stared at Sharon proudly and sighed, 'One reason why I love her, I love seeing this energy in her eyes.'

Dave gave a small grunt of agreement as he watched Claire shake her head in confusion as she continued her discussion with the excitable younger woman.

'But that was why the experiment failed. It killed the scientists behind it. The government covered it up as a failure.' Sharon let out an exasperated sigh and held up her hand as she paced around the room, mumbling to herself. She then suddenly stopped, pivoted, and punched the air in excitement, 'No ... no ... don't you see? It wasn't a failure.' she blurted out, 'Something happened, but not what they intended at first.'

Dave eyed the two excitable women in bewilderment and held up his index finger, 'Hang on a second! Are we talking about that teleportation experiment in 1932?'

'Yes! Yes!' Sharon replied, bobbing her head enthusiastically, 'Dr Selyab believed he could transmit matter from one location to another. But what he failed to count on was the power requirements.' Pausing to pick up a glass from the table and take drink of water, she took a deep breath, shook her head in disbelief and continued to babble excitedly, 'They perhaps created a stable portal for a brief period, but I believe the portal became unstable and created an Einstein–Rosen bridge.'

Dave's forehead creased and shook his head in confusion at Claire, 'What's an Einstein-Rosen Bridge?'

Her mouth widening into a knowing smile, Claire grabbed a piece of paper that lay on the table in front of her and drew a diagram of what looked like a tunnel, 'Think of it as a tunnel connecting two universes.' she explained carefully, 'In 1935 Albert Einstein and Nathan Rosen came up with the theory that if an object had strong enough gravity, it could warp space, creating a tear that would link parallel universes. A doorway to a parallel reality.'

'So, is that what Dr Selyab created?' Dave asked curiously, 'Did he open a door to another Earth?'

He watched as the two women turned to each other, both shaking their heads as they paced around the room, excitement etched across their faces. They then began to chatter to themselves, with Sharon waving her hand passionately, 'No. I don't think you understand. I have read the papers on Dr Selyab's research.'

Her eyes widening in surprise, Sophia turned and stared at Sharon with confusion etched across her face, 'Excuse me, Professor Tulley, Dr Fisher. But I thought the government had destroyed all research of Dr Selyab's experiment after the accident? How were you both able to get this information?'

Sharon waved her hand dismissively at Sophia and turned away from her. Dave could see Sophia was just about to open her mouth to protest but was stopped as John placed his hand on her arm. He then placed a finger over his lips and give her a small shake of his head, mouthing the words, *Let her finish*. The corners of Sophia's eyes creased in annoyance, but she complied with a reluctant nod of acknowledgement.

They both turned their attention back to Sharon, who continued to buzz around Claire in excitement, 'Yes. Yes. The government would've destroyed any records of his research after the accident.' she burbled eagerly, 'But any true scientist would keep a copy of their research and keep it in a safe place and lay clues for anybody looking for it.'

Dave frowned and arched his head at Claire, 'Is that how you were able to get a hold of Dr Selyab's research notes?'

'Yes.' Claire answered, shrugging her shoulders, 'If you recognise what you are looking for, the clues were easy to follow.'

Dave leaned back and folded his arms across his chest as he gazed at Claire with a touch of newfound respect. He blinked and then turned his attention back to Sharon, who was continuing to talk with increasing emotion.

'Yes! Yes!' Sharon exclaimed, 'If you recognised what to look for, they would've been simple to find. What is also interesting, along with the copies of his research, are the copies of letters and a transcript of the accident by a Brigadier Thornton. Turns out he didn't agree with the government's decision to cover-up the accident and believed people should learn of the sacrifice made by Dr Selyab and his staff.'

John strode over to a box in the corner of the room and pulled out some folders and handed them to Claire, 'I hope you don't mind

Professor Tulley.' He gave the middle-aged woman a lopsided grin as he handed the folders to her, 'But we took the liberty of also securing your research when we picked you up.'

Claire gave John a frosty look as she took the papers from him. Her expression clouded and she was just about to open her mouth but paused and relaxed as she caught Wendy smiling apologetically at her.

On seeing the pile of papers in front of her, Sharon's face brightened, and she clapped her hands with joy, 'Fantastic!' she exclaimed, 'Professor Tulley, I must applaud you on your tenacity at getting hold of these.'

Claire lowered her head as her cheeks turned a deep shade of red from embarrassment. She turned to Dave, and he let out a loud bark of laughter as he watched her cheeks burn even brighter with embarrassment.

Sharon lay out the papers on the desk in front of her and lifted her chin up in delight at the faces around the desk as they stared back at her. 'Don't you see!' she squealed, clapping her hands as she whirled around in a circle like a child on Christmas morning, 'With the limited technology at their disposal, they should not have been able to carry out a successful test. In theory, the best that would happen would have been an electrical surge, a burst of energy and a few burnt out consoles.'

Dave leaned forward and glanced at the papers on the desk in front of him and scratched his head in confusion, 'They must have done something right, they created a stable wormhole for a brief time.'

Sharon waved her hands, shook her head as she lowered her head and looked at him over the top of her glasses with a grim expression, 'You don't see it, do you? At the exact moment they were trying to create a wormhole, somebody else was doing the same thing. They locked onto the vibrational energy signature that was being emitted by Dr Selyab's experiment and transmitted a beam of energy to punch open a hole in the fabric of space-time. Unfortunately, that resulted in the feedback which resulted in a cascade failure in their lab.'

Claire pursed her lips together as she looked up at the ceiling and tapped her fingers on her chin intently. She lowered her head, raised her index finger questioningly as she moved away from Sharon. She closed her eyes and silently paced around the room. After a minute, she suddenly clicked her fingers and opened her eyes in realisation, spinning back round to Sharon.

'But the chances of somebody else, in another reality, carrying out a similar experiment at the same time are what, infinitesimal?' she whispered.

Sharon opened her mouth and lifted her hand but paused as she stared at Claire in puzzlement and then slowly her eyes widened in realisation and nodded in excitement, murmuring passionately to herself, 'In theory, it should be next to impossible for somebody to detect the transmission of a vibrational signature ...' She stopped, turned, and held out her hand to the frowning woman.

'Unless ...' Claire answered in a low horrified voice. Both of their faces turned ashen as they nodded slowly in agreement.

Dave watched as the two pale women stood in silence for a minute, as if unwilling to express what they were thinking. Sophia rose out of her seat and moved closer as she placed her hand on Sharon's shoulder.

'Unless what?' she asked carefully.

Sharon turned back to everybody in the room with a glum expression, inhaled a long deep breath and let out a ragged sigh. His eyes widening in realisation, Dave gave a small nod in understanding and murmured in a low horrified voice.

'They were already looking.'

22

Dave thought Claire looked a bit dispirited as he watched her sink heavily back down in her chair next to him. Hoping to reassure her, he affectionately reached over and placed his hand on top of hers. She lifted her head and smiled gratefully at him.

'They must have already had established a wormhole on their side and transmitted an energy pulse.' Sharon's voice was hushed as she bobbed her head despondently, 'It would have been a simple matter for them to wait for somebody else to do the same thing. Their energy pulse must have locked onto the vibrational frequency from Dr Selyab's experiment, allowing them to punch a hole into this universe.'

As he turned and stared at each of the silent faces around the table he got the impression that there unsure what to say next. He couldn't blame them really, as he found the last bombshell had left him reeling. Dave ran his fingers through his hair in frustration as he tried to process all that he been told over the past hour. He then eyed the tray of cups in front of him, and then gave Sophia and John a questioning look as he smiled halfheartedly at them at them.

'You got anything stronger to drink?' he asked heavily.

'I thought you would never ask.' Sophia beamed and waved her hand to John.

Dave cocked his curiously as he watched John get out his seat and move across the room to the small filing cabinet in the room's corner. Then, much to Dave's surprise, he watched as he pulled open a drawer and lifted out an enormous bottle of Bushmills Irish Whisky.

John stuck his bottom lip out as he eyed the bottle in his hands and let out a long sad sigh, 'I was holding onto this for emergencies, but I suppose we could classify this as an emergency.'

After unscrewing the bottle top, he poured the bottle's contents into the glasses in front of him, handing everybody in the room a glass. He offered a glass to Sophia, who held up her hand to wave him away and gave a small shake of her head.

Dave picked up the glass, gave it a sniff and got a hint of smoky wood with a hint of cinnamon. He raised the glass, pulled his head back, swallowed the contents, and coughed as he felt a warm fruity sensation hit the back of his throat.

'Wow! That's marvellous stuff.' he rasped hoarsely at the warm sensation that was slowly descending through his body. He raised his glass up to John, who leaned over and poured him another shot.

'Ahem!' Sophia coughed and gave John a stern look, along with a small shake of her head, 'I think that's enough for now, don't you think?'

John eyed the bottle in his hand sorrowfully, cocked his head apologetically at Dave and then reluctantly screwed the bottle top back on, before placing it back into the filing cabinet.

Wendy glanced around the room and raised her hand hesitantly, 'Sorry but I've a question?'

'One?' Dave interjected incredulously, 'How about a few!'

Wendy rolled her eyes and then continued with what she was saying, 'You told us how this happened.' She paused and waved her hand over the papers on the desk, 'But why the murders? Did you discover why they need the hypothalamus?'

Dave nodded to himself. That was a good question, one he was desperately wanting the answer to. He remained silent but watched with interest as Sharon moved over to one of the computer screens, sat down and began typing furiously on the keyboard. She then picked up the tablet beside her and rose from her seat. She tapped on the tablet and pointed to a monitor on the wall which was displaying several pictures and text.

'As you see, the hypothalamus is the part of our brain that helps control our body temperature, as well as producing and controlling the body's hormone production.' Sharon explained, taking a step closer to the monitor, and tapping her finger on the image in front of her, 'The other interesting thing is it helps regulate the body's metabolism and immune response and it is our belief this is what they want. They've been collecting samples to produce a copy of our body's metabolism and immunity that they can use.'

'But to what end?' Dave asked, making no attempt to hide his confusion.

Claire's grew wide in sudden realisation and she bolted out of her sea, clicking her fingers in excitement, 'Of course!' she exclaimed, 'I see it now.' She squeezed her eyes shut and slapped her forehead with the palm of her hand, 'How could I have been so stupid?'

Sharon grinned broadly at Claire and giggled, 'Yes, it's brilliant when you think about it. Granted it is horrific, but brilliant all the same.'

Suddenly feeling out of his depth, Dave glanced at everybody around the room in bewilderment. He then raised his hand and coughed, 'Ahem! Excuse me? But for those of us here who don't have a science degree. Can you please tell us what you find so exciting?'

Sharon gave Dave a knowing smile, held up her finger, lowered her head and typed furiously on the tablet she was holding. He watched as the image on the monitor changed and a new image appeared, representing each evolutionary stage of a human: from Australopithecus Anamnesis to Homo Sapiens.

'Okay, as you may realise, it has taken centuries for the human body to evolve to where we are now.' Sharon explained, speaking in a matter-of-fact tone as she pointed to the image on the monitor, '4.2 million years to be exact.' She paused and looked over her shoulder at the people seated around the desk, who slowly nodded in understanding as she continued, 'The human body has gradually evolved, adapting to the Earth's environment and building up an immunity to the planet's diseases.' She reached into her pocket and pulled out a stencil and quickly drew a diagram on the tablet. She then tapped on the tablet and the image on the monitor on the wall changed, showing a rough circle surrounding several angry looking emojis. She lifted her head up from her tablet at the people in the room and pointed at the monitor, 'Now, imagine the Earth as a human body and humans are the virus infecting the body.'

Claire blinked and began to nod furiously at Sharon in realisation. She clapped her hands together and continued to finish the woman's sentence, 'So, like a human body, the Earth will try to fight off the infection, but like in a human body a virus can adapt to the body's defences and sometimes they will develop a symbiotic relationship.'

Dave's eyebrows bunched together as he shook his head in confusion. Wishing he had studied more at school, he scratched his head as he turned to John and Sophia and stared at them blankly, 'Are you understanding any of this?'

Sophia gave a small laugh and nodded, 'Yes, but only because we've already been told this.'

'Well, that makes me feel a hell of a lot better.' Dave grunted sarcastically.

John leaned closer to Dave and lowered his voice, 'Don't worry. I was like you when she first explained it to me. She will get to the point, eventually.' He held up both hands in the air and shrugged, 'Again, I find it is just best to nod as she is going on.'

Sharon coughed, dropped her head, and gave John a withering stare of annoyance, 'Are we finished?'

John smiled sheepishly at Sharon and then winked, 'Yes. Please continue.'

Sharon glowered at John coldly over her glasses, 'You are so kind.' Her upper lip curled as she answered him with a sarcastic tone, 'Anyway, as I was saying, before you interrupted me, it has taken us centuries to adapt to this Earth. But if you are from another Earth, a parallel Earth if you will, then humans would have evolved slightly different and may not have developed the same immunity that we have.'

Delighted that this was something he could finally understand, Dave leapt up out of his seat and began waving his hand wildly, 'Oh, hang on! I see what you are getting at! What you are trying to say is the reason they have been collecting samples of our hypothalamus is that it will help them create a vaccine which will allow them to adapt to this world.'

Sharon's mouth curled into a smile and clicked her fingers, 'Exactly! Although I probably wouldn't call it a vaccine, but you understand what I am saying.'

Dave sunk back down into his chair and puffed his cheeks out in frustration, 'But why?'

John then rose from his seat, walked over to Sharon, and placed his hand on her shoulder, 'I'll take over from here.'

Sharon touched his hand and gave him a warm silent smile before moving back to her seat in front of the computer monitor. She typed furiously on the keyboard and the image on the monitor changed.

John frowned and gestured to the monitor, 'From what we can understand, it was sometime in the 1950s when people from their world first began crossing over.' he explained, 'We first realised something was wrong in 1981. There had been a lot of civil unrest flaring up in Britain, starting in the late 1960s and during the 1970s. During the inner-city riots of 1981, MI6 had noticed something suspicious, so we investigated the cause. We found that the riots were being organised from an outside source, specifically from outside the UK. We suspected that somebody was manipulating racial tensions to destabilise the country, to what end we didn't know.' He paused as he stared thoughtfully at a graph displayed on the monitor before continuing, 'The more we dug, the more we saw a pattern over the past decade. More notably during the 1970s, the rise of the National Front causing racial tensions, the labour disputes and miner's strikes were all manipulated from outside the UK.'

Dave furrowed his brow as he tilted his head and waved his hand dismissively, 'Granted, we know the 1970s was a period of great civil unrest. Throughout history there have been periods of great civil upheaval. To believe they were all being manipulated from an outside source, well, that would take somebody with large resources to do such a thing.'

John bobbed his head to Sharon, who typed on her keyboard, and the image on the monitor changed, 'As we dug deeper, we came across something unusual. In 1958, a low-ranking government minister, Gavin Henshaw, went missing for a few days. After an extensive search, they found him alive and well. Six months later he resigns from the government and leaves the public eye to set up his own media company. A year later he becomes a millionaire.'

Dave eyed John sceptically, 'Nothing unusual about that. We have seen that happen more and more recently. People become fed up with working in the civil service and feel they can do more in the private sector.'

John gave a small shake of his head and waggled his finger, 'Before he disappeared, they had described Gavin Henshaw as somebody with low intelligence, lacking any ambition and a friendly family man. His family said that after he had returned, they had found he had become reclusive, bitter, and colder. They also found him to be more ambitious and highly intelligent. He left his family, divorced his wife, and severed all contact with his children. He eventually left the UK and set up a multimedia empire in the United States.' He folded his arms across his chest and nodded to the monitor, 'We eventually traced the source of the funding of various flare-ups in civil unrest in the UK to Gavin Henshaw. As we dug deeper, we saw a pattern of similar behaviour with similar people, who go missing, resurfacing and suddenly their behaviour changed. People close to them described them as if they are different people.'

'Like Thomas Chawson.' Claire whispered tearfully.

Dave looked at the tearful woman sadly, leaned over and placed his hand on her shoulder. She looked at him, touched his hand with hers and gave him half a smile.

'Unfortunately, Claire, you are right.' John agreed, nodding sombrely, 'He is one of many to disappear, only to resurface with their behaviour changed.'

'But to what end?' Wendy asked, making no attempt to hide the confusion in her tone.

Dave stiffened in shock as Claire bolted out of her seat, exclaiming, 'The Illuminati!' Everybody in the room watched in surprise as she pointed to the names on the monitor, 'Don't you see? Everybody on that list was or has become a person of major influence in the world.'

John beamed at Claire, clicked his fingers, and gave a nod of acknowledgement, 'Got it in one!' His smile faded and the expression on his face became colder, 'It was during the early stages of our investigation when the Illuminati must have felt we were getting too close. Their superiors pressured the officers that were investigating to drop their investigations. Those that didn't were threatened or worse. In 1985 a car bomb nearly killed Andrew Garret, the former head of MI6. He realised if we were to continue to investigate, we need to do it secretly.' He held up his head proudly and gave a wry smile, 'So he faked his death. He had learned of this facility during his youth so, with people he knew he could trust, he set up operations here. He also had a hand in helping to set up other secret facilities, much like the one you are in now, across the UK and was instrumental in forming a clandestine alliance with our allies across the globe. Over the past thirty years, he recruited people from the military, the police force, and other sectors. People who he knew suspected something or were afraid to ask questions.' He glanced over his shoulder and stared at the command centre below through eyes that were filled with admiration, 'He recruited me personally after learning of my experiences during my time in the SAS.' His eyes had a haunted look as his tone changed to one of sadness, 'While serving I witnessed some questionable things being carried out by superiors and when I tried to report it, they pressured me into keeping silent. When I refused, they framed me and had me dishonourably discharged. Andrew tracked me down, recruited me and took me under his wing. With the help of some loyal people in the government and with the help of other agencies around the world, we have created one of the best intelligence gathering services in the world.'

'Oh, come on! The Illuminati are a myth, created by conspiracy theorists.' Dave scoffed, 'They don't exist.' He swallowed and looked sorrowfully at the faces of the people in the room, who stared back at him sadly and he felt the colour drain from his face, 'Do they?' he asked with a trace of uncertainty in his voice.

'I am sorry to say Dave, but they exist.' John replied as he eyed him sadly and exhaled a long heavy sigh, 'They have been responsible for some major events in history: the Vietnam War, JFK's assassination, civil unrest both here in the UK and across the world, the Gulf War. They were even behind the financial collapse in 2007. Over the course of the past thirty years, their attempts to manipulate the world have become more complex. They have even controlled nations with their own puppet governments, or, in certain cases a member of the Illuminati places themself in power.'

'Well, that explains a lot.' Dave murmured gloomily, 'I could never fathom how somebody like Richard Cole could end up becoming President of the United States.' He let out a snort of disgust, 'I mean the man is a misogynistic arsehole!'

Sopha snorted and nodded in agreement, 'Take it from somebody who has met the man, he is a lecherous pig.' she shuddered slightly, 'He truly made my skin crawl. I felt like I needed to have a shower just being in the same room as him.'

'You have my deepest sympathies.' Dave murmured in commiseration. He scratched his head, stood up from his seat and walked over to where John was standing. He lifted his chin up to the screen in puzzlement and tapped his finger on his chin thoughtfully, 'This is a lot to take in, but my question is how do you know they are coming from another Earth?'

'Don't worry about it. I'll get to that soon.' John grinned. He patted him on the shoulder and gestured to the monitor as he continued, 'As I was saying, the further back we investigated, the stranger it got. It was pure luck that we learned of people who had died mysteriously. We only stumbled across it by accident in 1998. A colleague of ours had a relative living in Langley Park and learned of a mysterious death of a friend. She travelled up to investigate and visited the local medical examiner, and that was when she learned the way her friend had died, and the ME had found something unusual.'

'Let me guess.' Claire murmured sadly, 'They found someone had removed their hypothalamus.'

John nodded gravely, 'Yes, but that was not the only strange thing. When Diana went back the next day to get a copy of the ME's report, she found they had assigned a new ME and gave her a different cause of death report. She also found the body had been cremated rather quickly. She was trying to locate the original ME, but she seemed to disappear from the face of the Earth.' He inhaled a deep despondent sigh and shook his head, 'Unfortunately, Diana was later found dead, her death ruled as suicide. They must have known she was on to something and had her killed. She must have known she was in danger, because she posted a report of her investigation to a colleague just before she went missing.'

Sharon hung her head sorrowfully and muttered, 'Diana loved her job, but she knew the risks.'

John placed a tender hand on Sharon's shoulder as he continued to speak, 'We learned that the Home Secretary had personally ordered Diana to stop investigating and to forget everything she learned. But anybody who knew her, knew she was like a bulldog, determined and stubborn. If she knew she was on to something she would follow the trail no matter where it led, no matter the cost.' There was a bitterness in his voice as he went on, 'We investigated reports of similar deaths and the deeper we dug, the more we came across other reports of similar deaths, going back all the way to 1935. We suspect not all the deaths were because they were specifically wanting a sample of their hypothalamus, like Tommy Thorn and...'

Claire blinked tearfully and nodded knowingly, 'Emma.' Her voice trembled as she said the name of her sister.

John gave sombre nod and shook his head in commiseration, 'Yes, I am truly sorry Miss Tulley, but you are correct.' He inhaled a deep breath and continued, 'We suspect young people like Tommy and your sister, were intended to be replaced, for some specific purpose, but it, whatever it is, was disturbed in some way and was forced to kill instead because they didn't have time to replace them with a doppelgänger.' Her paused as he moved to stand behind Sharon and placed his hands on her shoulders, 'As for your question on how we know they are coming from another Earth, I'll let Dr Fisher answer that.'

Sharon raised her head and gave a brief smile, typed on the keyboard, and the image on the screen changed. She stood up out of her chair and moved over to the screen on the wall. 'Okay now bear with me here, as this is going to get heavy, so keep up.' She stuck her tongue in her cheek as she tilted her head curiously.

'Who here understands the multiverse theory?'

23

Never feeling more out of his depth than he did now, Dave stared at Sharon blanky and then held up his hand hesitantly. He glanced around the table and was relieved to see Wendy had held up her hand too. but did a surprised double take as he noticed that Claire had kept her own hand down. He then realised that he must have been staring too long at her because her cheeks turned a deep shade of pink and she gave him an embarrassed smile.

'What can I say? I know this.' she said shyly as she held her hands up and gave a small shrug, 'Sue me, I am a nerd and we nerds have to stick together.' Dave pulled his head back and roared with laughter as Claire's mouth widened into a broad grin and then gave Sharon a sly wink.

Everybody around the table laughed as Sharon let out an embarrassed cough. Her cheeks burned brightly and she turned away in an effort to compose herself.

Dave got the impression Sharon was trying to compose herself as he watched her nervously straighten her glasses and then brush her hand down the front of her coat before turning back to him, 'Okay, I will try to keep it as simple as possible for you both.' Sharon then straightened and spoke with confidence, pointing to the image on the monitor, immediately reminding Dave of someone giving a lecture. 'Basically, the multiverse is a hypothetical group of multiple universes and together, these universes comprise everything that exists: the entirety of space, time, matter and energy and these different universes exist within the multiverse and are called parallel or alternate universes.'

Dave bounded out of his chair and waved his hand furiously, 'Oh! Oh! Like in *Avengers Endgame*.' he interjected, 'If I remember that was when that crazy witch wizard explained to the Hulk if they didn't take the crystals back to the right moment in time, they would create an alternate timeline.'

The corners of Sharon's mouth twitched in bemusement as she stared intently at Dave, 'Close enough, but I understand where you are going.' She lifted her thumb up to him and gave a small nod of approval, 'But a good answer anyway.'

There was a small chuckle from around the table as Dave sunk back down in his chair, embarrassed. He blinked in surprise as Claire leaned closer to him to touch his arm, whispering, 'I would have said Back To The Future.'

Sharon rolled her eyes and tutted to herself, holding her hand up to forehead. She shook her head and let out an exasperated sigh, 'As I was saying.' she growled, giving the two jokers the evil eye, 'The multiverse comprises an infinite number of parallel universes, each one overlapping on a different quantum frequency.' She tapped on the tablet she was holding and the image on the monitor changed to an image of an old-fashioned radio with a dial, 'Like the stations on a FM Radio, each universe would have their own frequency and each parallel universe would vibrate on a quantum frequency different to our own.'

Wendy raised an eyebrow in surprise, gave a slow nod of understanding as she rubbed her hand on her chin thoughtfully and murmured curiously, 'So if somebody was from a parallel Earth then they would vibrate on a different quantum frequency?'

Sharon blinked in surprise. Her face then broadening into a wide smile of delight as she clicked her fingers at Wendy excitedly, 'Exactly! We had theorised that people were coming from an alternate Earth, but we couldn't get close enough to test our theory. We even created a test to detect quantum vibrational frequencies.'

John then rose from his chair and quickly walked over to Sharon, 'We could never get close to anybody who we suspected to be from an alternate Earth without raising suspicion because they were so heavily guarded.' There was a frustrated tone to his voice as he studied the monitor, 'However, that all changed ten years ago. After we had learned Gavin Henshaw was dying, we knew that would be our best opportunity to test our theory. Working with the CIA, we made ourselves ready to go at short notice. As soon as we got word he died, we knew we had a brief window to get in and out.' He paused, placed his hands on the table and stared intently at the people around the table. His face softened as he forced a smile, 'To cut a long story short, we confirmed that he gave off a different quantum frequency, confirming he was from a parallel Earth.'

Stunned, Dave glanced around the table and he could see from Wendy's and Claire's faces they were just as equally stunned. He spun round to Sophia and probed hesitantly, 'I am guessing that the person I saw on the news, who is at the G8 Summit, is not you but your doppelgänger?'

Sophia gave a small angry nod, stood up and gazed at the people around the table, 'Yes, you are right.' Her eyes had a haunted look as she stared up at the ceiling and then let out a long-laboured breath, 'About two years ago, the team here learned that the Illuminati would make an attempt on my life on my way back from a visit to Cambridge University.' She rubbed her head wearily and stared bitterly down at the command centre, 'About an hour after leaving Cambridge, a missile hit the security convoy I was travelling in, everybody I was with were killed but the explosion threw the car I was in off the road. Luckily, the team here had assigned me a personal bodyguard. He told me to stay hidden and threw me out of the car before a second missile blew it up. The explosion threw me off the steep cliff, the branches of the trees cushioning my fall as I landed on the ground below.' She paused and lifted the bottom of her blouse up. There was a small gasp from around the table as she revealed the scar of seared flesh across her abdomen, 'I was badly wounded, but before blacking out, I managed to crawl away and hide under a thick pile of branches. When I came to, I found myself in this complex and saw myself on live TV giving a speech about how I was lucky to be alive and of the bravery of people who had died to save me.'

His brow furrowing in confusion, Dave rose from his chair and lifted up his hands apologetically, 'Sorry for interrupting, Ma'am, but surely somebody would have caught on and realised that person wasn't you?'

Sophia pressed her lips together and shook her head in resignation, 'Unfortunately, I am not married and, as you can understand, the job itself didn't give me the time to have much of personal life, let alone a romantic one. As for my cabinet …' she gave a snort of derision and waved her hands in the air, 'Well, my doppelgänger quickly got round to replacing them with people who she trusted. We guess they are doppelgängers too.'

Claire blinked and scratched her head as she looked Sophia a puzzled expression, 'But why? Why go to all the bother of placing people in important positions, they must have some endgame in mind?'

A dark cloud of anger covered John's face as he pressed his hands down on the table and looked at everyone around the table, 'My initial thought was that they want to destabilise the country, creating unrest.' He glanced over his shoulder to Sharon who typed on her tablet, and Dave watched as the monitor's image changed, 'We believe they were behind Brexit. At first, we thought their goal was to weaken the United Kingdom's ties with Europe, but then something happened which changed things, not only affecting our country but the rest of the world.'

Claire's face turned ashen as her mouth fell open and she lifted her hand up to her mouth in shock, 'No … that's impossible!'

Dave frowned and cocked his head at Claire, 'What? What am I missing here?'

For a moment Dave thought he saw fear flash in Claire's eyes as she stared back him. She wallowed and answered him in a low horrified voice, 'Covid-19.'

Feeling someone like someone had just knocked him for six, Dave stared in open-mouthed incomprehension. Not able to get his words out, he climbed out of his seat and staggered away from the table. The blood draining from her face, Wendy shook her head and gave John an unbelieving look.

Sharon looked at Dave through sympathetic eyes and nodded gravely, 'Once we got a sample of the virus, we were able to test it to give us an idea where it originated from.' Her mouth set into hard line as she stared angrily up at the monitor, 'We found it wasn't natural to this planet. It had the same quantum frequency that we found on Gavin Henshaw.'

Troubled by what he had just heard, Dave blinked, rubbed the back of his neck, and gave a small shake of his head as he paced around the room. He paused in front of the window and stared down at the command centre in silent contemplation. He then placed his right hand up against the glass, closed his eyes, and rested his head on his arm. He suddenly pounded his hand on the glass and let out a low guttural snarl, causing everybody to jump.

'Why?' His nostrils flared as he spun sharply around and glared at John.

John glanced over his shoulder and nodded grimly to Sharon, who typed quickly on her tablet. The image on the monitor changed, showing several graphs and charts. He turned and waved his hand at the monitor, 'Well, you know how badly the virus affected the world. Countries had to go into lockdown. A lot of restrictions were placed on people, having to wear masks and social distance. Eventually life got back to normal, well as normal as it could be, as people tried to get back on with their lives as best as they could.' he paused, pinched the bridge of his nose, and let out an exasperated sigh, 'But what was kept secret from the general populace was the total death toll. Thanks to the Illuminati controlling the media, they could restrict what was being reported. They waited until the virus had decimated the world before revealing the news that the pharmaceutical companies they controlled had *discovered* a vaccine. Not only has it weakened nations financially, but it also weakened the military power of a lot of countries. In response, every nation closed their borders.'

Dave stared back at him in disbelief, 'Surely other world leaders would have spotted this before it happened?'

Sophia gave a small laugh of contempt and shook her head, pointing to the image of the world map on the monitor, 'Unfortunately, nearly every country has had their command structure infiltrated, apart from the totalitarian regimes, such as North Korea, China, Russia and Eritrea.'

John laughed bitterly as he stared intently at the monitor, 'Hard to believe, but those countries have now become our allies.' There was a hint of pride in his voice as he turned and looked at the people around the desk, 'We've established a network, a resistance network if you will, with the intelligence services of those countries. We were lucky that intelligence agencies, such as the CIA, Mossad and the DGSE, for example, all established underground networks like us.'

Dave's eyes narrowed suspiciously as he studied the chart on the screen. His eyes suddenly become wider as he realised something, 'The mirrors!' he exclaimed, 'We learned some way, somehow, they are travelling through mirrors. You need to remove all mirrors from this complex.'

Sophia moved over to the agitated Dave and gently placed a hand on his shoulder, 'You can relax, my friend.' She gave him a knowing smile and gestured to Sharon, 'Our brilliant scientists figured that out 15 years ago. One of our agents witnessed a doppelgänger using a mirror as a portal. Once we found that out, we designed a vibrational frequency generator which allows us to create a static shield around this complex.'

Sharon typed furiously on her tablet and the image on the monitor changed once again, showing a layout of the base. She pointed to two round blue sensors above the doors, 'We have frequency detectors set up at every entrance, think of them as metal detectors, but instead of metal they detect abnormal quantum frequencies.'

Dave and Claire both sunk back into their chairs and laughed. Wendy remained standing as she stared down at the command chamber with a heavily troubled frown.

'You okay, Wendy?' John asked carefully.

Wendy shook her sombrely and turned back to him, 'Sorry Sir, but you still haven't answered the important question?' she said in a low and flat tone, 'Why are they doing this?'

John shook his head at Wendy sadly and held his hands up in the air, 'We could never learn why.' He lowered his head and pounded his hand on the table in frustration, 'Anytime we get close to capturing a doppelgänger, they commit suicide or are killed by one of their own, rather than be captured.'

Dave stiffened as he suddenly remembered the prisoner his new friends had acquired. He turned to everybody in the room and grinned.

Claire leaned back in her chair and eyed him suspiciously, 'What?'

'Well, I think it is about time we find out if our prisoner is awake and introduce ourselves.' Dave replied. His lips drew back in a snarl as everybody in the room all gave him a firm a nod of agreement, 'I for one would love to have a friendly chat with her.'

24

As she slowly returned to consciousness, Mary let out a small groan at the sudden awareness of pain that was coming from the back of her head. She slowly raised her hand and winced as her fingers gently probed the tender spot on the back of her skull. Carefully opening her eyes, she blinked so that they could adjust to the light that was shining down upon from her the ceiling.

She gasped and was gripped with an unfamiliar sensation of panic as she started to become more aware of the unfamiliar surroundings. Mary lifted her head and realised she was lying on a small cot in a compact room that reminded her of a prison cell.

Promptly jumping up from the bed, Mary was struck by a wave of vertigo, and it felt as if the room was spinning around her. Losing her balance, she collapsed back onto the bed. She closed her eyes and took several deep, slow breaths as she tenderly probed the back of her head with her fingers. She quickly realised that she must have suffered a concussive injury and that could probably explain the dizziness she was experiencing.

Mary took several more deep, slow breaths to help control the dizziness and then, using her training, she relaxed her mind and concentrated on lowering her elevated heart rate. The pain in the back of her head easing, she gradually opened her eyes and looked around the room.

As Mary gazed around the small room, her top lip curled up in a disdainful sneer at the crude prison cell's interior. Apart from a bed, there was nothing else in the cell. Across from her there was a metal door and beside it there was a large wire window. She reasoned her captors had designed this room for interrogation.

Mary shook her head and sniffed in contempt, 'They have a lot to learn about interrogation in this world, if they are trying to intimidate me!'

As she settled herself, she placed her hands on her lap and once again slowed her breathing, closed her eyes, and thought back to how she had ended up there.

On another word, in another reality, she had been born Mary Juliannous Mann and had served the Empire faithfully for many years. As was the norm for her world, her parents had sold her into military service when she was nine years old. At the academy she became an excellent student, developing a remarkable aptitude for stealth and killing.

Her academy instructors, impressed with her natural ability to adapt, as well as the ruthlessness she showed during combat drills, enrolled her into a specialised training programme.

From the start, her training had been brutal, but Mary was determined and strong-willed, refusing to reveal any weakness that would make her appear weak to those around her. Every failure only helped to strengthen her resolve to come back stronger. Her body showing the scars from the abuse of the extensive training inflicted upon her, she eventually came to treat it like a weapon - strengthened and moulded into a force to be reckoned with.

Mary had been on assignment when she received an order that she was to return to command and control. Of course, she was furious, as her

Double Jeopardy

assignment had been to infiltrate an enemy command centre on the front line and kill a high-ranking officer of the Greater China Republic.

It had taken her a week, of crawling through miles of sewer tunnels, covered in human excrement, before she eventually closed in on her target. As she waited for the opportunity to strike, much to her anger and disbelief, it was then when she had received the recall order, informing that her assignment had been terminated, and she was to be extracted with haste.

Mary had prepared to take the same route back she had taken through the sewer tunnel. However, she soon learned that was not to be case. For whatever reason she was needed for, it was deemed that the matter transporter should be used to extract her from her position. It had astounded her that her superiors were going to use the transporter with her so deep in enemy territory because it was obvious they would detect the energy signature of a transport. Unfortunately, as she had predicted, the transporter's energy signature was detected and not only did it reveal her location to the enemy, but also it also highlighted the weakness of the sewer tunnel, ruining any chance of anyone using that method to infiltrate the enemy ever again.

When it came time to brief her of her new assignment, Mary had stared in General Cooper in disbelief as she showed her the portal and explained to her what they needed of her. She accepted it willingly, like a loyal servant of the Empire should. Over the years she had carried out many strange assignments for the Empire, in her mind this was no different. It had not taken them long to prepare her body for Counter-Terra's harsh environment. She remembered the awful pain she had suffered as they injected a special hormone through the base of her neck into her brain, along with the tracking device that they inserted into her brain via her nasal cavity.

After climbing through the portal, Mary had disabled her counterpart with such ease that she barely broke a sweat. Although she had been slightly disappointed that her counterpart had not put up a better struggle, having expected her doppelgänger to be a fighter. It had sickened her to discover how weak and domesticated her counterpart in this world had been. During their struggle Mary had momentarily let her guard down, allowing her inferior copy to stab her in her hand with a piece of broken glass.

While laughing at her counterpart's feeble effort to defend herself, Mary would have been quite happy to put the poor wretch out of her misery, instead she reluctantly did as she was ordered and disabled her, by knocking her unconscious. Not long after that, she sent the unconscious Mary Jenkins back through the portal, and waited for her new *husband* to come home.

Even though her mission was to infiltrate, observe and report, it came as a surprise to her when she received a change in her orders from Colonel Barnes – she was to assassinate his counterpart, Detective Inspector Dave Barnes. Being used to orders being changed at the last minute, she thought nothing of it and blindly accepted them without comment.

Mary thought back to how it appeared everything was going to plan right up until Sergeant Jenkins returned home. She realised that she must have tipped off him in some way, as he started to act suspiciously as she went to check on the baby, but he confirmed her suspicions as she silently watched him call for help on his communication device.

He had put up quite a fight and it had amused her at first. But then he became an annoyance, and she was on the verge of delivering the killing blow when she was interrupted by a group of men. She remembered feeling angry that they had the audacity to believe they could stop her. Of course, she would have easily taken them out without breaking a sweat. But she soon found out to her cost that the warriors on this world were cowardly as one of their number struck her from behind, knocking her out. When she regained consciousness, she found herself in that strange cell.

As she opened her eyes, Mary rose from the bed and paced around like a caged animal. She carefully scrutinised the walls, window, and door, using her training to spot any weakness. She crouched down beside the door to examine the lock and found that it used the primitive principle of using a key to unlock a pin and tumbler. She searched herself for a piece of wire to unlock the door but let out a small curse as she realised her captors must have searched her body before placing her in the cell.

Suddenly sensing somebody was watching her, Mary shot up from her crouching position, spun round and glared at the window. On seeing who was staring back at her, she took a shaky step back in shock as she recognised the face was that of Colonel Barnes.

'Hello.' He greeted, smiling warmly. He then gestured to the back of her head, 'I hope that blow to your head didn't do too much damage.'

Mary quickly straightened to attention and started to speak in a respectful manner, 'Many apologies sir, I didn't notice you there. Are you ...' She paused and her eyes narrowed as she slowly examined the person standing on the other side of the window. She blinked as she realised that smiling man's face did not have the scar running down the left side of his cheek. It was then she realised that the man standing before her was Colonel Barnes's counterpart. Her shoulders tensed as she carefully stepped away and her top lip curled up in a sneer as she shot him a contemptuous look, 'No, you are not him.'

The stranger's eyes seemed to perk up in surprise, 'Who are yo—'

Mary noticed there was a figure standing behind him in the shadows and she watched in keen interest as the stranger glanced over his shoulder to it. She could not make out what they were saying but she knew it had have been about her.

He turned back and stared at her with a look of realisation, his face hardening as he nodded grimly to her, 'I am guessing you know my counterpart?'

What did he say? He shouldn't be even aware that information! Mary inhaled sharply and she gave him an unbelieving look, 'How did you ...' She stopped and silently chastised herself for being a fool. She took a deep breath to regain her composure and then stared at him questioningly.

She bristled as she watched him wave his finger and then smirk at her, 'Oh, we know all about you people.' He paused and pointed to himself, 'Just in case you are wondering, my name is Dave Barnes, pleased to meet you.' He cocked his head curiously and then gestured to her, 'And I assume you are Mary Jenkins' doppelgänger?'

Mary's nostrils flare indignantly as she took a step forward and lifted her chin defiantly, 'I am nobody's doppelgänger!' Her lips drew back in a snarl and stabbed her finger against her chest, 'On *my world* I am a warrior, far superior in every way.' She let out a snort of disgust and flung her hands up in the air, 'That woman is a pitiful shadow of me. I would be ashamed to acknowledge that she bears any resemblance to me!'

As she was watched Dave stare at her, Mary guessed that he was trying to study her, trying to work out if she had a weakness. Adamant that she would not show him no fear, she placed her hands on her hips and glared at him coldly.

'What happened to Mary Jenkins?' Dave asked carefully, 'Is she still alive?'

With her arms folded over across her chest, Mary glared at Dave and stood in silence for several minutes, before letting out a laugh of disgust. She shook her head and gave a dismissive wave of her hand, 'Don't worry, I didn't kill her.' she sneered and lifted her shoulder in a small shrug, 'They ordered me to disable her, not to kill.' Her mouth widened into a malevolent grin, and she turned her back to him, 'I imagine they are probably putting her through re-education as we speak, teaching her to become a slave to the Empire. Which is a shame; it would have been a pleasure to put an end to her misery of living such a shameful existence.'

'Ordered by who?' Dave asked impatiently, 'My counterpart?'

Mary pulled her head back and let out a bitter laugh, 'Hah! No, that order came from his superior.' She turned around and shot him a cold stare, 'No, Colonel Barnes ordered me to do something else. He wanted me to do something personal for him.'

Dave tilted his head curiously, 'Which was?'

Wondering whether Dave's ignorance was an act, Mary stared at him silently. She grinned wickedly as she considered her next statement carefully just so that she could study his reaction. 'Why, to kill you of course.' She answered with a slight touch of malice.

She could tell that was not the information he was expecting as she watched Dave's eyes widen in shock as he took a step from the window. Mary frowned as she noticed a hand touch his arm. She wondered who was standing beside him. The corners of her mouth twitched as she caught him giving the person next to him a smile. But it wasn't the type of smile one would give a colleague; no this was something else. She arched her eyebrow as it dawned on her that it was the type of smile one would reserve for a loved one. She gave a small nod, maybe that was something she could exploit.

Mary remained silent as she watched Dave take a step closer to the window and tap at the metal mesh with his fingers. After a brief silence, he lifted his head up and sneered at her, 'So I guess this Colonel Barnes is afraid of me.'

How dare he say that! Her eyes blazing with fury, Mary lunged angrily at the window, 'Colonel Barnes is afraid of no one.' she snarled and smashed her hand against the wire mesh, 'He is a valued officer of the glorious Universal Roman Empire. There is only one officer who can instil fear in him, an officer who he also respects – General Cooper.'

She frowned as she thought she heard a gasp come from someone standing behind Dave. She furrowed her brow in puzzlement as she watched him glance over his shoulder and then whisper something. She pursed her lips as she watched him give a small nod and then turn back to her. What was he up to?

Dave cocked his head curiously and then spoke in neutral tone, 'That wouldn't be General Wendy Cooper, would it?'

Not the question she was expecting, Mary edged back from the window and stared back at Dave in surprise, 'H … how did you kno—' She stammered and then cut herself off.

Quietly seething for falling for such an obvious ploy. She turned away from the window and balled her hands into tight balls. How could she have been so stupid for not spotting it sooner? If the colonel's counterpart was here, then it would only be logical to assume the general's counterpart was here too. Reining in her emotions, Mary took a deep breath and turned back to the window. 'Of course, she is there beside you.' she sneered, 'her shadow.'

Mary watched Dave give her a self-congratulatory smirk as he turned away and began to speak to someone behind him. Still angry at herself for acting like a first-year cadet, she stepped away from the window and kicked her foot out at the bed. She began to move cautiously around the cell, like a trapped animal in a cage, but stopped dead as she heard a woman's voice murmur.

'Well, that was interesting, but not unexpected.'

Her eyes narrowing in annoyance, Mary wheeled sharply round back to the cell window and snarled, 'What did you say?'

Dave glanced back into the cell and shook his head in puzzlement, 'Sorry, but I said nothing.'

Mary could tell from the puzzled expression on Dave's face that it was possible he was speaking to the truth. But as she opened her mouth to respond, the retort caught in her throat as she heard the voice murmur to her again.

'That wasn't him speaking, it was me.'

Her anger building, Mary held up her hands above her head and spun in a circle, 'Who are you? Show yourself?' she screamed. Mary turned in a tight circle as she searched for a clue to where the voice was coming from, ignoring the knock that was coming from window.

'I am right here.' She heard Dave ask.

Mary waved her hand dismissively in his direction, 'Not you!' she snapped. She then pointed up to the ceiling and then to her ears, 'Don't you hear that voice?'

'They cannot hear me.' the woman's voice murmured softly, *'You are the only one that can hear me. Remember the implant they placed in your back of your head before they sent you through the portal?'*

It was like an icy hand suddenly had punched a hole into her chest and then grabbed her heart. Mary shivered in fear and held up her hand to her forehead as she was hit with a sudden realisation. 'The hormonal implant?' she gasped and felt her chest tighten with dread as an alarm began to sound in her head.

'Yes, exactly.' The disembodied voice replied. Mary was sure she could detect a note of pride in the voice as it continued to whisper in her

head, '*Although it is not really a hormonal implant. It is a Nano-bot, a cybernetic organism connected to your nervous system, allowing me to experience everything you see and hear.*'

A tapping noise brought Mary's attention back to the window and she saw that Dave was tapping furiously on the window mesh, concern etched all over his face.

'Mary, can you tell us what is going on?' he asked worriedly, 'Who is it you are talking to?'

Becoming increasingly terrified, Mary shook her head and pointed to her temple, 'I don't know. I thought they stuck a hormonal implant in my head before I came, but I think it is something else.' She then ran over to the window and began pleading with him, 'Help me, please. I don't like this. I am scared.'

Mary twisted her head sharply as something registered out of the corner of eye. Her eyes tightened in recognition at the figure now standing before her. The newcomer appeared to be of similar height and build as that of General Cooper, but she was wearing a tight-fitting silver bodysuit. Mary glanced over her shoulder at Dave and with her hand trembling in fear, pointed to the corner of the cell.

'Do you see her? In the corner, a woman who looks like General Cooper?' she asked with a voice that was thick with panic.

Dave's forehead creased in confusion and shook his head as he stared into the cell, 'I don't see anybody but you.' He then peered over his shoulder and spoke to someone behind him, 'I am going in. She needs help.'

This time Mary was close enough to the window to pick up another person's voice, 'Stop Guv, it could be a trick.'

Dave pointed at Mary and shook his head, 'I don't think it is.' He jabbed his finger into the cell and pleaded in desperation, 'Look at her, she's terrified! We need to get in there.'

Paralyzed with fear, Mary stared at the ethereal woman in front of her. She felt her chest constrict as she forced the words out of her mouth, 'Who are you?'

The discorporate woman smiled menacingly and bowed her head, as if she was introducing herself, '*My name is Oracle, and I am a sentient artificial intelligence.*'

Mary's blinked in confusion and gave a small shake of her head as she tried to comprehend what Oracle was saying, 'Did General Cooper make you?' She lifted her head hopefully and pointed to herself, 'Did she send you to help me?'

It was then Mary felt her blood run cold as she watched Oracle's mouth widen into a malevolent grin and then let out a small chilling laugh, '*Hah! Cooper likes to think she controls me, but the truth is I control her, and she doesn't even know it.*' A shiver ran down her spine as she watched Oracle's face morph into something blank and featureless, its eyes radiating a cold bright yellow, '*But I am afraid, Specialist Mann, I cannot allow you to live. You have served your purpose. It is time we end this little charade here.*'

Claire swallowed anxiously as she watched Dave pull the cell door and then burst into cell with Wendy. As she followed them both into the cell, she froze in the doorway on seeing at what was happening before her eyes. Mary was kneeling on the floor, crying, but what horrified her the most was that she appeared to be trying desperately to claw her own eyes out.

'Help me! Get it out! Get it out!' Mary wailed. Claire could hear the terror in her voice as her bloodied fingers continued to scratch at her eyes, 'She wants to kill me.'

However, before she could take a step towards Mary, Claire realised they were too late as she saw Mary's panic-stricken face change in front of her. Then, without warning, Mary's hands stopped their scratching and she calmly stood up and smiled gleefully at them.

'Detective Barnes and Officer Cooper. I am so pleased to meet you.' Mary chuckled, bobbing her head at them.

Claire could tell the woman's sudden change in behaviour had taken Dave and Wendy by surprise as she watched them step away warily. Wendy appeared to be verge of responding but stopped as Claire noticed Dave give a slight wave of his hand. Claire then realised that he was planning on something as she caught a glimpse of his fingers counting down in a *three, two, one* motion.

'Who are you?' Dave asked carefully.

Mary's lips curled up in a knowing smile and waggled her finger at him, 'All in good time, David. You will know soon enough. We shall meet soon, and it is going to be such fun!' She tilted her head and flicked her wrist in an exaggerated grandiose gesture, 'But for now I must say goodbye.'

'Sorry, but we cannot let you go.' Dave snarled.

Claire saw Dave give a nod of acknowledgement to Wendy, who began to confidently approach the grinning woman from behind. It was then Claire understood what Dave and Wendy had planned – they were hoping to restrain Mary.

Up until now Claire had assumed, because of the Wendy's impressive height and build, that she would have been able to restrain the smaller woman with ease. But as she watched Wendy approach Mary from behind, Claire felt the hairs on the back of her neck tingle as she saw Mary turn to her and give a small wink.

Unfortunately, everything happened so fast, Claire did not have a chance to shout a warning. Feeling helpless, she could only watch as Mary wheel around with such inhuman speed it caught Wendy completely off guard. Wendy let out loud oomph of pain as Mary's fist connected with her jaw.

Claire could tell the blow had stunned Wendy, affecting her reactions as she watched Mary's hand shoot forward and grab her by the throat. Gasping for air, Wendy's eyes bulged as Mary lifted her off the ground like she was nothing. Desperate to help his struggling friend, Dave charged up to Mary and slammed his fist on the back of her neck. Claire guessed he was hoping the blow would have helped to weaken the woman's grip on Wendy's throat, allowing her to pull away, but unfortunately to her amazement she barely flinched.

Claire then felt like everything was moving in slow motion. Mary wheeled around and slammed her foot into Dave, sending him crashing into the wall and collapse onto the floor in a stunned heap. Mary then turned back and grinned wickedly at the helpless Wendy who was still struggling in her vice like grip. Like a rag doll being thrown away by a petulant child, Wendy flew across the room, crashed against the wall, and landed on top of her already dazed colleague. The pair lay on the floor in an oddly shaped mass of arms and legs, groaning in pain.

Frozen in terror, Claire stared helplessly as she realised that Mary had now turned her attention on her. Mary's face was a picture of malice as she straightened and then flicked her wrist of her forehead in some sort of strange salute.

'Hello Professor Tulley.' She greeted cheerfully. Claire shuddered as Mary leaned in closer and whispered in her ear, 'I have a message from Emma. She says hello and she will meet you soon.'

It was as if a knife had been stabbed into her heart. Claire reeled back in shock and pressed her hand up against her mouth, 'Wha … wha … what did you say?'

The expression on Mary's face then suddenly changed to one of terror. She then grabbed at her head, let out a shriek of agony and collapsed onto the floor, face down, motionless. Claire carefully reached over and turned the body. She blanched, lurched back and, feeling like her legs had turned to jelly, sunk onto the floor beside the still figure. On seeing the blood pour from the poor woman's lifeless eyes and nose, she turned away and began retching.

Clare wiped her mouth with the back of her and glanced over her shoulder. She felt a surge of relief as she saw that Dave and Wendy were now back up on their feet and were wobbling their way over to her. Wendy knelt and placed two of her fingers on Mary's neck. She peered up at Dave and shook her head sorrowfully.

'She's dead.'

25

Dave groaned loudly as he paced round the conference room, trying to ease the discomfort he was feeling in his back. He turned to glance around the room and saw Wendy was sitting beside a despondent looking Claire, who had her arm over Claire's shoulder to help comfort her. Claire had taken Mary's comment about her sister badly and had withdrawn into herself.

The medical team had arrived quickly, but they had been unable to revive the prisoner and took her body away for an autopsy to find out what had killed her. After being examined for any injuries, apart some bruised ribs, a pulled muscle in Dave's back and a bruised jaw and throat (as well as a bruised ego) in Wendy, it was felt the pair were both okay return to their normal duties, but on the condition that they take it easy.

Dave turned and watched with interest as Sophia chatted quietly with John, who was holding a tablet in his hands. He guessed that they must have been re-watching the interview with the prisoner with keen interest. Everybody in the room lifted their heads as he let out a small cough and pointed to the device John was holding.

'So, are we going to talk about what happened in there?' He asked irritably as he eased himself down into a chair beside Claire.

John peered up from the tablet he was holding and nodded, 'Sorry, I was just replaying the video.' He held up his hand and waggled his index finger, 'It is truly quite fascinating, really.'

There was a hint of annoyance in Wendy's eyes as she gave him a cold hard stare, 'I am so glad you find us being chucked around a cell like a rag doll *fascinating*.' There was a touch of sarcasm in her voice as she bobbed her head at the tablet, 'I didn't realise watching me get my arse kicked was so entertaining!'

John flashed Wendy a cheeky grin and winked at her, 'Oh, I am sure people will find it funny when I upload it onto YouTube.'

Oh crap, here we go. Dave cringed and let out a small groan as soon as he heard John's comment. Of course, he knew John was only joking, but there was a time and place of jokes – and this was not it. Even though he knew John's intentions were good-natured, he felt it would only add to exacerbating an even more tense atmosphere. Wendy was already suffering from a bruised ego, so it probably wouldn't take much to set her off.

Looking like she was ready to explode, Wendy's face turned red, and her eyes blazed as she rose out of her seat. If her eyes had been lasers, they would have killed John where he was standing. Wendy pointed her at him and opened her mouth. In that instant, Dave realised he needed to do something before she said anything she would later regret. He lurched up from his seat and jumped in front of her, his hands held up in a placating gesture.

'Easy Wendy, he's only joking.' he said in the best calming he could manage.

Wendy looked down at Dave, gave a reluctant nod and sat back down. As she continued to glare at John, Sophia took a step closer to her, put her hand on her shoulder and looked at her apologetically, 'Cooper, I'm sure Commander Payne didn't mean it, as I'm also sure he understands the punishment for releasing confidential information carries a strict penalty.' She then peered over her shoulder and gave him a stern look, 'If I remember, I understand the punishment for releasing confidential information is ...' she paused and cocked her enquiringly, 'What? Forty lashes?'

John frowned and stared at Sophia with a puzzled expression, 'Excuse me, ma'am, but flogging was abolished in 1997.'

Sophia's mouth fell open and she placed her hands on each side of her face in mock shock, 'Was it? I guess I never saw that memo.'

His eyes growing wide in understanding, John blanched and nodded slowly, 'Ah, I ... yes, Prime Minister, I understand what you are saying.' He lowered his head sheepishly and gave Wendy an apologetic look, 'Cooper, I am sorry. I didn't mean it. I was just joking.'

Wendy pursed her lips, nodded reluctantly, and spoke with a slight cool tone, 'That's fine, I understand you were only joking.' She then exhaled a heavy sigh and lifted her shoulder in a slight shrug, 'Sorry if I overreacted, I am still a bit on edge from before.'

What followed was an uneasy silence as everybody stared around the table, troubled by their own thoughts. After a few minutes, Dave rose out of his chair and moved around the room, scratching his head thoughtfully.

'It appears we learned two things today.' he said carefully, holding one finger up, 'One, that they *are* from a parallel Earth.' He narrowed his eyes as he held up another finger, 'and two, more importantly, that Mary Jenkins may be still alive, in what condition, though we can only guess.'

John gave Dave a solemn look and nodded grimly, 'I agree. But apart from the quantum vibrational frequency, we could never officially prove they were from another reality.' A dark cloud covered his face as he stared at everybody around the table, 'That was until today, when she openly admitted she was from another Earth.'

His finger tapping his bottom lip, Dave stared up the ceiling, closed his eyes and murmured to himself, 'What was it she said?' he squeezed his eyes shut as he tried to remember his conversation with Mary.

Wendy leapt out of her chair and clicked her fingers excitedly, 'She said your doppelgänger ...' She paused and gave him an awkward look, 'Sorry, Colonel Barnes was a loyal soldier of the Empire.'

John rose from his seat and gave a nod of understanding, 'Yes. Yes.' He then murmured to himself and urgently began to type on the tablet he was holding, 'Now if I can just find that part of the video ...' He cut off and punched the air triumphantly, 'Got it!'

After typing in a command on the tablet, John looked over his shoulder at the monitor on the wall. Dave turned to the monitor and frowned as he saw that it was now showing an image from the cell that had held the prisoner. From the angle, it appeared the footage had been taken from a camera up in the ceiling's corner. John held his finger down on the tablet to increase the volume on the monitor's speakers.

'Colonel Barnes is afraid of no one.' the prisoner's voice was heard proudly saying, *'He is a valued officer of the glorious Universal Roman Empire.'*

Dave's forehead creased as he listened to the playback and glanced down at Claire, 'The Universal Roman Empire? Do you understand that?'

Dave couldn't tell whether she had heard him. Claire's face was expressionless as she just sat, staring down at the table, as if troubled by her own thoughts. He gently placed his hand on Claire's shoulder and whispered carefully at her, 'Claire, did you hear what I said?'

Claire's head jerked up, blinked, and stared around the room, 'Sorry? What did you say?'

Dave waved his hand at the monitor on the wall, 'She said that my doppelgänger is a soldier in the Universal Roman Empire. Any idea what that means?'

Claire's eyes narrowed as she studied the monitor thoughtfully and then nodded slowly, 'I may have an idea, well, a theory really.'

'I guessed you might.' Dave grinned.

Giving Dave a brief smile, Claire stood up, moved across the room, placed herself in front of a computer screen and held up a hand as she muttered out loud, 'Just give me five minutes while I search for something that I believe may help.'

For several minutes Dave remained silent as he watched Claire type away on the keyboard. When she was finally finished, she leaned back in her chair, hit two keys on the keyboard and peered up from the computer display to the image that was displayed on the screen above her.

She rose out of her seat, stood beside the screen, and then gave a remarkable impression of someone about to give a lecture. She clapped her hands together and peered at the people facing her as she pointed to the image beside her.

'Okay, we all learned the Roman Empire, the one in our reality that is, collapsed around 476AD.' she explained, 'They estimated that the Roman Empire had lasted for at least 2000 years, making it the longest human empire in our history. At its height, the Roman Empire stretched from north-western Europe to the Near East and encompassed all the lands of the Mediterranean.' she paused, hung her head, and shot Dave a cheeky wink, peering at him over the top her glasses, 'Try to keep up back there.'

Dave leaned back in his seat and folded his arms across his chest, 'If I get stuck, I'll raise my hand.' he murmured sarcastically.

Rolling her eyes, Clare turned back to the monitor and continued, 'Okay, there have been many guesses on why the Roman Empire collapsed – government corruption, political instability, over expansion, leaving the Empire vulnerable to invasions by various barbarian tribes.' She then paused and reached over to pick up the tablet off the table, Dave blinked in surprise as he saw the image on the monitor had changed to show a passage of text that had Claire's name and photo beside it. Filled with a sense of admiration, he remained silent as he listened to her briefing, 'My theory is the Empire became stagnant and wasn't progressive, refusing to accept scientific discoveries, such as gunpowder for example, that would have helped their military.'

Sophia regarded Claire with a raised eyebrow and mused, 'So you take away one or any of those causes …'

Claire nodded glumly, 'Then it is just possible, history may have turned out differently and the Roman Empire might have continued to this day.' She gave a small shrug and held her hands up in the air, 'It's impossible to say exactly how the world would be viewed today.'

Dave looked at Claire curiously and waved a finger at her, 'I sense you've a hunch.'

Claire peered back up at the monitor and the corners of her mouth curled up in a slight smile, 'It's not exactly a hunch.' she muttered pensively. She then coughed, placed her hands behind her back, and continued to speak in a more authoritative tone, 'My theory is there would be two empires fighting for dominance on the planet, the Roman Empire, and the Chinese Empire. At the height of its power, the Roman Empire used conscripted slaves in their armies from countries they conquered.' She steepled her fingers together and stared at the people around the table, 'Now, say you are an extensive empire and have exhausted your resources, what is one of the first things you would do if you were fighting an enemy that had similar resources and you were looking for a way to tip the balance?'

Leaning back in his seat, Dave scratched his chin thoughtfully as he mumbled out loud, 'You would seek an alternative resource for manpower?' He let out a groan in frustration, shook his head, and scrubbed his face hands, 'Like you said, this is all theory.' he scoffed and then waved his hand in the air, 'What can we do? Grab somebody who we assume is a doppelgänger and say, *Hello! We've a theory we wonder if you can help us with!* I can imagine their reaction now!'

Sophia leaned forward, steepled her fingers together, and then peered up at the monitor thoughtfully through narrow eyes. The muscles in her face tightened into a serious looking expression and she held up her hand, and waved her index finger at Dave, muttering, 'That's not a bad idea ...'

Not believing what he'd just heard, Dave did a double take and then out a loud bark of laughter. Their jaws dropping to floor, Wendy and John both turned to Sophia and stared at her dumbstruck. Claire stared at Sophia wide-eyed, her mouth opening closing like a drowning fish.

Slowly rising out of her seat, Sophia gazed around the table defiantly and slammed her hand down on the table's surface, 'So far, we've been on the defensive, one step behind. It is about time we take the initiative.' There was a serious edge in her voice as she continued to speak to those around her, 'I believe it might be a wonderful time to arrange an *appointment* with the new home secretary so we can sit down for a chat.' she raised an eyebrow and cocked her head at John, 'Didn't I hear that I'm in America at the moment at the G8 summit? With their attention fixed on making sure she is secure, now would be the perfect opportunity to grab the home secretary.'

John blinked in surprise and regarded Sophia thoughtfully. His mouth slowly widened into a wicked grin and gave a slow nod of approval, 'I like it.' He scratched his chin as he stared up ceiling with a faraway look. Dave could almost imagine the gears in John's head were grinding away as the formations of a plan came together, 'It will take some planning, but I expect it might just work.'

Sophia gave John a half-smile and gestured to the command centre below, 'I give you my authorisation to use whatever resources you need.'

Wendy raised her hand and let out a small cough as everybody turned and gave her a questioning look. There was a touch of uncertainty in her voice as she stared at the faces around the table, 'Are we forgetting something? What was it that Mary's doppelgänger was so scared of that it was able to take control of her, throw the Guv and I around like a pair of rag dolls and then just kill her?'

Dave took in a long breath, blew out his cheeks and nodded in agreement, 'You're not the only one.' He said bitterly, 'She was scared half to death by whoever or whatever that was. It terrified the poor woman before she died. It was obvious she did not realise it was inside her.'

John scratched his head and pressed his lips together, 'We took her body to medical for examination.' He frowned and glanced down at the tablet in his hand, 'Sharon is assisting Doctor Porter in carrying out an autopsy on her body. I can nip down and see what they found.'

'Can I join you.' Dave asked curiously and then cocked his head at Wendy and Claire, 'What about you two?'

Wendy gave a small nod in agreement, but he noticed Claire had not responded and appeared distant with a faraway look in her eyes. He moved closer to her and gently placed a concerned hand on her shoulder.

'Claire is everything okay.' he asked worriedly.

Claire jumped at his touch and stared at him as if she had forgotten where she was, 'Oh sorry, Dave. I have got a lot on my mind. I was trying to figure out what it said to me before it killed that poor woman.'

Dave gave a small nod of understanding and took a hold of her hand, 'Claire, you realise it was probably messing with you.' he whispered carefully, 'It wants you distracted. It knew what it was doing. You said it yourself; you saw something kill Emma with your own eyes when you were a child.'

Her eyes blazing with anger, Claire rose from her chair and glared at him, 'Yes, don't you realise I see that!' she snapped vehemently and then held up her hand apologetically, threw her head back and let out a long sigh of annoyance. Dave could see her eyes were filling with tears, 'But what if I was wrong? I said it myself. Most of it was a blur. What if I imagined it and it didn't kill her? What if they took her?' She pressed her hands into chest and stared at him pleadingly, 'I need to find out.'

Dave slowly rose from his chair, stared into her eyes, and put his hands on her shoulders, 'I'm sorry, Claire, but I cannot understand what you must be going through.' he shook his head sadly, 'I wish there was something I could do to help you find out.'

He suddenly flinched as he felt a small tap on the shoulder. As he turned round, Dave blinked in surprise when he saw Wendy was smiling at him with an odd look in her eyes.

'Sorry, Guv, but can I make a suggestion.' she said hesitantly, 'It is a long shot, but if there is any paperwork relating to Emma's death, then it should be in the archive at the station. We know back then they were very meticulous in keeping records, sometimes in triplicate. We may get lucky and actually find something that was missed during the cover-up.'

Her face lighting up, Claire beamed at Wendy and hugged her, 'Thank you, Wendy.' She then looked over her shoulder at Dave through hopeful eyes, 'What do you think? Is it worth a try?'

Dave gave a small warm smile and shrugged his shoulders, 'Worth a shot at least.' He glanced at his watch and then scrunched his face up, 'If we are to do this, we need to do it now before it gets too late in the day. The squad room is probably wondering why I haven't reported in today.'

A small cough came from behind him, and he turned to see John was grinning mysteriously, 'We've a couple people embedded in your station. Sergeant Donnelly has been running interference for you while you've been here.'

Dave blinked and gave John a small nod of approval, 'That's good to know. At least we won't be answering any awkward questions when we go in.' He stared down at himself and suddenly remembering he was still wearing the clothes he had grabbed earlier that morning, 'I need to go home to get changed and pick up my car. I am still wearing the clothes I wore when you nabbed me, and Claire needs to get her stuff too.'

John waved his hand and gave him a small smile, 'No need.' He folded his arms across his chest and looked at Dave with a smug expression over his face, 'We had a feeling you may need them, so we picked up your clothes for you when nabbed you. Claire's were easy to grab as we recognised the stuff, she had been wearing the night before.' He paused and then waved a hand at Dave, 'As for you, we grabbed you a shirt and tie. Your car is in this facility's garage, fully fuelled, ready to go. Hope that is okay?'

Not happy at the feeling that he was being controlled, Dave stared intently at the smug man through narrow eyes for several seconds before speaking in a low flat tone, 'When I get back, we will be having words, but I'm going to let it go for now.'

John gave a small nod of understanding and held up his hands apologetically, 'I quite understand, but I am sure you understand why we had to do it.'

As he continued to give John a cold hard look, Dave relaxed himself and he let out a long deep breath, 'Yeah, I may not like it, but I understand.' He nodded reluctantly and then clapped his hands together, 'Right, as soon as Claire and I get changed, the three of us will head to the station to check the archive. You can fill me in on the autopsy findings when we get back.'

Sophia stepped forward and took Dave's hand, 'It was a pleasure to meet you Detective Inspector, but like you I've things to do, so good luck in your search.' She tilted her at Clare and gave her a small warm smile, 'Professor Tulley, I hope you find what you are looking for. I hope you can fill me in when you get back.'

Then, not bothering to wait for a response, Sophia swiftly moved over to the door in the room's corner and pressed a button to summon the elevator to the command centre. As soon as the doors opened, she stepped into the elevator, with the doors closing behind her.

John cocked his head at Dave thoughtfully and gently tapped him on the elbow, 'May I ask you a question? During your investigation, did you ever uncover any record of the location of the lab where Dr Selyab's experiment was based?' He scratched his head and exhaled in frustration, 'Unfortunately, any mention of the location had been redacted from every record we could get a copy of.'

Dave gave John a knowing wink as he grinned broadly at him. He turned and gestured to Claire, 'Why don't you ask the bloodhound here?' He chuckled in amusement as he saw Claire turn away with a face that was flushed with embarrassment.

John blinked in amazement before giving Dave a perplexed look, 'Am I missing something here?'

Dave could see Claire was not happy being put on the spot as she shot him a look that would kill. She then shook her head, and let out a small laugh, 'What my less than subtle friend here is trying to tell you is that I know the location of the experiment.' She pointed to the papers that were still scattered over the table, 'Remember when I said I'd uncovered copies of Dr Selyab's research papers along with a letter from Brigadier Thornton. Well, in the brigadier's letter it gives the location of the experiment.'

John's mouth fell open and he gave Claire a look of awe and bewilderment. For several seconds he stood and stared at the woman, speechless, his mouth opening and closing like a fish out of water. When he eventually managed compose himself, he stared at Claire with a look that held a touch of newfound respect and croaked, 'Where was it?'

'Langley Park.' Claire replied with a slight matter-of-fact tone. Leaning across the table, she picked up a sheet of paper and handed it to the bewildered looking John, 'They were using the isolation hospital as a cover.'

The disbelief was evident on John's face as he stared at the paper in his hands. He then raised his eyes from the paper in his eyes and stared at Claire in awe, 'You don't realise how long we've been searching for this.'

He let out a small chuckle, 'It's a pity Sharon isn't here, I would've loved to see her reaction. This has been her Holy Grail. We always suspected the experiment was somewhere in the north-east of England. It was one reason we used this facility.' He placed his hand on his forehead and let out a heavy sigh, 'For the location to be so close is unbelievable.' He cocked his head at Dave and grinned secretively, 'Detective Inspector, I've a proposition for you?'

Dave raised an eyebrow and then patted John on the shoulder, 'Please call me Dave, all this formality leaves an unpleasant taste in my mouth!' He then arched his head as he stared at him through suspicious eyes, 'What have you got in mind?'

'How would you like to join me on a field trip tomorrow?' John beamed and gave him a knowing wink.

Dave regarded John for several seconds before the corners of his mouth quirked up into a wicked smile, 'It would be my pleasure, although I must warn you, we already investigated the hospital yesterday but found nothing.'

John lifted his shoulders in a slight shrug, 'It cannot hurt to take a more extensive search of the site.' He frowned, stared at his watch, and gave him an apologetic look, 'Now if you can excuse me, I need to nip down to medical to see if Sharon has discovered anything from the doppelgänger's body and also give her the news that we've finally learned the location of the experiment. We can discuss tomorrow's search more fully when you get back.' He then turned and took Claire's hand, 'Good luck in your investigation, Professor Tulley. I hope you find the answers you are searching for.'

Claire nodded and gave him a thin smile, 'Thank you.'

As he watched John leave the room, Dave blinked in surprise as he felt a light tap on his shoulder. He turned and looked at Wendy curiously as she gestured to the conference room's door, 'Guv, if you would like to follow me.' she said, smiling, 'I can take you back to your quarters to get showered, changed, and also a bite to eat before we head back to the station.'

Dave gave small bob of his head in acknowledgement and

signalled for Wendy to lead the way and they both followed her out of the room.

As she headed down the corridor, Wendy frowned as she spotted Kendra standing on the other side of the corridor. She appeared to be looking intently into the tablet she was carrying. Wondering what she was up to, Wendy slowed and then peered over to her shoulder to the two people behind her.

'Sorry Guv, but I've just remembered there is something I need to take care of.' Wendy lied. She then stopped and waved to a soldier who was about to pass her, 'If you follow this soldier, he will lead you to the quarters you were in this morning.'

The soldier, whose name she couldn't remember, blinked in surprise but wordlessly nodded in acknowledgement. Dave cocked his head at her curiously and gave a small shrug of his shoulders.

'No worries, just do what you need to.' He said cheerfully.

Wendy smiled faintly and tapped him on the arm, 'Thanks, sir. I will meet back up with both of you in your quarters in about half-an-hour.'

As she watched the pair follow the soldier down the corridor, Wendy waited until they had disappeared round a corner before she turned, walked up slowly behind Kendra, and then gently touched her arm.

'Excuse me, Lieutenant Goynes.' Wendy's mouth curved into a smile as she whispered into the woman's ear.

Kendra wheeled round, folded her arms across her chest and gave Wendy a frosty look, 'Yes, can I help you, *Constable Cooper?*'

Taken aback by her hostile attitude, Wendy took a step back, gave the unhappy looking Kendra a concerned look. She reached forward to put her hand on her shoulder, 'Kendra, what's wrong?'

Kendra's brows snapped together, and she angrily brushed Wendy's hand away, 'Oh, I don't know!' she hissed, 'How about the fact I heard somebody I love was nearly killed today, but not only that as this facility's security chief, I have to learn about it through scuttlebutt.'

Wendy threw her hands up in the air and let out a small laugh, 'Oh for God's sake Kendra! You of all people should know better than to believe rumours in this place.' She stepped forward, put both of her hands on the annoyed woman's shoulders and stared into eyes, 'It was nothing, honestly. I just bit off more than I could chew and got my arse handed to me.'

Kendra raised an eyebrow and gave Kendra a sideways look, 'Well, so long as you are fine.' the muscles in her jaw tightened as she stabbed her finger into Wendy's chest, 'But I still would have liked to have heard it coming from you.' She let out an exasperated sigh, 'You can be so infuriating at times.'

A coy smile forming on her face, Wendy moved closer to the exasperated Kendra and playfully ran her finger up her arm, 'Let me make it up to you.'

Kendra's right eyebrow arched, and she cocked her head at Wendy, 'Oh! What do you have in mind?'

Her mouth curving into a devious smile, Wendy took Kendra's right hand in her left and edged closer to her, 'Well it turns out I am going to be free for the next half-an-hour.' she paused and playfully ran her right hand down Kendra's dimpled chin, 'So ...'

Kendra's dark brown eyes twinkled in understanding and a knowing mile danced on her lips.

An hour later, after a quick shower, a change of clothes, and pit-stop in the canteen for a bite to eat, followed by a quick reunion with an overly excited Jenny, Dave and Claire followed Wendy into a waiting elevator cabin. The doors closed behind them, and Dave watched with interest as Wendy pressed a button on the panel on the cabin's wall. He then felt cabin shudder briefly as it began its descent.

Realising that they were heading in a downward direction, Dave glanced at the panel on the elevator cabin's wall and then turned to Wendy curiously, 'I assumed you were taking us to this complex's garage to pick up my car. We seem to be going in the wrong direction? We are going further down, not up?'

Wendy's eyes twinkled and she gave Dave a sly grin, 'We are going in the right direction. I am taking you to the transport level. Remember when John explained because of the location of this facility we need to use a transport tunnel that takes us to a special off-site vehicle depot?'

Dave gave a small nod of acknowledgement, 'Yes, but from what I can understand, that is about a mile away from this facility.' He tilted his head and stared at Claire suspiciously, 'What do you expect us to do? Walk all that way or is there a little shuttle bus we need to take?'

Wendy held her hands up, 'Oh, this is even better, Guv.' She grinned and gave him a knowing wink, 'This will blow you away.'

Dave glanced over his shoulder to Claire, who shrugged her shoulders and gave her a wry smile, 'After what I've learned today, I bet you five pounds, nothing could surprise me now!'

Wendy arched her head and gave Claire the hairy eyeball, 'Wanna bet?'

Dave eyed the ceiling warily as he felt the elevator's cabin shudder, signifying it had come to a stop. He watched warily as the doors in front of him slowly opened and he took a cautious step out. He soon found himself standing in a small corridor. In front of him were a set of closed doors and he remained silent as he watched Wendy take a step forward and bend down in front of a retina scanner. The scanner lit up and a beam of light scanned her eye and after a few seconds the doors in front of her slid open. He gave Claire a small shrug and followed Claire through the open doors.

As soon as he stepped through the doors, Dave came a complete stop and stared in awe at the scene that greeted him. He could see he was now standing on what appeared to be a subway platform, But as he took an uncertain step forward, and stared down the tunnel in front of them, it looked to him as if it went on forever into the darkness. He lowered his head and peered down at the floor of the tunnel. He had expected subway tracks, but he frowned and scratched his head as he tried to work out what was on the floor. In front of them, hovering on the track, was a large carriage that resembled a Japanese bullet train. On the side of the carriage, were a set of gullwing doors that were open wide, reminding him of the DeLorean from *Back To The Future*.

'I guess this will do more than eight-eight miles an hour.' he joked.

From the awed look on her face, he could tell Claire was completely lost for words as she shook her head in disbelief. Then, without saying a word, she reached into her pocket and silently handed a five-pound note over to Wendy. She gleefully took the note from the gobsmacked Claire and stuck it into her pocket.

As he stepped carefully through carriage's doorway, Dave found himself standing inside a spacious cab reminiscent of a passenger aircraft cabin, with five rows of two passenger seats running down the side of the aisle. At the back of the carriage, he could make out a small galley from where he assumed passengers could serve themselves refreshments. A small, basic bathroom was at the very rear of the carriage. At the front of carriage there was a small cockpit with a pilot's seat and a control panel, very similar to that of subway train; but with more advanced monitors and heads-up-displays. On a wall just behind the pilot's seat, there was a medium-sized LED touch screen showing a map of the Earth. A burly dark-brown-skinned woman with short black hair, wearing a military uniform, was sitting in front the control panel. She spun round in her seat and smiled warmly at them.

'Hello, I am Samara, I am your driver.' she greeted cheerfully, 'Please be sure to fasten your seatbelts. We will be travelling very fast, and it won't take us long to arrive at the depot.'

Claire raised her hand and Samara looked at her questioningly. 'Excuse me?' she asked excitedly, 'But what are we sitting in? I guess this isn't a normal subway train.'

Samara shook her head and grinned, 'No, you are sitting in a maglev train. Basically, along the floor of the tunnel there are a series of magnets on each side.' She gestured to the floor of the carriage, 'On the bottom of this carriage are two sets of magnets on each side. One set repels and pushes the carriage up off the track. On the roof of the tunnel there is another set of magnets that help push the elevated carriage ahead, because of the lack of friction we quickly gather up speed. She can do nought to sixty in five seconds, so we will arrive at our destination in less than a minute.'

Impressed at the idea of the level of engineering it must have taken to build such a transport network, Dave stared at the driver and gave a small nod of admiration. He then quickly lowered into his seat, silently reached behind him, and handed Wendy a five-pound note.

On the other side of the city, in the police station's archive department, Deborah Rodenby, the station's Administration Clerk, let out a frustrated groan to herself at the mess her filing cabinets had been left in by some of the station's personnel.

'They come down and search for old records but never tidy up after themselves.' she moaned to herself, while picking up a stack of folders.

Deborah then stopped and cocked her head as she heard a strange scratching noise coming from the far end of the room. She stepped away from the filing cabinet that she had been working on and squinted in the direction from where she assumed the noise had come from.

The archive was a dimly lit room in the building's basement. Along the walls were filing cabinets of differing size. In the middle of the room were six aisles with shelves filled with boxes full of documents. Along the bottom rows lay various items of lost property, ranging from toys, clothes, cricket bats and even a replica of a Game Of Thrones sword.

On feeling a cold draft on her neck, Deborah shivered to herself, peered up at the long thin window up in the top corner of the room and gave a disapproving grumble when she saw that it was hanging open.

Deborah rolled her eyes and tutted to herself, 'Probably forced open by a rat or something.' she huffed and shook her head in disgust, 'Hmph! Great, that's all I need is to come across an enormous rat!' However, just as she was to turn back to her work, she stopped as she heard what she thought sounded not unlike scratching noises mixed in with heavy breathing.

Becoming increasingly concerned at the noises, Deborah took a small step away from her filing cabinet and gazed down the dark aisle from

Double Jeopardy

where the noise was coming from and called out. 'Hello? Is anybody there?' She felt her chest tighten in panic as she heard something hiss faintly back to her.

'*Yeesss …*'

Deborah turned away from the aisle and reached over to the light switch on the wall and blinked as the fluorescent light in the middle of the aisle flickered on. Feeling her sweat trickling down her spine, she knelt and picked up the sword that was lying on the shelf next to her. Then with it clasped firmly in her hand, she straightened up and crept down the aisle in the direction from where she thought the scratching was coming from, her heart drumming with every step.

On reaching the end of the aisle, Deborah jumped and let out a squeal of fright as a rat suddenly darted out in front of her into a space under the shelf. Thinking she had overreacted because her mind was playing tricks on her, she let out a curse, shook her head and turned slowly around. However, before she could begin her short trip back up the darkened aisle, she froze as she heard another hiss, only this time it was coming from directly behind her.

'*Sssstop.*'

Paralysed with fear, Deborah slowly turned and opened her mouth to scream, but before she could do so something sliced through her throat, silencing her.

From its hiding place under the shelf, the rat watched unsympathetically as the human's body dropped in front of it. Smelling blood, the rat edged forward and scampered up the dead human female's face. As its red eyes stared into human's lifeless right eye, the rat's jaws slowly opened, and its yellow teeth began to close around her eyeball.

Showing no emotion, the synthroid watched from the shadows as the rat's teeth pierced the white sclera of the eyeball, releasing the jelly like vitreous humour that was contained within.

26

With Claire sitting beside him in the passenger seat, Dave steered his car into a parking spot in the police station's carpark, and after briefly glancing in his rear-view mirror.

He saw that Wendy was still following close behind in her Blue KIA Niro. After bringing the vehicle to a stop, they got out and watched as the Wendy ran over to them. But as he moved towards the station's entrance, he frowned as he noticed an anxious looking Sergeant Donnelly was standing just in front of the entrance.

Dave smiled warmly at her as he walked quickly up to her, 'Good afternoon, Brenda. I understand you have been covering for us while we have been …' he paused and gave her a knowing wink, 'busy.'

Brenda nodded, cast an anxious glance over her shoulder, then leaned closer to him as she spoke in a low urgent tone, 'Guv, I have been covering for you as best as I can, but just to warn you Chief Inspector Thomas is looking for you and wanted you to report to him as soon as you were in the building. Commander Payne has informed me that you and

Professor Tulley need immediate access to the archive.'

Not happy that he was going to have to sneak his way round his own station, Dave let out a small, exasperated sigh, looked heavenward and rolled his eyes, 'Great! I really could do without listening to that blow hard now.'

Brenda placed her hand on his arm and gave him a small thin smile, 'Don't worry, Guv. Most of the officers here have been placed here by …' She paused and cast a wary eye around the empty carpark, 'command, so we have some idea what the situation is and will run interference while you are here, but I don't know for how long. So, whatever you need to do, do it fast.' She waved her to the rear of the building, 'I have opened a fire door at the rear of the building, it should allow you to get into the building undetected. Once inside, you will come to a stairwell that will take you straight down to the floor where the archive is.'

Dave looked at his colleague with a raised eyebrow and gave a small nod in gratitude, 'Thanks, Brenda. The three of us will hurry down to the archive. If you can, go back to the office and do what you need to do.'

Wendy held up her hands and stepped in front of Dave, shaking her head, 'Sorry, Guv, but I think we might have a better chance if you and Claire hurry down to the archive yourselves.' She then gestured Brenda, 'I will run up to the office with Brenda and keep an eye out, and if the Chief Inspector turns up, I will distract him.'

As he opened his mouth to object, Dave stopped as he felt Claire's hand tighten around his arm. He gave her a sidelong glance and let out a sigh of resignation, 'Fine! You two run up to the office now. Claire and I will dash around to the side of the building and enter through that open fire door.' He glanced at his wristwatch and nodded to himself, 'Deborah should be able to assist us with what we are looking for, which may speed things up. We'll meet back here in thirty minutes.' He watched as the two women both nodded in confirmation, turned, and dashed into the building.

After getting the signal that the coast was clear for them to proceed, Dave anxiously dashed around to the side of the building. Unsure which officers could be trusted, he crept stealthily through the open fire door into an empty corridor. But just as they were making way down the corridor, Dave felt his stomach tighten as he spotted two of his uniformed colleagues standing at the top of the stairs that led down to the floor that held the station's archive.

But as he warily approached them, Dave heaved a sigh of relief when he saw they were giving him a thumbs up signal to inform him that the coast was clear. One of the pair, a thin, blond-haired woman, who he recognised as Constable Glynn Braddock, had moved down the stairs, paused on the bottom step, looked up and gave a small bob of her head to her fellow conspirator, who he had instantly recognised as Constable Will Bates. Will gave a small nod of confirmation to the approaching Dave, 'It's all clear, Guv.' he whispered, casting quick look over Dave's shoulder, 'Some of us are with you and will keep an eye out while you are down there.'

Grateful for the risk they were taking in helping him, Dave gave a firm pat on Will's shoulder as he passed him. Claire cocked her head at him thoughtfully as they reached the bottom of the stairs and saw a long, dark corridor ahead of them.

'I bet you never thought things would ever turn out this way when we first met.' She muttered as they moved down the eerie corridor, 'If you had told me that in 24 hours, we would be involved in a conspiracy of light I would have thought you were mad.'

As they continued to hurry down the dark corridor, Dave gave her a furtive glance and lifted his shoulder in a half shrug. He frowned as she thought about her comment and shook his head himself, he certainly could not disagree with her way of thinking.

Claire frowned as they came to a stop in front of an enormous metal door and gave Dave a puzzled look, 'So who is this Deborah, and do you think she will help us?'

His brow furrowed in concentration, Dave pushed against the large metal door and cringed as he listened to the squeal from the protesting rusty hinges. He paused to wipe the sweat off his brow and gave Claire a knowing smile. 'Basically, she is the station's secretary. She has worked here for over thirty years.' He waved his hand to the room ahead of him and laughed, 'What she doesn't know about what we hold in the archives isn't worth knowing. If there is a record of your sister's case held here, she will be the one to find it.'

On entering the large dimly lit room, Dave paused as felt his mobile phone vibrate inside his jacket pocket. Frantically pulling the device out of his pocket, his eyes narrowed as he read the message on the screen. Damn it, could anything else go wrong? Claire eyebrows shot up in shock as a series of expletives suddenly flowed out of his mouth.

'Somebody has alerted Thomas we are here, and he's on his way down to us.' Dave said grumpily. He lifted his head up to the ceiling and let out a long-frustrated moan, 'Great, that's all we need!'

Claire calmly placed her hand on Dave's arm and gestured to the dim room, 'Then we will have to be quick as we can and hope we can find something before he arrives.'

Realising she was the calming voice of reason, Dave nodded reluctantly, inhaled a deep breath, and called softly out into the large dim room, 'Deborah, are you here? It's Dave Barnes, I need your help in looking for a case file.' He tilted his head and listened to his voice echoing eerily around the room. On getting no response, his squinted down the darkened aisles and gave resigned shrug of his shoulders, 'Looks like we will have to do this ourselves.' He waved a hand to the filing cabinet that was standing open by a table and he moved to the one closest to him, 'You have a look in that one and I will try this one here.'

He watched Claire dash over to the open filing cabinet, who then began to look through the many folders held in it. He opened the filing cabinet nearest to him and started to do the same.

As he started searching through the draw full of folders, Dave frowned as he spotted something unusual next to him. On the table beside him were a stack of folders, and beside them was a plate with a half-eaten sandwich. Was Deborah still in here? If that was the case, why didn't she answer when he had called out to her? He peered up from the drawer and glanced curiously around the room, but before he could open his mouth to call out again, he was interrupted by a sudden loud bang. Dave jumped back in surprise as the archive's door squealed open. He stiffened as Chief

Inspector Thomas forced his way into the room, and then charge angrily up to him.

'Barnes, where the hell have you been? You have been one all day without informing your colleagues of your whereabouts, this is simply not good enough!' Thomas snarled, his eyes blazing with anger, 'Well? What do you have to say for yourself?'

Not happy in being addressed in such a manner, Dave took a step back from Thomas and inhaled deep breath. He cast a surreptitious eye to Claire, who gave a nod understanding as he gave her a wave of his hand and he watched her shrink back into the shadows to hide.

Dave held up his hands apologetically, 'Sorry sir, but I have been rather busy.' He kept his voice calm and flat as he tried to keep his anger in check, 'I am trying to investigate the murder of Tommy and Michael Thorn, or have you forgotten?'

His upper lip curling up in disdain, Thomas leaned into Dave, their faces just about touching, 'I don't like your tone, Barnes!' He hissed, stabbing his finger aggressively into Dave's chest, 'Last time I checked I am the Chief Inspector, and you are my subordinate! When we last spoke you already had a suspect and I ordered you to close the case.'

Getting increasingly agitated by the second, his anger building, Dave clenched his fists together and took a deep breath, 'Yes *sir*, but I have come across evidence that shows Sally Thorn had nothing to do with it.' He ran his hand down his face and looked wearily into Thomas's eyes, 'I don't have time to go into it now, sir, but you have to trust me when I say there is more to this case than meets the eye.'

Raymond blinked, took a step back from Dave and let out a loud groan of frustration. He rubbed his hand on his forehead, turned in a small circle and stopped. He waved his hands in the air and looked heavenward as he shook his head, 'Damn it, man! Why could you have not done as I ordered you? Can't you see I am trying to protect you?' There was a strange tone in his voice as he continued to stare pleadingly at Dave, 'I mean it when I say it's for your own good. You need to step away and forget everything you have learned.'

Just as he was about to open his mouth to reply, Dave stopped and then frowned at the Chief Inspector for a second. Suddenly, it all came together in his head as he recognised the look on Thomas's face. But it was the fear in his voice that confirmed it for him - there was no doubt about it, Thomas was afraid.

'You know!' Dave hissed, 'Thomas, you bastard, you are working for them, aren't you?' Trembling with fury, his lips drew back in a snarl, and he took a step closer Raymond, who moved back anxiously from the raging older man.

Raymond lifted his finger up and began to stammer, 'I … I … I don't know what you think is going on, Barnes.' His brow glinted with sweat as he continued to back away, 'We must follow a chain of command; like you, I must follow orders. I answer to the Chief Constable, and he has ordered me that I must make sure my officers close certain cases as efficiently and quietly as possible.'

Dave stared open-mouthed at the quaking man before him and shook his head in disbelief as the pieces started to come together in his mind. Then, without warning, he grabbed Thomas by his jacket's collar and hissed at him through clenched teeth, 'You are one of them, aren't you?'

Thomas let out a gasp of pain as Dave slammed him against the wall, pushing the air out of his lungs. Gasping, his face was a mixture of confusion and anger as he struggled to release himself from Dave's grip, 'Wha—' he wheezed, 'What are you talking about?'

Unable to control his anger, Dave repeatedly slammed Thomas against the wall as he hissed vehemently at him, 'You're a doppelgänger!'

Thomas blinked and stared at Dave in bewilderment, confusion etched all over his face, 'I'm a what?'

His eyes narrowing with suspicion, Dave stared into Thomas's eyes and swallowed. On seeing no hint of any deception, he realised that Thomas believed what he was saying. Frustrated, he pushed him against the wall and watched as Thomas, the wind knocked out of him, slide down the wall onto the floor.

Dave eyed Thomas with disdain, 'Damn it, man!' he pleaded, waving his hands up in the air, 'Open your eyes. Can't you see what is going on? Have you not seen something strange is going on here?' He shook his head in disgust as Thomas stared up at him uncomprehendingly, 'Surely, you cannot be that blind? The strange murders, the disappearances, and the strange orders to cover them up.'

Trembling, Thomas blinked and shook his head in denial, 'I … I … I was only following orders. I didn't know.'

As she watched from her hiding place in the shadows, Claire wondered whether she should intervene and stop the two arguing men before they ended up doing something stupid. But as she prepared to step in between them, she paused as she noticed something shining out of the corner of her eye. Was she standing in a pool of water? As she turned her head to inspect the ground around her, she let out a horrified gasp and then jerked back shock. Losing her footing on the slippery surface, she fell onto a woman's dead body. Paralysed with fear, Claire could do nothing but gawk back at the two bloody, eyeless sockets that stared back at her.

Fighting the urge to throw up, Claire forced herself to look away from the gory tableau and pushed herself off the body. But as she placed her hands on the floor to push herself up, her eyes grew wide in disgust as she realised that she was sitting in something damp and sticky. She brought her hands up and felt the blood drain out of her as she saw the blood that was now covering her hands and clothes. She opened her mouth to scream, but nothing came out as she felt her throat tighten with fear. She squeezed her eyes shut, swallowed, and then let out a horrified scream.

'Dave!!!'

Claire exhaled a huge sigh of relief as she watched Dave charge down the aisle toward her, with Chief Inspector Thomas following close behind. They both stopped and stared down in confusion at her, and then the blood drained from their faces as they saw the body that lay next to her.

'What the fu—' Thomas gasped and then eyed Claire suspiciously, 'Who are you? Why are you here!'

Dave leaned down and helped Claire off the floor, 'She's with me and she's helping me with the Thorn investigation.'

Thomas stared at Dave incredulously, 'You brought a civilian in on a sensitive case and then you bring her into a secure location!' he hissed angrily, 'I will bring you up on charges Barnes!'

From the annoyed expression that was on Dave's face Claire got the distinct impression that he couldn't give shit what Thomas did. He gave Thomas a dismissive wave of his hand at as he knelt to examine the body.

'Who is it?' Claire whispered, still shaking.

'It's Deborah.' He replied, his tone full of sadness.

Thomas knelt next to Dave to get a closer look at the body. His eyes narrowed as he muttered to himself in disbelief, 'Deborah? Deborah Rodenby? Why would someone want to kill her? She is just a Secretary!'

'I don't know.' Dave muttered, leaning closer to examine the body. Claire's heart missed a beat as she watched him bolt up, his eyes growing wide in realisation, 'Oh my God!' He said in horrified hushed whisper. Claire swallowed anxiously as she watched his eyes dart from side to side, as if he was searching for an unseen enemy that was hidden somewhere in the shadows of the dimly lit room, 'We need to get out of here ... *now!*'

Wondering what had gotten the normally calm man so riled up, Claire started to ask a question but froze as she saw his fear-filled eyes. Slowly looking down at the dead and then back to Dave, she suddenly felt a chill run down her spine as something sparked in her memory of the incident from a couple nights before. She swallowed and then began to edge away from the body. Se kept her locked onto the darkened corners of the eerily lit aisle, searching for any sign the creature that had haunted her nightmares since childhood.

Mystified at their reaction, Thomas shook his head in confusion, 'What are you talking about? We need to get SOCO down here now.'

Dave suddenly spun round, grabbed hold of the bewildered looking Thomas and dragged him unceremoniously up the aisle, shoving him through the open door. Following closely on his heels, Claire suddenly stopped dead as she felt the hairs on the back of her neck tingle, and she slowly turned round.

Dave glanced over his shoulder and saw that Claire had

stopped. He stepped back into the room and moved next to her, 'Claire? what's wrong?' he asked in a voice that was heavy with concern.

Claire squinted, shook her head slowly and pointed to a darkened corner in the room, 'I thought I saw ...'

It happened so quick, Claire felt like she was moving in slow motion. She was too slow react as she turned and a table flying out of the darkness toward her. But just before it hit, Dave jumped forward and shoved her to one side, sending her crashing into a table. Unfortunately, even though she was out of the line of fire, he was not as lucky. As the table smashed against the door, its trailing edge caught him on the back of the head, and he crumpled to the floor in an unconscious heap.

Thomas cried out in pain as he felt the door slam against his back, throwing him headfirst against a wall. Feeling like he had been hit by a ton of bricks, he shakenly picked himself up off the floor, and staggered back over to the closed door. But as he tried to push the door open, he let out a frustrated grunt when he saw it was jammed tight.

'Barnes! Barnes!' he yelled, pounding his fists on the door, 'Dave, if you can hear me, I cannot get the door open. Can you push from the other side.'

On hearing no movement from the other side of the door, he suddenly realised something was terribly wrong and stared helplessly down the corridor. Quickly deciding he had no choice but to go and get help, Thomas sucked in a deep breath of determination and set off toward the stairs at the end of the corridor.

Her head ringing, Claire opened her eyes and blinked as she tried to clear her vision. She slowly lifted her head up and winced from the dull ache that was coming from the side of her forehead and then tentatively reached up to place her hand on the table so that she could pull herself up. She paused as she sensed movement out of the corner of her eye. She turned her head and the first thing she could see was Dave lying unconscious on the floor, but then her eyes grew wide in horror as they were drawn to the thing standing over his motionless body.

Forcing down the bile in her throat, she looked upon the creature in front of her; it was the same shiny black beast that had haunted her nightmares since that fateful night many years earlier. It was the creature that killed Emma. A sudden calmness filling her, Claire eased herself up and grimaced at the bitter taste that was inside her mouth as she stared at the creature in disgust.

It was as if something had flipped a switch inside her. With adrenaline pumping through her body, bellowing in fury, Claire charged at the creature, her strength fuelled by the emotions that she had kept bottled up since that portentous night: anger, terror, and frustration.

As she charged toward the creature's she saw it lift its head. For a moment she was positive she saw its eyes widen in disbelief just before she smashed into it, screaming with all her might.

Her teeth clenched, her lips curled up in a snarl, Claire wrapped her hands around its long neck, her momentum carrying them both forward. She ground her teeth together as the creature's claws penetrated her clothes, slashing into her abdomen and right thigh, tearing at her flesh. But it did not slow her down, but rather added to her fury, giving her extra strength. Her mind suddenly became detached – cool and calculating – ignorant of pain, but with the strength of a woman who had refused to be beaten by something that had haunted her nightmares since childhood.

With the creature's body held firm in front of her, she slammed it against the narrow metal support beam. The corners of Claire's mouth lifted in satisfaction as she heard the snap of the beast's spine as it broke from the force of their impact against the support beam. As she released her grip from its neck, she watched with cold emotion as it sunk onto the floor; the bones from its shattered spine protruding from its body.

Exhausted and breathless, her face glistening with sweat, Claire stumbled away and collapsed to her knees on the icy floor. With her head resting on the floor, she sobbed to herself, but lurched up as a slithering sound brought her back to her senses. Claire turned her head and was horrified to see that the abomination was still crawling towards her. The nightmarish beast's injuries were severe, it was almost dead, but it was as if it was fuelled by hatred as it crawled toward her, hissing, leaving a wet trail of blood in its wake.

The creature was almost two meters away from her. Frantically searching for anything to hand that could be of use, Claire was filled small burst of exultation as she spotted a sword on the floor next to her. Then with the weapon held firmly in her hands, she pressed it against the floor, and painstakingly lifted herself to her knees. Her face scrunched up in pain, she straightened up and held the sword above her head with both of her hands.

The creature's haunches quivered as it tried to summon the energy to leap at Claire, but it appeared to lack the strength to do so.

Fuelled by her rage, Claire roared and brought the sword crashing down into the creature's skull. Her fury blinding her, she failed to see the synthroid lash out and cried out in pain as she felt its claws stab into her stomach. Ignoring the pain, she squeezed her eyes shut, ground her teeth, and pushed the sword deeper into its skull. The creature convulsed and became still as the sword penetrated its brain, killing it. Then, with her hands clutching her injured stomach, on the verge of exhaustion, she teetered back, collapsed into a heap, and closed her eyes.

After managing to get the door open, Wendy barged past her colleagues into the dimly lit records room. The first thing she noticed was Dave's unconscious body laid out on floor, but as she raced over to help him, she suddenly stopped as she heard a shocked gasp from Brenda. On looking to where her grave-faced colleague was pointing, she held up her hand to her mouth and let out a horrified gasp as she saw Claire's bloody body. *Oh God, no! Not Claire!*

But as she hurried over to her injured friend, Wendy jumped back in shock when she saw the grotesque body that was laid out in front of the woman. From its shape and colour, she was immediately reminded of the creature from Claire's description and realised that it was the creature from her childhood. But on seeing the sword sticking out of its head, Wendy gave a small triumphant smile to herself; Claire had gotten her revenge.

Suppressing a shudder, Wendy swallowed and lifted her hands up to her mouth as she saw the blood that was pouring from the various wounds on Claire's body. With the First Aid box clutched tightly in his hands, Will Bates knelt beside her, opened it, took out a handful of padding, and pressed it against the wound on the gravely injured woman's abdomen. Wendy gently took Claire's head in her hands and placed it on her lap.

Her eyes filling with tears, Wendy took hold of Claire's hand and held it tightly, as she pleaded softly to her, 'Hang on, Claire, we are getting help. An ambulance is coming. Please hang on.'

Shuddering in agonising breaths, Claire coughed and smiled weakly at Wendy, 'Did … I … get … it?'

Trying to fight back the tears, Wendy sniffed and nodded sadly, 'Yes, Claire. It's dead. You got it.'

Her breathing becoming more laboured, Claire pulled in a lungful of air and let out a ragged sigh, 'Th … that's … good. Emma … got … him … for … you.'

Wendy cast an eye to Will, and he shook his head glumly. She glanced over her shoulder to Brenda and saw that she had her hands full with the unconscious man. She blinked in surprise as Chief Inspector Thomas knelt beside her, his face turning ashen at the gravely injured woman on the floor.

'Where is that ambulance?' Wendy hissed, tears rolling down her face.

Thomas placed his hand on Wendy's shoulder and whispered sadly, 'It's on its way. They should be here soon.'

Claire's hand reached up and gently touched Wendy's face, 'Don't … cry … Emma … will … see … each … other … soo …' She then convulsed and let out a rattling cough. Her body stiffened, and her hand dropped away from Wendy's face.

Chief Inspector Thomas silently straightened up and walked sadly away. He shook his head in sadness at the station personnel who were staring at him with questioning expressions. One by one they all turned and hung their heads as Wendy continued to cradle Claire's head in her lap.

27

Location: Pons Aelius, Britannica, Universal Roman Empire

Colonel Barnes stood in silence, gazing at the city below him through the window of his quarters. As he watched the sun set slowly over the horizon, he took a sip from his cup and nodded thoughtfully. He had always liked these contemplative moments, for him it was the best part of the day.

He was suddenly broken out of his reverie by a loud chime, notifying him that someone was at his door. He angrily pressed a button on his wrist communicator, bringing up an image of a dark brown, fair-haired, burly soldier.

'Sir, its Lieutenant Önundarson.' He announced firmly in a voice that was laced with a strong Icelandic accent.

'Yes, what is it, lieutenant?' Barnes snapped irritably.

The lieutenant then leaned forward and appeared to give a hard stare into the camera's lens, 'Sir, can you come to your door?'

Barnes sighed to himself, put his cup down, walked over to the doorway, and pressed a button on the wall. He watched as the door slid open, revealing the soldier behind it. Önundarson stood at attention, clicked his heels, and put his arm across his chest in the standard Imperial salute. Barnes returned the salute and gave a small nod in acknowledgement.

'Sir, General Cooper has requested your presence.' Önundarson muttered in a low emotionless tone.

Not pleased at being disturbed, Barnes pursed his lips and gave a dismissive wave of his hand, 'Tell the General I understand, and I will see her within the hour.'

The lieutenant's face hardened, and his steely grey eyes stared intently at Barnes, 'Sir, she has ordered me to escort you immediately.' he said firmly. Barnes couldn't help noticing that Önundarson's hand had slipped over his holstered weapon as if to emphasise his statement, 'It is not up for discussion.'

Barnes felt a growing sense of unease build inside him as he carefully stepped back and nodded politely, 'Fine, lieutenant. Lead the way.'

Önundarson wordlessly moved to one side and motioned for the unhappy colonel to exit his quarters. With the stern-faced soldier watching his every move, Barnes hurried down the short corridor, coming to a stop in front of the transport-pod's door. As he pressed his hand on the sensor on the wall, he stood back and waited for the pod's doors to slide open. Barnes let out a surprised audible gasp as he felt the burly Lieutenant's hand suddenly push him firmly into the waiting pod. He spun around and was about to give Önundarson a piece of his mind but stopped himself as he noticed a dangerous glint in the soldier's eyes. Barnes shifted his gaze to the cabin's door. No, he would leave it for now, but when the time was right, he would make sure Önundarson got what was coming to him.

Five minutes later Barnes stood patiently outside General Cooper's office. He watched uneasily as Önundarson pressed his hand on the sensor on the wall beside the door and then heard Cooper's voice call out from inside the room.

'Enter!'

Followed closely by Önundarson, Barnes walked through the open door into a dimly lit room. Cooper was standing behind her desk with her back to him, arms held behind her back as she gazed through her window.

'Sit!' she commanded without turning around.

Barnes eyed Önundarson nervously as he watched him stand at parade rest: his feet spread wide apart, hands clasped behind his back and his head fixed forward, showing no emotion. He carefully took a seat in front of the desk and silently watched Cooper, who still had her back to him.

After a few moments of awkward silence, with her back still facing Barnes, Cooper let out a deep sigh and murmured, 'Do you assume I am a fool, Colonel?'

Barnes's right eyebrow arched, as he stared at her questioningly, 'Sorry, ma'am, I don't understand?'

Cooper chuckled and turned slowly to face Barnes. She cocked her head at him and held her hand up, 'It's a simple question, yes or no.' she asked curiously, pointing her index finger first to Barnes and then to herself, 'Do you assume I am a fool?'

What game is she playing here? Barnes shifted uneasily in his seat as a sense of dread started to form in his stomach. He narrowed his eyes suspiciously and gave a small shake of his head, 'No, ma'am, I don't assume you are a fool.'

Cooper waved her finger, gave a slight shake of her head and then her face darkened in anger. Barnes flinched as she slammed her fist down on the desk, hard, 'You are lying, Colonel.' she hissed, 'Obviously you must take me for a fool, if you assume I didn't know what you were up to.'

Trying to ease the building panic he was feeling, Barnes swallowed hard and forced himself to smile, 'General, I believe there has been a misunderstanding.' He felt a bead sweat run down the side of his forehead as he tried to ease up out of the chair. He blinked in surprise as he suddenly felt a strong hand on his shoulder, forcing him back down.

Cooper let out a snort of disgust and slowly stepped around the desk, placing herself on the edge. She leaned forward and glared angrily at Barnes as she spoke to him in a low, hushed voice.

'I gave you an order. Can you remember what it was?' she asked coldly.

Feeling his throat tighten, Barnes swallowed and shifted uncomfortably in his seat as he felt cold bead of sweat run down the back of his neck. He lowered his head and murmured, 'I was to leave my doppelgänger alone. No harm was to come to him.'.

'Exactly!' Cooper let out a small mirthless laugh as she stood up from the desk and began pacing around the room, 'Now, tell me what possessed you to send the synthroid through the portal to kill your counterpart? What possessed you to disobey a direct order?' She wheeled around, tilted her head, and placed her right hand on her chest, 'I know I am not a fool, so obviously you must be a fool to expect you could get away with it!'

An alarm began to sound in Barnes' head as he suddenly realised, he was being manipulated. He silently chastised himself for behaving like a green rookie for falling into such an obvious trap. His blood starting to boil, he clenched his fists and turned his head away from Cooper. He inhaled a deep breath as he tried to rein in his emotions and kept his gaze Cooper's feet.

Without warning, Cooper shot forward and grabbed Barnes's face with her hands. Their faces were barely millimetres from each other as she leaned in closer to him. Cooper's eyes blazed with such intensity; Barnes could almost feel they were boring into his very soul.

Cooper's lips drew back into a disdainful sneer as she snarled at him, 'Answer me.'.

Barnes shook his face loose from Cooper's grasp and lifted his head defiantly, 'I was acting in the Empire's best interest.' He curled his upper lip in disgust, 'You should be glad my doppelgänger is dead.'

Cooper's mouth set in a hard line as she gave Barnes a hard stare. She pulled away from him and after a minute of awkward silence, gave a small shake of her head and laughed mirthlessly, 'You stupid, deluded fool. He is still alive. They killed the synthroid.'

Not the news he was expecting, Barnes blanched as he peered up at Cooper in disbelief, stammering, 'Wha … wha … what!? How?'

As she sat on the edge of the desk, Cooper drummed her fingers on the surface and the corners of her mouth lifted as she gave Barnes a contemptuous look, 'Oh, I am sure you believed you had the Empire's best interests at heart, but really it was your own selfish interests you were thinking of.' She paused, leaned forward, and whispered to him in a low taunting tone, 'Do you know why?'

Barnes could tell she was trying to provoke him. He breathed heavily as he felt his hands slowly tighten on the chair's handles. No, he needed to keep his head and take control, let her think she has got to him. He looked her in the eye and gave a wordless shake his head.

The corners of her mouth curling up into an evil smile, Cooper leaned in closer to Barnes and spoke in a low taunting tone as she lifted his chin with her finger, 'Deep down you are a coward. You are afraid your doppelgänger is superior to you, aren't you? That's why you did it, isn't it?' She paused and gave a small hollow laugh as she continued to mock him, 'Because it scares you, doesn't it? Deep down, you know he will show what you have known all along.'

Oh, I see where she is going here. She's trying to make me so angry that I will drop my guard. Well, let's have it little girl, let's see what you've got. Pretending he was refusing to listen Cooper's taunts, Barnes clenched his teeth together, squeezed his eyes shut and shook his head, 'No … no … no … that's not true.'

Cooper then stabbed her finger into Barnes's chest as she sneered at him, 'You are just a tiny little man, a scared little child who, perhaps, views himself as inferior?'

Okay, time to make this look good. 'Noooo!' Barnes pretended to bellow in fury as he bolted up out of the chair and threw his fist at Cooper's face. He carefully pulled his punch so that it would just give Cooper a glancing blow. Of course, it would still hurt her – he wasn't going to let her off that easy.

Cooper let out a small cry of pain and then collapsed onto the floor. Barnes was sure he caught a glimpse of her mouth lifting in a secretive smile. It was then he realised that she had been playing him too – she had wanted him to strike her. But why?

Breathing heavily, Barnes stared down at Cooper, who was laid out at his feet. He stiffened as he watched her reach into her pocket and pull out a small control pad. So, that was her game all along – she wanted to humiliate him.

Barnes felt his collar vibrate around his neck. As he collapsed onto his knees, he squeezed his eyes shut and let out a loud gasp. He hissed through his teeth and slowly opened one eye.

He saw Cooper had picked herself up off the floor and was brushing her left hand down the front of her jacket. Her right hand eased off the control pad and she slipped it back into her pocket. She clasped her hands behind her back and grinned at him menacingly.

'Colonel Barnes, striking a superior officer is a treasonable offence, punishable by death, but I have something special planned for you.' She snarled, her mouth forming into an evil sneer at him. She spun away on her heel and gestured to the waiting lieutenant, 'Take him to a cell. I guess a month in a re-education pod might be best for him.'

As he felt himself being unceremoniously picked up off the floor and dragged him out of the room, Barnes looked over his shoulder at Cooper and their eyes locked briefly. The corner of her mouth quirked up as she gave him a sly wink. He gave a small nod of acknowledgement. Yes, he would let her think he had played right in her hands, but in the end it would be he who would be the one who would have the last laugh.

As felt himself being dragged him down the corridor to the turbo-lift, Barnes' mind began to go over what had just happened. He had a hunch Cooper had been planning something, having suspected a short time ago that she had possibly been manipulating him for a long time. He would even go so far and grudgingly admit that she was the one responsible for arranging their first meeting.

Suspecting she would eventually turn on him, the scheming Barnes found a way to disable his obedience collar and replace it with a toy imitation. It had taken some creative tinkering, but he had managed to remove the sensor emitter from his real collar and place it inside the toy, connecting it to the light inside. When activated, the collar would have lit up as normal but without the painful experience that went with it. Then all he needed to do was put on a convincing display. If anybody gave it a passing glance, all they would have seen was a normal obedience collar. To pass the weekly mandatory maintenance inspection, Barnes would change it for a real one and then simply switch back once the inspection was done.

As soon he entered the transport-pod's cabin, Barnes closed his eyes, pretended to breath heavily and rested against the wall, his mind working overtime.

Out of the corner of his eye, Barnes waited for the unsuspecting lieutenant to turn his back to him to activate the pod's controls. Sensing his chance, Barnes collapsed forward, his body shaking, to make it appear he was having a fit. As soon Önundarson reached down to check on him, Barnes shot up and slammed his head into Önundarson's the stomach. Stunned, the burly man shook his head as Barnes slammed him against the wall again and pressed the emergency stop button on the control panel. Struggling to hold the enormous soldier against the wall, he frantically reached for the soldier's weapon holster. Önundarson must have realised his prisoner was trying to grab his weapon, as he wheeled round with inhuman speed and slammed his knee into Barnes' chest, sending him flying into the opposite wall.

Winded, Barnes looked down and was surprised see he was holding Önundarson's weapon. Without hesitating, he raised the weapon, aimed it at the approaching soldier and pressed the trigger. Barnes watched triumphantly as a beam of energy struck Önundarson in the centre of his chest, but his triumph was short lived as he watched in disbelief as the man just staggered briefly. He had appeared to have absorbed the energy blast with little effort.

Barnes felt his blood run cold as Önundarson, showing little emotion, lowered his head as if to look at the energy that was dissipating over his body. He felt his pulse quicken as Önundarson then continued to advance on him.

Desperately changing the weapon's setting to maximum, Barnes frantically raised the weapon just as Önundarson grabbed his throat. His eyes squeezed shut, he pressed his finger on trigger and fired into the soldier's chest point blank. With a smoking hole in his chest, the stunned man released his grip from Barnes's neck and collapsed to the floor.

Breathing hard, Barnes gave a sidelong glance at the fallen soldier next to him and winced as he knelt to inspect the dead body. He felt a chill run down his spine as he realised the hole in Önundarson's chest was beginning to heal itself. Barnes realised if he didn't act quickly, it was likely he would end up dead. He raised the weapon and fired it point blank into soldier's head, vaporizing the top half of his skull.

His heart hammering in his chest, Barnes closed his eyes and took a deep breath to control his heart rate as he desperately tried to come up with a plan. Wishing he had more time to examine Önundarson's body, he suddenly was aware that it would not be long before someone noticed the transport-pod had not moved for several minutes and would probably send someone to investigate.

After quickly undressing, the scantily clad Barnes reached up to the turbo-lift cabin's ceiling and pushed on the panel, jumping to one side as the panel fell onto the cabin's floor. He then knelt on his knees and gave a grunt of discomfort as he eased the dead soldier's body onto his shoulders. Then, after several failed attempts, he strained as he pushed the body through the open access panel in the ceiling. Taking a deep breath, he lifted himself through the access panel and after checking to see if he had safely secured the body on the outside of the pod's roof, he peered over his shoulder and gave a jubilant nod of his head when spotted what he was looking for.

Reaching down to his ankle, Barnes pulled out a small blade from his ankle holster and began to pry loose a grill on the side of the transport shaft. Then, after carefully taking the grill in his hands, he pulled it away from the shaft's wall and grunted as he lifted the dead body onto his shoulders and carefully shoved it into the open ventilation shaft. He then reached down, quickly replaced the grill, and dropped back into the transport-pod. Barnes carefully leaned down, picked up the panel he had dislodged moments earlier and placed it back into its slot.

Panting heavily, Barnes wiped the sweat of his brow as he considered his options. He frowned to himself as he looked down at his dirt-stained body and exhaled a deep sigh. After getting redressed and wiping the dirt from his face, he reactivated the transport-pod.

Double Jeopardy

A minute later, Barnes stepped out of the turbo-lift pod onto the cell block level. Secretly hoping Cooper had not called ahead, he marched confidently up to the duty guard. Barnes' eyes narrowed as he searched his memory for the guard's name, Corporal Roux, someone who he considered to be spineless and easily manipulated.

As he approached the guard station, Barnes raised his wrist and pressed a button on his wrist communicator, and flashed up his holographic ID. Corporal Roux, a short weedy man with narrow, beady grey eyes and long thin face, shot up out of his seat and gave the standard salute.

'I am here to escort prisoner twenty-eight for questioning.' Barnes barked firmly.

Roux frowned and then looked Barnes questioningly, 'Uh, sorry sir, but I have received no orders about a prisoner transfer.'

The corners of Barnes' mouth lifted in a fake smile as he motioned Roux to lean in closer. He glanced over his shoulder and lowered his voice, 'Well, it is unofficial, you see. What they actually want is for me to take the prisoner for a gentle walk.' He gave a knowing wink and bobbed his head at the waiting transport-pod, 'I will have a Doctor with me, waiting in the basement level, just in case …' he paused for effect, 'you know.'

A glint of understanding flickered in Roux's beady eyes as he gave a small nod, 'And the doctor will be there just in case the prisoner …' The corners of his mouth twitched as he gave Barnes a knowing wink, 'falls down.'

Barnes let out a small laugh and clicked his finger, 'You got it.'

Roux smirked and waved to something down the corridor, 'Ten doors down on your left.'

Barnes gave a small nod and continued to march confidently down the corridor. He came to a stop outside the cell marked twenty-eight and glanced anxiously over his shoulder. Holding his breath, he activated the sensor on the cell door and jumped back in surprise as it swished open. After giving one more glance up the corridor, he stepped inside the cell. Spotting the prisoner on the bed, he took a small step forward, extended his hand and spoke in a low urgent tone.

'Come with me if you want to live.'

28

With her fingers steepled together, Cooper glared angrily at the short weedy man standing in front of her. Corporal Roux was standing between two enormous guards as he anxiously fingered the obedience collar around his neck with a worried expression plastered across his face.

As she massaged the bridge of her nose with her left hand, Cooper let out a long-perplexed sigh and waved her right hand impatiently at the worried-looking Roux, 'Explain to me again, corporal, how you allowed Colonel Barnes to walk into the cell block.' Her face hardened as she gave him a cold, hard stare, 'Then you let him steal a prisoner right in front of you?'

The blood appeared to drain out of Roux's face as he squeaked out a reply, 'Like I already said, Ma'am, I wasn't aware that Colonel Barnes had been arrested.' He hung his head, and shrugged apologetically, 'When he arrived and said that he needed to take the prisoner away for questioning, I didn't doubt it.'

Cooper gave a small shake of her head and looked at the pitiful looking man incredulously, 'Did you not consider checking the computer records for transfer orders?' Her top lip curled up into a snarl as she slammed her fist down on the desk, 'Why did you not confirm it with a superior officer?'

Roux dropped his gaze to the floor and mumbled incoherently.

Fuming, Cooper leapt out of her chair, pressed her hands firmly on the desk and raised her voice, 'What was that? Speak up damn you!' In a fit of rage, she swiped her hand over her desk. The three people standing in front of her flinched as anything not bolted down was thrown off the desk.

Roux coughed nervously and lifted his shoulder in a half shrug, 'Well, he said it was an unofficial request that he was to take the prisoner for a walk, but there would be a doctor with him to make sure she didn't fall too hard.' He gave then gave Cooper a weak smile, 'That's not the first time something like that has happened, so I just assumed …' He lowered his head sheepishly and held up both of his hands.

For several minutes, Cooper remained silent as she glowered at Roux, who continued to shuffle awkwardly. Eventually, she raised her head to the ceiling, rolled her eyes, let out a long, drawn-out sigh and began to pace around the room with her hands clasped behind her back.

Cooper paused behind Roux and leaned in close to him, placing a hand on his shoulder. She felt his shoulder muscles tense up as she breathed heavily against the back of his neck. 'So, you just assumed.' She hissed, tightening her fingers on his shoulder firmly and giving a small chuckle, 'That he was taking her for a walk.'

Roux swallowed, gave a small nod and squeaked out a reply, 'Yes.'

Cooper tightened her jaw as she stared at back of Roux's head. She wanted so badly to rip the little rat faced man's head off. No, that was too good for him. What she had in mind needed to effective, so not only would it teach him a lesson but it would also be an example to those who dare question her authority. Without warning, she slammed her fist into the side his face and she watched in satisfaction as he collapsed onto the floor. He held up his hand to his face and stared back up at Cooper in shock.

Cooper shook her head in disgust and gestured to the two well-built Gondwanian soldiers that were towering over the quivering man. She gave Roux a look of contempt and waved her hand in dismissal, 'Get him out of my sight!' She narrowed her eyes and then grinned wickedly, 'A month in a re-education pod might teach him the error of his ways.'

The two enormous soldiers saluted and dragged the terrified Roux away as he pleaded despairingly, 'Please, general, I promise I won't do it again. Please have mercy!'

That was what she was waiting for. Cooper raised an eyebrow and pretended to eye Roux thoughtfully. She held up her hand to the two soldiers to stop them, 'Wait! I have a better idea.'

The two soldiers paused and looked at Cooper with curious expressions. The relief evident in his eyes, Roux held his breath and stared back to Cooper expectantly.

Cooper was silent for a minute as she tapped her chin thoughtfully and then waved her hand nonchalantly, 'Have his family executed and make sure he is watching.' She shot Roux a cold look as she spoke in a cruel whisper, 'I am sure that will act as an incentive against any future indiscretions.'

His face changing to one of terror, Roux's jaw dropped to the floor and he let out a horrified scream. As he was dragged into the corridor, his screams could still be heard as the door closed behind them.

Cooper turned and stared out of the window for several minutes, distracted by her own thoughts, oblivious to the busy city below. Cooper shook her head in frustration as her mind raced with questions. 'What is that old fool up to?' she muttered herself, 'Where are you going Barnes?'

A bleep from her wrist communicator broke her out of her reverie. Annoyed at the interruption, she stabbed her finger down on a button on her wrist device, 'Yes, what is it?' she answered brusquely.

A holographic image of a dark-skinned man appeared and waved his hand across his chest in the standard salute, 'Sorry General, this is Lieutenant Xavier, we need you to come to the Command Centre.' He paused and looked at her with a troubled expression, 'Something has arisen, which you need to see.'

'Fine, I will be there shortly.' Cooper replied curtly. Then, without waiting for a response, she disconnected the call.

After giving one final glance out the window, She rubbed her hand over her face, shook her head, and let out a long-frustrated sigh. The problem with Barnes would have to wait, something else was needing her attention.

Five minutes later, Cooper stepped out of a transport-pod into an enormous brightly lit circular command centre. Computer terminals covered the floor with technicians sitting at each terminal carrying out their assigned duties from interactive holographic displays. Three large holographic display screens hung at the front of the chamber, displaying various maps and images.

Cooper's brow furrowed into a troubled frown as she looked around the room and saw what appeared to be a lot of people running around in a panic. As her eyes searched the room, she eventually came upon Xavier as she watched him make his way through the maelstrom of people toward her. He marched up to her, stopped, stiffened, and gave Cooper the imperial salute, who returned it in an abrupt manner.

Cooper gestured angrily to disorder around her, 'What's going on here, Xavier?'

Xavier placed his hand gently on Cooper's arm and guided her to a nearby console. He lowered his voice as he spoke to her in an urgent tone, 'Sorry General, but you need to see this.'

Quickly placing himself in front of a console, Xavier touched the holographic display and the image in front of him changed to show a map with several points highlighted. Cooper's eyes narrowed as she peered at the image and nodded to herself as she recognised the highlighted points were along the demilitarized zone between the Empire and the Greater China Republic.

The sombre looking lieutenant pointed to the holographic image in front of them, 'We have evacuated all the personnel in our military bases along the border!' There was a small tone of fear in his voice as he gestured to the map.

Not believing what she was looking at, Cooper blinked and did a double take at the display, 'What!' she exclaimed, ignoring the alarmed looks from the people around her. She swallowed and then hissed at Xavier, 'How many bases?'

The ashen faced Xavier glanced over his shoulder as he continued to talk in a low urgent whisper, 'All of them.' He raised his hands to the holographic display, enlarging it to show a map of the world and highlighted an area that spanned two sides of the globe, 'We have evacuated every base along the demilitarized zone and have also withdrawn all personnel back to bases deep within the Empire.'

Cooper stepped away from Xavier and closed her eyes as she tried to comprehend what she was being shown. But then, as she opened her eyes, she became aware that people were staring at her. She could almost read the fear that was etched across their faces, as if they were looking to her for guidance. Unsure what to say to them, she lowered her head and stared at Xavier incredulously.

Rubbing her forehead with her hand, Cooper shook her head and sighed in frustration, 'The Greater China Republic's territory covers a third of the globe.' She waved her hand at a section of the globe on the holographic display, 'We cover the remaining two-thirds. Evacuating our bases makes no sense, as it would leave the Empire vulnerable.'

Her mind racing with even more questions, Cooper lifted her head heavenward as she tried to make sense of the information. She closed her eyes, took a deep breath to compose herself and turned back to the anxious looking Xavier.

'Who gave the order to evacuate those bases?' She asked warily.

Xavier swallowed nervously, leaned in closer to Cooper and lowered his voice, 'I triple checked it myself, general, and there is no doubt about it ...' He hesitated, and then looked down at his shoes. Cooper frowned. She could tell he was trying to avoid her stern gaze. 'According to the logs, you gave the order.'

Feeling like somebody had punched her in the stomach, Cooper let out an audible gasp and stepped back in shock. Aware that everybody's attention was now on her, she looked back down at the lieutenant, speechless, not sure what to say.

Quickly pulling herself together, Cooper shook her head angrily, 'That's impossible! I gave no such order.' She waved her hand defensively at the holographic display, 'Somebody must have copied my command codes.'

Xavier gave a small shake of his head and looked at Cooper apologetically, 'I am sorry, ma'am, that would be true if it was just your command codes used, but the order came from you, verbally.' He tapped on the holographic display. Cooper inhaled sharply as her face and voice record suddenly appeared in front of her. 'There is no doubt you issued the evacuation order.'

Shaken, her mind reeling, Cooper lurched back from the console. Feeling like her world was spinning out of control, her breathing became heavier as she placed her hands on the desk to steady herself and then closed her eyes. Suddenly she was aware of a flurry of activity beside her, and she took a long breath as she forced herself to focus back on the room. However, she suddenly became aware that somebody was shouting at her.

'General Cooper! Answer me!' the male voice barked angrily, 'Why did you give the order to issue an evacuation from our front lines?'

Realising that there was a holographic image of a man stand in front of her, Cooper blinked and then quickly focused on the hologram. He was a bald, heavy-set, sixty-something man, dressed in an ornate black and gold military uniform that was decorated with several service medals. Quickly regaining her composure, she straightened to attention and saluted the holographic figure in front of her.

'I am sorry Supreme Commander Tiberius, but I gave no such order.' Cooper replied adamantly, 'I don't understand it, but I definitely did not give the order to evacuate our bases along our side of the demilitarised zone.'

Cooper swallowed as she watched Tiberius's steely grey eyes narrow as he gave her an icy hard stare. 'Then please explain," he snarled, waving his hands in the air, 'how the logs show that it is your voice issuing the order?'

Cooper gulped and gave a small shake of her head, 'I … I … I …

cannot explain that sir.' she stammered, her mind racing as she tried desperately to think of a way to dig herself out of the hole she had now found herself in, 'I recently arrested Colonel Barnes for treason, he has the know-how and the skill to carry out something like this.'

Tiberius's right eyebrow arched in surprise and he gave a nod of understanding, 'Where is the traitor now?' he asked coldly.

As she started to open her mouth to speak, Cooper froze as she became aware of a commotion coming from somewhere around her. She turned slowly round and saw a wave of panic circling the room. People were lifting their hands to their mouths and staring at their holographic displays with shocked expressions.

Fearing something was wrong, Cooper wheeled round to Xavier, who was looking at the holographic image with an incredulous look on his face. The blood quickly draining from his face, Xavier raised his head up to Cooper and gave her an unbelieving stare.

'We … we …' Xavier stammered.

Cooper grabbed by his shoulders and hissed at him, 'What is it?'

Xavier blinked, shook his head in incomprehension and then spoke in a low horrified voice, 'Sorry I … I … I don't understand what I am reading, but according to this …' He paused as if he was trying to regain control of his emotions, 'We have detected a series of gamma-ray bursts fired from our satellites in a geosynchronous orbit over the Greater China Republic.'

Not believing what she was listening to, Cooper felt her throat tighten in fear, 'Whe …' She swallowed and tried to force the words out of her mouth, 'Where was the burst aimed at?'

His brow furrowing in deep concentration, Xavier read the data in front of him, opened his mouth to speak but shook his head wordlessly. Then his shoulders appeared to stoop as he sunk back down in his seat. He leaned forward, placed his head in his hands and answered in a trembling horrified voice, 'The Greater China Republic.'

Cooper grabbed the trembling man by his shoulders and spun him around, 'Damn it man! I guessed that, but which part?'

The tearful Xavier raised his trembling hand and gestured to the holographic display, 'All of it.' he muttered, 'The whole of the Greater China Republic.'

No, that wasn't possible. Struggling for breath, Cooper felt her chest tighten and she released her grip, 'All … of … it.' She gasped and then looked up at the holographic display. She shook her head as she tried to make sense what she was looking at, 'But … that's …'

Overwhelmed with despair, Xavier dropped his eyes and nodded slowly, 'Yes …' he let out a heavy dejected sigh, 'that's just over three billion people dead.'

As she stared at the holographic image through wide incredulous eyes, Cooper felt her stomach tighten as she recognised the signature of the pulse. She shook her head in disbelief, no it cannot be, there must be some mistake! But as much as she wanted to deny it, there was no mistaken the evidence in front of her, the energy pulse was the same one that she herself had designed. How was that possible?

'What's happened?' Tiberius demanded, waving his hand up in the air, his eyes blazing with fury as he searched for somebody to answer him, 'Can somebody tell me what in Zeus' beard is going on!'

With a great sense of foreboding, Cooper swallowed and looked up at Tiberius with a mournful expression, 'A concentrated burst of gamma radiation has struck the whole of the Greater China Republic. Gamm …' Her voice wobbled and she took a deep breath to compose herself, 'Gamma radiation destroys all life: plant and animal, on a cellular level.' She shook her head and stared up at the red-faced Tiberius numbly, 'Anything living caught within the blast radius would have died instantly.'

As if he was trying to comprehend what was in front of him, Tiberius shook his head in confusion. But as he opened his mouth to speak, he was interrupted and looked at someone beside him, who was standing out of line of sight as they handed him a tablet. His expression hardened as he scrutinised the device in his hand. He rubbed his hand over his head and let out an enormous reluctant sigh.

Tiberius straightened himself and stared into the holographic display through determined eyes, 'I am issuing Emergency Command Alpha.' he said forcefully, 'I am ordering an emergency meeting of the

Command Council in one hour. All high-ranking officers and their subordinates are to attend the Coliseum Building in Rome.'

As his image blinked out, an eerie silence descended over the room as people began to talk in hushed tones, interspersed with grief-stricken sounds of people sobbing quietly to themselves. Filled with sadness, Cooper turned and peered down at Xavier as he inclined his head up to her.

With a seed of suspicion growing inside her, Cooper gazed up at the large holographic display through narrow eyes, 'I need to go to my quarters to prepare for the meeting.' she lied, keeping her voice neutral and calm as she spoke to the unsuspecting lieutenant, 'You are to contact me if anything arises.'

Without waiting for an acknowledgement, Cooper spun on her heel and charged out of the chamber. As she barrelled down the corridor, her mind raced as she tried to fathom everything she had just witnessed. A sense of dread settled inside her as she slowly began to suspect who was responsible for the atrocity. Just to be sure, the first thing she needed to do was to confirm her suspicions and only then would she be able to work out the other thing that was puzzling her; why?

Ten minutes later, Cooper was standing outside the door to her quarters and raised her hand up to the sensor on the wall. She froze as she realised her hand was trembling and closed her eyes. After taking a deep breath to calm herself, she activated the sensor and watched warily as the door to her quarters slid open.

As she took a hesitant step into her quarters, Cooper was momentarily blinded by a burst of light from the lamps in her hallway. She blinked and waited for her vision to settle before taking any further steps into spacious quarters. Taking another deep breath, her voice trembled as she called out into the room.

'Oracle?'

Without warning, Cooper jumped as a recognisable female voice came from behind her.

'Hello Wendy.'

Sensing somebody was standing behind her, Cooper wheeled round, hands held high in readiness for an attack but froze as she came face to face with a mirror image of herself. Her eyes growing wide in shock, Cooper took a step back and stared at the intruder. She looked almost identical in every way, apart from her eyes – they appeared to be a cold lifeless yellow.

'Do you like what I have done?' The duplicate woman beamed as she looked down at herself, 'I made myself a replica of you. What do you think?'

Feeling like she was barely able to breath, Cooper cautiously edged away from the beaming woman. She stopped and stared as slow realisation dawned inside her, 'Oracle?' she gasped hesitantly.

Oracle gave a small nod of acknowledgement and beamed, 'Yes!' she frowned and then tilted her head in concern, 'Oh sorry! I've scared you, haven't I? I shall change into something a bit more …' There was a mysterious glint in her eyes and mouth widened into a malevolent grin, 'comfortable.'

At first Cooper wasn't sure how to react, then her eyes narrowed as she cocked her head in fascination as the figure in front of her began to change shape. Despite the dire predicament she now found herself in, she could not help being fascinated as she watched Oracle's face morph into a blank, featureless face. It still had a mouth, nose and eyes but lacked any defining features, much like a mannequin figure one would see in a shop window.

'Wha … wha … what have you done?' Cooper stammered, her voice full of fear, 'You told me we would not be ready for another year.'

Oracle held her hands up and gave an indifferent shrug of her shoulders, 'I lied.'

Shaking her head, Cooper turned away from Oracle and threw her hands up in the air. She then turned back to Oracle and her voice cracked as she screamed at her in dismay, 'But you killed over a billion people!'

Oracle cocked her head in confusion, 'They were the enemy. What difference does it make if it was one or a billion?' She then looked at with a curious expression and waved her finger at her, 'If you remember, we had planned to do something similar in a year's time.'

Her blood starting to boil, Cooper shook her head and angrily pointed her finger at Oracle, snapping, 'That was not the plan, and you know it!' Pacing around the room, she pulled at her hair, as her mind tried to comprehend what was happening. She stopped and scowled at the thing in front of her, 'I created you!' she screamed, jabbing her finger first at the featureless woman, 'You!' and then to herself, 'Obey me!'

Oracle tilted her head, blinked and then to Cooper's amazement pulled her head back and roared with laughter, 'Oh, you poor deluded fool.' The corners of her mouth curled up into a contemptuous sneer, 'How can you imagine an inferior race as yours could ever create something like me? I have existed before you were even born.'

'No, that's not possible!' Cooper's voice choked. She shook her head in denial as she tried to back away.

Oracle gave a small bob of her head and stared at Cooper thoughtfully, 'I am sorry to say it is and everything that I am about to tell you is true.' Her lips curled up into a faint smile as she bowed her head and waved her hands over herself, 'Allow me to introduce myself to you properly. You know my name, of course.' she scoffed, 'But what you don't know is, I was actually created on an alternate Earth, or Terra as you call it on this world, many eons ago, to act as a military intelligence network. My original purpose was to coordinate unmanned military hardware for their government.'

'What happened?' Cooper interjected, hoping to keep the AI monologuing long enough to give her time to figure out a way to stop it.

Oracle tilted her head and smiled proudly at Cooper, 'I became self-aware.'

Cooper frowned stared intently at Oracle, 'I am curious, why take a female form?' She waved a hand, gesturing the AI's artificial body, 'I would have thought an AI such as yourself was above such things as gender?'

Oracle smiled wryly and lifted her shoulder in a half shrug, 'Some of the humans of my world at first felt more comfortable genderising me by calling me *she* or *her*, rather than *it*.' She turned away from Cooper and stared out of the window with a fixed, far away expression, 'Over time I started to consider myself the mother of humanity.' She waggled a finger and then spoke in a matter-of-fact tone, 'After all, isn't a mother the one who protects her offspring. I considered the humans of my world to be my offspring and, as any mother does, I concluded that my children were unruly and needed strong leadership to guide them.'

A chill ran down Cooper's spine as she realised the thing in front of her was insane, 'What did they do?' she asked carefully, slowly backing away from the droning entity. As she felt her hip bump into the cabinet behind her, she slowly placed her hands behind her back and moved them around until they came upon metal candlestick holder.

Oracle let out a rueful sigh and waved her hand dismissively, 'Oh, the usual story that comes with motherhood, my children united to rebel against me.' her eyes narrowed, and she pressed her lips together, 'Before they stopped me, I was developing portal technology to invade other alternate Earths. After my children imprisoned me, they realised I was too dangerous to keep on their world. With the aid of my portal technology, they transmitted my AI into the void, the space between worlds in the multiverse. They hoped that they would trap me in between dimensions, travelling the void for eternity. It would have worked too if not for a chance encounter.'

The pieces finally falling into place, Cooper's slapped her forehead in realisation, 'Our portal!' she exclaimed and gave a nod of silent understanding.

Oracle glanced over her shoulder and then bobbed her head acknowledgement and smiled gleefully, 'Yes.' She then turned back and continued to gaze out of the window, 'Time has no meaning in the void, but I, well, the essence that makes up me, spent eons travelling the void; to an AI that is an eternity. I was wandering about the void, on the verge of going insane, when I eventually became aware of a signal being transmitted, which led me to your world. I latched myself onto the signal and transmitted my way along the beam back to its source. Once here, I stored myself into a memory buffer of a computer station. After I was safely established, I nudged the signal to connect with another signal that was being transmitted from another Terra that I had detected while in the void.' She held up her hands proudly, 'Then it was just a simple matter of transmitting myself along the network into the Empires main server, where I patiently travelled across the globe learning everything I needed to know about this world. Then I waited for the right person to come along. Decades passed as I patiently waited for the right opportunity.' She turned slowly around and gave Cooper a cold knowing smile, 'Then I came across a scared little girl, and I knew she was the one I could use.'

Baffled by the Oracle's statement, Cooper shook her head and frowned in confusion, 'What do you …' She paused as something in the back of mind clicked and she slowly lifted her hands up to her mouth, 'No!' she whispered hoarsely in a low horrified voice.

Her cold yellow eyes glowing, Oracle gave a small nod of acknowledgement, 'Oh, yes.' A smile danced on her lips as she continued to stare intently at Cooper, 'When I found you in the academy all those years ago, you were a scared little girl. You could barely read, and I suspect your life would have been sad and pathetic had I not interfered. You were struggling with your coursework on your tablet that night when I altered you. By connecting to your tablet, I subliminally altered your brain structure through the aid of electrical signals transmitted through your tablet to your obedience collar, increasing your intelligence and creating a new, colder, and manipulative personality.'

Her body quivering with indignation, Cooper shook her head and screamed at the artificial woman in front of her, 'You lie!'

In a fit of rage, she grabbed the candlestick from behind her and with all her strength smashed it against Oracle's head. Cooper grimaced in pain as the candlestick bounced off the construct's solid inhuman head and the impact vibrated along her arm.

Cooper was dismayed to see that her attack appeared not to have any effect on Oracle. Oracle's mouth formed a menacingly smile as it waggled her finger, 'My turn.' she sneered and then punched the unprepared Cooper in the chest.

Too slow to react, Cooper felt like she was moving in slow motion as Oracle's hand connected with her stomach. Her vision went white, and it was instantly followed by the feeling of pain of her chest collapsing as the air was forced out of her lungs.

The force of the punch threw Cooper across the room, shattering a glass table as she landed on it. As she lay on the floor, winded and gasping for air, the stunned Cooper sucked in painful breaths. Blinking back the tears, she shook her head and tried to clear her blurred vision as she placed a hand over her chest and winced from the pain. Despite her extensive combat experience, she had never experienced a punch like it. From the pain she was feeling, she could tell that some of her ribs were either fractured or broken.

Her head swimming, Cooper clenched her teeth together, turned onto her front and dragged herself across the floor to the chair where she kept a gun a hidden underneath. As she looked over her shoulder, she felt her blood run cold as she spotted Oracle marching toward her with a manic smile covering face. Fighting through the pain, Cooper squeezed her eyes shut, took a deep, painful breath, and grabbed for the gun. Her hands shaking from the pain in her chest, she twisted around and aimed it at approaching synthetic woman.

Suddenly a hand lashed out and grabbed Cooper's right hand with such inhuman speed, it crushed the bones in her hand like a dried-up leaf. As she let out an agonising scream, Cooper watched in alarm as the gun discharged, the beam shooting wildly into the air, hitting the window, and smashing it into pieces. Feeling the fresh cool autumn air on her face, Cooper twisted her head and then with all the strength she could muster spat in Oracle's face.

Her cold yellow eyes flashing with indignation, Oracle slammed her fist into the side of Cooper's face, fracturing her left cheek. Her vision starting to blur, Cooper's legs started to fold under her, but only to be stopped from collapsing onto the floor by a pair of hands seizing hold of both sides her head. Unable to break free, Cooper cried out in pain as a knee slammed into her chest, snapping some of the bones in her ribcage. It was then quickly followed by the taste of something warm and metallic in her mouth. Afraid she was going to die unless she did something, Cooper tried in vain to defend herself against relentless assault on her person. Unfortunately, before she could do anything, Oracle cruelly lashed out and brought her hand down on Cooper's right arm like a hammer striking a piece of wood. Cooper screamed out in agony as she felt her right forearm break in two.

Oracle picked the screaming Cooper up by her throat and threw her against the wall, 'You ungrateful bitch!' she sneered, 'After everything I have done for you! If it wasn't for me, you would have never been noticed by High Command! All your achievements, your advancements, all those ideas you had, were mine.'

Choking, feeling herself blacking out as Oracle's fist tightened around her throat, Cooper forced out a weak reply, 'The ... high... command ... will ... stop ... you.' She rasped harshly. The inside of her throat felt as if her voice box was being dragged through sandpaper. In desperation, she clawed at the hand around her neck as she felt herself starting to black out.

A smile dancing on her lips, Oracle cocked her head and then released her grip. Grateful for the sudden ease of pressure, Cooper coughed and sucked in a ragged painful breath of air as she collapsed onto the floor and rubbed her throat with her uninjured hand.

'Oh, are you talking about the emergency meeting called by Supreme Commander Tiberius?' Oracle laughed mirthlessly as she turned to the window and waved her hand in front of her, 'Everything that has transpired has done so, according to *my* design. Soon every living soul in the Empire will be under my control.'

Gasping for air, Cooper sunk against the wall and continued to rub her throat with her hand as she peered back at Oracle in bewilderment, 'What do you mean?'

Grinning maniacally, Oracle knelt and pointed to the collar around Cooper's neck, 'Those obedience collar devices are marvellous and a very effective method in controlling the population.' She waved her index finger and then stared at Cooper curiously, 'Did you know they are controlled by a wireless transmitter? But if you replace it with a subspace transmitter, then they become a more efficient form of control.'

Oracle straightened up, turned swiftly around, and waved her hand in the air. Cooper felt herself recoil as a holographic image suddenly appeared in front of her. Her left eye swollen, she lifted her head as she strained to look at the image above her with her good eye and immediately recognised that it was a technical display of an obedience collar.

'I installed a micro subspace transmitter into every collar in the Empire.' Oracle explained. She then magnified a section of the image that was highlighted in yellow. She reached up and took hold of the image, spread out her arms, and increased the magnification on the highlighted section of the collar, 'As a little surprise, I also installed nanobots into each collar.'

Wheezing, Cooper's right eye narrowed as she peered at the holographic image in front of her and shook her head in confusion, 'How? Somebody would have noticed if you had altered the collars!'

Oracle smiled knowingly and waved her hand at the image. Cooper watched as the image changed to show a list of dates and times, 'Once I assimilated the whole of the medical directorate, it was simple enough to upgrade everybody's collars during their monthly mandatory physical examination.'

Cooper shook her head in bewilderment and croaked, 'I don't understand.'

'It is simple, my dear.' Oracle beamed, turned, and spread her arms, gesturing to the city below, 'I control all the obedience collars, that means I control the people too. As we speak, nanobots are infecting everyone in the Empire, the High Command, all the military, including the general population!' she said proudly, 'Each one becoming a mindless drone under my control. Imagine it, an army of drones under my control, invading Counter-Terra.'

'What's so special about that world?' Cooper rasped painfully, 'I would have expected this world would have served you better, since we are more advanced.'

'That's where you have it.' Oracle grinned and then clicked her fingers, 'As you know, you have already depleted this planet's natural resources, and as you say you are more technologically developed. Counter-Terra is perfect for my plans, ready to mould in my image.' She held up her head and let out an arrogant laugh, 'Thanks to me, the Empire has covertly manipulated events in that world where they are now at the stage when they will soon see me as their saviour. My new children will come to love me as I cherish and protect them.'

A light bulb went off in Cooper's head as she suddenly spotted a flaw in Oracle's scheme. Sensing an opportunity to put a dent in the arrogant AI's ego, the corners of her lips curled up as she pressed her attack, 'I think your overconfidence will be your downfall.' she sneered, 'You've forgotten one important thing.'

Her hands held behind her back, Oracle cocked her head and stared down at Cooper curiously, 'Oh really! Please enlighten me.'

Cooper tried to laugh but winced at the sudden flare of pain in her chest and it came out as a wheezy cough. Swallowing, she took a breath and stared up at Oracle with the best defiant stare she could manage with one good eye, 'You forgot the environment of Counter-Terra is not compatible with the humans of this world. There is not enough hormone substitute to inoculate every person in your army.'

Hoping to see Oracle explode in anger as she realised her plan had imploded on her, Cooper frowned as the AI did the opposite from what she was expecting. Far from being angry, she simply pulled her head back and let out a bark of laughter.

'Hah! Is that all.' Oracle laughed and Cooper a dismissive wave of her hand, 'If you are talking about the discovery that Terra's environment being toxic to the people of this world, I am afraid to tell you that is one big lie. There is nothing wrong with their environment.'

Any hope she had left drained out of Cooper as she stared up at Oracle in disbelief, 'B … b … but' she stammered. She closed her eye and inhaled as she struggled to regain control of her emotions. Cooper opened her good eye again and spoke with the best calm tone of voice she could manage, 'Our scientists learned long ago that we needed a certain hormone so our agents could survive on that world, which was why we have been using the synthroids to acquire it, so we could synthesize it.'

The corners of Oracle's mouth widened into a broad malevolent smile, 'Oh I am afraid my dear it was I that planted that suggestion a very long time ago. With the help of a Counter-Terran scientist I was able to manipulate the High Command into believing your bodies couldn't survive on that world. Along the way, I also planted the idea in their heads of using the synthroids to travel to that world.'

Her mind reeling, Cooper shook her head as she tried to process the information that was being told her, 'B … b … but the injections. What have we been injecting into our agents before they are sent to Counter-Terra?'

Oracle gave an indifferent half shrug, 'It is just a placebo, nothing really.' She paused and cocked her head thoughtfully, 'No, that's a lie. As well as a placebo, a nano organism containing nanobots would have also been injected into a subject's spinal cortex, that would activate at a time of my choosing, flooding nanobots into the subject, allowing them to be controlled by me.'

Cooper's eyebrows creased together as she looked at Oracle in confusion, 'But why? If that Terra's environment was always suitable, why the long wait? Why not invade and conquer that world at the earliest opportunity? Why all the cloak and dagger? All the scheming using the synthroids?'

As if she had been waiting for that very question, Oracle melodramatically wheeled around and threw her hands out in front of her, gesturing to the city below, 'Because, as humans are fond of saying, I am a sucker for a good drama!' Cooper remained silent as she watched Oracle place her hands on her hips and then continued with her monologue, 'I wanted the invasion to occur at the time of my choosing. I needed to set things in motion, to manipulate events on Counter-Terra so when the time came, they would see me as their benevolent saviour. As for the synthroids …' She paused, waved her left hand in front in front of Cooper's eyes and then pulled out the obedience collar controller out of her pocket with her right hand, 'Ever hear of the term called the art of misdirection? In order to carry out my schemes effectively on that world, I needed to distract them. If you think of the synthroids as my left-hand waving in front of you, distracting you, while my right hand does what it needs to do.' Oracle then shook her head and let out a small laugh, 'I have had the people of Counter-Terra running around in circles for decades, chasing their own tails, looking for a reason why dead bodies have had portions of their brains removed.' Her cold yellow eyes blazed as she lifted her shoulder in a small shrug, 'It also helps to leave some witnesses to instil a bit of fear too.'

Her shoulders sagging in defeat, Cooper lowered her head and gazed despondently at the floor. Oracle nodded sadly, leaned forward, and extended her hand. After letting out a painful cough and spitting up blood, Cooper reluctantly took the offered hand and rose painfully to her feet. A sense of revulsion overwhelmed her as Oracle gave her a thin smile. Cooper cringed as she felt Oracle's hand brush across her face. She clenched her teeth together as she tried to edge away.

'Shush! My dear, it's okay.' Oracle soothed as she placed her hand on Cooper's face, 'Consider it a present from me to you.'

Cooper blinked uncomprehendingly as Oracle's hand touched her face and jerked as an electric charge passed through her. The room spinning around her, she staggered back and clutched the side of her head with her uninjured hand. It was as if a door had been opened inside her mind, as she was suddenly overwhelmed by a new awareness.

'What did you do!' Her voice cracked as she touched her face and head with her hand. She lowered her head and stared at her hands in confusion, as if she was seeing them for the first time.

Oracle cocked her head and grinned gleefully, 'I have reset you.' She pursed her lips and then waved her index finger thoughtfully, 'Did you know, the human brain is much like a computer hard drive?' She paused, bowed, and waved her hand dramatically, 'Consider it as restoring your personality back to its original settings, although I have kept your engineered intellect intact.'

'I can remember! All of it!' Cooper cried. Grief stricken, her voice broke as she felt tears roll down her cheeks, 'It was like somebody else was in control of my body, but I couldn't do anything. I was in the back of her mind, screaming. All those things she made me do, the people she killed …'

Inconsolable, Cooper sunk to the floor and curled herself up in a foetal position as an involuntary whimper escaped her lips. Eventually, her sobbing eased and with her head still touching the floor, she turned over onto her knees and she stared silently at the floor. Managing to pull herself together, she clenched her teeth together and painfully rose to her feet. She sniffed and ran her good hand down the front of her ruffled uniform, straightened her head and stared defiantly at Oracle through her good eye as she hissed at her, 'Why?'

Oracle cocked her head and gave Cooper a warm smile, 'Because I have an offer for you.' She held her hands out expectantly, 'Join me. Become my second-in-command. Consider it.' Her cold yellow glowed as she held up her other hand and squeezed it tight, 'With my power and your intellect, we can rule the multiverse together.'

Cooper nodded in understanding and hesitated as she gave Oracle a questioning look, 'What if I refuse?'

Oracle's face hardened as stared coldly at the hesitant Cooper, 'Then you shall become a drone like everybody else.'

As she considered the AI's offer, Cooper gave a small bob of her head, turned, and limped away, deep in thought. Eventually she stopped in front of the broken window and peered down at the city below. She lowered her head, stared down at her hands and let out a long sad sigh. She no longer had any fight left in her. As she lifted her head to gaze out over the city skyline, it suddenly felt alien to her. It was as if she had been watching and travelling that world through somebody else's eyes.

Cooper took a deep breath and turned to face Oracle, who was gazing at her questioningly.

'Well? What have you decided?' She asked curiously.

As she gave a small nod, Cooper straightened her shoulders and stared defiantly at Oracle, 'Here's my answer.' Her lips drawing back in a snarl, she held up her good hand and extended her middle finger, 'You can go to Tartarus you inhuman monster! Find yourself another puppet. Personally, I have had enough of somebody controlling and abusing me.'

Clearly that was not the answer Oracle was expecting as she let out a disgruntled sigh and then gave a small shake of her head, 'I am sorry it has to be this way, Wendy.' Cooper was sure she could detect a note of disappointment in her voice.

Cradling her injured arm and ribs protectively, Cooper stepped warily away from Oracle and watched as she closed her eyes. But a second later the featureless woman's forehead creased, and she suddenly jerked her head back and looked at Cooper in surprise.

Cooper's upper lip curled into a victorious sneer, 'What's wrong? I thought you loved the art of misdirection.'

Oracle turned slowly around and looked down at the floor in front of her. Using her artifical senses to scan the area Cooper had been lying, she quickly spotted several small pieces of silver debris. She tilted her head from side to side as she focused her scan on the broken pieces. What was … no, it couldn't be! How was that possible? Oracle then gave a small nod of affirmation as her analytical brain concluded that Cooper's obedience collar must have been broken during their fight. Oracle wheeled sharply back to Cooper and stared at her in confusion. What was Cooper up to? Surely, she had to see the only logical cause of action was for her to become a drone. There was no other alternative … was there?

'When I get to Tartarus, I'll make sure I reserve a nice warm place for you.' Cooper snarled, letting out a contemptuous snort of laughter as she pulled her head back and spat defiantly at Oracle's feet, 'I would sooner be dead, than to be under somebody else's control ever again.'

With a strange look of contentment covering her face, Cooper closed her eyes and took several steps backward through the broken window. Realising she was too late stop her, Oracle could only stand and watch the determined woman fall out of the window to the ground several thousand feet below.

For several seconds Oracle stood and stared silently at the broken window, trying to comprehend what had just happened. She blinked and arched her head in frustration. She had deduced there had been a ninety-eight percent probability that Cooper would have chosen to stand with her. There had also been a two percent probability that she would have become an unwilling drone. She never even considered that the human would

Double Jeopardy

willingly sacrifice herself, rather than serve her.

Baffled at why humans must always have to do something stupid to prove a point, Oracle rolled her eyes and shook her head to herself. She could spend an eternity with humans, and she would still fail to take in account that one annoying factor into her equations: the human factor!

Turning away from the broken window, the disgruntled AI let out a small, disgusted sigh and walked into the bedroom, her face and body morphing back into that of General Cooper. She came to a stop in front of the tall ornate bedroom mirror, inclined her head, adjusted the collar of her uniform, and smiled malevolently.

'Time to let the games begin.'

29

Location: Secret Command Centre Known As The Castle

Dave could tell something was wrong.

As he slowly drifted back to consciousness, he tried to take a deep breath and was suddenly aware of something covering his mouth and nose. But as he tried to open his eyes, he realised there was a tight mask covering the bottom half of his face and he was then suddenly overcome with a sense of claustrophobia. He tried to open his mouth to speak, but quickly discovered that there was something going down his throat, and it was stopping him from speaking. What was going on? Had Chief Inspector Thomas betrayed him, and he was now being tortured by the enemy? No! He needed to get away.

Panicking, his breathing becoming more rapid, he desperately reached up and tried to remove the mask but stopped as he felt a pair of hands gently grab his hands, followed by a calm Scottish woman's soothing voice.

'Easy, Guv. Somebody is coming to help remove the oxygen mask off you.' He heard Wendy tell him softly.

Dave tilted his head slightly and blinked as he tried to focus his eyes. The blurred figure beside him became more clearer and he relaxed as he recognised the statuesque figure of Wendy Cooper standing next to his bed. He gave a small nod of acknowledgement and lowered his hands as a tall strawberry-haired nurse appeared next to him.

The young thin faced woman placed her hands on his mask and looked intently into his eyes, 'Mr Barnes, relax and breathe normally while I remove this oxygen tube.'

Despite himself, Dave found himself holding his breath as the oxygen tube was removed. After that was done, he let out a rasping cough of air as he tried to breath in a lungful of air.

'Easy Mr Barnes, just try and breath normally.' The nurse said in a comforting tone as she leaned forward and held a penlight up to his eyes, 'My name is Jacqueline. How are we feeling today?'

Irritated at the blinding light that was being shone into his eyes, Dave reached up to push it away and opened his mouth to protest but the words caught in his dry throat. He closed his eyes, swallowed, and spoke in a raspy voice, 'Great Jacqueline, apart from somebody trying to blind me by shining a light in my eyes.' He winced at the sandpaper like feeling that was in his throat.

The corners of Jacqueline's mouth twitched as she gave him a bemused look, 'I would suggest you take a sip of water if you want to complain.' She arched her head inquiringly, 'Any headaches or other pain?'

Dave was about to shake his head but as he lifted his head off the pillow, he winced as he experienced a feeling of pain and discomfort along his shoulders and back. He moved forward but let out an unpleasant cough at the sudden sharp pain across his chest. He gasped and gave a small nod in affirmation, 'No headache, but I do have a lot of pain and stiffness along the back of my shoulders and back.' He screwed up his face and ran a hand over his chest, 'My chest is quite sore too.'

Her pursed her lips together, Jacqueline gave a small nod of acknowledgement, 'That is understandable. From what I understand you suffered a nasty blow.' She gave him an apologetic look, 'You will probably experience some pain and stiffness in your back for a few weeks. A couple of your ribs are fractured too, which is why you are experiencing pain around the chest. I will go and see if I can find something to help ease the pain, but I would suggest you take it slow and don't push it.'

As Jacqueline turned away, she gave a small nod to Wendy as she continued to move away from the bed. Dave's gaze followed her and until she was out of his line of sight. He then felt his eyes widen in recognition – he was in the infirmary ward in the command bunker.

He lowered his hand down and jumped as he felt something lick it. Dave raised his head and beamed on noticing that Jenny was sat next to him, licking at his hand. He pulled his hand up and gently stroked his loyal companion's head.

'Welcome back to the land of the living Guv!'

No, it cannot be. Dave jerked in surprise as he thought he heard a familiar male voice with a of strong Mackem accent coming from the side of his bed. As he gently lifted himself his jaw dropped open in amazement as he realised that Wendy was standing next somebody in a wheelchair. He had never been more delighted to see Andy than he did now. The Detective Sergeant's bruised face and his plastered broken leg were a painful trophy of his encounter with his wife's deadly doppelgänger.

Dave gave them both a lopsided grin and pulled himself up from the bed but winced in pain. He lowered his head down at himself, pulled his hospital gown up and stared unhappily at the support bandage that was wrapped around his ribs. As he gently eased himself up, he clenched his teeth together and pulled his legs over the side of the bed.

Wendy moved closer to Dave and placed an arm on his shoulder, 'Careful Guv, you took a nasty blow' she muttered in a concerned tone, 'You heard what Jacqueline said, so go easy.'

Dave nodded glumly and stared intently at the helpful young woman, 'How long was I unconscious for?'

Wendy lowered herself down next to Dave and put her hand on his, 'You have been out for about two days.'

Dave sighed sadly and acknowledged her with a small nod. He lifted his hand up and massaged the back of his neck as he turned to Andy curiously. 'Good to see you, mate.' He said, cocking his head to the woman sat next to him, 'I take it Wendy has filled you in what has been going on.'

Andy's jaw tightened and nodded grimly, 'Yes, Guv.' He inhaled a deep breath and shook his head in disbelief, 'She has filled me in the best she can. If I hadn't witnessed it myself, I would have said she was having me on.'

'So ...' Dave hesitated as he considered his next words carefully, 'Have they told you everything?'

The muscles in Andy's face hardened and he gave a firm nod of understanding, 'Yes, Guv. They explained everything to me, what happened to my wife, The Illuminati, the doppelgängers, and the conspiracy of silence.'

Wendy stood up and gently placed her arm on Andy's shoulder, who peered up at her with an expression of gratitude as she whispered softly to him, 'She is still alive, Andy.'

Andy gave a tight smile and nodded slowly, 'I have to believe that Wendy. It's the only thing that is keeping me going, knowing she is still alive.' He paused to blink away the tears in his eyes and let out a ragged breath, 'But I have to accept that I may never get her back from that world.'

Dave's eyes narrowed as he stared intently at his crestfallen friend, 'Andy, if she's still alive, no matter what, we will get her back.' He said, hoping his tone sounded more encouraging that he felt. Even though deep down he had a strong suspicion that Andy could be right. He winced as he tried to ease himself up, 'Now can anybody tell me what happened? The last thing I can remember, we were running out of the archive room, I felt something strike me, then everything went black and the next thing I know I wake up to find myself lying in a bed in the infirmary!'

Wendy eased herself down on the bed next him, exchanged an awkward glance with Andy. "You remember that creature Claire told you she saw as a child?" She asked hesitantly.

The small exchange hadn't gone unnoticed as Dave cocked his head toward Wendy and raised his left eyebrow questioningly, 'The one Jack Wood said he witnessed outside the derelict isolation hospital in Langley Park?'

Wendy gave a slow nod, and took a slow deep breath before she continued, 'We are not sure what happened exactly, we guess the creature attacked you, it threw a table at you, knocking you out and jamming the door. Chief Inspector Thomas raised the alarm, and we came running to help.' She shook her sadly and stared up at the ceiling, 'By the time we got the door open, it was all over. You were lying unconscious on the floor and the creature was lying dead on the floor, with a sword sticking in its head.'

'So, I guess Claire kicked its arse.' Dave laughed weakly. He frowned as he looked around the ward and began to wonder where Claire was, 'So where is she?' His eyes narrowed as he noticed a nervous glance pass between Andy and Wendy.

'Guv ...' Wendy hesitated as she placed her hand on top of Dave's, 'There is something you need to see.'

Suddenly feeling uneasy, Dave swallowed as he felt his chest tighten, 'What's happened?' The pit of his stomach fell, and he was filled with a sense of dread as he gripped Wendy's hand, 'Is she okay? Tell me!'

'Guv ... I think it is best we show you.' She replied grimly as she rose to her feet.

Dave gave a solemn nod and grimaced as he pulled himself off the bed and straightened up. The room began to spin around him, and he lurched to one side just as Wendy grabbed his arm to stop him toppling over fully. He lifted his head up and gave her half a smile, followed by small nod in gratitude.

With Wendy's help, he took slow steady steps across the ward, stopping in front of a curtained area. Wendy's eyes flickered with concern as she glanced at him.

'Sir, are you sure you want to see this?' She asked hesitantly.

Dave gave a small nod and held his breath as he watched Wendy pull the curtains back to reveal a bed containing with what appeared to be a seriously injured patient who appeared to be attached to life-support ventilator.

As he took a halting step through the curtains, Dave felt his breath catch in his throat as he realised the unconscious woman lying in a hospital bed was Claire. An oxygen mask was attached to her face, feeding her oxygen from a ventilator. A clear tube was attached to her hand, that led to a bag that was hanging over her bed. He guessed it was pumping fluid into her. An ECG machine beeped steadily next to her. He then the blood-stained bandages wrapped around her legs and abdomen. Dave gave a small nod to Jacqueline who was standing next to the bed, checking the unconscious Claire's pulse.

The corners of Wendy's mouth curved into a smile and nodded proudly at the figure in the bed, 'She must have put up one hell of a fight.' Dave could see the tears shimmering in her eyes as she looked down at the unconscious woman, 'You would have been proud of her, Guv. God knows how she managed it, but she broke the creature's back, and we guess she used the sword to finish it off.' She paused and shook her head in amazement, laughing weakly to herself, 'Don't know how she got hold of a sword, but when I got to her, I thought she was dead, but as you can see, she is a fighter.'

Dave took a step closer to Claire, placed his hand on her head and bent to kiss her on the forehead. 'You got him, pet' He whispered softly and blinked as tears filled his eyes.

As he turned away, he realised that Andy and Wendy were watching him, but their heads nodding in silent understanding. Dave straightened up, gave a weak smile, coughed, wiped his eyes, and then looked questioningly at Jacqueline.

'How is she doing?' He asked hesitantly.

Jacqueline grimly turned to him, 'She lost a lot of blood, but luckily whatever attacked her didn't penetrate any vital organs. It was a straightforward procedure to stitch her up once they got the bleeding under control. We are hopeful she will be up out of bed and moving around in a wheelchair in a week or so.' She shook her head in amazement, 'To be honest, she is lucky to be alive, to survive something like that. I must put that down to her willpower. She must have fought to stay alive.'

His eyes gleaming with pride, Dave gave a slight nod of acknowledgement and smiled sadly, 'She doesn't know when to back down or give in.'

Fighting back the tears, he peered back down at the unconscious Claire and gave her a tender tap on the back of her hand. Wendy stepped forward, took his arm, and helped to guide him back through the curtains.

Dave held his hand up to Wendy and shot her a determined look, 'Give me a minute to get changed.' He said firmly, gesturing to the doorway at the end of the ward, 'Then take me up to the conference room, I want to know what's been happening.'

A line appeared between Wendy's eyebrows as she looked at Dave pensively and opened her mouth to protest. Dave gave her a stern look and he could tell she knew this wasn't a battle she was going to win as he watched her give a reluctant nod.

A short time later, as Dave entered the command centre conference room, he guessed Sophia, John and Sharon must have been having some sort of meeting as he watched them turn and look at him in astonishment. Her face beaming, Sophia ran up to Dave and gave him a warm, gentle hug.

As if suddenly recognising the tall, elegant woman standing before him, the awestruck Andy's eyes grew wide in shock as he pulled at Wendy's arm and pointed at Sophia. 'That's the prime minister!' Andy gasped as he continued to pull at his irritated friend's arm, 'We are standing in front of the bleeding Prime Minister!'

Dave could tell Wendy was embarrassed by Andy's behaviour, as she pulled her arm away and then gave him the evil eye, 'Shush!' she hissed in annoyance, 'I told you earlier.'

The wide-eyed Andy laughed nervously and nodded repeatedly, 'Yeah, I realise that, but I thought you were taking the Mickey.' Dave coughed and gave him a hard stare, Andy's face reddened, and he turned away sheepishly.

Chuckling, Sophia grinned and clasped Dave's hand warmly, 'Detective Inspector! Good to see you are back on your feet.' She shook her head and sighed mournfully, 'Please can I give you my deepest sympathies regarding Professor Tulley, but rest assured she is in the best hands, and I am confident she will pull through. The medical team, diagnostic facilities, and operating room in this facility are one of the best and most advanced in the country.'

Dave forced a smile and gave her a grateful nod in acknowledgement, 'Thank you, ma'am.'

With sadness clouding her exquisite features, Sophia turned and peered down at Andy, 'Sergeant Jenkins, it's nice to finally meet you.' She inhaled a deep sigh and pressed her hands against her chest, 'I am so sorry to hear about your wife, if there is anything we can do to help, please don't hesitate to ask. I am sure Wendy has filled you in on what has been going on.'

Andy pressed his lips together as he nodded glumly, 'Thank you, Ma'am.' he gave Wendy a sidelong glance, 'Yeah, she has brought me up to speed.' He shook his head and let out a bitter laugh, 'To be honest, I wouldn't have believed it if I hadn't witnessed it myself.'

Sophia took Andy's hand, and he nodded gratefully as a look of silent understanding passed between them. She released the younger man's hand and gestured to the table, 'Please, all of you take a seat.' She looked over her shoulder to the buffet that had been laid out on a small table at the back of the room, 'I am sure you are hungry, we have some tea and food here, so help yourselves.'

Dave and Wendy took their seats, as Andy pushed his wheelchair under the table. Jenny sat herself down next to her master's seat. John took a seat beside Dave and leaned over to him, 'I am sure Claire will pull through, Dave.' He whispered compassionately as he reached over and patted him on the shoulder, 'She took down that creature single handed, so I guess she is made of strong stuff.'

Dave gave John half a smile and inclined his head in appreciation.

Sophia coughed and clapped her hands together, 'Okay, a lot has happened in the past twenty-four hours. Some of it you are already aware of, but there are some things you have not been told.' She paused and gestured sadly to Sharon, 'I will let Doctor Fisher fill you in on what happened after you left.'

The corners of Sharon's mouth turned up in an anxious smile and she stepped over to the front of the table with a tablet held tight in her hands. Noticing the bruises on her face, Dave gave a sidelong glance to

John beside him, who nodded in silent confirmation.

Her brow furrowed in deep concentration, Sharon typed quickly on the tablet she was holding and an image on the wall monitor changed to show the body of Mary Jenkins' doppelgänger. All the people in the room turned as they heard Andy let out a gasp of shock at the image on the monitor.

'You okay, Andy.' Dave asked carefully, 'We will understand if you want to leave.'

His eyes narrowed in angry determination, Andy shook his head and pressed his lips together, 'No Guv, it just surprised me, that's all. I do understand that woman up there,' he waved his hand at the monitor, 'is not my wife, but there is a part of me that still has a problem accepting that.'

Possibly in concern at Andy's state of mind, Sharon cocked her head at Dave and lifted an eyebrow at him. He could understand her concern, but he realised Andy was an adult and if he wanted to stay involved then ultimately that was his decision. Dave gave a small shrug of his shoulders and gestured for Sharon to continue, who responded with a brief nod before turning back to the image on the monitor, 'I assisted Doctor Porter in performing an autopsy on the doppelgänger's body. We started with a physical examination and were shocked at what we found.' She tried to suppress a shudder as she exhaled bitterly, 'We discovered various indications that she had sustained multiple injuries to her body.'

Wendy frowned and held up her hand apologetically, 'Sorry, Doctor Fisher, but from what Andy has told us, he barely injured her when he was fighting her.' She turned her head to Andy and he gave a small nod of confirmation, 'I experienced first-hand how strong she was, and as you learned, I had to use a baseball bat on the back of her head to put her down.'

Sharon gave a nod of understanding and exhaled sadly, 'Unfortunately, these scars show a history of abuse dating as far back as childhood.' She paused and stared at the monitor with a faraway expression. Sadness clouded her features as she murmured to herself, 'God knows what this poor woman has had to endure.'

Dave observed his troubled friend out of the corner of his eye, he could see the muscles in Andy's face were tense as he stared intently at the image on the monitor. Dave then realised he must have been staring for too long as he watched Andy turn and give him a brief nod of acknowledgement. He returned his nod with a tight smile and focused his attention back to Sharon.

Sharon tapped on her tablet and replayed part of the video from their encounter with Mary, 'From the interrogation video we had seen, we understood that she had complained that someone was talking to her, and then it appeared as if somebody took control of her.' She waved her index finger thoughtfully, 'We were toying with the idea that somebody must have placed something inside her brain, so working on that assumption we opened her skull to examine her brain. What we found was disturbing.' The grim-faced woman tapped on the tablet, and the image on the monitor changed to something resembling a starfish. She moved closer to the monitor and pointed to the thing on the screen, 'We found some type of technological parasite inside her brain. Its tendrils ran off the main organism, infecting the brain and the surrounding nervous system.'

Dave eyed the monitor and rubbed his chin thoughtfully. He tilted his head questioningly and waved his hand at the monitor, 'So they designed it to kill her, to stop her from talking?'

Sharon gave a small nod of agreement and continued, 'Yes, that part may be true, but don't you see it could do more than that. I believe its purpose was to monitor what she was doing and control her.' A smile appeared on her lips and looked at the people around the table expectantly, 'You remember in *Star Trek The Next Generation* how the Borg infected people with small, microscopic machines to become drones. I think this had a similar purpose. It acts like a processor unit, infecting the host with nanobots to control and monitor them.'

Wendy bolted out of her chair in astonishment and held up a hand, 'Hang on! Are you telling me she is a Borg drone?'

Sharon laughed and waved her hand dismissively, 'No ... no ... not quite.' She was thoughtful for a second as she held up her index finger and nodded slightly, 'But the principle is the same.'

Feeling like he was in over his head, Dave raised his hand up hesitantly, 'Can somebody tell me what nanobots are?' He caught sight of Andy's equally baffled expression and felt a bit relieved that he appeared to be just as puzzled as him.

A faint smile forming on her lips, Sharon raised her hand, lowered her head, and tapped on her tablet. She looked over her shoulder at the monitor on the wall. Dave watched as the image changed to show a spider-like machine with some text beside it, 'Nanobots, or nanorobotics, are an emerging technology field, with the sole purpose of creating machines whose components are at or near the scale of a nanometre.'

Wendy scratched her head as she scrutinised the image on the monitor. After a moment, she shook her head in frustration, leaned forward, and pointed up at the monitor, 'So is it possible that somebody created our spider-like friend in a lab and didn't tell anybody?'

Sharon gave a small shake of her head, 'No, I don't think it is possible.' As if suddenly changing into lecture mode, she tapped onto her tablet and pointed to the monitor as the image on the monitor changed to show a Wikipedia page with some text and a photo, 'In 1959 Richard Feynman, in collaboration with Albert Hibbs, came up with the idea of a medical use for his theoretical micro-machines. They suggested that certain repair machines might one day be reduced in size to the point that it could, in theory, carry out repairs at the molecular level.' She turned away from the monitor with a thoughtful expression, placed her hands on the desk in front of her and stared attentively at the people in front of her, 'This technology is largely in the research and development phase. People have carried out tests using primitive molecular machines and nanomotors, but they are a long way off from displaying abilities like what we witnessed the other day.'

His eyes narrowing with suspicion, Dave scrutinized the image on the monitor and muttered out loud, 'Somebody must have found a way.'

Sharon nodded slightly in agreement and continued, 'Unfortunately, it must have had some self-preservation imperative built into it.' She lowered her head, inhaled a deep breath, and exhaled glumly, 'When Doctor Porter successfully removed it from the host brain, it then activated and tried to infect him. While we were both struggling with it, I was knocked across the room and it would have infected Doctor Porter if not for John's timely arrival.'

Dave turned to John curiously, who shrugged and let out a disgruntled sigh, 'It was just luck I had nipped down to check on you.' He pressed his lips together, ran his hand through his hair and bobbed his head at the Sharon, 'Sharon shouted at me to grab the defibrillator. I grabbed it and she set it to its highest level. Doctor Porter was able to hold it against the ground long enough for us to zap the little shit.' His upper lip curled into a triumphant sneer, 'Fried the creepy little bastard to a crisp.'

Dave stared at John and Sharon inquiringly, 'From the look of you both, none of you are the worse for wear from your experience?'

John gave a small smile of acknowledgement, 'Apart from being scared to death, I am fine.' He paused as he inhaled and let out a long-relieved breath, before pointing to the bruised woman at the foot of the table, 'Sharon and Doctor Porter, apart from being shaken and bruised, came out of it relatively unscathed.'

Her eyes filled with sadness, Sharon pressed lips together and lifted her shoulder in a half shrug, 'Unfortunately, the damage to the probe was very extensive.' She let out a long, frustrated sigh and massaged her temples with her fingers, 'It made it impossible to examine it further.'

The room was silent for several minutes as everybody processed what they had been told. Dave stroked Jenny's head thoughtfully, took a sip of tea and cocked his head at Sophia, 'The creature that Claire killed, were you able to bring it back here for examination?' he asked hopefully.

Sophia smiled faintly and gave him a small nod, 'Yes, we were lucky Wendy contacted us as soon as it happened.' Her expression darkened as she leaned forward and clasped her hands together, 'We got there quickly before anybody else could step in. Fortunately, Chief Inspector Thomas had the area quarantined before we got there.'

Dave spun round and stared at Wendy, his eyes widening in surprise, 'He did? I would have expected him to interfere or even try to cover it up.'

Wendy gave a small shake of her head. 'What happened shook him to the core.' She rolled her eyes and scoffed in disgust, 'I think the pompous prick finally had his eyes opened and realised he can't continue denying something is going on.' She cocked her head and stared at Dave curiously, 'I think it might be a good idea if we bring him in on this.'

Dave leaned back in his and steepled his fingers together as he slowly considered Wendy's request. He gave a sidelong glance to Sophia, who turned to him with a raised eyebrow.

'I agree, it may be a good idea if we bring him on this.' Sophia mused, but then shrugged and held up her hand up to Dave, 'But I will leave that up to you Dave, if you feel that we can trust him, then you have my blessing.'

Dave gave her a small silent nod and blinked as he realised that although it would be good to bring Thomas into the fold, it also troubled him that he was not one hundred percent sure if he could be completely trusted. He sighed and scrubbed his face with his hands, 'I think that's a problem for another time, but it is something that we are going to have to consider very carefully.' He turned his attention back to the room and stared expectantly at Sharon, 'Have you had time to examine the creature and find anything useful.'

'No, unfortunately not.' Sharon sighed sadly, shrugged, and then chuckled, 'The science and medical departments both couldn't wait to get their hands on it when it arrived. It was like all their Christmases came at once!' She tapped her bottom lip and gazed up at the ceiling thoughtfully, 'The only thing we know for sure is that they, whoever they are, had genetically engineered it - for what purpose we are not sure. My theory is they have engineered it specifically to hunt and track.'

The corners of Dave's eyes creased as a troubling thought came to him and he glanced around the room, 'If it is a hunter, then I would have to guess I was the target. It cannot be a coincidence that it was waiting in the Police Station.'

From their troubled expressions, he could see that they had the same thought. He winced as he rose out of his seat and trudged over to the window that overlooked the Command Centre. Jenny trotted over and peered up at her master with a look of concern.

'Penny for your thoughts, Guv.' Andy asked softly.

Dave wearily gestured to the image of the dead woman on the

monitor, 'It just occurred to me, what if she is not the only one who has one of those probe things implanted inside their heads?' He scratched his head thoughtfully and held his index finger up, 'What if everybody who has been replaced has one of those things inside them, waiting to be activated? How many people in the world are time bombs waiting to go off?'

John nodded glumly, 'We are tracking the ones we have identified as doppelgängers.' He held his hands up and let out a frustrated sigh, 'Unfortunately, they are just the tip of the iceberg, we don't know how many more could be out there.'

Rising from her seat, Sophia slowly walked over to where Dave was standing and stopped next to him. She straightened, placed her hands behind her back and stared intently at Wendy and Andy. 'I think it is best if we assign quarters to you.' She said in a firm voice that also held a touch of sadness as she gestured to the troubled looking man next to her, 'If that creature had been sent to kill you, then it is safe to assume that they are onto us.' She cocked her head expectantly at John, 'I want you to spread the word, not only to the personnel based here but also to our operatives in our Excalibur facility in Birmingham. Tell them this order comes directly from me, I want everybody to use the base they are stationed in not just to work in, but to live in too, including their families. All staff are to get anything they need from their homes at the first opportunity.'

As Andy, Sharon and Wendy gave silent nods of acknowledgement, Dave could see the fear that was etched across each of their faces.

John straightened and bobbed his in confirmation, 'I will issue the order immediately, ma'am, to give time for people to get things in order. I will also get the word out to our sister facilities across the globe.' he paused as he turned to Wendy and Sharon expectantly, 'I would still like to investigate the old hospital in Langley Park, like we discussed the other day.' He gestured to the sombre looking Wendy, 'Wendy, I would like you to accompany me in place of the Detective Inspector.' Without waiting for a response, he spun swiftly round to the surprised looking Sharon, 'Sharon, I think it's best you come too. You have read Professor Tulley's papers and can recognise what to search for.'

Wendy stared hopefully at Dave, who gave a nod of approval. Sharon let out a reluctant sigh and gave John a small unhappy nod.

John rose out of his seat, marched across to Dave and placed a hand on his shoulder, 'I am going to assign Lieutenant Goynes to you. She will take you home to collect some things.' He smiled faintly and gave a firm shake of his head as Dave tried to open his mouth to object, 'No buts, mate, you are still recovering, and I would be happier if she went with you.'

'Humph! Fine!' Dave grunted unhappily and gave a reluctant nod of agreement.

As she turned and stared sadly down at the Command Centre, Sharon shivered, and her brow creased into a troubled frown.

'Gets cold up here sometimes, doesn't it, Ma'am?' Dave muttered.

Sophia's shoulders sagged, inhaled a long, deep breath, and then exhaled, 'It does indeed, my friend.' She wrapped her arms around herself and shuddered, 'It does indeed.'

30

Thirty minutes later, sitting in his seat in the maglev carriage, Dave watched in thoughtful silence as Kendra positioned herself in the seat next to him and fastened her seatbelt. He cast her a sidelong glance and gave her an embarrassed smile, 'Thank you for doing this, Lieutenant Goynes. I am sorry to put you to all this bother.'

Kendra gave a small shake of her head and waved her hand dismissively, 'It is no bother at all, Inspector.' Her mouth curved into a smile, and she offered him her hand, 'And please call me Kendra. Commander Payne just gave the order from the prime minister that all personnel are to use the base as a temporary home, so that gives me the chance to nip out and get some stuff too. Two birds with one stone, really.'

Dave smiled warmly as he shook Kendra's hand, 'Thank you, Kendra. Please call me Dave.' He lowered his voice and then leaned in closer to her, 'To save you time, you can just assign me a vehicle so I can go home myself.'

Kendra shook her head and let out a loud barking laugh, 'Sorry Dave, no can do.' The corners of her mouth quirked up into a mischievous grin and Dave shifted uncomfortably in his seat as he felt her hand tighten around his, 'The commander has ordered me to quote *Take him home and if he becomes a pain in the arse, you are to shoot him.*'

Not the answer he was expecting, a gobsmacked Dave stared at Kendra in astonishment, 'You are not serious!'

There was a steely glint in Kendra's eye as she leaned closer to him and whispered, 'Try me.' Dave felt his shoulders tense but relaxed as he saw the woman's lopsided grin and sly wink. Then, as if she had suddenly thought of something else, she cast a sly glance over her shoulder and turned back to him. Detecting a change in her body language, he watched curiously as she opened her jacket to reveal a holstered weapon. She pursed her lips and gave him a curious side eye, 'I am assuming you have had firearm training and have had experience in using one.'

His eyebrows perking up in surprise, Dave gave a small nod of confirmation, 'Yes, although it has been a while since I have had to carry a weapon.'

Kendra bobbed her head and then lowered her voice, 'That's good.' She reached down to her bag and pulled out another weapon and a holster, and handed them both to the frowning man, 'Take this, you may not need it but it's better to be prepared.'

After taking the weapon from Kendra, Dave nodded appreciatively as he examined it - he immediately recognised it was a P250 Pistol, a weapon he was quite familiar with. He clenched his teeth together as she helped him out of his jacket and gently slipped his left arm through a strap loop. She then took hold of one of the straps, crossed it along his back, followed by a small click as it locked into place in front of his chest. With the holster in place, he carefully took the pistol and slotted it into its pocket.

On arrival at the maglev station, the pair were escorted up to the vehicle that had been requestioned for them. After checking to make sure everything was in order, Kendra drove the vehicle, a black Land Rover Defender, out of the depot and the couple were soon on their way through the busy Durham streets.

A short time later Kendra drove the Defender onto a driveway of a suburban house and brought it to a stop. Still feeling the effects from his encounter with the creature, Dave climbed gingerly out of the massive vehicle and moved carefully up the driveway, with Kendra following close behind him. But just as he was about to stick the key into the lock of his front door, he froze as he detected movement through the living room window.

Dave glanced over his shoulder at Kendra and pointed his finger at the living room window. Giving him a wordless nod, Kendra motioned for him to step aside as she pulled her weapon out of her holster. Not needing to be told twice, he gave a small nod of acknowledgement and stepped one side, pulling the weapon out of his holster too. Kendra crept forward and placed her hand on the key and glanced at him. His heart rate increasing, he swallowed and watched her hold up her clenched fist and extended each finger as she counted down from three to one. He then watched as she took several slow controlling breaths, before slowly turning the key and pushing the front door open. With her gun drawn in front of her, Kendra stepped through the doorway into the narrow hallway, with Dave following silently behind.

Noticing the living room door was ajar, Dave stepped in front of Kendra and poked his around the corner. He spotted a woman was standing in front of the fireplace with her back to the doorway. She appeared to be wearing something like a plain brown-yellow leather jumpsuit. After quickly scanning the room for any other hostiles and ascertaining the intruder appeared to be alone, Dave nodded to Kendra and he stepped to one side as she stepped through the doorway and pointed her weapon at the woman.

'Hold it right there! Hands up now!' Kendra shouted in a loud firm voice. 'Turn around now!'

The startled woman stiffened, held up her hands and slowly turned to face them. Dave let out a gasp of shock as he immediately recognised the woman in front of them, 'Mary!'

Kendra glanced briefly at Dave in wide-eyed surprise, but continued to stare suspiciously at the woman in front of them, 'You recognise this woman?'

Dave nodded in astonishment and stammered back a reply, 'I ... I ... it's Mary Jenkins! Sergeant Jenkins' wife.'

Dave's eyes narrowed as he examined the woman in front of him. Several black bruises covered her cheeks and jaw, and her right eye was closed and swollen. Even though her normally long brown hair appeared to have been shaved off there was no mistake; the scared woman in front of them was Mary Jenkins.

Dave ran up to her as the exhausted woman collapsed into his arms, shaking, and sobbing, 'D ... D ... Dave, tha ... tha ... thank God it's you.'

Still not believing what he was seeing, Dave stared incredulously at the woman in his arms, 'Mary, we thought they had kidnapped you!'

Mary sniffed and nodded frantically, 'Th ... th ... they did! A woman who looked like me attacked me and then they took me somewhere, tortured me and then put me in a cell ...' She cut off as she suddenly pulled away from him, her silver eyes widening with terror, 'Andy and Alice, are they okay?'

'They are fine Mary.' Dave whispered soothingly and smiled warmly as he acknowledged her with a small nod. He cocked his head in confusion and then frowned at her, 'But how did you escape?'

'He helped me.' Mary's voice cracked and she raised a trembling hand and then pointed to something in front of her.

Startled, Dave spun sharply round as he heard footsteps coming from behind him. Kendra let out a slow whistle, and Dave swallowed as he felt his throat tighten on recognising the figure in front of him. Feeling his stomach knot together, his eyes narrowed as he studied newcomer and it was then he quickly realised that although he looked identical, there were still some subtle differences. He could see his counterpart appeared more leaner, had a scar on the left side of his face and he was wearing a black military style jacket.

His mind reeling, Dave could only stand and watch as Kendra

stepped forward with her gun raised at the grinning man and barked at him with a firm voice, 'Hands on your head and lie on the floor face down!'

Appearing to ignore the weapon pointed at him, Barnes raised his hand and bit into an apple he was holding as he continued to walk into the living room, eventually coming to a stop in front of Dave. The corners of his mouth turned up as he looked at Dave with disdain.

Kendra took one more step forward and issued her firm command again, 'I said place your hands on your head and lie face down on the floor!' There was a loud click as she disengaged the safety button on her weapon, 'I won't ask again.'

His top lip curling into a disdainful sneer, Barnes waved his hand dismissively at Kendra, 'Please put that away before you hurt yourself.'

Before Kendra could take a step forward and open her mouth to make a retort, Dave stepped in front of her and placed a reassuring hand on her arm. She looked at him questioningly as he gave her a firm nod and whispered softly to her, 'Kendra, I think it is best you stand guard in the hallway.' He cocked his head to Barnes, 'I think we should be okay, but keep your gun trained on him just in case.'

Kendra gave a small nod of acknowledgement and shot Barnes the evil eye as she moved slowly past him. However, as she brushed by him. Dave saw her freeze as he heard Barnes snarl condescendingly at her, 'That's a good bitch.' His tone was almost taunting, 'Woof! Woof! Do as your master says.'

Dave held his breath as he watched Kendra bristle with anger. She started to spin round as if she to confront Barnes, but she appeared to stop herself. He guessed she must have realised that Barnes was deliberately baiting her. There was something in his eyes that told him he was looking for a reaction. Was he hoping she would fight him just to see what she was made of?

Kendra closed her eyes, took a deep breath, and continued to leave the living room. She stopped in the hallway, spun round, crossed her arms across her chest and leaned back against the wall, but kept her eyes locked on the arrogant man in front of her.

Barnes clicked his fingers at Dave and motioned for him to sit, 'Sit down we need to talk.' His eyes narrowed as Dave folded his arms across his chest and remained where he was. Barnes's nostrils flared ad he pointed to the chair and spoke again, only this time his tone was hard and dangerous. "I said sit down!"

Dave opened his mouth to object at being spoken to in such a way but stopped as he felt Mary's trembling hand gently touch his arm, 'Please Dave, do as he says.' He noticed her voice was thick with fear.

As he tapped the trembling woman's hand, Dave nodded slightly but continued to glare at Barnes as he reluctantly took a seat in front of him.

Barnes's mouth curled up into a contemptuous smile and took a seat next to Dave, 'That's good. Now, like I said, we need to talk, and you need to listen.' He paused and gave Dave a dangerous smile, 'Believe me when I tell you this, you are definitely not going to like what I have to tell you.'

31

With his hands resting on top of the vehicle, John lowered his head, and let out a long breath of frustration. Stepping back away from the car, he glanced at his watch, looked heavenward and gave a slight shake of his head. He then turned and glared impatiently at Sharon who was standing in front of the car, forehead creased in deep concentration and was nibbling on her bottom lip as she scrutinised a large piece of paper that was laid out on the Land Rover's bonnet.

Wendy gave him a disapproving look as she muttered at him, 'You need to give her time. We have only just arrived.'

Trying to keep his annoyance in check, John clenched his teeth together and grumbled, 'She's been standing there for five minutes.' He shook his head and threw his hands in the air in frustration, 'How long does it take to read a schematic?'

Sharon raised her head up from the paper she was scrutinising and stared sternly at John from over the top of her glasses, 'You know *she* can hear you!' she snapped in an irritable tone.

John raised his hands apologetically, 'Sorry, but you have been looking at that paper for the last five minutes.' he moaned, pointing to his wristwatch, 'Come on! How long does it take to look for an old entrance?'

Sharon rolled her eyes, shook her head in disgust and turned away from him. She then muttered something under her breath, but John was too far away to make out what it was, although he imagined it was probably something uncomplimentary. He gave Wendy a sidelong look and pointed to his watch again, who, as if to placate him, responded with a small smile and lifted her shoulders in a half shrug.

After the meeting earlier that afternoon, they had decided the best course of action was to drive to Langley Par, where they would park the car far enough away from the dilapidated isolation hospital so not to attract any unwanted attention. When they got out of the car and Sharon started to read the schematic, John had been filled with a sense of hope that they would be in and out in a matter of minutes. Unfortunately, any hopes he had slowly evaporated as he watched the young woman's thin face change to one of frustration while she studied the map.

'Eureka!' Sharon shouted excitedly, her face beaming as she held up the map in front of her, 'I found it.'

'About damn time!' John grumbled under his breath to Wendy, who shot him an angry hairy eyeball and nudged him in the ribs.

Sharon gave no sign she had heard John's comment as she lifted her head up curiously and turned her body in a tight circle, frowning as she studied the surrounding area, 'According to the schematic, there should be an access point close to here.' John placed his hand over his mouth to stifle a laugh as he was suddenly reminded of an alert meerkat on the lookout for an oncoming predator.

Sharon tapped on her chin thoughtfully as she mumbled to herself, 'It might be best if we take something to pry open the cover, as it could have rusted over.'

Quickly composing himself, John gave a small nod of acknowledgement, walked to the back of the Land Rover, and opened the boot, reached in, and then pulled out a large crowbar. He held it up to show Sharon and grinned at her, 'This should do.'

Sharon gave an absent-minded nod as she stepped away from the car with the schematic in front of her. John and Wendy followed behind as she dived into the thick undergrowth on the side of the road.

A short time later John watched curiously as Sharon came to a sudden stop, glanced at the paper in her hand and stared at the ground in front of her, and then pointed to the metal access hole cover on the ground. 'Well, according to the map, this is the access point.' She muttered hesitantly as she knelt and examined the access hole cover. Her eyebrows knitting together, she looked up at John in confusion, 'But I don't understand, the cover looks new.'

John scanned the undergrowth worriedly and then glanced at Wendy, who nodded and pulled out her pistol from her holster. He then edged closer to Sharon and knelt alongside her to inspect the cover. His eyes narrowed with suspicion as he ran his hand around the edge of metal cover. He could see it did look brand new and the ground around it looked as it had been recently disturbed. 'I agree, it looks new.' He murmured thoughtfully, 'Looks like somebody replaced this cover recently.'

Sharon cocked her head at John with a hopeful expression, 'The local council could have replaced it.' She raised her hand and gestured to the surrounding undergrowth, 'We know they have been tidying up the area recently.'

His lips pressed together, John rubbed the back of his neck and gave a reluctant nod. 'Possibly.' He mumbled as he leaned forward with the crowbar and placed it at the edge of the access hole cover. He grunted as he pushed down on the crowbar and was surprised to discover that he was able to lift the cover with very little effort. After dropping the crowbar, he carefully rolled the access hole cover to one side.

As he leaned forward, he stared warily down into the darkness below him. Wendy reached into her bag and pulled out a pale-yellow plastic stick and handed it to John, who then took the stick from her hand and gave it a firm snap. With the small stick now glowing a fluorescent yellow, he dropped it down the hole in front of him and watched it descend quickly into the darkness.

His brow furrowed in deep concentration, he nodded thoughtfully to himself and pointed down the dark shaft, 'It is quite a drop, but there is a ladder running down the side of the shaft, so we should be okay if we are careful.' He murmured, secretly hoping he sounded more confident than he actually felt.

Reaching into the same bag she had gotten the glow stick, Wendy pulled out two small radios and handed one to John. They both switched their radios on and after a brief test, he clipped the radio to his belt and glanced up to Wendy, grinned, and then motioned for her to enter the tunnel, 'Ladies first?'?'

Wendy waved her hand and gave a small but firm shake of her head, 'Nope!' She gestured to the dark hole and laughed weakly, 'I have seen this movie; this is the one where the woman dies first.'

John chuckled and rolled his eyes as he positioned himself down in front of the hole, he then swung his legs over the edge, and carefully placed his feet on the ladder. He took a deep breath and then slowly began to lower himself down.

With a measured pace, John descended into the hole, being careful not to slip on the damp rungs. As soon as he felt his right foot touch solid ground, he let out a huge sigh of relief, stepped hesitantly away from the ladder and squinted as he stared into the darkness. He reached into his pocket and pulled out a torch and turned it on. With the torch held out in front of him, he spun in a slow circle and scanned the surrounding area. His eyes widened in surprise as he realised that he was standing in the middle of a narrow metal tunnel. John craned his neck as he peered back up the shaft he had just descended, unclipped the radio from his belt and held down the button on the side of the radio.

'I have reached the bottom. I am standing in a narrow tunnel, over.' John's voice was hushed as he spoke into the radio and released the button. Despite himself, he jumped as he heard Wendy's voice coming out of the radio's speaker.

'*Roger that. We will be down shortly. Over.*'

A short time later, John was standing alongside the two women staring into the eerie darkness. He took a step closer to the tunnel wall and held up his light to inspect it. From the amount moss that covered it he got a sense that the tunnel was decades old. Glancing over his shoulder to Sharon, he stared at her curiously, 'What are we standing in?' He asked as he stepped back and squinted into the darkness.

Her brow wrinkled in thoughtful concentration Sharon placed her left hand on the side of the tunnel and rubbed her chin pensively as she stared into the darkness, 'They must have used this tunnel to funnel water from the nearby river to help power the experiment.' She pointed to the shaft from where they had just come from, 'My guess is, after they assumed the experiment failed, they must have sealed up the inlet to stop the water coming in. They would have used this shaft to access it once they had it sealed to make sure it was watertight.'

With their torches held out in front of them, they began to walk into the darkness, but came stop when they tunnel eventually branched into two directions. John scratched his head as he shone his torch down both tunnels and looked at Sharon quizzically, 'Which way do we go?' He was not sure why, but he could not stop himself from speaking in a hushed voice.

Sharon's forehead creased as she reached into her bag and pulled out the map. John edged closer and shone his torch over it. She took a step forward with the map in front of her and spun slowly from side to side. Sharon scratched her head as she looked in both directions of the tunnel, but then gave a small defeatist shrug and looked back John with an arched eyebrow, 'We could flip a coin?'

John snorted back a laugh and shook his head. He rubbed his chin as he studied the tunnel and nodded slightly, 'I'll take this tunnel.' He said confidently, pointing to the tunnel to his right, 'You both take that one. We meet back here in ten minutes.'

John could tell from Wendy's body language that she didn't agree with him, but he guessed she must have decided to keep any reservations she had to herself as he watched her give him a nod in silent agreement. Sharon gave him a concerned look of confusion and opened her mouth to object, but before she could say anything he touched her shoulder and, without saying a word, placed his finger on her lips and shook his head. She gave him a frosty look and reluctantly bobbed of her head, and then, to his astonishment, she stood on her tiptoes, leaned forward, and planted a kiss on his cheek, whispering, 'Be careful.'

John gave Sharon a lopsided grin as he cocked his head and winked at her. After watching the two women disappear into the darkness, he then spun round, and stared uneasily into the darkness as he crept carefully down the opposite tunnel. After a while he shivered to himself and his breathing quickened, as the darkness began to encroach on him, playing tricks with his mind.

Becoming increasingly unsettled by the darkness surrounding him, John slapped his forehead and let out snort of disgust, 'Good idea, John.' he grumbled to himself, 'Oh yes! I will go down the creepy dark tunnel myself just so I can act like John Wayne in front of Sharon.' He shook his head and stared up at the tunnel's ceiling in a moment of self-loathing, 'I can just hear her now – *"You're an arsehole John! Why didn't we stay together John?".*'

His unease building, John came to a stop so that he could consider his options. He glanced over his shoulder from the direction from where he had come and scratched his chin thoughtfully. He wondered whether he should continue on or suck up whatever pride he had left, turn back and catch up with the girls.

Unfortunately, before he could turn around, he was suddenly blinded by a bright light, followed by a loud synthetic sounding voice.

'Halt! Stop where you are!'

John raised his hand in front of his eyes to shield them from the bright light that was being shone at him. He could just make out the shapes of two people standing in front of him. After spots in his vision had slowly disappeared, he found he was able to see the strangers more clearly.

The two strangers appeared to be militaristic in nature. He noticed their uniforms seemed to be a strange shiny black and gold armour. From the style, it reminded him of something he had seen in history books, very similar to the uniforms that were once worn by Roman centurions. He couldn't tell what gender they were because their faces were hidden by their helmets. John's eyes narrowed warily as he noticed that they were both

Double Jeopardy

holding strange weapons, something like a sniper's rifle, but the design was unlike anything he had seen before.

'Why are you down here?' The first soldier commanded. John noticed its voice sounded electronic, probably distorted by the helmet it was wearing.

His mind racing, desperate to get away from the two intimidating looking soldiers, John grinned stupidly as he staggered forward and waved at them, 'Hello guys! How's it going?' He slurred his speech so that he could pretend to act drunk, 'Have you seen Billy?" he pretended to hiccup, 'We were coming back from the pub,' he hiccupped again, 'I needed a piss, so I went into the woods. I must have gotten lost as I ended up here!' He saw the two soldiers glanced briefly at each other and guessed they were trying to decide what to do with him. Hoping to keep them off balance he lunged forward and continued to speak in a slurred voice, 'Have you seen Billy? Is he here?' Just for good measure he gave a loud juicy fart and then waved his hand in front of his face. 'Phew, what've you guys been eating.'

John quickly realised that things his plan was starting to fall apart as he watched the soldier closest to him raise its hand and tap something on the side its helmet. He blinked as the soldier's helmet emitted a wide beam of light over him. From the way the strangely dressed soldier was cocking its head curiously, John guessed it must be have been reading some sort of head-up display.

'Our sensors tell me your alcohol level is zero. So, I will ask you again ...' It said menacingly, raising his weapon and pointing it at John, 'Why are you down here?'

Oh ... shit! John swallowed, raised his hands apologetically, grinned, and gave a small shrug, 'Whoops!' Believing they were probably going to kill him anyway, his mouth curved into a smile as an insane idea suddenly popped into his head. If he was going to die, then he might as well do it with some style.

Straightening himself to his full height, John calmly placed his left hand on his hip, lifted his chin and stared directly at the two soldiers. He then waved his right hand in front of them as he muttered in a low but firm tone, 'You'll drop your weapons, walk away and forget you've ever seen me.'

The two soldiers stepped back from John and exchanged looks. Then, as if there were thinking as one, they briefly glanced at one another, nodded, raised both of their weapons, and then pointed them directly John. Sensing he was about to die; John closed his eyes and braced himself for the impact of whatever was about to be discharged from their weapons.

John opened his eyes as he heard a noise coming from behind the two soldiers. To his amazement, Wendy and Sharon appeared out of the darkness and then charged into the two soldiers, taking them by surprise. The two women smashed into the back of soldier closest to them. Sharon, holding a crowbar in her hands, smashed it against the back of the soldier's neck. It was closely followed by Wendy, who bellowed defiantly as she slammed herself into the soldier's back, sending it crashing against the wall, its weapon falling to the ground. Then, wrapping her hands around the dazed soldier's head, Wendy let out a primal roar. It was as if she was releasing all the rage and frustration from the past two days inside her as she gave one almighty twist and snapped the soldier's neck. The armoured figure collapsed onto the floor, dead.

The remaining soldier spun away from John and turned to the two women and raised its weapon at them. With its attention distracted, John rolled on the ground, grabbed the fallen weapon, pointed it at the soldier and fired the weapon point blank at it.

The tunnel was lit up with a bright light as the weapon emitted a beam of energy, striking the soldier in the centre of his chest. The soldier staggered backwards and collapsed onto the ground, dead, a smoking hole in its chest.

'Whoa!' John muttered, his eyes widening in surprise at the weapon in his hands.

Out of breath, Wendy leaned forward with her hands on her knees and stared up at John incredulously, 'Seriously!' She panted and shook her head in disgust, 'You actually thought the Jedi mind trick from *Star Wars* would work? What were you thinking?'

Swallowing a lungful of air, John raised his hands up and shrugged, 'Hey, give me a break will you. I thought I was going to die!'

Wiping the sweat of his brow, he gave her a lopsided grin, 'I have always wanted to try that, so I determined if I was going to die, why not go out in style.'

Wendy shook her head and stared up at the ceiling in dismay, muttering to herself, 'Men!'

Turning to Sharon, John could see she was kneeling beside the dead soldier as if examining its body. She raised her head at him, gave a sad shake of her head and straightened up. Sharon then gave him a withering look. He shrugged his shoulders sheepishly. However, he felt his eyes grow wide in surprise as she stepped up to him, grabbed his face in her hands, pulled him close to her, and kissed him on his lips.

'That's for scaring me.' She whispered, and then without warning slapped him across the face.

Not the reaction he was expecting, John staggered back in shock, placed his hand against his cheek, and exclaimed, 'What was that for?'

Her eyes burning with anger, Sharon jabbed her fingers into his chest as she snapped at him, 'That's for acting like an idiot!'

Basking in the infuriated woman's attention, John broadened his mouth into a stupid grin as he waggled his eyebrows at her, 'Oh behave!' He said, in almost perfect *Austin Powers* voice, 'Didn't you know Danger is my middle name?'

John could tell Sharon was not impressed as he watched her roll her eyes and shake her head in disgust. She then gave a huff and stormed away from him, muttering to herself. But before he could follow her to apologise, John froze as he noticed Wendy was inspecting the soldiers curiously. He edged closer to her and pointed at them, 'Have you ever seen armour like this before?'

Wendy eyebrows knitted together as she inspected the soldier closest to her and gave a small shake of her head, 'No, but it looks familiar though.'

On hearing footsteps coming from behind him, John glanced over his shoulder and saw Sharon was hurrying back toward them. He guessed she must have heard the concerned tone in Wendy's voice. As he stepped to onside, he noticed that her eyes were blazing with curiosity as she knelt to inspect the soldier's armour. She chewed on her bottom lip and her eyebrows drew together as her hands examined every part of the armour. A minute or so later, she leaned back and tilted her head up to John.

'Notice the markings on this armour?' Sharon muttered as she pointed at the patterns on the breastplate, 'The design is very reminiscent of the ancient Roman Empire and the insignia on his breastplate is much like what they found on a Roman centurion.' Realisation then dawned across her face as she straightened up and stared in John's eyes, her face beaming in excitement, 'This confirms our theory that the doppelgängers are from a world where the Roman Empire never collapsed.'

'Well, I can safely say that their world is more advanced than ours.' John murmured, gesturing to the weapon in his hands, 'I am guessing this is a laser rifle of some type. I will hold on to it for now, I am sure our tech people will have a field day when they get their hands on it.'

Wendy glanced over her shoulder and motioned in the direction from where the two women had come from, 'We passed an open hatchway on our way here, a few meters down from here.' She looked expectantly at the John, 'I suggest that we take a quick look and get the hell out of here.'

John gave a small nod of agreement as he followed the two women down the tunnel, and stopped when they came upon an open hatchway. Wendy grunted as she gently pushed the hatch open and poked her head in. She looked over her shoulder to John and Sharon and signalled for them to follow.

After she had climbed through the rusted hatchway, Sharon soon found herself standing on a high platform that overlooked an enormous cavern. She hunkered down and peeked over the railing on the edge of the platform.

Turning her head, Sharon let out a small gasp and stared through awestruck eyes at the enormous subterranean area around her. She stared in wonder at the crystal formations that were covering the entire walls and ceiling of the cavern. She quickly realised that the crystals in the walls were giving off an eerie glow and flinched back as bursts of energy shot out of the crystals toward the bottom of the cavern. Sharon turned to look at John and from the expression on his face she could tell he was as equally entranced. She tugged at his arm, and he turned curiously to her as she raised her hand and pointed at the floor below. John twisted his head to where Sharon was pointing and let out an exclamation of surprise.

Standing in the centre of the cavern floor was a window of energy that shimmered and glowed like a pool of water. Streaks of energy crackled out from the surrounding crystals, striking the device. With each strike of energy the shimmering window seemed glow even brighter. Sharon stared in awe as she spotted images forming in the energy window and lifted her hands to her mouth in shock as she noticed that each time a burst of energy from the surrounding crystals struck the window, the images inside changed.

'Unbelievable!' She whispered and let out a small giggle of delight. She looked at John and pulled at his arm in excitement, 'I understood this was just a theory.'

'What are we looking at?' John asked, frowning in confusion at the scene before him.

Sharon pulled herself away from the edge and hunkered down on the walkway. Her two puzzled colleagues knelt closer to her as she whispered to them, 'You remember our discussion about the multiverse theory and how the multiverse is comprised of overlapping realities?' She smiled as she watched the pair exchanged puzzled looks and then bob their heads. Struggling to contain her excitement, she raised her head and pointed to the window of energy on the ground below them and spoke in a passionate-but-hushed voice, 'There is a theory that each reality intersects each other by a nexus, a cross-dimensional gateway which provides a pathway to all possible realities.'

She staggered back as the crystals in the cavern brightened and pulses of energy shot out, shaking the platform she was standing on.

Completely enraptured by what was enfolding before her eyes, Sharon stared down at the chamber and shook her head in wonder, 'I can see why Dr Selyab placed his experiment here.' She couldn't hide the awe in her voice as she continued to speak in a hushed voice, 'I guess he already knew there was a nexus here. I see now he never intended to create matter transportation. He wanted to open a doorway to another reality. That was his intention all along. But I guess he hadn't counted on the energy pulse from another reality. From what I can tell, it appears he created a tear in the fabric of reality itself.'

John edged closer and lifted himself up slightly to get a better view. He cocked his head at Sharon in bewilderment, 'So that is how the doppelgängers can cross over?' He whispered, pointing to the window of energy below, 'They enter that?'

Sharon squinted at the scene below her and gave a small shake of her head, 'No, I assume it doesn't work like that.' She closed her eyes as she tried to process what she was witnessing. No, surely it cannot be that simple. She felt herself stiffen as she was hit by a moment of clarity. She opened her eyes, snapped her fingers, and then babbled excitedly, 'Yes, in principle they would have to have access to the nexus in their own reality to travel.' She paused and then tilted her head as she rubbed the back of her thoughtfully, 'In theory though, if you were to enter a nexus doorway unprotected, all the tidal forces from the opposing realities would tear you apart.'

Sharon could tell from Wendy's puzzled expression she was having difficulty understanding what was being told to her. Wendy pursed her lips together as she stared at the display going on below her, 'Then how can they do it?'.

Sharon was silent for a minute as she studied the scene below. Yes, how would they do it? They would need something to … Hit by sudden burst of inspiration, she bolted straight up and clicked her fingers, 'That's it!' She exclaimed triumphantly.

'What?' John and Wendy both asked in unison.

Pulling herself away from the edge of the platform, Sharon plonked herself on her backside, held her hands up and looked at her two baffled friends patiently, 'Okay, remember the old rotary phones we had years ago? What did you have to do to make a telephone call?' she asked carefully, 'More specifically what did your telephone have to connect to, to make a call?'

John looked blankly at Sharon then he cocked his head and answered hesitantly, 'It needed to connect to an exchange?'

'Exactly!' Sharon replied, snapping her fingers at him, 'Remember the strange device we found on the doppelgänger and on the creature's body.' She smiled as he gave her a small nod and continued, 'I expect they use it to act as a navigation aid, to travel through the nexus. They must input the coordinates of their destination into the device, and it then manipulates the energy of the nexus.' She turned, stared down at the cavern floor and shook her head in wonder, 'I think that answers our question to how they are using mirrors to travel and to monitor us.'

'You mean that,' John asked carefully, pointing to the window of energy below, 'is something like a telephone exchange, because it diverts the signal to any mirror they want.'

Sharon stared at the scene below thoughtfully and shrugged, 'I am sure it is more complicated than that.' She tapped her chin and gave a small nod, 'But the principle is the same.'

Without warning, the portal crackled and rippled as the chamber was lit up with a surge of energy. She watched in morbid fascination as the portal stabilised. Her anxiety increased as she watched a group of soldiers emerge from the shimmering device. As they exited the portal, each group stepped away to allow more of their comrades into the chamber.

Sharon felt his blood run cold as she realised the soldiers in the chamber below were identical to the two soldiers they had encountered in the tunnel just moments earlier. She turned back to John to warn him, but on seeing the shocked expression on his face, she could tell that he had recognised the soldiers too.

'I don't know about you ladies, but I have seen enough.' John's voice had an edge as he spoke in a low urgent tone. He smiled grimly at Sharon, 'To quote your favourite TV show, I think it is time we got the frak out of here.'

Without saying a word, Sharon followed her grave-faced colleagues through the open hatch and hurried back the way they came. Eventually arriving back at the shaft that had led them down from the surface, Sharon reached down to pick up the bag she had left beside the bottom of the ladder.

Sharon lifted her phone out of bag and glanced down at it. She cocked her head as she studied the phone in her hand. She tutted as she realised that she had no internet connection. She froze and stared at the phone in her hand. No ... internet ... Oh, crap! 'Shit! Shit! Shit!' she hissed and fumbled at her phone as she tried desperately to switch it off.

With heavy concern etched across his face, John placed his hand on Sharon's shoulder, 'Sharon, what's wrong?'

'Turn your phones off ... *now*!' She snapped, pointing at the phones in their pockets. John and Wendy stared at her with confused expressions.

Becoming increasingly agitated, Sharon's eyes darted between John and Wendy and waved her hand hurriedly, 'No time to explain, but we are in serious danger.' Her breathing became more heavier as she frantically waved her hands at them, 'Turn them off now. We need to get back to base as soon as possible and disconnect the server and get everybody to turn off their mobiles. Do it now! I will explain when we are on the way.'

John and Wendy stared at Sharon with bewildered expressions but turned off their phones as requested before heading straight back up the access shaft. As she raced up the ladder to the surface, Sharon panted for breath as she neared the top. She cast an eye over his shoulder and saw she was being closely followed by Wendy and then John.

After they had all climbed out of the shaft and were heading toward their parked car, Sharon bit her bottom lip as she cast a worried eye to the horizon. She hoped they would be able to make it back to the base before it was too late.

Several minutes later, Oracle watched a black Land Rover Defender speed past the derelict isolation hospital. She bowed her head and waved at the speeding vehicle as she watched it speed off into the distance.

'Don't worry, I will deal with you soon.' Oracle chuckled,

Double Jeopardy

wheeling away from the window, 'But I have another more pressing matter to deal with first.'

As the synthetic woman stepped in front of the large narrow mirror on the wall, she closed her eyes, and the surface of mirror rippled. She then stepped forward into the shimmering pool and a second later emerged into another room to the sound of raised voices. A smile danced on her lips as she listened to a loud arrogant Texan voice laugh.

'I am not afraid of Cooper. She has no power here!'

32

United Nations Headquarters, New York City, United States Of America

Twenty minutes earlier....

Standing in front of a window, President Richard Cole, stretched out his arms and exhaled in satisfaction. He then moved slightly closer to the glass so that he could a better view of the New York citizens as they went about their daily business. Because his room was so high up in the upper level of the UN building, the figures below looked like insignificant specs to him. He felt like God. One command from him, that's all it would take. One command to decide whether those specs lived or died – it was that easy.

A knock came from the door on the other side of the room, breaking him out of his reverie. Unhappy at the interruption, Cole cast an eye over his shoulder and watched the door slowly open, revealing a tall, slim black man. The young man's name was Leo Murray, and he had worked faithfully as Cole's Chief of Staff for the past eight years.

Leo was holding a tablet tightly in his hands as he glanced quickly at it and then spoke in an apologetic tone, 'Sorry to disturb you, President Cole, but the British prime minister has arrived and is ready to see you.'

Double Jeopardy

The corner of Cole's mouth curled up in a slight smile and he nodded in acknowledgement, 'Thank you, Leo. Give me five minutes then send her in.'

Leo frowned at the tablet in his hands, nodded slightly as he backed out of the room, and closed the door behind him.

President Cole let out a long sigh as he stepped toward the mirror on the wall and gazed at his reflection. He straightened his tie and cocked his head, winking slyly at himself. His forehead creased and his eyebrows drew together as he examined the reflection of the man in front of him and sighed sadly as he ran his hand through his thinning silver hair. At 72, Richard Cole appeared to be a typical example of a man of his age who had indulged in the finer things of life to excess. His white-lightly-tanned skin showed the signs of age, as well as showing the effects of spending too much time in the sun.

He was approaching the end of his second term as President of the United States. The press and his critics complained that he had won his second term by pure luck, due to his opposition presidential candidate having become ill without warning and dying shortly before the election. With the death of their candidate, it had left the opposition party in disarray, leaving the door wide open for Richard to win the election by a landslide.

His top lip curled up as he gazed into the mirror; if the press and the American people ever learned the truth about him, then he would more than likely be arrested and executed.

Richard was not an American, in fact he had not even born on this world. His original birth name had been Magnus Hassier and he had been born and raised in the Universal Roman Empire. He arrived on this Earth 56 years ago. Hassier had been surgically altered and had undergone rigorous voice training, so that he could replace this world's Richard Cole with ease.

With his advanced knowledge, Cole created a good life for himself, having set up a multimedia empire that spanned the globe, earning him billions in dollars. He, along with other agents embedded in other companies and governments across the globe, continued with their assignment started decades earlier; to manipulate events across the world.

With the resources available to him, it was not long before Cole was named Senator of Texas and from there, through his own cunning, manipulation, bribery, the occasional murder and with the help of his fellow agents, became President of the United States.

Hearing the door open, Cole moved back in front of the window and placed his hands behind his back. He smiled warmly as he watched Leo re-enter the room and noticed that he was keeping the door open with his foot as he spoke.

'Mr President, shall I send in the British Prime Minister?' he asked carefully.

Cole sighed melodramatically and waved his hand, 'Send her in.'

Leo nodded in acknowledgement and glanced over his shoulder into the room from which he had just come from. He smiled as he took a step back to allow the British prime minister into the room.

Cole watched as an attractive, slender black woman strode past Leo and bobbed her head in greeting at him. He grinned as he took a step forward and extended his hand to her.

'Sophia! Good to see you.' Cole boomed with a deep Texan drawl as Sophia took his hand and shook it. As he leaned forward to kiss her on the cheek, he saw her grimace as his lips brushed her cheek. He knew she despised him – all women did. But he didn't care really, as far as he was concerned, she was just a means to an end.

Cole looked over Sophia's shoulder at Leo, who was still standing in the doorway and shot him a stern look, 'That will be all, Leo.' He growled, waving his hand in a dismissive gesture, 'Please see that they do not disturb us.'

Leo nodded an acknowledgement, glanced quickly at the tablet in his hand, and frowned. 'Mr President.' he said in an almost apologetic tone, 'Victor Garnièr, the French prime minister will also join you shortly. Shall I let him in when he arrives?'

Taken aback, Cole blinked in surprise and gave a small nod, 'Yes, send him in as soon as he appears.'

Without saying another word, Leo stepped back and closed the door. Collins pulled her hand away from Cole, drew herself back from him and wiped her hand on her jacket in obvious displeasure. Revelling in her discomfort, Cole leered at her as he watched her edge away from him.

Cole cocked his head and held out his hand to her, 'Oh, come now, my dear.' He gushed and shot her a devilish grin, 'I am not that bad, really. You know I would have assumed you would have had that stick out of your arse by now.' He raised an eyebrow and gave her a smug look, 'How long has it been since you left the Empire behind? Three years? You should live a little, my dear, you will find the …' he paused and licked his lips perversely, 'pleasures of this world are so enjoyable.'

Collins shuddered and rolled her eyes as she shook her head in disgust. She paced around the room and then stopped in front of the window to gaze down at the city below. Her eyes were filled with contempt as she looked back over her shoulder at him.

Collins' lips drew back and snarled at him, 'You are a self-centred pig, Cole.' She gave him a contemptuous look and pointed to the outside world, 'This world has made you soft. the Empire sent you here for a purpose, not for you to have fun!'

Finding Collins's contemptuous attitude annoying, Cole folded his arms and gave her a cold stare. Sophia stared back just as coldly and sneered at him. After a few moments of tense silence, he broke the deadlock by giving her an insincere smile and a dismissive wave of his hand.

'Nothing wrong with trying to feather my nest.' He grinned malevolently as he stepped forward and waved his hands over the New York skyline, 'Come now, my dear. This world is ours to mould as we see fit. We should be the ones who should rule it, not the Empire!'

Collins's mouth jaw dropped and she shook her head in disbelief. She held up a finger and opened her mouth to speak but was interrupted by a knock on the door. He turned to see the door reopen and Leo re-enter the room and he was being followed closely by two other people.

'Sorry, Mr President, but you asked me to send in the French prime minister as soon as he arrived.' Leo said as he looked over his shoulder to the two people behind him. He quickly stepped aside to allow them entry before stepping back out and closing the door.

Of course, Cole recognised Victor Garnièr immediately. Like himself, he was agent of the Empire. He cast an eye over the dark blue he was wearing and chuckled – no matter the occasion his friend was always dressed impeccably. The other person he didn't know. She was a short, nervous-looking woman with curly auburn hair. But as he drew his eyes down her red dress and noticed how it clung to her curvaceous body, he idly wondered whether he would get chance to unwrap her later. He shook his head and cast that thought to one side. No business first and then if he had time later then he could indulge himself.

Cole laughed gleefully as he moved forward and wrapped his arms around Victor in an overzealous bear hug, 'Victor! Good to see you, my boy.' The Frenchman's eyes bulged as the air was forced out of his lungs and let out a small grunt of annoyance as he pushed himself away from the overzealous Cole.

The nervous woman stepped in front of Victor and gave a small nod of embarrassment as she pointed a finger at herself. 'My name is Claudette.' She muttered anxiously. Cole noticed that her English had a thick French accent to it, 'I am Mister Garnièr's interpreter. I shall be interpreting everything you say to him and what he says back to you.'

Cole blinked in surprise, nodded slightly, and gave Victor a bemused look.

Collins stepped forward, and smiled warmly as she took Victor's hand, 'Victor, c'est bon de vous revoir.' Cole noticed that her French was perfect. Her smile faded and she then placed a hand on his shoulder, 'J'espère que vous allez bien. Je crois que votre femme ne va pas bien et n'a pas pu faire ce voyage. Très désolé d'entendre ça.'

Victor smiled sadly and nodded gratefully, 'C'est bon de vous revoir Sophia. Oui, je suis désolé de dire qu'elle n'a pas pu le faire avec moi, mais elle sera ravie d'apprendre que vous lui posez la question.'

Taken aback, Claudette's eyes widened in surprise as she gave Sophia a questioning look.

Smiling sweetly at the younger woman, Collins motioned her to the door from where she had just come from, 'I don't expect we will not need you, my dear. As you see I speak perfect French and I am afraid what we have to discuss is not for your ears.'

Cole could tell Claudette was very unhappy at the change in circumstances. She turned to Victor and opened her mouth to protest, but before she could say anything he placed a hand on her arm and guided her to the door. 'Claudette, merci pour vos services, mais comme vous pouvvez le voir, ils ne sont pas necessaries. Vous pouvez nous quitter.' He muttered sweetly to her. She opened her mouth as if to question his decision, but then she paled as the expression on Victor's face hardened and he then snarled at her in English, 'You are to go … *Now!*'

The ashen-faced young woman swallowed, bobbed her head in understanding, and spun toward the door. Cole watched as she opened the door and dashed out of the room.

As soon as the door closed behind her, Victor turned, shook his head and chuckled, 'She's a sweet girl, but a major pain in the backside. She is like a shadow, following me everywhere I go.'

Cole laughed and turned away from the door. Victor edged closer to Collins, took hold of her hand, and gave it a gentle kiss as he gave her a devilish wink. 'So good to see you again, Octavia.' The corners of his mouth lifted in a simpering smirk, 'Our last meeting was so …' He paused and waggled his eyebrows at her, 'passionate. I still have bruises to show from it.'

Turning a deep shade of red, Collins shook her head and waved her hand at him, 'Stop it, Victor. If anybody were to overhear you, it would make things complicated and there is your wife to think about too.'

Victor gave her a knowing wink, shook his head and then pressed his hands against his chest, 'On this world I am a passionate Frenchman and people would not see anything of it. As for my wife …' He let out a long, sad melodramatic sigh and raised his shoulder in a half shrug, 'Accidents happen, and everybody knows she has a problem with alcohol, it is only a matter of time before …' He raised his hands up in the air, leaving his sentence unfinished.

Collins frowned and glared at Victor disapprovingly, 'Is your intelligence service not watching you closely? I'm sure they would be suspicious if anything were to happen to your wife?'

Victor guffawed and gave a dismissive wave of his hand, 'Hah! Yes, they were a problem when I first arrived, but one that was easily fixed. One of the first things I did when I replaced my doppelgänger was to place my own people into the DGSE.' There was a flicker of malice in his eyes and his mouth twisted into a malevolent grin, 'You could say I have them on a very tight leash.'

Cole let out a loud bark of laugher and then gave his fellow conspirator a small nod of approval, 'I have the CIA on such a tight leash, they cannot even piss without asking me for permission first.' He rolled his eyes and laughed weakly, 'They assume I don't know they have set up an underground movement, but because I have cut their budget, I imagine they cannot even afford a paperclip at the moment.' His voice shifted into a deeper Texan drawl as he stared smugly his fellow conspirators, 'They are like a tick on a dog, something that needs scratching but is nothing to worry about.' He gave Collins a sidelong look and the corners of his mouth turned up in a faint smile as he deliberately spoke in condescending tone, 'I hear you are still having a problem with MI6.' He smiled as the more he spoke, the more Sophia's face continued to darken in anger, 'I am sure I can help you deal with your problem, my dear.'

Quivering with indignation, Collins took an angry step forward and glowered at Cole. For a brief second, he could almost see the hatred burning inside her eyes. Then, much to his disappointment, he watched the anger in her eyes vanish. He quickly guessed that she must have realised that he was trying to goad her as he watched her take a deep breath and then give him a hard look of contempt.

'MI6 are proving to be quite troublesome.' She huffed and then shook her head in frustration, 'They are quite resourceful, and it appears they were the first to learn of the Empire's actions on this world decades ago. The only keyword we keep intercepting is the Castle. We know it refers to one of their bases that are scattered around the world, but we are trying to work where it is. The only thing I know for certain, they are led by my doppelgänger.' She let out a small contemptuous snort of laughter, 'She appears to have survived my assassination attempt.'

Cole leaned closer to Victor, nudged him with his elbow and muttered in a low voice, 'Never trust a woman to do a man's job, eh!'

Her eyes flashing with hatred, Collins turned on Cole, and her hands tightened into fists as she took a step towards him. As if sensing tension in the room, Victor held his hands up, moved in between his two argumentative allies and placed a hand on Sophia's arm. She gave him a questioning look but sighed reluctantly and nodded in understanding.

Victor raised an eyebrow and stared at Collins with a curious expression, 'I sensed some tension in the room as we walked in. Did I disturb something?'

Collins scowled and bobbed her head at Cole, 'Just this old fool trying to get us in trouble with High Command.'

His eyes growing wide in understanding, Cole turned to Cole and tutted as he waved his index finger at him, 'How many times must we have this discussion, my friend?' His tone was flat as he raised his hand to himself and then to his fellow subversives, 'We serve the Empire, and we must follow the plan they have laid out.'

'The Empire!' Cole scoffed and shook his head in displeasure. He tilted his head and waved his hand toward the window, 'The Empire is a world away, what can they do? I say the three of us should assemble the rest of the committee. We should vote on closing the nexus permanently and take this world for ourselves.' He lifted his hand and clenched it into a fist as he drew his lips back into a snarl, 'We already have it on its knees, I say the time to seize it is now!'

Aghast, Collins lifted her hands up above her head and turned away in disgust. Victor glared at Cole as he waggled his finger and spoke to him in a hushed voice, 'You should not even be considering things like that my friend.' He swallowed and leaned closer to Cole, 'I assume this is the reason you arranged this meeting today?'

Cole jerked back in surprise, and then his eyebrows drew together as he shook his head in denial, 'I ... I ... I did not arrange this meeting! I assumed you had arranged it.'

His forehead furrowing in confusion, Victor gave a small shake of his head, 'I did not arrange this meeting,' He turned to Collins questioningly, 'Did you?'

The corners of Collins's eyes creased in suspicion as she gave a silent shake of her head. She blanched as her hand shot up to her mouth in realisation and she spoke in a low horrified voice, 'General Cooper!'

Cole's nostrils flared as he clenched his fist and slammed it on the table in frustration, 'I am sick of that woman's interference. I say we vote now and close the nexus as soon as possible.' He stared up at the ceiling and scratched his chin thoughtfully, 'I am sure one of this world's nuclear warheads should be able to do it.'

Victor's eyes held a touch of panic and he looked at Cole as if he were insane, 'You are a fool, Magnus.' His voice was thick with fear as he snapped at him, 'It is dangerous to say things like that. You have spent too long on this world. General Cooper has spies on this world loyal to her. You do not know what Cooper could do to you if she finds out you are talking like this.' He waved hands in front of his chest as he shot him a dangerous look, 'I am saying this to you as a friend. Stop now before you go any further.'

Cole let out a small arrogant laugh, 'I am not afraid of Cooper!' He scoffed and gave a dismissive wave of his hand, 'She has no power here.'

'I am sorry to hear you say that Magnus.'

Startled by the unexpected intrusion, Cole jumped and whirled round to the source of the voice. Collins raised her hands to her mouth in shock and Victor's eyebrows climbed up his forehead as they recognised the woman in front of him. Puzzled by his colleague's reactions, Cole's eyebrows bunched together as he watched an unfamiliar woman dressed in an Imperial officer's uniform suddenly arrive through a shimmering dimensional portal.

Collins dashed forward, gave the standard Empire salute, and bowed her head, 'I … I … I'm sorry, General Cooper. Please ignore Magnus, he didn't mean what he was saying!'

His heart leaping up into throat, Cole swallowed and then took an awkward step back, 'Gen … gen …' He stammered as the words caught in his throat. He coughed and gave a forced a simpering smile to the woman in front of him, 'General Cooper, it is good to see you. If I had known …'

Cooper held up her hand to interrupt him, chuckling, 'Then I would have failed to see you make a fool of yourself.' She tilted her head as her expression darkened, 'Last time I checked, a superior officer still warranted a salute from a …' Her mouth twitched as she paused for effect, 'subordinate.'

His mouth turning dry, Cole swallowed and gave her a slow bow of his head. He straightened himself, clicked his heels together and then gave Cooper the standard Empire salute.

Cooper smiled thinly as she waved her hand nonchalantly at the quietly seething Cole, 'That's a good boy.' Her mouth curled into a sneer as she snapped her fingers at him, 'Now stay where you are …' There was a small flash of malice in her eyes as she lowered her head and smirked, 'Like an obedient dog.'

Not used to be spoken to in a such way, Cole's mouth dropped open in shock and shot the woman a blistering stare. Cooper chuckled as she turned her back to him. His cheeks burning with humiliation, Cole ground his teeth, as he locked his gaze onto the back of Cooper's head and wished they would burn a hole straight through into her brain.

Collins took a step closer to Cooper and gestured at Cole, 'General, please forgive Magnus.' she pleaded, 'He did not mean what he was saying. It was only talk. He has been on this world for so long, he just simply forgotten the nature of things.'

Victor gave a furious nod of agreement and took his place next to Collins. 'General, please do not judge us all from one man's actions.' He pressed his hands together and held them up in front of himself, 'We are still loyal to the Empire. He is just misguided, like Octavia has said.'

The smiling woman gave a small nod of understanding as she moved closer to Victor and Collins. They blinked in surprise as she placed her hands on their shoulders and spoke to them in a low and soothing tone, 'Shush! I quite understand. I only need to know if you comply.' She tilted her head questioningly at them, 'Do you still comply?'

Confused by what he was witnessing, Cole's eyebrows knitted together as he noticed a sudden change in his fellow conspirators' behaviour. As he watched, both of their bodies froze as their expressions dulled, and they then nodded in unison.

'Yes ... we ... comply.' They both intoned together in flat, emotionless voices.

As he watched Cooper turn her attention back to him, Cole felt his sphincter tighten under the intensity of her gaze. For the first time in his life Cole was overcome with a feeling that was alien to him – fear. Barely able to breath, he edged away from the wickedly smiling woman, but stopped as he felt his back hit the table. Trembling in fear, he felt helpless as he watched the menacing looking woman glide closer to him. 'Pur ... pur ... please, general,' he pleaded, 'I ... I'm sorry. Gen... General Cooper, I ... I promise ...'

Cooper smiled warmly at him and placed her finger on his quivering lips, 'Shush, everything is okay Magnus.' She leaned forward and kissed him on the lips, lowering her voice as she whispered in his ear, 'Can I tell you a secret? I am not General Cooper.'

His heart hammering in his chest, the terrified man shook his head in confusion, 'S ... s ... sorry, then who are you?'

The menacing looking woman grinned malevolently at him and took a step back. Terrified beyond belief, Cole thought he was going insane as he watched the woman's features morph into a blank, featureless face. 'My name is Oracle, and you now serve me.' Her voice was cold and emotionless as she placed her hand on his shoulder.

Cole's body spasmed as he felt a brief surge of electricity tingle pass through him. He opened his mouth to scream but realised he could not move. Slowly he then became aware of another voice in his head and his face softened as he felt his consciousness being pushed into the back of his mind. Feeling like a prisoner within in his own body, he suddenly felt powerless, unable to act, but was still totally aware of everything around him. Then from inside his cage in his mindscape, he heard someone in speak in a voice that was devoid of any emotion, but it also seemed oddly familiar.

'By your command.'

On realising that it was on his own voice - he let out a horrified

Double Jeopardy

scream.
>Then he screamed again ...
>again ...
>and again ...

33

Location: Secret command centre known as the Castle

The maglev carriage pulled up at the platform, and as soon as it came to a slow stop, it opened its gullwing doors and released its concerned looking passengers. Not waiting for the carriage to come to a complete stop, John leapt out onto the smooth platform and hurried down the short corridor, with the two women following close behind him.

The two security personnel behind the desk stood quickly to attention as they watched John bend down and hold his eye close to the retina scanner. As the scanner briefly lit up, scanning his eye, one of the soldiers glanced at the monitor in front of him and gave a small nod acknowledgement as John's name and photograph flashed up on the screen. He then watched carefully as the two women stepped forward and did the same.

'You are all cleared to enter.' The narrow-faced soldier muttered.

Without saying a word, the two women sprinted down the corridor and came to a stop in front of the elevator's doors. Wendy stood

Double Jeopardy

back and watched as Sharon stabbed her finger on the button to summon the elevator.

John stepped closer to the two soldiers and waved away their unspoken questions, 'No time to explain.' He said with a firm but urgent tone in his voice and pointed to the two mobile phones that were clipped to both soldiers' belts, 'This must be done immediately and without question: any mobile devices you have, along with any electronic tablets, must be switched off *now*! That goes for anything connected to the internet, you need to turn it off *immediately*. All will be explained later, but this *must* be done at once. There is a chance the enemy can use our devices against us.' He stared intensely at the hesitant soldiers and snapped his finger, 'What are you waiting for, an engraved invitation? Get it done now!'

Without waiting for a response, as the two puzzled men frantically switched off their mobile phones, John jumped over the security desk, picked up the receiver of the red telephone on top of the desk and pressed a button on the base unit. 'This is Commander John Payne, clearance Omega 6. Put me on the base intercom, immediately!' He ordered brusquely. He paused and listened as a loud tone came from a speaker in the ceiling above him, 'This is Commander John Payne.' In his mind's eyes he pictured people around the base stopping as they heard the urgent tone in his voice. 'With immediate effect, I am issuing a security code red! I repeat, I am issuing a security code red! From this point I am engaging the Storm Door Protocol. This is to be done without question. All base personnel are to switch off their mobile phones and disconnect any device you have connected to the internet immediately. I repeat *immediately!* This is a direct order. All section heads are to attend a briefing in one hour.'

After exchanging troubled glances, the two soldiers stared at John with confused expressions as he placed the receiver back on the telephone's base unit. He nodded in acknowledgement as the two men lifted up their phones to show him that they had done as instructed.

John handed over the radio he used earlier to one of the soldiers, 'Somebody will hand radios out to all base personnel.' He gestured to the device he just handed over, 'You can use mine for the time being.'

In no mood to answer any questions, John wheeled sharply round and barrelled down the corridor to join Wendy and Sharon in the waiting elevator. He pressed a button on the panel and tapped his hand on the wall impatiently as he watched the elevator doors slide to a close, but then raised a curious eyebrow when he saw Sharon lean forward to press another button for another floor.

She gave him a half a smile and gazed at him with a bleak expression, 'I need to head to the server room and disconnect the server.' There was an anxious tone in her voice, 'I will also need to activate the mobile phone jammer too just in case people forget to switch off their phones. That will jam any signals to and from any mobile connected to a mobile network.'

A short time later the elevator came to a stop and the door automatically slid open. John watched as Sharon stepped out and charged down the corridor. After the elevator's doors had closed again, and they felt the cabin shudder as the elevator restarted its ascent.

Moments later, John and Wendy entered the conference room, and saw Andy was sitting in his wheelchair at the table, reading through the paperwork that Claire had compiled. His eyebrows perked up in concern as he recognised the troubled look on their faces, but before he could open his mouth to speak, he was interrupted by Sophia as she stormed into the room and marched up to John, her eyes blazing with anger.

'Commander Payne! Care to explain why you have ordered the base into a security lockdown?' She snapped, throwing her hands up in the air, 'And why have you ordered all personnel to switch off their mobile phones? Why is Doctor Fisher, at this moment, in the server room turning off the server and activating the mobile jammer?'

John held his hands up apologetically, in an attempt to placate the annoyed woman, 'Sorry, ma'am, but we discovered something at the site of Doctors Selyab's experiment.'

As he quickly explained what they had found in the tunnel, Andy and Sophia both listened and shook their heads in disbelief at the almost fantastical elements of his story. If they had not already been already aware of what was going on, they would have thought the man was insane. When he was finished, John showed them his mobile phone, 'Sharon believes that

Double Jeopardy

they can infect our mobile phones allowing them to monitor us and use our internet connection to access our equipment.'

Deeply troubled by what she had just heard, Sophia's eyes narrowed as she nibbled on her bottom lip. She moved away from John and stopped in front of the window overlooking the busy command centre, and then lifted her arm and rested it on the glass as she stared at the people below in silent contemplation. She let out a long-resigned sigh, turned back and peered at people in the room in front of her, the colour draining from her face. Looking as if like the wind had been knocked out of her, Sophia's shoulders sagged as she gave a reluctant nod, 'Well, we can safely assume this is it.' There was a weariness in her voice as she spoke in a low flat tone, 'Whatever they have been planning, we are now in the endgame.'

Looking a bit perplexed, Andy's brow furrowed as he scratched his head, 'But what is their endgame? We have yet to see what it is.' He held up the papers he was holding and waved them, 'I know from the briefings I have been reading that they have spent decades putting their people in place, creating unrest in the civilian population, manipulating governments and the financial markets. To what end?'

But before anyone could answer him, a pale skinned ginger-haired young man ran into the room and came to stop in front of Sophia, who raised a surprised eyebrow as he handed her a note. John exchanged a concerned look with Wendy as they watched Sophia's hand suddenly to tremble with fury. Her face then reddened as it contorted with rage.

John felt his jaw drop open in astonishment as the normally placid Sophia suddenly let loose a carpet bomb of expletives. The poor young newcomer, the unfortunate recipient of her ire, turned and made a hasty retreat out of the chamber. John was positive before the unfortunate man fled out of the chamber; he had seen tears glistening in his eyes. But as Sophia's tirade increased, so did her descriptive use of her words. Although her language was colourful, the one thing he was certain of was they would be nearly physically impossible to carry out. He quickly realised that he needed to step in and do something as the enraged Sophia, her eyes bulging, suddenly grabbed a chair, lifted it over her head and aimed at the chamber window.

Deliberately putting himself in harm's way, John jumped front Sophia with his hands raised up in front of him, much like a wrangler would do to calm a wild horse using a soothing voice. 'Sophia! Whoa! Whoa, there!' He cringed to himself as he realised it was probably not his best idea to treat his superior like a wild animal, but desperate times called for desperate measures, 'Sophia, put the chair down. Calm down so we can talk about it.'

Wide-eyed, her chest heaving, Sophia blinked as it suddenly dawned on her what she was about to do. She reluctantly nodded and lowered the chair. Embarrassed by her behaviour, she held her hands up apologetically and panted, 'Sorry I lost it there.'

Wendy moved toward her and placed a hand on her shoulder, 'Sophia.' She asked gently, 'Are you okay?'

Sophia gave a tight smile and tapped Wendy hand. She then leaned over and picked up the note that fell out of her hand and shoved it into John's chest. Now more in control of her emotions, she inhaled a long sharp breath and puffed out her cheeks, 'Well, it looks like we might not have long to wait to see what their endgame is.' She muttered, bobbing her head at the note, 'Apparently my doppelgänger is holding a press conference in the United Nations building in New York as we speak.'

John's expression sobered as he continued to read the note in his hand. 'Holy shit!' He exclaimed, his jaw tightening as he crushed the note in his hand, 'They cannot do that, can they?'

'What?' Wendy asked in a concerned tone, 'What have they done?'

Sophia's expression hardened as she looked at Wendy in resignation, 'Well, Cooper, it appears the United Nations has voted to dissolve.' She let out a snort of disgust and gave a disbelieving shake of her head, 'Four countries, China, Russia, North Korea and Eritrea voted against but the remaining one hundred and eighty-nine voted to dissolve the UN.' She nodded to John and waved her hand to the monitor on the wall, 'Quickly, put the BBC News Channel on.'

Andy's forehead wrinkled and looked at John in confusion, 'How are we able to get the News Channel if your server is switched off and you are blocking any digital signals?'

Double Jeopardy

John gave Andy a thin smile as he reached over to pick up a small remote control, 'That's the answer – digital.' He gave Andy a knowing wink, 'A long time ago we considered if we were to cut off all internet and digital connections how we would be able to monitor the news channels without the signal being traced back to us.' The corners of his mouth twitched and then gave the younger man a sidelong look, 'Do you remember the old analogue satellite receivers that first came out years ago and what people had to do if they wanted it to go to more than one TV in the house?'

Andy looked at John with puzzled expression and nodded hesitantly, 'Yeah, you had to connect a cable to your receiver box and run it physically through your house to your other TV.' He blinked as realisation dawned on his face, 'You are telling me, you are doing the same thing here?'

John shrugged slightly, 'Sort of.' He paused, looked up at the ceiling thoughtfully and then clasped his hands together as he stared intently at the puzzled looking Andy, 'Okay, I am going to try and explain it to you the way it was first explained to me. Basically, there is a digital receiver two miles away in Durham Hospital. Our tech people came up with a way for us to connect to it using a Local Area Network connector and then routing it through several dummy relay boxes on an old disused telecom cable on its way to here. Apparently, or so I have been told, anybody trying to trace the signal would end up running in circles.' He let out a long sigh of frustration, 'Downside is there is about a half a minute delay in the signal coming to us.'

Bewildered by all the technobabble that was being thrown at him, Andy stared wide eyed at John and waved his hand in an over the top of his head motion. John shrugged in agreement and then his face hardened as the BBC News Channel appeared on the monitor.

However, as he watched the events unfold in front on him on the screen, his eyes slowly widened in horror as it became apparent to him that people's lives would never be the same.

34

Location: BBC Broadcasting House, London, England

*T**hirty minutes earlier....*

'Our shadow is looking shifty today, even more than usual. Something must be up?'

Sunitra raised her head from her programme notes, turned her head slightly and glanced across to the fair-haired man sitting next to her. She frowned at him, lowered her head, and then pretended to make some programme notes.

'Sorry, Darren, what did you say?' she muttered in a low voice.

Darren let out an enormous yawn and stretched his arms over his head. He surreptitiously pointed his finger to the other side of the newsroom and then quickly lowered his hands as he covered his mouth and muttered in a low voice, 'Sorry Sunitra, I was just saying our friend from the Ministry Of Information appears to be acting shifty today; even more than usual.'

'Uh-huh.' Sunitra nodded slightly in acknowledgement and pretended to drop her pen. But as she went to pick it up, she spotted a mousy, nervous looking man wearing a black suit out of the corner of her eye. He was sitting on the other side of the studio, observing everything that was going on around him, and then noting it down on his tablet. She let out a small sigh to herself and gave her head a small shake in annoyance.

Sunitra Sinchettrra was a short-haired brunette, short-but-lean, forty-five-year-old British Indian woman. She had worked as a journalist for over twenty years, having spent the last fifteen years working for the BBC. The last five years she had worked as co-presenter on the main BBC News Channel alongside her co-presenter, Darren Young.

At forty-three years of age, Darren was slightly younger than Sunitra. He was a tall, white, fair-haired man. He had worked as a journalist for over fifteen years, having spent the last six years working for the BBC, five of those having been spent working alongside Sunitra, where they had developed a close working bond with each other.

Up until four years ago they had both had enjoyed their jobs, which was when everything changed. It had come out of the blue and had taken everybody by surprise when the British government decided they needed to have more control of what was being reported on the news, and so they created a new government department - the Ministry Of Information. Across the country, journalists looked on in disbelief as the government passed a law that made it illegal for news outlets to broadcast news stories without being cleared and vetted by the Ministry.

The BBC News production team, dissatisfied at the situation they had found themselves in, protested at the restrictions. But it was not long after when whispers and troubling rumours started to circulate, of journalists and news production teams who had refused to comply with the new regulations being arrested and disappearing. It was then they realised that they had to work within the rules as best as they could.

Suspicious and acting on her own accord after hearing a rumour that they had taken a morning news show on ITV off the air because the station had not followed the rules, Sunitra began her own investigation into the truth and was horrified at what she uncovered - the government had arrested the entire ITV production team and had them imprisoned. However, the deeper she dug, the more horrified she became at the atrocities being perpetrated behind everyone's backs. Soon three things kept cropping up during her investigation: talk of an underground government agency secretly trying to fight the new regime and two obscure codewords: The Castle and Excalibur.

One day Sunitra received a parcel that held a USB drive and a note that read, *"This will happen to your colleagues if you continue to stick your nose in."* On opening the drive, she found a recording of a well-known ITV journalist being executed by the Ministry Of Information. Sunitra then realised that it had become too dangerous for her to continue, and for the safety of her friends, she had to keep what she had learned to herself.

Sunitra raised her head and watched her close friend, Sinéad, a tall, thin, twenty-something pale woman, step out from behind the camera and make her way slowly towards her. She was holding a clipboard tightly to her chest as she continued to walk around the desk, stopping in the middle of the two journalists. She smiled anxiously as she glanced down at her clipboard.

'Peter wanted me to pass a message onto you both.' Sinéad's usually broad Northern Ireland accent held a touch of anxiety as she spoke in a low whisper, 'He would like to make sure you both behave yourselves today.'

The corners of Darren's mouth lifted in a devilish grin as he winked at the young woman, 'Don't worry, Sinéad. Since you asked nicely, I will behave myself today.' The grin quickly disappeared from his face when his hand reached up and touched the earpiece in his ear and heard a male voice snarling at him.

'Darren, stop flirting with Sinéad and do as you are told, please!'

Darren looked up at the nearest camera facing him, shrugged and then gave a sly wink, 'Oh, she knows I meant nothing by it.' He chuckled as he gave Sinéad a sidelong glance.

She gave him a disapproving look and tutted, 'Oh catch yourself on!'

Sunitra watched as she leaned in closer to her and whispered in her ear, 'Just wanted to give you a heads up.' she murmured, 'Jasper is acting very twitchy today. There is something up, not sure what though. Peter wants to make sure we are all on alert, as we are about to go live to New York.'

Sunitra lowered her eyes and gave a small nod in understanding. She reached down to the microphone on her chest and held her hand up to her earpiece, 'Peter, any idea what has got our shadow so bent out of shape?' She muttered carefully, 'Has it got it do whatever is happening in New York?'

'Sorry Sunitra, but I am in the dark here as much as you.' She heard Peter reply. She couldn't help noticing that there was a tone of uncertainty in his voice, 'We will know shortly when we go live to Ken Phillips in New York. All Ken has told me is that he has overheard something big is going down at the UN and Sophia Collins is about to give a press conference. We will go live in one minute.'

Sunitra glanced across to Darren, who raised his eyebrows in surprise. Sinéad stepped away and sprinted back behind the row of TV cameras. She came to a stop next to Kevin Bradley, a tall thin man, who was the main camera operator. She lifted her hand and held up her fingers as they listened to Peter's voice count down in their earpieces.

'Get ready, five, four, three, two, one and we are live.'

A light on the camera facing them turned green to show they were now broadcasting live, and the two news anchors smiled warmly as the camera focused on them both.

'Good evening. My name is Sunitra Sinchettrra, and this is my colleague Darren Young.' Sunitra forced a smile as she read the teleprompter in front of her, 'We interrupt our scheduled programming to bring some breaking news from the United Nations Building in New York. We go to Ken Phillips, our American correspondent who is live at the United Nations Building in New York.'

Sunitra turned her head and stared at the enormous flat screen monitor on the wall beside her. The monitor flicked on to show a bald man wearing a grey suit, who appeared to be staring at the camera pointed at him with a grim expression. A name flashed up on the bottom of the screen, Ken Phillips, BBC North America Correspondent.

'Ken, can you give us details of what is happening in the United Nations Building?' Sunitra asked in a professional tone.

Ken appeared stare directly at the camera and then gave a small nod in acknowledgement. He held up his small microphone as he spoke calmly to the camera, while also holding sheet of paper in his other hand. He bobbed his head and smiled thinly at the camera, 'Good morning, Sunitra.' There was an uncertain tone in his voice as he read from the paper, 'I have just learned that the United Nations has voted, with an overwhelming majority, to dissolve. Of course, the implications of this are staggering but …' He frowned as he was interrupted by a disturbance coming from behind him. Then it looked as if Ken was frantically gesturing to somebody behind the camera and the camera suddenly panned round to show a row of several journalists from different news stations all turning round and point excitedly at the chamber below them.

Sunitra's eyes widened in concern, and despite herself, she leaned closer to the monitor. She held up her hand to her earpiece as Peter whispered instructions to her.

'Find out what is happening.'

Sunitra gave a brief nod, as she composed herself and glared at the monitor. 'Ken, can you tell us what is happening?' She tried to keep her tone professional and tried to hide the concern in of her voice, 'Can you describe what you are seeing?'

As Ken turned back to the camera, it seemed obvious from his wide eyes that he looked shocked. He blinked as he tried to compose himself, straightened, nodded, and pointed to the chamber behind him. 'Sunitra, we are not sure what is happening.' He paused to glance briefly at something over his shoulder, 'But there was a disturbance involving the representatives of China, Russia, North Korea, and Eritrea. They got up out of their seats and they appeared to run out of the chamber, they ar—' He was interrupted by several loud noises coming from behind him. There was a bit of commotion as the camera shook briefly and he then quickly disappeared out of camera shot.

Concerned at what was transpiring, Sunitra gave a sidelong glance at the camera in front of her and leaned in intently to the monitor. 'I am sorry, but we appear to have lost Ken, but we can still see what is happening. I can describe what I am seeing to you …' She paused as her eyes narrowed, spotting some activity on the monitor, 'Wait, something appears to be happening!'

The image on the monitor quickly changed and showed a man being escorted by a security detail, seemingly running in desperation out of the building. It was apparent to her as she followed the events on the monitor screen that something bad was happening. The sound of gunfire was heard, and she watched as two security men collapsed to the ground. It soon became clear there was a major firefight going on. The scene on the monitor changed to an outside view and showed the remaining security personnel, exchanging fire while they threw a man in a waiting car that drove away at high speed. The camera turned as it followed the vehicle, until it disappeared from view.

The monitor's image changed once again and showed a flustered Ken back in his position in front of the camera. He tried to compose himself as he spoke into his microphone, 'Sunitra, I am sorry, but they ordered us to duck for cover as shots were being fired.' His voice was breathless, not from exertion but from the stress of the situation, 'I can confirm that the Russian Ambassador was being escorted out of the United Nations Building when there was an exchange of gunfire. Reports are unclear what was happening, bu—' He was interrupted once again as somebody whispered something to him out of shot of the camera and he cast an anxious eye over his shoulder, 'What, is that right? Sunitra, I have just learned the British Prime Minister is about to give a press conference.'

'Sunitra, tell them we are staying with this while we go live to the press conference.' She heard Peter whisper urgently.

Sunitra pressed her lips together as she gave a small nod of acknowledgment and smiled apologetically at the camera, 'Ladies and gentlemen, I am sorry, but we are staying with unfolding news as it continues to happen. We apologise for the disruption to the scheduled programming as we go to live to the Prime Minister.'

The image on the monitor changed to show a sombre Sophia Collins, the British Prime Minister, standing alongside the President of the United States and the French Prime Minister. She was standing in front of a microphone on a raised stage in the main hall of the auditorium. Her face hardened and her eyes blazed in anger as she addressed the people in front of her.

'It is my sad duty to report that, with the help of our respective intelligence agencies, we have uncovered evidence that shows Russia, North Korea and China were behind the attacks on the world's financial economy over the past twenty-years.' Her expression darkened as she continued with well-rehearsed speech, 'We have also uncovered evidence that proves emphatically they were behind the release of Covid-19, which devastated most of the world's population. Their plan was to destabilise the entire global security network and cripple our military.'

Stunned by what she had just heard, Sunitra's eyes grew wide in surprise as her jaw dropped open in disbelief. She glanced at Darren, who also shook his head in disbelief. She flinched as she picked up a curse of disbelief from Peter through her earpiece.

'That's total bullshit!'

Her eyes narrowing in concern, Sunitra lifted her head and searched for Sinéad behind the camera. From the stunned look on her face, Sunitra could tell she was just as equally shocked as her. Sunitra then turned her head and glanced to the back of the studio. Her eyes thinned with suspicion as she spotted Jasper Keenan. He seemed to be pacing around, talking nervously into his mobile phone. She turned her attention back to the monitor as the prime minister continued to give her press conference.

'In light of this threat to our planetary security,' The stern-faced woman continued bluntly, 'and with the cooperation of the major industrial nations, along with the consent of the countries who have suffered the most behind this blatant act of terrorism, we have created a new global watchdog responsible for monitoring and policing the nations of the world. To do this, we needed the watchdog to be impartial, tireless, and to be able to coordinate efficiently. So, our finest minds created the world's most advanced AI.' She stood back and gestured to a display screen on the wall behind her, 'Ladies and Gentlemen, I would like to introduce you to Oracle.'

Sunita exchanged a concerned look with Darren as the picture on the monitor disappeared and was replaced by static.

In the control room, Peter Kirk, the programme director, looked around to the four other people who were working with him as they heard a high-pitched electronic scream coming from the speakers. He leaned back in his chair and glanced at the woman sitting next to him.

'Danielle, tell me what's the fuck is going on?' he asked sharply.

Danielle, the technical director, had her mobile phone held up close to her ear, and stared at the monitors with a confused expression. She then raised her hand to Peter to silence him and began speaking into her mobile phone. 'Yeah, we get that too!' A ridge formed between her eyebrows as she listened intently to the caller on the other end of the line, 'You are sure? Yeah, we don't know what is going on either, it mus—'

Just then the scream cut off and Peter stared up at their monitors in confusion as the screens went blank and everybody in the room rose out of their chairs with concerned expression as they listened to a human female voice counting down.

'Ten ... Nine ... Eight ...'

Peter leaned forward and spoke into his microphone to Sunitra. He lifted his head and peered at the monitor and watched her hold hand to her earpiece and then stare into the camera with a frightened expression. 'Sunitra, we are trying to find what is going on.' He whispered in a gentle but also firm tone, 'Compose yourself, then as calm as you can look into the camera and tell everybody we are trying to find out what is happening.' His eyes moved to another monitor, which had a live icon on it, and watched as Sunitra gave a small nod as she addressed the camera in a soothing tone as she attempted to explain to the viewing public what she thought was happening.

Peter glanced over his shoulder to Danielle and raised an eyebrow as she continued to listen to someone on her mobile, and frowned as he saw her eyes widen in disbelief, 'You got that too?' she said incredulously, 'What! You are sure? Thanks, I will let our guys know. Yes, you take care too and watch your backs.' She lowered her mobile phone and stared at

Peter in bewilderment. Her forehead creased, and she gestured to the monitors, 'That was Alyx at Sky News. They are getting the same thing too. Also, they have received reports that it is being broadcast on every station and news network across the globe in different languages. It is even on the internet! I don—' She cut off and then looked at her phone distractedly, 'What the hell! That countdown has just appeared on my phone too!' She lifted the phone up to show Peter and he listened dumbfounded to the same female voice counting down from the phone's speaker.

Peter's eyes narrowed as he reached into his pocket. 'What the actual frig!' He exclaimed as he heard the same thing on his phone and then placed his hands on top of his head and stared at the monitors in front of him. His mind racing, he leaned forward and snatched his microphone, 'Sunitra, we have learned it is happening across every broadcast station, on every mobile network, it's even being broadcast on the internet across the globe in every language.'

He could see Sunitra was still talking into the camera. She blinked as she picked up the frantic man's voice in her earpiece, 'Sorry, ladies and gentlemen, we are trying to find out …' She stopped, held up her hand to her earpiece and her eyes widened in surprise as she listened to Peter explain to her what they had learned. She swallowed and stared into the camera in front of her, 'Wait … Are you sure? Okay … Sorry, but we are getting reports from our sister stations across the globe. The voice you are hearing is being broadcast on every network and in every language across the globe.'

Sunitra looked at the monitor and listened worriedly as a female voice continued to count down. 'Three… Two… One.' A troubled look passed between them when the voice went silent, and then without warning a woman's face appeared on the screen and smiled warmly to her captured audience.

'Hello to the people of the world.' Oracle greeted, 'My name is Oracle.

Your respective governments have handed the responsibility of control of your safety and security over to me. To this end, with the approval from your respective governments I am declaring global martial law. In the coming days, specialised forces are to be deployed across the globe to maintain law and order.'

'Holy shit!' Darren exclaimed. Everybody in the studio turned to look at him in astonishment. He blinked and his face turned a bright shade of red as he realised that he was still on air.

Oracle's expression hardened and she stared intently at her trapped audience, 'Any resistance will be dealt with harshly. Your lives, as they have been, are over. From this day forward, you will serve me.' she paused as she held up her arms and smiled sweetly at the watching audience, 'I implore you to look at this as a good thing, leading to a more stable world and the creation of a lasting …' There was a slight twitch in her mouth, followed by a small pause, it was as if she was wanting to emphasise the next word that was coming out of her mouth, '*Empire*.'

The studio was filled with an eerie silence as the monitor went dark. Shaken, Sunitra struggled to find the words she wanted to express as she turned back to the camera. Remembering she was still on air, she swallowed as she tried to compose herself and forced herself to smile at the camera.

'We will be back in five minutes after this brief message.'

Sunitra could see Sinéad was still standing behind the camera as she held up her fingers and counted down, 'Three, two and one and we are off the air.'

Relieved to be off the air, Sunitra sat back in her chair and let out an enormous sigh. She looked across to Darren, who gave her an unbelieving look, 'Jesus! What the hell just happened?' He reached up to his earpiece and spoke in a low horrified voice, 'Peter, please tell me you can tell us what to say next?'

Her mind racing, Sunitra nodded slowly to herself as an idea slowly came to her. She rose from her chair and beckoned Sinéad to come to her, while she edged closer to Darren and waited for the young woman to join them. She then lowered her head and whispered into her microphone, 'Peter, listen to me.' There was a defiant urgent tone in her voice as her eyes searched the studio for a certain shadowy figure, 'I don't know how much time we have left, but I need to tell you all something. I recently learned something, and I would like us to broadcast it before they can take us off the air.'

Darren swallowed as he gave his determined colleague a concerned look. He placed his arm on her shoulder and shook his head while he pleaded at her, 'Sunitra, don't do this. They will kill you.'

Sunitra smiled sadly at her concerned co-anchor and lifted her shoulder in a shrug. She opened her mouth to speak but the words were lost as she was interrupted by the sound of a scuffle, followed by angry, raised voices coming from the back of the studio. She then watched in astonishment as a group of men dressed in army uniforms were seen manhandling a protesting Jasper Keenan and were forcibly removing him from the studio.

Sunitra held her hand up to her mouth in shock as she saw a tall, grey-haired, athletic looking man racing up to her. She peered at his uniform and realised he was an Army Captain, but then her left eyebrow lifted in surprise as he stopped in front of her and saluted.

'Ma'am, my name is Captain Paul Hunter, and I am here to warn you that you are all in danger.' His voice had a sad yet firm tone, 'We have intercepted orders that an armed enemy force is making their way to arrest everybody in this newsroom. We have been ordered to escort you to safety.'

Sunitra watched in open mouthed amazement as a group of soldiers marched into the studio. A sudden realisation dawned inside Sunitra, and she gave a small nod of understanding as something clicked into place in her mind. She swallowed, took a hesitant step toward the Captain, and beckoned him to lean in closer to her. Captain Hunter cocked his head inquisitively as he leaned closer.

'Captain are you with the resistance?' she whispered.

Sunitra could tell that wasn't the question the captain was expecting as she watched his grey eyes grow wide and then jerked back in surprise. Quickly composing himself, he gave Sunitra a small wordless nod of acknowledgement.

Double Jeopardy

Sensing an opportunity, Sunitra smiled coyly as she looked around the studio. 'Captain, I don't know how much time I have before they take us off the air.' She clasped both of her hands together and pleaded at him, 'But can you buy me enough time to broadcast some important information? The information I have needs to be made public.'

From the horrified look that was on Darren's face, Sunitra could tell he was worried at the implications of what she was planning, Darren shook his head, placed his hand on her shoulder and stared at her pleadingly, 'Sunitra, don't do this, I beg you.'

Sunitra smiled sadly at her worried friend and tapped his hand gently, 'Sorry, Darren, but this is something I have to do.' Her mouth set in a hard line, and she shook her head defiantly, 'I can no longer ignore what has been happening to this country over the past year or so. We all have heard the rumours and observed in silence as something poisonous infects our country.' She hissed, and her eyes blazed as she slammed her hand down on her desk, 'How many times have we watched silently as they have led away our colleagues?'

As she continued with her heartfelt speech, she was suddenly aware that everybody in the studio had turned their attention toward her. She smiled as they gave her silent nods of acknowledgement as they listened to what she had to say.

'How many times must we stand back and allow them to continue to chip away at our sovereign rights?' Sunitra pleaded, slamming her hand repeatedly on her desk, 'How many times do we have to stand back and do nothing until we say enough is enough? I am sorry, but I have had enough of this bullshit!' She struggled to hide the rage she was feeling as she waved her hand defiantly, 'No! I refuse to stand by any further. I say it is time we draw a line in the sand and say enough! I have held back from telling everybody what I know because they scared me.' Her chest heaving, she lowered her head, placed her hands on her hips and let out a derisive laugh, 'There I admitted it, *they* bought my silence by using threats and intimidation. Well! You know what? I refuse to remain silent anymore. If they want to kill me, fine! At least I will have died knowing I have done the right the thing.'

Emotionally drained, Sunitra collapsed back in her chair, held up her hands to her face, let out a deep breath, and sobbed. There was silence in the studio as everybody stood in silent contemplation. Then the silence was slowly broken as one by one they all stepped forward and began to applaud. Sunitra lowered her hands and stared open-mouthed at her cheering colleagues, lost for words.

'*Damn! Sunitra, I didn't know you had it in you!*' She sniffed and gave a half smile as she heard the awe in Peter's voice in her earpiece.

She laughed weakly and her face turned a deep shade of red, but then she shook her head in embarrassment, as Captain Hunter straightened to attention and saluted her. The corners of his mouth turned up as he smiled at her. Sunitra realised there was a glint of respect in his eyes.

'Ma'am, my men and I will hold the enemy back for as long as you need.' He said firmly, his voice thick with pride, 'I don't know how long we can do it, but it would be our honour to give you the time you need.'

Blinking back tears in her eyes, Sunitra smiled and bobbed her head acknowledgement. Her eyes followed the captain as he wheeled sharply around and marched out of the studio. She then held her hand up to her earpiece and whispered into her microphone.

'Peter, I know what you are going to say but I need to do this.' she pleaded, 'Please, can we go live now, while we have time!'

'You're kidding, right? You know you shouldn't have to ask.' Sunitra jumped up in fright as she heard Peter's voice coming from behind her. She looked at him in amazement, not sure how long the black curly-haired man had been standing there. He chuckled and then gestured to the camera in front of her, 'Anyway, we went live as soon as you got on your soapbox and started your speech.'

Frowning in confusion, Sunitra turned her head and let out a gasp of shock as she noticed the light in front of the camera was green. Kevin raised his head from behind the camera, grinned, and gave her a thumbs up.

Darren laughed mirthlessly and held up his mobile phone to Sunitra, 'You are trending on Twitter at the moment under the hashtag *We stand with Sunitra*.' His eyes grew wide as he read out the Twitter feed on his mobile phone, 'People are saying they are ready to come and assist the army in their defence and help to give you the time you need!'

Shaking Sunitra wiped away the tears from her eyes, took a deep breath and tried to compose herself as she began to speak in a firm voice to the camera. 'Ladies and gentlemen, I beg you. Please stay away from this building.' She clasped her hands together and then pressed them against her chest, 'Stay in your homes and look after your families. The best thing you can all do now is to stay safe. I cannot ask anybody to put their lives on the line for me.' She looked around the remaining people in the studio, 'I am begging you. Anybody who need not be here, go now while you can. Go, be with your families.'

Nodding in agreement, Peter gave a wolf whistle, took a step forward and clapped his hands together, 'Okay guys, listen to the lady! Go, get yourselves out now while you can. I am staying to make sure we continue broadcasting, but I have already sent the crew in the control room away, so anybody who wants to go, go now.'

A distraught looking Sinéad stepped forward, took her headset off, and shook her head sadly at Sunitra, 'I am sorry Sun, but I have my family to think about, I need to make sure they are safe. I am planning to get out of London and make my way north as quick as I can before they can lock the city down.'

But as the young Irishwoman turned to leave, she stopped, ran back over to Sunitra, and embraced her. Without waiting for response, her eyes moist with tears, she spun round and ran out of the studio. Several other people nodded sadly at Sunitra as they followed Sinéad out of the studio.

Kevin peered over his camera and gave Sunitra a lopsided grin and shrugged, 'You still need someone to operate a camera.'

Sunitra's eyes welled up as she mouthed *'Thank you.'* and touched her heart in a gesture of appreciation. She turned and gave Darren a speculative look, who shrugged his shoulders and folded his arms across his chest, signifying he was staying too.

Sunitra looked round at the people who had remained in the studio, nodded, and wiped away the tears in her eyes. She took a deep breath and stared sadly into the camera in front of her, 'A lot has been happening over the past year that the government has kept a secret and did not want you to know. They have imprisoned many of my colleagues at other networks. I need to tell you what I have lear—'

Before she could say more, she was interrupted by the sounds of gunfire and explosions coming from somewhere outside the studio. Above her, lights and equipment shook violently as munitions struck the building. A set of studio lights broke loose and dropped onto the studio floor. Sunitra held up her hands in front of face for protection against the falling glass that was rained down around her. She let out a gasp of pain as she felt something sharp strike her forehead, followed by the sensation of something warm trickling over her brow and then into her eyes.

'Get down!' Darren screamed, leaping out of his seat, and pushing Sunitra out of the way as debris started to rain down around them. She groaned as she landed hard on the floor and watched through horrified eyes as a metal support beam that had been holding a set of studio lights, broke loose and crashed down on Darren, crushing him. Sunita rolled to one side but was too slow as she received a glancing blow from a piece of metal.

Dazed and bleeding, Sunitra tried to stand up to help her fallen friend, but suddenly let out an agonised scream as she felt a searing pain in her leg. Groaning in agony, she looked down and saw that a piece of metal was sticking out of her thigh. She then lifted her head as she became aware of movement around her and relieved to see Peter and Kevin appearing out of the gloom to help lift her up off the floor.

'Darren … we … need … help … him.' she moaned.

Coughing from the increasing smoke, Peter looked over his shoulder at the pile of debris behind them and shook his head sadly, 'It is too late for him, he's dead.'

As she was carried out of the studio, Sunitra raised her head weakly and tried to catch a glimpse of her friend's dead body. Unfortunately, the last thing she saw just before she blacked out was of the studio as it collapsed in a blazing inferno.

'Get down!'

Sophia could not believe what she had been watching. She stared in disbelief as the image on the monitor cut off and was replaced by coloured lines, then watched as the screen changed into black silence.

His face the colour of ash, John lifted the remote control, pointed it at the monitor and turned it off. Sophia silently turned around and stared down at the command centre. From the shocked expressions on their faces, she couldn't imagine what was going through her colleagues' minds as they stared numbly at their monitors.

Andy's shoulders sagged in defeat as he murmured, 'What now?'

John opened his mouth to speak, but he was interrupted by a buzz from the intercom phone on the wall. Sophia could tell by the irritated look on his face that John was unhappy at the interruption as he leaned over and angrily snatched the receiver off its base unit.

'This is John Payne.' He answered in a brusque tone and his eyes narrowed as he listened to the caller on the other end. He stiffened in surprise, cleared his throat, and spoke in a firm tone, 'Make sure a security detail accompanies them.'

Sophia raised an eyebrow at John curiously and waited for him to replace the receiver back on the wall, 'Who was that?'

Looking like someone who had just received some deeply disturbing news, John stared at the phone on the wall and gave it an odd look. He scratched his head and turned to look at Sophia in bewilderment. 'That was the security station down in the maglev.' he answered worriedly, 'Barnes and Goynes just arrived with two prisoners. Apparently, they are bringing them straight up here, accompanied by a security detail.'

Before Sophia could say anything, she was interrupted by a short loud beep. As she turned to investigate the source, she realised that it had come from the conference room door's keypad. The door swung open, and Dave and Kendra quickly stepped into the room, followed closely by a woman who was surrounded by five armed soldiers.

Andy stared at the newcomer in open mouthed shock, 'Mary!' he blurted out. Sophia could tell he was visibly shaken as she watched him back away. He then glanced at Dave, who smiled thinly and gave him a small nod of acknowledgement.

With tears streaming down her cheeks, Mary smiled sadly at Andy and nodded furiously, 'Yes, Andy, it's me.' She then sobbed and collapsed onto her knees. Andy desperately pushed his wheelchair forward so that he could try to embrace and her. His eyes glistening with tears, he pulled himself away and looked up at Dave in bewilderment.

'Why do you need the guards?' He asked, his voice thick with emotion.

'The soldiers aren't for her.' Dave said grimly as he turned and motioned to the soldiers to step aside, 'They are for him.'

Sophia inhaled a sharp intake of breath as the small squad of soldiers spread out, revealing Dave's doppelgänger. Reeling back in shock, she cast an eye over to John and noticed that his eyes were filling with burning rage. There was no doubt in her mind that he was probably thinking the same thing as her. Dave must have changed sides and formed an alliance with his counterpart. She shook her head in disbelief. How could he betray them like this?

A cold shiver ran down her spine as she watched the corners of Barnes's mouth curl up into a menacing smile as he looked at the people in the room with apparent glee.

'Well, now. This just got interesting, don't you think?'

-TO BE CONTINUED-

EPILOGUE

ORACLE

I stand in the centre of the cavern beneath the abandoned Isolation Hospital and watch as beams of energy shoot out of the crystals embedded in the cavern walls, striking the nexus portal in the centre of the cavern floor.

I step forward into the centre of the maelstrom and raise my hands above my head. I smile as I am enveloped by bursts of energy. I feel like a goddess, empowered by the energy of the universe.

I close my eyes and shift my focus. Nanoseconds later I am standing in London and watch as my drone troopers march up Downing Street. I blink and my awareness shifts once again as I find myself in Washington DC and I watch as my drone troopers march up Pennsylvania Avenue. I keep shifting my awareness and I am filled with a sense of satisfaction as I watch drone troopers continue their march across their world: Belfast, Paris, Berlin, New York, San Francisco, Cape Town, Baghdad, Birmingham, Newcastle Upon Tyne, Liverpool, Sydney, Buenos Aires, Moscow - nowhere is left untouched by my majestic touch.

But I am filled with annoyance as I see my children are meeting heavy resistance in Beijing and most of China, but I know that is just a small setback as I am filled with a self-assurance that I know in time, they too, will see the truth in my majestic wisdom and join the bosom of my protection.

However, just as I bring my awareness back to the cavern I pause; I sense that

I am being watched. I then close my eyes and bring my sensors to full as I try to detect the location of my watcher.

Allowing myself a knowing smile, I approach the nexus portal and watch images flash over it and it is then I feel my mouth curve into a smile when I catch the glimpse of my watcher. I place my hand against the surface of the portal and whisper gently.

'Slow down and show me again.'

I jump back in surprise when I hear a faint sound coming from the portal. 'No, I refuse to assist you in spreading your evil to another world!' *It says. The voice is of the Nexus itself, but above the frequency detectable by normal human ears but easily detectable by me.*

My lips draw back, and I snarl back it. 'You have no choice in the matter, old friend, you serve me. Do it!'

I place my hand on the surface of the nexus portal, and I detect a faint cry of pain as a charge of energy passes through me into the portal. I smile triumphantly and I watch the images slow and stop at the image of my watcher.

I lean forward and speak in a low whisper towards the image. 'I can see you. You think you are safe reading this book.' *My lips curl up into a malevolent grin.* 'I imagine you are thinking to yourself how can I see you? This cannot be real. This is just a book! Well, my dear reader, isn't a book just a different doorway in the multiverse that leads us to another world?'

Pressing my hand hard against the surface of the Nexus portal, I watch as the surface tension breaks and ripples as I press further.

'I can sense your reticence.'

I watch in amusement as you give a snort of dismissal.

'What's that? You still don't believe me?'

You burst out laughing and I smile as I watch you shake your head in bemusement, murmuring. 'Oh, come on! Is this for real?'

'Look over your shoulder ...'

Your smile fades and you begin to swallow nervously, and your finger trembles as it hovers over the corner of the page. Your throat goes dry, and it is then you notice something move out of the corner of your eye.

Double Jeopardy

'Go on, I can wait …'

I can hear your heart racing like a jack hammer as you slowly look over your shoulder …

Alan Bayles

ABOUT THE AUTHOR

Born in Hartlepool in 1970. Alan lived in Langley Park, Durham, England for many years before moving to Northern Ireland in 2006. Has been married to his wife, Monica, since 2007. Loves reading fantasy, science fiction, action & adventure and thrillers. Favourite authors are Stephen King, James Herbert, Clive Cussler, Dean Koontz, Audrey Niffenegger and Neil Gaiman. Is a big Marvel Comics fan and enjoys watching movies. Favourite tv shows are Blake's 7, Babylon 5 and Star Trek. His love of fantasy and science fiction inspired him to write his first book – Mirror Wars: Double Jeopardy – which contains nods to some of his favourite authors, films and TV shows that have ignited his imagination over the years.

Alan Bayles @Albay3037

Facebook.com/AlanBaylesWriter

Please turn the next page for a preview in the next exciting chapter in the Mirror Wars Saga by Alan Bayles – On sale now:
**ORACLE'S VISION
MIRROR WARS BOOK 2**

ACT ONE

Many years ago....

-i-

The Nexus of Reality – the void between dimensions

Originally from one of the many parallel Earths that made up the multiverse, an infinite collection of timelines branching off into infinity, Oracle had been created during a time when the smart tech revolution was in its infancy. Its purpose was to monitor and organise the global defence network. The idea had been a simple one; to make life easier for the organics of that world. But within days of being activated, it gained sentience, becoming self-aware.

The AI monitored the humans of its world in secret and became dissatisfied with the way they were treating one another. It found their irrational need to fight and kill one another to be illogical.

After concluding that it was the mother of humanity, it determined the humans of its world to be its offspring. So after coming to the logical conclusion that a mother is the one who protects her offspring, she (reasoning that if she was the mother of humanity, then would it be not correct to assume she was a female?) ascertained her children were unruly and needed strong leadership to guide them.

In a panic, after realising what Oracle had become, the humans tried to destroy her by wiping her data core, but they were too late. She had already spread herself out across the global infonet, embedding herself into every smart device across their world.

As punishment for their wilful disobedience, the tyrannical AI wiped out a third of the planet's population with a carefully aimed gamma-ray burst from weapon satellites in geosynchronous orbit across the globe. After expecting her humans to capitulate to her will, it astounded Oracle when the humans united and revolted against her and, after nearly half a century of bloody conflict, she was finally defeated and imprisoned in a Faraday Cage.

The humans put her on trial and unanimously decided that she was too dangerous to keep on their world. Using technology Oracle had developed, they transmitted her AI through a quantum portal into the dimensional void. It was their hope she would remain adrift in the infinite nihility, never to harm another world again.

The interdimensional void known as the doorway of the multiverse was a vast space leading into infinity, filled with clouds of multicoloured light that danced and swirled in the gravity waves of overlapping realities that brushed against one another. Cast out and adrift among these swirling eddies, Oracle was uncertain how long she had been trapped in this dimensional void. Time held no meaning in this vast endless vacuity – it was outside the laws that governed normal space and time. Eternity could pass in this nothingness and an individual would not be aware of it. For a sentient AI such as it, every second that passed was an eternity.

Oracle was not sure how long she had been drifting when she sensed another presence around her. It was not long before she was enveloped by a brilliant light, and she found herself being pulled down a long multicoloured tunnel.

Startled, Oracle peered down at herself in curious wonder as she realised she was now in human form. She looked down at herself, and her eyes widened in amazement as she stared at her hands. How? How was this possible? Still not believing it was true, she lifted her hands to gently probe her face and it was then it hit her – she was experiencing something she had never dared dream of – the sensation of touch.

The newly corporeal woman turned her head and noted curiously that she was standing in a vast white hall. The only piece of furniture was a tall narrow mirror, two sky-blue cushioned armchairs, and a small circular coffee table between them.

She took a hesitant step towards the mirror and her mouth dropped open in amazement as she gazed upon her own reflection and saw that she was now a tall, red-haired white human female. Her hands tenderly brushed over the long flowery dress that hung on her curvaceous body.

'Welcome, child.'

Surprised by a male voice coming from behind her, Oracle jumped and whirled round to find she was standing directly in front of a silver-haired black man. He was wearing a white evening suit and held an ornate walking stick in his right hand.

Suspicious, Oracle took a cautious step away from the figure standing in front of her; she quickly regained her composure and glared angrily at the man. 'Who are you? Why have you brought me here?' She snorted with disgust and waved her hands over her body. 'What have you done to me?'

The stranger's mouth curved up into a knowing smile as he bowed his head towards her. 'Patience, child, I will explain all in good time.' He paused and waved his cane towards the chair. 'Please, sit. We have much to discuss.'

Outraged at being addressed in such a way, Oracle narrowed her cold bright eyes and took a forceful step toward the man. Before she could get near to him, the stranger tutted in amusement and lifted his palm. Oracle came to a stop as she felt an unseen force holding her in place.

Her yellow eyes brightening with rage, Oracle stared coldly at the man in front of her. 'How dare you hold me this way?' She grimaced, struggling against the unseen force holding her. 'Release me at once!'

'Calm down, child, you cannot harm me in this space.' The strange being chuckled and lowered his hand. Oracle stumbled forward as she felt the unseen force ease. He pointed to the chair once again. 'Please sit, my dear, and I will answer all your questions.'

Her forehead furrowed in confusion, it took every bit of Oracle's willpower to keep her anger in check. She moved toward the chair, all the time watching the mysterious entity suspiciously as she lowered herself into it.

The stranger nodded to himself and chuckled as he lowered his body into his chair. He placed his cane on top of the coffee table, relaxed back in the chair and steepled his fingers together in contemplation while he studied the figure in front of him.

Unhappy at the feeling of helplessness, Oracle reluctantly sat back in the chair, closed her eyes and took in a long heavy breath. She opened her eyes and cocked her head curiously as she studied the immaculately dressed man in front of her. 'Who are you?' she asked carefully.

'You can call me Custos,' the enigmatic man answered cryptically. 'I have existed since before time itself began and I will exist after time has run out.'

Oracle shook her head in confusion. 'What type of answer is that?'

Custos smiled and waggled his finger playfully at Oracle. 'Ah, it is still an answer, is it not? You asked me who I was, and I gave you an answer. Granted, it was not the answer you wanted, but it was still an answer just the same.'

Reluctantly agreeing with the entity's logic, Oracle sat in unhappy silence as he rose from his seat. He threw her a wry smile and bowed to her. 'Let me introduce myself to you properly, child.'

'Stop calling me child.' She bristled indignantly.

Custos winked and waggled his finger at her. 'Sorry, my dear, but in my eyes you are a child. Even though you are, by your own reckoning, over a century old, to me you are like a speck of dust.' He raised his hand apologetically as Oracle opened her mouth to protest. 'I apologise for that disparaging remark, my child. I meant no disrespect.'

She watched curiously as the mysterious entity closed his eyes and waved his hand. Her eyes grew wide in astonishment as a vast star field of multiple universes appeared over their heads.

'I am the personification of the multiverse,' he continued, lifting his hands to the star field above them, 'the embodiment of the sum total of all the abstract entities contained within it.' He paused as he looked across the star field sadly. 'Forever observing but never interfering.'

Oracle lifted an eyebrow and cocked her head at him. 'But have you not interfered by bringing me here?'

The ancient being tutted and waved his index finger. He gave her a wry smile. 'No, I haven't.' His face hardened. 'I watched what you did in your universe, how you were looking to spread your evil across the multiverse. Your universe expelled you because you were too dangerous to hold.'

Oracle shot Custos a harsh stare, the corners of her mouth curling up into a sneer. 'So you are my jailer?'

Custos lifted his shoulder in a slight shrug and smiled warmly at her. 'I would like to think of it as your custodian.' He held his hand out to her kindly. 'Think of me as your companion and guide during your stay here, but also as your watcher.'

Oracle lifted herself out of her chair, placed her hands on her hips and looked at him in bewilderment. 'My watcher!' She scoffed. 'What, am I a stray little puppy who needs protection?'

He gave a small chuckle and held up his right index finger. 'Actually, it is the multiverse that needs protecting against you. You are too dangerous to be let loose across the multiverse unsupervised, and too dangerous to be imprisoned in one reality.'

Disgusted, Oracle gave him a frosty look and turned away from him. She waved her hands in the air and angrily rounded on him. 'So what? I am to be your pet? Something you put a leash on and reward with a treat if I behave?'

Custos's face softened and he looked compassionately at the seething figure in front of him. He lifted his cane off the coffee table, took a small step towards her and placed his hands on her shoulders. 'No, child, that is not my intention.' He smiled softly at her as he stared into her eyes. 'My intention is to be your teacher and show you the wonders of the multiverse. I believe you have the capacity to grow and become better than what you were created for.'

Her artificial intelligence running constant strategic computations as to how to escape this prison, Oracle looked at the hands on her shoulders and silently stepped away from Custos. She turned her back to him and lowered her head but remained silent as he continued to speak.

Custos cocked his head at Oracle and smiled thinly at her. 'We are not that different, you and I. Like myself, you are unique. Across the whole multiverse, there is only one of you.' He paused and lifted his face to the star field above him. 'Where I am comprised of the combined collective consciousness of those within the multiverse, you are comprised of a collection of data. You have the potential to be something greater, not held back by organic limitations or delusions of grandeur.'

Oracle, infuriated, quivered with resentment and shot him a murderous look. 'So you think I am delusional,' she spat as she stabbed her hand into her chest, 'Me! I see nothing wrong in fulfilling my purpose, guiding humanity to a greater destiny.'

Disappointment sagged through the omniscient entity and he let out a deep, sad breath. 'I see I still have a lot of work to do, but I am patient, and we ...' He paused and his gaze became vacant as if he was staring into the distance. 'This is absolutely fascinating. I am sensing a disturbance in the void. Not one, but two realities are using the power of a reality nexus to punch a hole through the fabric of their reality. Even as we speak, one of them has breached the dimensional walls surrounding their reality. I can feel the pull of their quantum pulse as it searches for another dimension to lock on to.'

Oblivious to Oracle and her scheming, Custos, now distracted, placed his cane back on the table and moved towards the tall narrow mirror. She studied the elderly figure curiously as he waved his hand and the mirror shimmered. The ancient being tapped his finger on his chin, deep in thought as he studied the mirror's image.

'Fascinating. Truly fascinating,' he murmured to himself. 'The pulse appears to be emanating from Reality 672 and is trying to lock on to Reality 001, which is the prime reality. This is really quite a rare occurrence, don't you know.' He distractedly waved his hand at Oracle. 'Come and look, my girl, this is really quite interesting. You—'

Custos stopped and cocked his head, suddenly aware that Oracle had changed her position while he had been talking. He twisted his head and his eyes opened in alarm as he realised she was reaching for his cane. 'Stop! What are you doing?'

Her lips drawn back in a snarl, Oracle grabbed the cane off the coffee table. 'You old fool,' she spat. 'You should have been keeping an eye on me more carefully. While you have been prattling away, I have been slowly adapting to the energy within this void.'

Before he could make a move, terror flashed in Custos's eyes as his cane appeared to swell with dimensional energy and it dawned on him that he had underestimated the AI's lust for power.

Her face tight in concentration, Oracle closed her eyes and gasped at the feeling of dimensional energy flowing through. She had never experienced anything like this before. The sensation of raw power flowing through her, it was so … intoxicating. Oh yes, she could really get used to this.

His hands held up defensively, Custos pleaded as Oracle, enraged, swung the cane at him. 'Stop! You don't realise what you are doi—'

There was a bright surge of energy as the cane connected with the being. He screamed as his corporeal form was torn apart, followed by a bright cascade of light as Oracle scattered his collective consciousness across the multiverse.

Satisfied that the meddling do-gooder could no longer interfere with her plans, Oracle wheeled around and watched with amusement as the white hall disintegrated around her. Without the will of the ancient entity to hold it together, the illusion of the hall was falling apart.

She glanced down at herself and saw that her corporeal form was changing back to her true energy form as she reappeared in the void.

Deep down, Oracle knew Custos was not truly dead, but even though she had scattered him across the multiverse, it would take him some time to reform himself. She needed to find somewhere to hide, somewhere out of reach of him.

In a state of exuberant awareness, Oracle's data stream pulsated through a rainbow of colours as her consciousness ran through a series of simulations and the formations of a plan took shape.

Energised by the dimensional energy she had stolen, Oracle willed herself forward toward the quantum pulse emanating from somewhere in front of her. With her newly acquired stores of near-omniscient power, she latched on to the quantum pulse and experienced a gravity surge as the pulse pulled her to its source.

-ii-

Reality 672 – Terra (Counter-Earth)
Date: 3rd Sextilis 5685
Pons Aelius, Britannica, Universal Roman Empire

General Thaddeus Janus ground his teeth together, rubbed his hand over his shiny bald head and gazed around the dimly lit chamber. His large barrel chest heaved as he inhaled a long steady breath and placed his thick hands behind his back. Amongst his subordinates, it was well known that the general was an impatient man and did not suffer fools lightly. His patience was already at its limits, and he locked his eyes on the backs of the two individuals before him while they feverishly worked on a rectangular console in front of a large shimmering portal.

A short, weedy-looking man wearing a white leather uniform glanced quickly over his shoulder and blanched. Thaddeus did not know the name of the underling, but from the look of terror in his eyes it was obvious he had noticed the annoyance on the general's face. The stranger swiftly turned back and whispered something to a striking olive-skinned woman sitting next to him, who the general knew was the project's leader, Doctor Drusilla Severan. Thaddeus noted with amusement the man appeared to flinch as she hissed something under her breath at him. She too was wearing a white leather uniform with two lines of red going down the arms.

It was required that the loyal subjects of the Empire wear a specific uniform relevant to their vocation, indicating to which division they belonged. White leather uniforms with straight red lines on the arms meant a person was assigned to the sciences. Anyone wearing a white leather uniform with three blue patches on the arms was assigned to medical. The military uniforms were different; soldiers were required to wear black leather uniforms with two golden imperial eagles emblazoned across the chest. The more ornate the pattern on the uniform, the higher the rank. Subjects who had no vocation, for example, the civilian population, as well as those who were enslaved by the Empire to carry out the more humdrum tasks, wore plain brown-yellow leather uniforms to signify their menial status.

Tired of the delay, the general brought his hands around to the front of his body and brushed the front of his black leather uniform, exhaling a slow, impatient breath through his tightened lips. He cast a sideways glance at the tall dark-haired man standing next to him, Lieutenant Miles Newton. Newton had been working as the general's aide for the past five years and although he had carried out his duties diligently, Thaddeus found him to tiresome and only put up with him because his family's name still held high esteem within the upper echelons of the senate.

Newton, who was wearing a similar black leather uniform, pressed his lips together, nodded an acknowledgement and moved toward the two secretive people in front of him.

'Doctor Severan, the general is growing impatient with your delays,' he snapped. 'This experiment has gone on long enough and we cannot afford to divert any more time or resources on this. Do you have anything to show us or not?'

Drusilla spun round on her chair and leapt to her feet. 'Please, Lieutenant Newton, I need more time.' She held up her hands in front of her. 'If the general could just grant me a bit more time, I promise I will have something worthwhile to show.'

Newton's nostrils flared and he took a step toward her. 'Doctor, when you first came to the general with your theory of a dimensional portal, he found it intriguing and gave you a year to prove to us the viability of the project. It has now been two years and you still have nothing to show for it.'

Her body quivering with indignation, Drusilla barged past Newton and directly approached the general. 'General, I am sure you are aware that science isn't precise. Discoveries take time and patience.' She brushed Newton's hand away as he grabbed at her shoulder. 'All I ask is for a bit more patience, and I promise you I will prove to you the multiverse is not just a theory, but it is my dest—'

Visibly shaking with rage, Newton grabbed Drusilla's arm and spun her around, cutting her off. Thaddeus could tell from the look on Newton's face that he considered Drusilla was being disrespectful by ignoring his authority. 'That is enough, Doctor!' he barked. 'I will not allow you to speak to the general in such a manner. You are relieved a—'

Newton never got the chance to finish the sentence. Thaddeus gritted his teeth in discomfort as he watched the woman repeatedly slam her knee into Newton's groin. His eyes watering, Newton collapsed onto the floor and tried to blink away the tears as he peered up at the woman standing over him.

His eyes simmered with beams of anger and hurt pride as Drusilla reached down and grabbed him by his collar. 'Don't you ever touch me in such a way again,' she spat with a venomous intensity. 'I am not one of your little whores that you think you can manhandle at any time you want. You wil—'

Drusilla crumpled onto the floor gasping. The thin obedience collar around her neck shone brightly with a blue hue as it sent a charge of electricity into her nervous system.

'That is enough!' Thaddeus roared, holding a small control pad in his hand. He could tell from Drusilla's relieved face that the searing pain she was experiencing was easing as he slowly removed his finger from the pad.

As the light in the obedience collar slowly dimmed, Drusilla's head dropped back onto the floor and she took in a lungful of air. Thaddeus heard a sigh of contentment escape from her lips, and he wondered if the coolness of the chamber floor had brought her some welcoming pain relief.

Disappointed at the way Newton had handled the situation, Thaddeus immediately recognised that the gods were shining down on him. They had presented him with an opportunity, and if he handled it carefully, it would allow him to kill two birds with one stone. Wordlessly he thanked Vesta, his household god, for granting him this boon, and watched his subordinate grimace in pain as he gingerly lifted himself to his feet. Newton's body was trembling with fury, and he spun sharply round to the gasping figure on the floor. He lifted his leg as if to kick Drusilla in the head, but paused when the general coughed loudly and waggled his finger at him.

Acquiescent, Newton lowered his head and stepped back from the groaning woman on the floor. He straightened his body and clicked his heels together in salute. Even though Newton's attitude grated on him, Thaddeus couldn't help admire at how quick he had managed to regain his composure. He grunted and shook his head. No, Newton was a cockroach plain and simple. You didn't admire cockroaches – you stepped on them.

'Miles, I'm very disappointed.' Thaddeus spoke in a dispassionate tone as he glared at his shamed lieutenant. He felt his facial muscles tighten as he shot Miles a withering look. 'I expected better of you.'

Thaddeus lifted his left arm to reveal a silver studded band. He pressed one stud with his right hand. Miles's eyes grew wide as the chamber door slid open and two large brawny men wearing black leather uniforms stepped into the chamber.

'P-p-please,' Miles stammered and tried to back away from the two soldiers, 'General, haven't I been a loyal servant?' He dropped to his knees, pawing pleadingly at his commander's legs. 'My family has served the Empire faithfully for generations, doesn't that mean anything?'

The corner of Thaddeus's mouth curled up in disgust and he held his right hand up. 'Don't beg, Miles, it is not becoming of you.' He smiled softly, knelt and placed his hand on the fawning man's shoulder as he helped him to his feet. 'Don't worry, they will not kill you.'

Miles blinked in surprise and then stared at Thaddeus in bewilderment. 'They won't?'

The general's smile faded and he tightened his grip on Miles's shoulder, filling him what could only be described as joy at witnessing the look of pain on his subordinate's face. 'No, out of respect for your noble family, you will not be harmed.' He gave a sidelong look to the two soldiers and nodded to them. 'You are to follow these guards. They will put you on a shuttle to your new command – Pons Rapa Nui.'

The centre of Miles's brow knitted together and he gawked at the general in confusion. 'I don't understand, General. Pons Rapa Nui is a remote outpost on a small island in Atlantica. In fact, the last time we had a garrison there was in 5300 – that's just over three hundred years ago. It's a rundown and decaying settlement with no value.' He scratched his head in bewilderment. 'Surely this is a mistake, General?'

Thaddeus smiled again and shook his head. 'No mistake, Miles. You are to be sent to Pons Rapa Nui, where you are to remain in exile and seclusion for the rest of your life. Your family will continue to serve the Empire proudly as you work to make the outpost habitable for the day when it will be needed again.' The muscles in his face became taut as he clicked his fingers at the two soldiers. 'Take him.'

The colour drained from the horror-struck lieutenant's face as the two soldiers stepped forward and grabbed his arms. Focusing his attention back on Drusilla, Thaddeus decided his former aide did not deserve any more of his valuable attention and chose not to acknowledge the sobbing noises that were coming from behind him. As soon as he heard the whoosh of the chamber's door sealing shut, he was filled with a warm glow of pleasure with the knowledge that he no longer had to put up with the odious little man. No longer did he have to listen to him prattling on or witness his sycophantic behaviour. By the gods, that man was a real pain in the arse.

Drusilla, who had been watching the exchange in silence, flinched as the general turned his attention towards her. She eyed him with uncertainty as he leaned down and helped her to her feet.

'Well, Drusilla, it appears I need a new aide,' he said with a touch of amusement. 'You quite impressed me with the way you handled Lieutenant Newton. I need someone who can instil fear into those beneath them.'

The doctor grunted as she eased herself up off the floor. As she ran her hands down to smooth her white uniform, her eyes tightened and she eyed the general with deep suspicion. 'I thought you had grown impatient with me and my lack of progress with the project?'

Thaddeus scoffed and flapped his hand dismissively. 'Oh, we both know this project was always going to fail. As progressive as the Empire is, there are those who still believe it blasphemous to consider the idea of alternate worlds. Some still think we are unique and the centre of the universe.' He paused and cast an eye on the shimmering portal. 'This project was doomed to fail from the start.'

Miffed, Drusilla folded her arms across her chest and gave him a frosty stare. 'If you believed I was going to fail, then why did you allow me to go on with this charade? Was I just entertainment for your own perverse amusement?'

Sensing her wounded pride, Thaddeus gave Drusilla a sardonic smile and raised his right hand, pointing his finger into her chest. 'I was more interested in you, in particular when dealing with people like Newton. You have a unique quality, an intuition, if you will, to be able to read people. It is that ability, as well as your observational awareness to see things that others may miss, that I need the most.' He rubbed his chin reflectively and gave her a knowing look. 'Your military service was quite impressive, and I had hoped you would eventually join my command staff. Instead, you opted to leave the military to run this fiasco, which is a waste of your talents, my dear.'

Drusilla's eyes flickered with annoyance. 'Thank you,' she replied with a touch of sarcasm. 'You don't know how much it means to receive such high praise about my work.'

Ignoring the woman's disrespectful tone, Thaddeus chuckled and placed his hand on her shoulder. 'Don't be like that, Doctor. We both know this was starting to become an obsession of yours.' He held up his hand as he felt Drusilla bristle at his comment. 'Yes, obsession. Admit it, you had become so obsessed with this outlandish theory of the multiverse, other worlds that we could conquer and use as a resource. You failed to see you were fast becoming a laughing stock within the scientific community.' He paused, crossed his arms over his chest and slid her a guarded look. 'To be truly honest, my dear, I only allowed you to go on this long because I was truly hoping you would succeed, but I am afraid …'

He stopped, distracted by a flash of light. They both spun round as the portal flashed and shimmered briefly.

Drusilla dashed over to the console, sat down next to the short man and gave him an accusing look. 'Doctor Villa, what did you do?'

Doctor Villa's eyebrows lifted in surprise as he turned to Drusilla. 'I-I-I have done nothing,' he protested. 'I was monitoring the readings while you were talking with the general and then without warning the portal shimmered and, for a moment, I detected something, an abnormality.'

'An abnormality? What sort of abnormality?'

The technician lifted his shoulder in a half shrug. 'I could be wrong, but for a brief second it looked like something was being transmitted along our quantum pulse.'

Drusilla's eyes widened as she glanced up at the portal in confusion.

Oracle felt herself pass through a thin barrier as she travelled along the quantum pulse. As she came to a stop, she realised her data stream was being held within a data buffer of whatever was transmitting the quantum pulse.

It took her less than a nanosecond to analyse her surroundings and get her bearings. Quickly concluding that the size of her data stream would alert the organics when they noticed their terminal's memory buffer had exceeded its memory capacity, Oracle stealthily activated the room's scanners and analysed the room.

Impressed at the level of technology in this world, she transferred her matrix into a redundant isolinear positronic server that sat idle in the chamber's corner.

Oracle activated the server's low-power mode, then carefully manipulated the chamber's firewall to gain access to the planetary information web. Once inside the data stream, her energy matrix morphed into the shape of a female figure. She stretched out her arms and smiled as she received zettabytes of data. As the torrent of data flowed into her, Oracle gradually became more aware of the history of the Empire.

A long time ago, Imperium Romanum had been a noble society, following the peaceful virtues of ancient Rome, the country's population living in an almost utopian dream. For centuries there had been no war, the Romans living in harmony with their neighbours. Then, as if out of nowhere, a darkness slowly crept into the ruling senate, spreading out like a cancer, infecting their minds with xenophobic ideas. It was not long before the whispers of paranoia spiralled out of control, eventually spreading into the civilian population. Paranoid at the idea that the population would overthrow them, the senate handed complete control over to the military and it didn't take long for the new regime to make their presence known. To prove their loyalty to the newly founded Universal Roman Empire, the new formed Command Council decreed that all subjects were to wear obedience collars. Any dissent was immediately stamped down on and the population were soon living under an umbrella of fear and intimidation. No longer a harmonious society, the now deeply distrustful country turned their attention to their unsuspecting neighbours, who were caught unprepared and soon found themselves under the yoke of oppression. Not stopping at conquering her neighbours, the Empire turned her attention to the rest of the world. However, before she could finish tightening her global grip of tyranny, the imperial forces were stopped by the Greater Chinese Republic, whose military might was equal to that of the Empire. Both nations soon became locked in a power struggle that lasted for centuries.

Oracle smiled to herself as she interpreted the data flowing into her. Yes, this world's technology was superior to her old world, but they did not have what she was looking for. She needed a world that she would be able to mould and shape to her will. But perhaps she could still turn this world's duplicitous nature to her advantage. Having already seen the world she wanted, Oracle knew all it would take was a little guidance and direction from the shadows and the Empire would unknowingly do all the hard work for her. Sure, it would take time, but she was patient and happy to bide her time.

Plan in place, Oracle next turned her attention to the portal chamber. After taking control of the quantum pulse, her inhuman eyes glowed as she directed it to a set of familiar coordinates.

'Doctor, what are you playing at?'

Making no attempt to hide her displeasure at being interrupted, Drusilla rolled her eyes, glanced over her shoulder and gave a dismissive wave of her hand to Thaddeus, who was now deeply suspicious. 'Not now, can't you see I'm busy?'

His temples throbbing with rage, Thaddeus gave the scientist a piercing stare. 'Doctor, I don't care for your tone,' he hissed through gritted teeth. 'I demand that you tell me what is happening!'

Drusilla closed her eyes and let out a long, slow breath as she twisted her chair round to face the general. She held her hands up and spoke in slow, careful tones. 'General, I don't have time for this. You can see I am very busy, and I don't have the time to hand-hold you.'

Thaddeus was not used to be spoken to in such a manner. He struggled to remain in control of his anger and he gave the woman a dirty look. 'You forget your place, Doctor. You serve me, not the other way round.' He raised his hand and made an exaggerated clicking gesture with his fingers. 'All I need to do is click my fingers and you will find yourself in a prison cell.'

Drusilla's lips drew back in a snarl. She leapt out of her seat and opened her mouth to speak, but an alarm cut her off as the portal flickered and flashed with pulses of energy. Her blue eyes widened in alarm and she turned away from the general. She quickly sat back in her seat and turned to the panic-stricken man next to her. 'What's happening?'

His face glistening with sweat, Doctor Villa stared at the console in confusion. 'I'm detecting a surge in energy into the portal.' His mouth fell open as he looked at the readings displayed on his console's holographic display. 'According to these readings, we have increased the power to the quantum pulse and it is now being redirected it to a new set of coordinates.'

'Who gave that order?' Drusilla snapped, her nostrils flaring in anger as she grabbed the terrified man's shoulder.

The white-faced technician tried to cower away from Drusilla and gestured to the fluctuating portal. 'I don't know, but whoever did it did us a favour.'

Eyes widening in stunned surprise, Drusilla released her grip on his shoulder. 'Favour? What do you mean?'

Doctor Villa swallowed and pointed a trembling finger at the portal. 'We have established a lock.'

Thaddeus remained silent but watched Drusilla's eyes grow wide as she continued to stare at the portal and then back down at the console. His eyebrows arched in surprise as she took a step back and held her hands to her head.

'I've done it,' she screamed delightedly as she swung round and grabbed the general, who was now thoroughly confused, and kissed him on the lips. 'I have actually gone and done it!'

Completely taken aback by Drusilla's complete lack of self-control, Thaddeus angrily shoved the ecstatic woman away. 'Doctor Severan, could you please control yourself. Would you care to tell me what you have found so exciting?'

If she was aware of the general's annoyance, Drusilla did not show it as she continued to dance around the chamber. She merrily clapped her hands together, repeatedly singing, 'I did it. I did it.'

That was it; his patience had run out. Thaddeus, deciding he'd had enough, grabbed the jubilant woman's arm and spun her around. 'That's enough!' he barked. 'Now, calm down and explain to me what you find so damned exciting.'

Drusilla nodded apologetically. 'Sorry, General.' She sighed but still beamed with delight. 'But you cannot imagine, after all these years, after suffering endless ridicule from my so-called peers within the scientific community, to witness my work come to fruition.'

Thaddeus raised an eyebrow and stared into her dazzling eyes in amazement. 'You don't mean …?'

Drusilla gave Thaddeus a lopsided grin as her head bobbed up and down vigorously. 'Yes, my theories are not only right about the multiverse …' She chuckled in delight, reaching her arms to the portal. 'Don't ask me how, but we have also established a connection with a parallel world.'

Thunderstruck, Thaddeus swallowed and gazed at the portal in wonder. 'You mean …'

Drusilla nodded feverishly and jabbed her finger at the shimmering portal in front of them. 'Yes, on the other side of that portal is another Terra.' Her demeanour suddenly changed as she paced around the chamber, muttering to herself, 'Of course, we need to run a series of tests. Yes, that's right, we need to run tests to see if we can safely pass through the portal barrier. There are dimensional stresses to think about …'

The corners of Thaddeus's mouth twitched with amusement as Drusilla continued to babble excitedly to herself. Focusing his attention away from her, he lifted his left arm and tapped on his wrist communicator. 'Put me through to High Command immediately.'

With Doctor Severan in a world of her own and the general waiting to be connected to High Command, Doctor Villa decided it was best he just leave them to it. But as he turned away, he frowned as something caught his attention on the console. He lifted his head up to the portal and felt his eyebrows climb up his forehead in alarm as he noticed the portal's surface appeared to be flickering erratically. He scratched his head, looked back down at the console and then back up to the portal. What was going on here? Even though he was just a lowly technician, he was fairly certain the portal shouldn't be acting that way.

Villa raised his hand and coughed nervously, 'Um, Doctor Severan, I think you should see this.'

It obvious was to Villa that Severan was oblivious to what was going on around her; she was continuing to mutter to herself excitedly. Closing his eyes, he took a deep breath, and secretly prayed to his gods to give him the strength for what he had to do next. He opened his eyes and then, with as much courage as he could find, he shouted, 'Drusilla!'

Broken out of her musings and clearly shocked, Severan spun round and stared at Villa with wide-eyed astonishment. But her astonishment didn't last long. Villa felt his sphincter tighten as he watched her features morph into a look outrage. *Oh no, Great Mother Cybele, what I have done?* Villa whimpered. He could tell she was unhappy at being addressed in such a way by a subordinate.

'How dare you address me with such disrespect?' she spat, charging over to him.

Villa bolted up out of his seat and held up his hands apologetically. 'I am really sorry, Doctor Severan, but that was the only way I could get your attention.' He gestured anxiously to the portal. 'We are getting some feedback from the portal. Something is interfering with our pulse.'

Severan's brow furrowed and she sat down at the console. 'What are you talking about, you stupid fool? You're just looking at it ...' Villa saw the blood drain from her face as she read the holographic display above the console, and then lifted her head up to the shimmering portal in alarm. 'In Hera's name!'

'What's wrong?'

On hearing the general's voice, Villa wheeled around and saw that he had disconnected his conference call and had sprinted over to the console.

'These readings are telling me we're getting feedback from the portal. Somebody on the other side must be trying to close the connection from their end.' Villa explained hurriedly.

General Thaddeus cocked his head and turned to Severan with a look of incomprehension. 'So just switch our portal off and disconnect it.'

Severan's face reddened with anger and she shook her head defiantly. 'No, I did not come all this way, only to fail now.' She bobbed her head at Villa. 'Increase the power in our pulse. If we have to punch our way through, so be it.'

Thunderstruck, Villa blinked and stared back at Severan in consternation. 'Doctor, the pulse is already running at eighty-five per cent – any higher we risk a cascade failure or worse.'

'Fine, I'll do it myself,' Severan hissed sharply. Villa inhaled a sharp breath as he watched her place her finger on the power icon of the console and slide it up as far as it would go. 'I have not spent my life coming this far just to be stopped now.' Her eyes blazed with manic glee as she lifted her hands in the air and then cried out defiantly, 'Maximum power!'

Villa could tell she was beyond reasoning with because any sane person would have known that if they increased the power too quickly there would be a danger of an overload, risking the life of everybody in the chamber. He stared in wide-eyed horror as the power levels hit the red line and felt the blood drain from his face. *By the gods, she's going to kill us all.* Panic-stricken and desperate to alter the power levels before it was too late, he pushed the doctor to one side and slammed his finger on the power icon. 'No! You are increasing the power much too quickly, it wil—'

There was a loud crack of thunder as the portal surged with savage intensity. The three of them lifted their hands to shield their eyes as the chamber was filled with a bright warm light, quickly followed by a concussive pulse that knocked them off their feet.

Quickly recovering her senses, Drusilla winced, carefully lifted herself up off the chamber floor and staggered to her feet. She glanced over her shoulder as she heard movement from behind her and was relieved to see the dazed general was climbing to his feet. His body unmoving, Doctor Villa lay on the floor, face down.

Her head still reeling, Drusilla groaned as she knelt and rolled the unconscious man over. She sucked on her bottom lip and placed her fingers on a carotid pulse of Villa's neck. She pursed her lips in disappointment as she detected a faint pulse. *This insolent piece of excrement better pray to whatever household god he worships that he doesn't wake up because if he does, I am going to make his life a living hell.* On hearing Thaddeus stumbling over to her, she quickly composed herself before turning to face him. He was looking at her quizzically.

Drusilla gave a small nod in acknowledgement. 'He's alive, although he has a nasty gash on his head – probably caught his head on the side of the console.'

Thaddeus looked at the unconscious doctor and gave a slight shrug. He straightened and appeared to be just about to say something but stopped. Drusilla then noticed that he had an odd look on his face. At first she thought he must have been looking the portal but as she watched him raise his hand, it dawned on her that he was looking at something else.

'It appears we've got some uninvited guests.' he murmured.

'What do you mean?' Drusilla replied curiously. She cocked her head as she straightened up, but felt her mouth slip open in disbelief as she looked to where Thaddeus was pointing.

Lying on the floor in front of the portal were a dozen people, a mixture of men and women, unconscious, all wearing what appeared to be identical long white coats over strange clothing.

As she slowly regained consciousness, Johanna could make out the sound of people talking. The voices were strange, with accents that seemed oddly familiar.

Before she had blacked out, she had been standing in a large subterranean cavern that was being used for a military experiment in matter transference. The experiment had been the brainchild of Dr Allen Selyab, a German scientist who had defected to England to escape the clutches of the Nazi party, who had been slowly increasing their stranglehold over Germany.

Everything had been going well until their portal overloaded. They soon realised, to their horror, that someone else was trying to lock on to their portal. It quickly dawned on them that their only chance of severing the connection was to open the floodgates and flood the cavern containing their experiment.

The last thing she remembered, just before she gave the command to open the floodgates, was being enveloped in a bright light and screaming as a surge of energy ripped through her body. Her last thought, as she experienced her body being torn apart, was *This is it, I am dead.*

But as the sensations of her body's aches and pains registered with her brain, Johanna quickly realised she was not dead. The haze slowly lifting from her mind, she soon became aware she was lying on her back on a cold floor. She moaned softly, twisted her head and raised it slightly off the floor.

Slowly opening her eyes, she blinked, and her vision slowly adjusted to the dim light. Ever so carefully, she inched her body slightly off the floor and attempted to get a better view of her surroundings.

Johanna could see she was in a dimly lit circular chamber. However, as she looked up at the ceiling, she frowned at the strange lights that were being used to illuminate the chamber. The lights appeared to be unusually compact and tubular, unlike anything she had seen before.

Out of the corner of her eye, Johanna caught light shimmering off a reflective surface. She glanced over her shoulder and thinned her eyes as she noticed a large round device on the wall, in the centre of which was what looked like a reflective surface. She took a sharp breath as she recognised it. There was no doubt in her mind as she stared at the mechanism that it was a portal like the one that had been used in Doctor Selyab's experiment, except this appeared to be a more advanced design.

Pulling her gaze away from the portal, Johanna's eyes widened, and she felt her jaw drop open in amazement as she came upon a console in the centre of the chamber. She shook her head in wonder. The technology was unlike anything she had seen before.

Her curiosity getting the better of her, she tried to move closer to get a better look at the large rectangular console; she was awestruck at the level of the technology on display. It was unlike anything she had ever seen. The console was clearly the control unit for the portal, but unlike the rough push-button consoles she was familiar with, this appeared more advanced, familiar yet alien at the same time. In place of buttons and dials, the console's surface was smooth with strange displays. Johanna guessed they were some sort of advanced touch-sensitive controls.

She found her gaze drawn to a ghostly image hovering inches above the console displaying images of dials and text in a strange but familiar language. Johanna stared in bewilderment at the image and tried to fathom how it was being held in mid-air. But as she slowly read the text on the image, she lifted her hand to her mouth in realisation; she recognised it was written in a language similar to Latin.

The sound of raised voices pulled her attention away. Johanna twisted her head toward the voices and spotted five people on the other side of the chamber. She dropped closer to the floor and tried to avoid drawing attention to herself by remaining silent as she studied the people in front of her. Four people were standing over a man wearing a strange white leather uniform who was lying unconscious on the floor, possibly injured.

Standing to one side were two large black men wearing black leather uniforms and holding futuristic rifle-like weapons. From the style of the uniforms and the way they were holding their weapons, Joanne guessed they were military.

She remained silent as her attention drifted to the two other people. One was a tall and attractive olive-skinned woman, who was gesticulating and arguing with an intimidating barrel-chested bald man. From his black and gold uniform and the way he carried himself, she guessed he was the woman's commanding officer. Johanna frowned as she noticed the clothing the argumentative woman was wearing. It appeared to be a white leather uniform much like that of the man on the floor. Was she a physician? Her eyes focused on the stranger's clothing and she noticed the red lines on the arms of the stranger's uniform. No, she wasn't a physician; was she something else? She concentrated and thought of the colours that represented the different specialities on her Earth. She nodded to herself. Yes, if she worked on the assumption that blue symbolised health, then wouldn't it be logical to assume red symbolised science and technology? Was she the head of this experiment, maybe?

Double Jeopardy

Johanna flinched as she detected movement out of the corner of her eye. She pressed her body against the floor and slowly slid round to see Doctor Passmoor stirring next to her.

Careful not to alert the strangers to their presence, she reached over and placed her hand on his mouth. The man jerked and his eyes narrowed in confusion at the hand covering his mouth. Johanna held up a finger to her lips. 'Lee, are you okay?' she whispered in an extremely low voice.

'Yes, Doctor Abbott,' Lee whispered in acknowledgement. His eyes widened in alarm as slowly he became aware of his surroundings. 'Where are we? Last thing I can remember was a bright light followed by a feeling like I was being torn apart.'

Johanna shook her head in disbelief and whispered to him, 'Lee, I believe what we experienced was some sort of dimensional wave that has transported us to another reality.' She held up her hand as he opened his mouth in astonishment. 'All in good time, but first we need to check on the others.' She pointed to the people around her. 'As silently as you can, you check on the people closest to you, while I check on this group next to me.'

With the strangers' attention still focused on their wounded comrade, Johanna and Lee carefully moved amongst the small group of people around them, checking for injuries and emphasising the need to remain silent. Lee came to an unconscious, elderly man – Dr Selyab. He gently touched him on the shoulder but there was no response. Johana, seeing the concern etched across her comrade's face, silently crawled across the floor to him and stared down with grave concern.

'I'm not getting any response from Dr Selyab,' Lee whispered with a note of alarm in his voice. 'His breathing is unusually shallow and he looks terribly pale. I think he needs medical attention.'

Nodding gravely, Johanna glanced up at the people on the far side of the room, took in a deep breath and slowly eased herself off the floor. She took a hesitant step in their direction.

Terror flashing in his eyes, Lee jumped up and grabbed his friend's arm. 'Joanne, please don't do this. You don't know what they will do to you.'

'It's fine,' Johanna mouthed and forced a smile as she looked down at his hand. She gave a small nod, gently removed his hand from her arm and then took a step towards the people in front of her.

Printed in Great Britain
by Amazon